PENGUIN BOOKS

beautiful collide

Ava Harrison is a *USA Today* and Amazon Number One bestselling author. When she's not journaling her life, you can find her window shopping, cooking dinner for her family, or curled up on her couch reading a book.

beautiful collide

USA *TODAY* BESTSELLING AUTHOR
AVA HARRISON

PENGUIN BOOKS

PENGUIN BOOKS

UK | USA | Canada | Ireland | Australia
India | New Zealand | South Africa

Penguin Books is part of the Penguin Random House group of companies
whose addresses can be found at global.penguinrandomhouse.com

Penguin Random House UK,
One Embassy Gardens, 8 Viaduct Gardens, London SW11 7BW

penguin.co.uk

First published in the United States of America by AH Publishing 2024
First published in Great Britain by Penguin Books 2025
002

Copyright © Ava Harrison, 2024

The moral right of the author has been asserted

Penguin Random House values and supports copyright.
Copyright fuels creativity, encourages diverse voices, promotes freedom
of expression and supports a vibrant culture. Thank you for purchasing
an authorized edition of this book and for respecting intellectual property
laws by not reproducing, scanning or distributing any part of it by any
means without permission. You are supporting authors and enabling
Penguin Random House to continue to publish books for everyone.
No part of this book may be used or reproduced in any manner for the
purpose of training artificial intelligence technologies or systems. In accordance
with Article 4(3) of the DSM Directive 2019/790, Penguin Random House
expressly reserves this work from the text and data mining exception

Edited by Editing4Indies
Content editing by Readers Together
Proofread by Proofing Style
Typeset by Jouve (UK), Milton Keynes
Printed and bound in Great Britain by Clays Ltd, Elcograf S.p.A.

The authorized representative in the EEA is Penguin Random House Ireland,
Morrison Chambers, 32 Nassau Street, Dublin D02 YH68

A CIP catalogue record for this book is available from the British Library

ISBN: 978-1-405-97394-6

Penguin Random House is committed to a sustainable future
for our business, our readers and our planet. This book is made from
Forest Stewardship Council® certified paper.

beautiful collide

prologue

Molly

I HAVE A MONSTER. A CRUEL, TWISTED NIGHTMARE THAT HAUNTS the shadows of my mind. It lurks in my memories, waiting to strike when I'm not ready.

You're fine, Molly. You're safe.

"Hurry up."

I whip my head to look over my shoulder at the words. The girl isn't speaking to me, but my back still goes ramrod straight.

Tonight is supposed to be exciting. It's the Frost Cup. The biggest weekend in high school hockey. Teams from all the neighboring states flock to Redville to play in my school's infamous tournament.

Every inch of the hall leading to the rink is packed. On a typical night, the crowd is chaotic during home games. Tonight, it's even worse.

Apparently, this team is the best.

That's why more people are here than usual.

This is the game of the year. Scouts are in the audience. College scouts. Pro scouts. Hell, even my brother's coach for the Saints is here.

I'm surprised Dane didn't insist on coming with me. He barely lets me go anywhere alone.

But when he stopped me at the door earlier, I put my foot down.

Told him I was going alone.

I'm a senior, for crying out loud.

And just because my older brother is my guardian doesn't mean he has to act like an overprotective dad.

"For fuck's sake, will you people just walk?"

This time, it's a guy speaking. A real douchebag, by the looks of it.

I keep going, pushing my way through the crowd.

I'm almost there when I see someone familiar standing a few feet away. It's him. And suddenly, my monster isn't some faceless shadow in my mind. He's real, and tangible, and terrifying, and *here*.

He can't see me. The world might end if he does. For me, anyway.

A shiver works its way down my spine. I duck to the left, hoping the crowd will hide me.

I can't talk to *him*.

I can't even look at him.

Shit.

I know, without a measure of a doubt, he's waiting for me.

He wouldn't be if Dane were here.

How does he know I'm alone?

It doesn't matter. Escape first. Questions later.

The walls start to close in on me. I can feel my chest tightening.

With a force that rocks my feet, I'm ripped away from the stadium, falling into my memories and succumbing to my vicious monster.

I'm there again.

In the dark . . .

No.

You're not.

You're at school. Going to a hockey game. Because everything is normal now.

I'm safe.

I'm protected.

Maybe if I repeat it enough, I'll believe it.

Someone bumps into me from behind.

"Move, freak."

I don't even know the girl scowling at me, but I'm sure she knows me. Thanks to Dane, every student at Redville High knows me.

She turns to her friends and giggles. "I don't care that her brother is some NHL hotshot. The girl's a weirdo."

Her insults barely register. My feet are still weighed down. It feels like someone dumped concrete in my shoes, and for the life of me, I can't lift my legs to keep going.

Move. Now. He'll catch you if you don't.

The sound of rushing water fills my ears, and I know it's only a matter of time before the darkness pulls me under.

You're going to die.

My heart thunders in my chest. It's impossible to breathe.

Great. I'm going to die of a heart attack at seventeen.

I shake my head. No. I won't let this happen now.

I've researched panic attacks, and if I let the intrusive thoughts break in . . .

"Who is she saying no to?" the girl whines, still mere inches away from me in the gridlocked crowd. "Is this bitch for real?"

A shoulder hits me, and I stumble forward.

She laughs. "Careful."

Usually, I'd say something.

Normally, I also wouldn't be a sneeze away from a full-fledged panic attack.

I thought I had them under control.

But every time I see *him* . . .

Without a word, I head in the opposite direction, away from the entrance to the rink. Toward anywhere but here.

I'm almost to the door. Just a few feet away. The exit sign blares red with promises of my escape.

Hopefully, the alarm doesn't sound when I push open the door and add yet another embarrassing memory to my long list of high school fiascos, but I'm so close to losing my shit, I don't even care.

The cool metal handle ices my fingers. I push it forward, the door creeping open slowly.

No alarm.

Makes sense. It's a game day, after all.

I'm sure all the doors are unlocked tonight.

It takes a surprising amount of strength to prop open the heavy door, and the second I do, the cold night air hits me in the face.

It's dark outside. Much darker than it was in the front of the building, where lights illuminate the black sky.

Here, a halo of stars and a giant moon are my backdrop.

I walk until I can see a faint light from the other side of the building and take a seat on the gum-dotted pavement.

Eyes closed, I try to calm my racing heart. My jaw chatters from the cold. Or maybe it's the nerves.

A roar of cheers shatters my quiet solitude. It fades a moment later, leaving me alone with the thought of my monster looming over me.

He's here.

He's here, he's here, he's here.

No matter how hard I try, I can't stop the way I shake.

"I'm just cold," I try to tell myself, my teeth chattering between each syllable. "It's not because of him."

I'm stronger now . . .

But even my strength can't stop the shadows from creeping in when the lights go out.

The faint shuffle of footsteps behind me sends a jolt down my spine. My body locks tight like a coiled spring.

Please, not now.

I don't want to talk to anyone.

Please, don't see me.

I close my eyes, willing whoever it is to leave.

Don't let it be him.

It can't be him.

It has to be him.

I'm spiraling. I know I am. But no matter how hard I try, my head and heart no longer feel tethered to reality. It's too late. The monster struck and won. I've flung the door to my brain wide freaking open, and now all my intrusive thoughts batter their way in.

He found you.

A footstep closer.

Another one.

My body clenches.

My breathing stops.

I brace for impact.

Warmth.

All I feel is warmth.

My eyelids fly open at the sound of the door opening and closing nearby.

I peer over my shoulder, searching for the stranger. But I'm alone.

No one is here.

Did I make it up?

But it's warm. So warm.

My fingers brush against the fabric draped over my shoulders. It's thick and worn and smells like pine trees.

A jacket.

Whoever it was left me a jacket.

SEASON ONE

chapter one

Hudson

DON'T FUCK THIS UP.

My heart thunders like I drank too much coffee or took speed.

Neither actually happened, but here I am, pacing the large arena, needing to calm down.

Today is important. It's my first game with the Redville Saints. Hence why I'm a fucking mess.

Get out of your head, Wilde.

It's not like this is my first game.

But it's your first game in the NHL.

My hands start to shake at my sides.

Shit.

I can't walk into the locker room for my first game, shaking like a pussy.

My eyes scan the vast space, landing on a door just up and to the left of the large hallway.

I should head to the locker room and get myself sorted. I came early to do just that, but I still need a second to myself.

Crossing the distance, I see that the door is half open already. Fuck. Hopefully, no one is in there.

Fuck it. I can't risk seeing anyone I know now. It's either get caught by however many people can fit in a tiny closet or however many can fit in the giant locker room.

I step inside the room, pulling the door closed at the same time.

The second it shuts behind me, I take a deep breath and survey my surroundings.

Just as I thought. A storage closet.

There's shit everywhere.

Great location, Wilde.

Couldn't have picked a better spot to gather your thoughts.

Just as I'm about to turn around and find a bathroom or something, I hear a sound.

I narrow my eyes, trying to figure out where it came from. Then I hear it. A grunt. A deep sigh follows the grunt. I'm not alone in this storage closet.

Fucking fantastic.

It would be just my luck to stumble into a new teammate jerking off on my first day here. Nothing screams great first impression like trauma bonding over some perv's idea of a game-day warm-up routine.

I shut my eyes, debating whether I'm curious enough to investigate. To see or not to see? My curiosity wins out, and I weave around a shelf, spotting someone in the far corner, wedged between stacks of discarded hockey sticks and cleaning supplies.

She's bent over at the waist.

And just like that, the nerves are gone.

My hands don't shake.

My mind stops racing.

My heart rate, however, picks up for an entirely different reason.

Holy shit, this girl has an ass. It's probably not the most polite reaction, yet I can't help but stop where I'm standing and stare.

Since my timing obviously sucks, she chooses that exact moment to look up.

"Seriously? Creeper."

"What?" I raise my hands in the air, feigning innocence. "Can't hate a guy for looking."

"Actually, I can." She straightens up, then spins to face me, her arms crossed.

If I thought her ass was nice, it's got nothing on her face. For a second, I forget how to breathe. If this is how I go out—trapped in a closet before I even play my first pro game—I can't complain. She's stunning in a way that doesn't feel real. Like someone plucked her straight out of my dreams and dropped her into my lap.

She looks young, probably around my age, early twenties, but there's something timeless about her. Long brown hair spills over her shoulders, catching the light. Her skin glows, flawless and warm, and her lips—God, her lips—are full and slightly parted like she's about to say something clever.

But her eyes hit me hardest. Seafoam green, bright and sharp, like they're daring me to get too close. They lock on to mine, and I swear she sees right through me, peeling back every layer with one glance.

The world narrows to just her. Us.

I'm not the kind of guy who believes in fate, but right now, I'm wondering if maybe it believes in me. If this girl didn't just catch me staring at her ass, I'd probably ask her out right this second. But unfortunately, she seems unimpressed by me.

In fact, she props her hand on her hip, her eyebrows narrowed.

Fine. Someone doesn't appreciate me gawking at her. Duly noted.

I lean a hip against the shelf and kick one foot over the other. "What brings you to . . ." I spin a finger around, gesturing to the closet. "This part of town?"

Her eyes flare for a moment before she moves fast, grabbing the nearest object off the shelf, which happens to be a wrench. She waves it around as if it explains everything, frowning once she realizes what she grabbed.

She recovers fast, though, and pulls her shoulders back with fake confidence. "None of your business."

"Wow. Touchy, touchy." I don't bother hiding my amused grin. "Let me guess—you're an over-the-top fangirl who broke in disguised as maintenance staff."

She's not even in the maintenance uniform I spotted when I entered the stadium, but the need to fuck with her is strong. I'm not sure why. I've never been like this with anyone else.

"The opposite, actually. I'm hiding in here to avoid people like you."

"People like me?" I bring a hand to my chest, mock-offended. "You wound me. FYI, I'm a great person."

"Oh, really?" She raises a brow. "Because staring at a stranger's ass totally screams 'upstanding citizen.'"

"Would it scream 'upstanding citizen' if the ass didn't belong to a stranger?"

"What are you doing here, anyway? You can't be here." Her tone catches me off guard. She's openly hostile, something I'm not used to.

It's my turn to pop up an eyebrow. "And you can?"

She rolls her eyes at me. "Of course I can. I practically work for the team."

I almost expect her to say duh. Like everyone should know who she is. Which makes me wonder why I don't.

I narrow my eyes. Then it hits me. I know exactly who she is—Molly Sinclair, Dane Sinclair's little sister. I've seen her before, and every time, she looks just as beautiful as she does today.

"And you are?" She tilts her head slightly as she looks me up and down. "Do you even work here?"

"*Technically*, I work here."

She raises a brow. "Technically?"

"Fine. I play here," I correct. "For someone who practically works for the team, shouldn't you know?"

"Ah, a hockey player," she says as if it explains everything.

"What's that supposed to mean?"

She shrugs, shoving the wrench onto the nearest shelf. "Hockey players are basically toddlers with money. Let me guess," she adds, throwing my earlier words back at me. "You were wandering looking for snacks?"

"Snacks?" I laugh. "I'll have you know that, in addition to being a great guy, I'm responsible, too. I brought all my snacks with me."

"Then why are you here?"

"I came in because I thought someone was—" I stop myself, realizing how ridiculous it would sound if I admitted I thought she was a teammate jerking off. "Never mind," I finish lamely.

A sudden smile takes over her face, and holy shit, I really wish we'd met on better terms. Specifically, terms that don't include me getting caught staring at her very, very nice ass.

"No." She smacks her forehead. "You heard a noise and thought you'd walk in on something R-rated, didn't you?"

"Absolutely not," I say quickly. Too quickly.

"Oh my God." She's laughing now, and I can't even be mad at it. She's that beautiful. "You did. That's why you're acting so weird."

"I'm not acting weird."

"You're still here, aren't you?" She brushes past me to grab something from a shelf. "That's weird."

"Well, excuse me for being concerned about strange noises in a closet," I shoot back, helping her grab the grip tape off a shelf a solid two feet taller than her. "Next time, I'll let the angry lady with the wrench handle it."

"Good plan." She slides the tape into her back pocket. "And for the record, it's Molly, not angry lady."

"Hudson." I relax my arm when she ignores my outstretched hand.

She narrows her eyes, studying me in a way that both thrills and unnerves me.

"Oh." Her head bobs up and down. "You're the new player."

I take a step forward.

She takes a step back.

Interesting.

"I am."

"And what exactly are you doing in the storage room?" She swallows, pulling her shoulders back. "You would've already had to be in here to hear me dig for the tape."

I shrug, trying to downplay it. "Wrong turn."

Her eyes squint, scrutinizing me. "I find that hard to believe."

"How do you figure?" I ask, defensive.

"This hallway is at the opposite end of where a player would ever be, so the fact that you're in here feels pretty targeted. Are you following me?"

I scoff. "Why would I be following you?"

"No idea. Just asking."

"No. I took a wrong turn. That's all."

"Yeah, okay. Well, on that note, new guy, I have to go." She starts walking toward the door but stops in her tracks. "Oh, no."

I rub my brow, getting whiplash from this conversation. "What?"

"Tell me you didn't close the door."

I follow her gaze to the now closed door. "I did. So what?"

"No." Her hands shoot to her scalp, tugging at her thick hair. "No, no, no."

"What's the problem?" I inquire, sensing her rising panic.

She tosses her hands up. "Seriously?"

"Yes. Seriously."

"The door is broken."

"Okay." I shrug. "So what?"

"Not so what." She shakes her head, beginning to pace, not

even looking at me. "We're trapped in here." Her voice rises, urgency creeping in.

"Now you're just being dramatic," I say, trying and failing to lighten the mood.

"Yeah? Why don't you try to open it?" she challenges, finally peering over her shoulder with an arched eyebrow.

So I do just that.

I stride over to the door, my hard steps echoing in the small space as my shoes clap against the concrete floor.

Once I'm standing in front of the door, the possibility that she's right starts to sink in. I have a game soon. I can't be late. There'll be hell to pay if I am.

I reach my hand out, my fingers grasping the cold metal, and try to turn the knob.

Nothing.

It won't move.

It doesn't even budge.

A flash of brown catches my eyes. I pivot to see what it is. Her hair. It sways with the movement of her body.

I'm not sure what I'm witnessing.

Her tiny hands fist.

Her lips move fast, stumbling over incoherent mutters.

Is she *shaking*?

Fuck.

chapter two

Molly

I TAKE A DEEP BREATH. *NOT THAT IT HELPS.*

No matter how hard I try, I can't breathe.

The air feels dense around me, reminding me of the early morning fog when it clings desperately to the windshield of a car.

Why are the walls closing in?

The storage closet isn't small.

This shouldn't be happening.

I thought I was better. *I'm not.*

A heart shouldn't race this fast.

I drop down to the floor, my legs no longer able to hold the weight of my body.

A strange, metallic scent clogs my nostrils, and my ears start to ring.

Cue the dizziness.

I press myself down lower until my head kisses the concrete. Invisible hands tighten around my heart, constricting the organ in my chest.

I'm trapped.

Again.

Always trapped.

"You need to breathe." An unfamiliar voice breaks through my haze. "Come on. Inhale."

I shake my head back and forth.

"I promise you can," he coos.

I try. I really do. But my breaths still come out in short, frantic gasps.

It's pointless. I'm going to die in here.

"It's okay. You can do it."

The space around us feels dark, and the ringing in my ears intensifies as I search for something—*anything*—to calm me.

"Take a slow inhale for me."

I do what he says, allowing him to guide me.

"That's good. Now, slowly exhale." The voice is closer now, almost as if he's beside me.

"I can't."

"Yet you are."

I can't help but let out a shaky laugh.

"See? Even laughing is breathing."

I hear movement, and then I feel his warmth. He must be right beside me, and that makes my heart beat even faster.

"Shh." Rough fingers touch my hand. "In. And out."

I hesitate at first but eventually follow his lead.

"In. Out."

The tightness in my chest loosens. It's definitely better than moments ago.

"Can you open your eyes?"

I shake my head, immediately dizzy from the movement. "No."

"Come on, Molly. Please."

His smooth baritone as he says my name forces an eyelid open. I stare at him out of one eye. "You do know who I am."

"You gave me your name," he points out.

Shit. I totally forgot. I hate that I get like this. Panicked. Messed up. Unable to push myself out of it.

"You didn't need to, though," the new guy, whose name I'm still not privy to, admits. He squints, and small lines form at the sides of his temples. "Of course, I know who you are."

"And you? Do you have a name?"

"Hudson Wilde."

Hudson.

I realize he gave it to me earlier as we argued. He held his hand out, and I didn't even shake it. I almost feel bad about it. Almost.

Consider it the price of admission for staring at my ass.

Which, to be fair, I would've enjoyed, since he *is* hot. But he caught me at a bad time. Or rather—I caught *him* at a bad time. It's game day, the closet must be a zillion degrees, and I absolutely loathe enclosed spaces.

If Hudson remembers that he already gave me his name, he doesn't call me out on my panic-induced memory lapse. He just helps me ride this out, patting my hand every now and then.

"Fun name," I manage to groan out.

"I think so." The corner of his mouth tips up into a smirk, and I swear it's the sexiest thing I've ever seen.

That's one way to calm a panic attack.

As if on cue, my gaze darts around the room, and it all comes rushing back. I'm locked in the storage closet. No way out. And I doubt anyone will come for us for some time. Not with the game starting soon. I don't even have my phone with me. Even if I did, it's pointless. Huge chunks of the stadium have no signal.

My heart thumps in my chest again.

"Hey, you're okay." It's shocking how fast he catches on to my changes. "What's going on?"

I don't answer.

I can't.

My fingers start to tremble.

"Please, keep breathing for me." Hudson leans closer, his voice soft. "Forget the world. Pay attention to me—and only me. You can do it."

I focus on him. On the steady cadence of his voice, as he prompts me again.

"In . . . out . . ."

I release another breath, feeling some of the weight lift from my chest. "What if we don't get out?"

"Impossible." He shakes his head with such certainty I almost believe him. "Someone will eventually need something. That wrench, maybe?"

A tiny laugh tries to claw its way past my throat and fails. I'm too choked up. Too antsy and amped up, and the only reason I haven't completely lost it is this total stranger.

A warm feeling spreads across my back when I realize he's touching me.

"Is *this* okay?" The concern in his voice nearly makes me sob.

I can't remember the last time anyone cared for me like this.

Sure, Dane loves me. But he's never been affectionate.

Not like this.

It's not in his DNA. The man's idea of love is patting my head like I'm a Labrador and telling me to suck it up.

I nod, welcoming Hudson's comfort.

It takes me a few minutes of breathing before I can see again, and when I open my eyes, his bright blue gaze is staring into mine.

To say Hudson Wilde is very good-looking is an understatement.

He's the kind of good-looking that makes you forget how to form sentences. All broad shoulders, sharp jawline, and a smile that screams trouble. I would bet that the second he makes his NHL debut, he'll have advertisers lining up, begging for his face on a billboard. I would know. I have several on speed dial.

From a marketing standpoint, the team landed an ace. He'll have the fans screaming from their seats each time he zips past. I can see the viral videos already.

I knew the Saints were bringing on a new player, but I never cared to research him.

I work exclusively with my brother, and while I often interact with the team, the other players aren't my concern.

Making sure my brother is okay is.

Dane gave up his life for me.

He'd say he's not struggling, but I see it differently. He's hollow inside. A shell of a person.

I know the feeling.

Losing our parents, mainly Mom, changed us both to the marrow of our bones.

And here I am, trying to keep myself together, but instead, I'm losing my shit in a storage closet with one of his teammates.

A wave of nausea hits me.

Dane can never find out this happened.

How would I ever explain it?

He would want to know how and when this started.

I can't tell him that.

I'll have to think of an excuse for where I've been. Not trapped in a closet. And certainly not with his new teammate. Nope. The second he finds out about this is the second ten years of lies unravel. The darkness. The panic attacks. *Him.*

That can never happen.

Dane can never know.

Even if I have to lie through my teeth to make sure of it.

Lifting my hands, I bury my head in them.

"What's going on?" Hudson rubs small circles on my back. "Is it being locked in, or is it more?"

"I hardly think that's any of your business," I can't help but snap.

This is my own personal sin bin. I don't talk about this stuff with anyone. Ever.

"Good." He brushes off my tone, unbothered. "There's the fire you need."

"What?"

"You were about to lose it again, and I needed to stop you. Having you think I'm a nosy asshole is better than the alternative."

"You're diabolical."

"I like to believe I am."

Despite the fact we're virtual strangers, I *do* feel the need to tell him something. Anything. He's been so kind. But I can't spill too much. Even *I* don't want to admit to myself why I'm like this.

"I have issues with closed spaces . . ."

"You're claustrophobic?"

"Not really. It's a bit more than that, but I don't want to get into that right now. If I think about it, I tend to spiral."

"Tell me something else . . . Molly."

The way he says my name sends chills down my spine.

Easy, girl. You're trapped in a closet with a stranger. This is not the time or place to get all hot and bothered.

Wait. My mouth drops open. I'm trapped in a closet, and my libido is working?

This is new to me.

I've never felt anything but complete fear when locked in enclosed spaces.

I look over at Hudson.

What about you is different?

Sure, he's stupidly cute. With gorgeous dirty-blond hair that looks brown at certain angles, crystal-blue eyes you can get lost in, and a killer body that would make me feel tiny under it.

But I've met many hot men.

Hell, most of the team regularly graces the center spreads of *Sports Illustrated*.

And still, I have never, *ever* thought of anything but suffocating behind a closed door in a small space.

He's the first person who has made me feel like maybe the walls aren't here to trap me.

Maybe—just *maybe*—they're here to protect me.

chapter three

Hudson

I DON'T KNOW HOW LONG WE SIT THERE.

I didn't bring my watch, and if I check my phone, it will just piss me off that I'm going to be late for warm-ups. It's the twenty-first century, and engineers still haven't managed to douse the earth with proper cell service.

Instead, I concentrate on helping Molly.

I'm about to speak when a creaking sound echoes in the small space, followed by a crash as the metal door bangs into the wall.

I jump to my feet and spin to see an older woman in a stadium uniform standing in the doorway, mouth open as she meets my gaze.

"My God, thank fuck," I say before turning to look at Molly.

"I'm fine." She shoos me away with a wave of her hands. "Go."

I don't think twice. Too much time has passed, and I'm sure Coach will be pissed.

I bolt from the small space, adrenaline pumping through my veins. Warm-ups should be starting soon. There's no question.

This is bad. Real bad. Not only am I still in my street clothes, but if everyone else is dressed and ready, I won't be able to warm up with them.

I dash toward the locker room, but I don't even make it inside before I realize how truly fucked I am. Half the team is already walking in the opposite direction toward the rink. The air crackles with tension as a few of my new teammates spare me disapproving glances and shake their heads.

Some look amused. Others annoyed. A few—like Dane fucking Sinclair—look ready to murder me on the spot.

There's not even a second to soak in my success.

I made it to the NHL.

It's all I've ever wanted. The only real goal I've ever had in life.

Fine. Even super late and in my street clothes, I can't help but give myself a moment to soak it in and—

"Where the hell have you been?"

The voice slams through the tension like a bulldozer.

Shit.

I might not know him well yet, but it doesn't take a rocket scientist to realize who that voice belongs to and that I'm about to get my ass handed to me.

I pivot slightly to meet the owner of the voice head-on, and just as I suspected, it's Coach Robert.

"Well, well." He strides to me, his expression carved from stone. His voice drips with sarcasm as he continues, "Look who decided to bless us with his presence."

I wince. I've been here all of two minutes, and I've already managed to piss off the man who controls my ice time. Not great.

He weaves through players, stopping just short of me. "You think you can just waltz in here late?"

My heart begins to race, guilt mixing with panic. "Coach, I—"

"Save it." He holds up a hand, and I swear the hallway gets colder. "I don't care if your dog ate your alarm clock or if aliens abducted you. The only thing I care about is the fact that you're late."

I stand there, clutching my gear bag like a scolded kid. The weight of every player's stare burns into my skin.

It takes everything in me not to hop from foot to foot. "But I—"

"This is professional hockey, Wilde." Coach plants his feet, his eyes hard, the message clear. "No excuse will make this okay."

"I'm sorry. It won't happen again—"

"You're damn right it won't." Coach starts to pace, a predator in this confined space. "I don't care if you were the top player in the minors, the second coming of Gretzky, or the goddamn tooth fairy. When I say show up, you show up. Got it?"

I know what I should say.

That I should keep my head down and mutter *got it*. Anything to appease him.

But I can't.

I grew up in a fair household—one with parents who valued honesty and always listened when I had something to say.

Like an idiot, I try to explain.

"I was locked in a closet," I blurt out.

I can see the disbelief etched on his face. The way he crosses his arms in front of his chest and sneers down at me like I'm some kind of idiot.

Just then, I catch a set of footsteps approaching me from behind.

I turn, relieved to see Molly.

Finally.

Desperation claws at my throat.

"Tell him," I all but beg her, too worried to register the flash of alarm in her eyes before she smooths over her expression.

In its place is a calm, cool mask.

A mask of a stranger.

Dane bristles instantly, his broad shoulders squaring like he's prepared for a brawl. He moves like a wall between us. "How do you know my sister?"

Molly's lips part, and for a split second, I think she's going to tell him the truth. That I actually showed up early. That all of this is an innocent mix-up. That I'm not the asshole Dane clearly thinks I am.

But then she hesitates, her blue-green eyes darting to mine with something I can't quite read. Guilt? Panic? An apology?

"Molly . . ." Dane keeps his voice low. Gentle. "Are you okay?"

His eyes narrow as he takes in his sister, clearly soaking up her distressed appearance. She can paste on a blasé expression all she wants, but it won't hide her messy hair and wrinkled shirt.

Dane's face takes on an even harder edge. "Did this guy upset you?"

Shit. Shit. Shit.

This is even worse. Now, I'm basically being accused of harassment on top of being late.

My stomach drops as Molly stands there, motionless. The tension thickens the air around us. The entire hallway is silent, awaiting her answer.

A part of me can't believe this is happening.

Why isn't she saying anything?

I expected her to jump in and back me up.

Instead, she remains silent, her eyes fixed on the floor like it holds all the answers.

"Just say something," I urge, the plea coming out rougher than I intended.

I hate that my voice cracks a little.

I hate the injustice of this all.

Dane steps closer, and even though we're about the same height, his towering frame casts a shadow over me.

His jaw tightens, and his glare sharpens into something deadly. "Leave my sister alone." The *or else* is silent but there.

"I didn't do anything to her. I swear." I lift my hands up defensively, trying to de-escalate the situation before it blows up even further, if that's possible at this point. "I don't even know her."

"So you *don't* know her."

It escapes his mouth like a *gotcha*.

I glance at Molly, desperate for her to explain.

But she doesn't.

Her shoulders are tense, her arms crossed tight against her chest as she stares at a spot over my shoulder, refusing to meet my eyes.

"Molly," I say, quieter now. "Tell him the truth. *Please.*"

I feel like I'm in the fucking twilight zone.

Molly's lips press into a thin line.

I think she won't ever speak again.

So it shocks me when she finally says something, her voice steady. Too steady.

"We don't know each other," she says in a cool and detached tone. "He must have me confused with someone else."

The lie lands like a slap.

I'm too stunned to react.

Molly's gaze flicks back to Dane, her calm facade unshaken. "I've never met him before."

The ground around me opens up.

She lied.

She lied.

Dane lets out a low, disbelieving laugh. "You mistook my sister for another chick. That it?"

"What?" I ask, genuinely stunned.

"I know guys like you. You're all the same. You string along puck bunnies whose names you don't even bother to remember." His tone is sharp, each word laced with accusation. "Players that play on and off the ice."

The insinuation hits hard. My blood starts to boil. "That's not who I am."

"Oh, really?" Dane edges closer, sneering down at my street clothes. "Because you sure as hell look the part."

I clench my fists at my sides, fighting to keep my temper in check. I've never had a problem with it. But I've also never been accused of being a player for getting locked in a storage closet and helping a total stranger come down from a panic attack. If anything, I should be canonized into the sainthood.

I should've shut up and agreed with whatever they said when I had the chance.

I'm late without a reason? Yes, Coach.

I'm benched? Yes, Coach.

I'm a fucking player, even though I've never been into casual hookups. Fucking yes, Coach.

"Believe whatever you want," I snap. "But I *was* in the closet with your sister. Molly Sinclair. Not anyone else."

Dane raises an eyebrow, his gaze hard and unyielding. "Then why the hell didn't she back you up?"

His question lands like a sucker punch. I glance at Molly again, searching for something—*anything*—in her expression that might give me a clue. But she's still staring at the floor, her face unreadable. Hell, she can't even meet my eyes. I don't understand.

"Dane." Mason's voice cuts through the tension like a blade. "Chill. Let's get to warmups before Coach has all our asses running suicides for the next week."

Dane doesn't look away from me, but his shoulders relax slightly at Mason's interruption.

"Fine," he mutters, his voice still laced with warning. I guess I don't blame him. My little sister is annoying as shit, but I'd be the same way in his shoes. "But this isn't over."

With one final glare, he steps back and turns to Molly. Placing a protective hand on her shoulder, he leads her out the door as the rest of the team files toward the rink.

My new teammates snicker as Coach glowers at everyone with a pulse.

"Damn." Mason grins at me, chucking my shoulder. "Sinclair didn't hold back, huh?"

I don't say anything, my eyes still on Molly's retreating back.

"Don't worry about it." Mason pats my back before he leaves.

"Dane is protective as hell over Molls. None of us are even allowed to sneeze in her direction."

He's being nice and trying to make me feel better about this mess. I appreciate it, but I can't help my anger. It simmers within me, just below the surface.

You can't afford to lose your cool, Wilde.

I feel like I've been suspended in time.

The weight of Molly's lie bears down on me, heavier than the thick air in that closet we just escaped. I replay the past two hours in my head, searching for something I missed. A signal. A reason. Anything that explains why she didn't back me up. But no matter how many times I try to make sense of it, the outcome doesn't change.

She lied.

She lied, and there's nothing I can do to undo the fallout.

This is not how I wanted to start my professional career. As the resident bad boy. Late, undisciplined, and prone to skirt chasing.

My reputation is fucked.

There's no sweet-talking my way out of this. Not with Dane. Not with the team. And definitely not with Coach Robert. They've already written my story for me. The new guy who showed up late and caused a scene, probably thinking his talent is enough to carry him.

But that's not me. Not really. Sure, I'm confident in my skills—I have to be—but I've spent years proving I'm more than just a kid with a quick stick. Now, with one mistake—one lie—all my hard work is slipping through my fingers.

It's a hard pill to swallow.

It lodges in my throat, choking me with the bitter taste of frustration. I don't just feel misunderstood. I feel betrayed.

I thought Molly and I had something.

I glance at the door Molly walked through, her silence still ringing louder than any accusation Dane threw at me. She left me to take the fall. And for what? To hide something? To protect herself? It's not like we did anything wrong.

My jaw clenches as my mind spirals into questions I don't have answers to.

"Rough first day, huh?"

The question startles me out of my reverie. It came from our center, Aiden Slate, which is almost as shocking as this whole debacle. The man has a reputation for being silent. One time, he managed to field questions at a press conference without a single word.

"Don't worry about it." Aiden wipes something off his laces, rubbing until his skates are shiny enough to reflect light. "Coach benched Wolfe three games for missing warm-ups last season. He starts now."

I suit up as fast as I can, knowing there's no chance in hell I'll actually be allowed on the ice. "Three games?"

"Well, he missed warm-ups *and* called Coach 'Gramps.'"

Coach barrels out of his office, where he dipped in to retrieve his clipboard, and stops just long enough to bark at me again.

"Enough of this. Don't bother getting changed. You're sitting this one out." He pivots to the doorway, calling over his shoulder. "You better not make this a habit, or I might decide you're more useful as a benchwarmer."

chapter four

Hudson

THE AIR FEELS HEAVY WITH ANTICIPATION.

This isn't just another game.

It's *my* game.

My first as a Redville Saint. My first shot at proving I belong here.

I've spent the past few days replaying every moment of that disastrous first game in my head.

The closet fiasco. The late arrival. Molly's silence. Dane's anger. Coach's barely concealed irritation.

It all circles back to one thing: I have something to prove.

Mason claps a hand on my shoulder, his grin easy. "You ready, Wilde?"

I glance at him, and for the first time since that disaster of a morning, I feel a flicker of something close to gratitude. Mason's been in my corner since the second I stepped into this locker room, and he hasn't stopped trying to lighten the load.

I force a smirk. "Born ready." My answer might come off as cocky, but it's better than admitting I'm not.

"Good." He leans in. "Because if you fuck this up tonight, Coach will have your ass. The man is no joke. If you're not careful, he's liable to have you weeding the courtyard of Lancaster Arena. And when you pass out from the exertion, he'll step over your body without a backward glance."

I laugh despite myself, shaking my head. "Wow. Um . . . thanks for the pep talk."

Mason grins. "Anytime."

Together, we make our way onto the ice.

It's pure chaos. The crowd cheering is like nothing I have ever heard before.

It's deafening, and I fucking love it.

This is what I've worked my whole life for.

The minors were nothing like this.

Even the lights here are more blinding, the energy in the arena more palpable. My heart pounds in my chest.

All the doubts creep back in.

Then the puck drops and everything else fades away.

From the second my stick touches the ice, I'm locked in. The Colts are fast, but I'm quicker. I push hard. My lungs tighten from the exertion, but I have too much to lose, so I push through the pain. My skates slice across the ice as I dart down the rink. The puck finds my stick, and instinct takes over.

I pass it to Aiden, who maneuvers around the defense with the ease of a veteran. Now I see that he lives up to the hype. He's that good. He fakes left, then sends the puck back my way. I barely have time to think before I shoot it past the goalie and into the net.

The horn blares, and the crowd erupts.

One goal.

My first.

I don't have time to celebrate. The Colts push hard after the face-off, and suddenly, I'm being crushed against the boards.

Before I can react, Dane is there, barreling into the guy like a freight train. He doesn't even glance my way. He skates off like protecting me is just another part of his job, which I guess it technically is. It still pisses me off, but I don't have time to dwell on it.

The puck's back in play, and I'm moving again, faster this time, more aggressive. I force myself to play harder than I ever have, desperate to prove I belong here. Every pass, every shot, every stride feels like a test, and I. Will. Not. Fail.

I block a pass from one of the Colts forwards, stealing the puck and driving it up the ice.

Another pass. Another shot. Another goal.

Two goals.

By the end of the first period, I'm drenched in sweat but buzzing with adrenaline.

Mason nudges me as we head toward the locker room, his grin wider than I've ever seen. "Not bad, rookie."

"Not bad?" I scoff. "I'm carrying this team already," I joke, or at least attempt to, but seeing as Aiden scowls at me, I don't think it hit the way I wanted. Oh, well. I can play the role of the cocky bastard.

"Easy there." Aiden pushes past us. "You're still a rookie, remember?" he says, confirming my suspicions. He's not my greatest fan. *Yet.* I'll win him over eventually.

I roll my eyes but can't help the smile tugging at my lips. At least I'm starting to prove myself.

Before we leave the rink, I catch sight of Molly in the stands, and my stomach twists. She's sitting near the glass, her face unreadable. Her silence in the hallway still stings, and the fact that she's watching me now only adds fuel to the fire.

Fuck.

The second period is brutal.

The Colts are relentless. Their weak defense from the first

period is tight now. They are trying to close the gap. That much is obvious.

At one point, I'm slammed into the boards again, harder this time. My vision blurs for a second, but before I can even process the hit, Dane is there. He grabs the guy who hit me and makes quick work of putting him in his place.

The penalty box door slams shut behind him, but not before he shoots me a look. I can't tell if it's a warning or an acknowledgment. I hope it's the latter.

It's bad enough that I already got off to a bad start with him. I intend to be with the team for a long time, and since Sinclair is a veteran of the Saints, I'd rather have him on my side than against me.

The whole period is a blur.

Must be the adrenaline.

Because the next thing I know, it's time for the second intermission. Once in the locker room, Dane approaches me.

"Not bad." His tone is dry, and for a moment, I wonder if he's fucking with me.

I glance up to assess his mood. Even though he isn't smiling, I can tell this is the real deal. He means it. "Thanks."

He nods, crossing his arms. "You're a good addition to the team."

The compliment catches me off guard, and I'm not sure how to respond. I feel like I'm at a crossroads with him, and I don't want to fuck this up.

"Thanks," I say again, more sincerely this time.

He studies me for a beat longer before nodding. "Just . . . keep it together, Wilde. We don't need drama."

"I'm not the one causing drama." *Shit*. It slips out before I can stop myself.

I tense, waiting to see how he'll take it. If the olive branch he tossed my way is genuine enough to withstand a snarky comment or two.

Dane's jaw tightens, but instead of snapping back, he exhales heavily and offers a reluctant nod. "Fair enough."

It's not exactly an apology, but it's the closest thing to a truce we've had since I joined the team.

As he walks away, I can't help but feel a flicker of relief. Maybe, just maybe, things are starting to look up.

By the time the final horn sounds, we're up by two goals, and the arena erupts in cheers.

As I skate toward the bench, Mason greets me first, clapping me on the back. "Hell of a debut, Wilde."

"Thanks." I nod.

Dane is next, his expression unreadable but his nod of approval clear.

"Good game." Note to self: Dane isn't a talker. This is the best I'm going to get.

"I did kill it," I tease. This is who I am and always have been. Hell, I was voted class clown for my high school superlatives. It's best they know my personality now if we're ever going to get along.

He doesn't say or do anything for a second. *Fuck, did I read this wrong?*

Then he shakes his head, but I swear I see his lips twitch.

Good.

This can work.

Even with the rocky start, I can make a home here on the Saints.

For now, I'll take that win.

SEASON TWO

chapter five

Hudson

It's not a good look for me that I'm running late. Again. It's starting to be the story of my life, but this time, I had no choice.

Family shit.

And unfortunately, my family lives just far enough to cause problems if I ever have to jet off to see them.

The team is set to leave any minute now.

Shit.

Please tell me I didn't fuck this up.

The light turns red. I pull to a stop and reach over the center console to grab my phone.

Dammit. It's off.

I switched it off earlier when I was with my mother and never switched it back on.

The moment my phone powers to life, I know I'm in trouble.

It chimes a million times. Texts. Messages. Missed calls.

I mean, sure, I'm running late, but it's not like we are leaving for another . . . I look at my phone. Well, fuck.

Now. We're set to take off now. Shit. That doesn't make sense.

The time change between Illinois and Ohio always messes me up.

I might have left at eleven, but the moment I crossed over the state line, I lost an hour.

Aiden: Where you at?

Then there's Mason's nonstop bombardment.

Mason: Bro, answer your phone.

Mason: Wilde. Fuck, dude. Where you at?

Mason: Seriously. Where the hell are you, Wilde?

And more texts from Aiden.

Aiden: Coach is about to freak out.

Aiden: You've got five minutes before Coach loses his mind.

And finally . . . Dane.

Dane: Call Coach. Now.

Dane isn't one to message me, so I know shit is serious.

"Goddammit."

I close the app and open my email instead.

Just as I suspected, there's one from Coach. No question, he's pissed.

While they haven't technically left yet, I won't be there before they take off. The light turns green. I flick on my turn signal, pull into a random parking lot, and park, dialing Coach's number.

He answers on the first ring.

My back clenches in anticipation, bracing for impact.

"Where are you, Hudson?"

Shit. When he says my name like this, I feel like a schoolboy about to get scolded by my dad for coming home after curfew.

The only difference is the consequences are worse this time.

"Sorry, Coach." I run a palm down my face. "I thought I'd be back in time."

"Don't give me that," he barks, louder than anyone has a right to be on the phone. "You're not on the plane, and we're wheels up in two. This is a pattern with you, Wilde. Late for your first warm-up. Late for your first game. Hell, you were probably late being born."

I was. Forty-three weeks. Mom harps about how difficult her post-term pregnancy was whenever she begs me to come back home for the holidays. Not that she needs much convincing. I love my family more than anything.

"I had a family emergency," I try to explain, my voice tight.

"Yeah?" Coach snorts, clearly unimpressed. "What is it this time? A long-lost brother in need of a kidney? Your dog ate your skates?"

The man has never let me live down my first game.

It's been one year. And still, he hasn't let it go.

Will he ever take me seriously? Or am I always destined to be the class clown?

The big disappointment that he'd be happy to trade me if it weren't for how good I am.

Since the owners are here to make money, trading me wouldn't go easy for him. I bring in a crowd.

Which is most likely why he hates me.

"Coach, it's not an excuse. I was needed at home. I'm on my way, but I won't be there on time. Can you guys—"

"Absolutely not. This is the National Hockey League, Wilde. You don't just show up when it's convenient for you. Find your own way to the game, or don't bother coming at all. You understand me?"

Boy, do I ever.

Before I can reply, the line goes dead.

Shit. That was rough.

Okay. Off to the rink. I need to grab something and head out.

By the time I make it to the arena, the parking lot is eerily quiet.

Just as I suspected, no one is here. It's empty. Actually, there *is* one car here, most likely owned by someone who works in security.

I park my Mustang in my usual spot and fling open the door, hopping on my hood. The morning light glints off the glossy paint as I pull out my phone and add all the guys who texted me to a group chat, one by one.

And then I name it: All Hail Hudson.

Hudson: Since my time is valuable, this was easier.

Aiden: What is this?

Hudson: It's a group chat. Duh.

Mason: One called HUDSON IS AN ASS.

Mason changed the name of the chat to "Hudson is an ass."
Hudson changed the name of the chat to "Saints of Redville."

Hudson: I thought it was cute. Guess not.

Dane: Why do we have a group chat?

Hudson: It's easier.

Aiden: For whom?

Dane: Not for me, that's for sure.

Mason: I like it.

Hudson: I knew you were my favorite.

Dane: Why am I here?

Hudson: Cause we're friends.

Dane: Are we?

Hudson: Ouch.

Aiden: It's a legit statement.

Mason: Damn, guys.

Hudson: I'm on my way. There was a complication.

Dane: Again, why are you telling us this?

Hudson: Ouch again. I'm starting to get a complex and think you don't like me.

Dane: . . .

I pocket my phone and jog into the locker room, my steps echoing in the empty arena. It's darker than I'm used to. The place feels weird without the usual chaos. Just silence. A small light from the office is the only thing illuminating the space.

If I didn't know better, I'd think no one is here.

I head straight to my locker, digging for my keys. I need to grab something. While I might not have as many pregame rituals as Aiden, I do always carry a picture of my family with me to every game I go to.

Opening my locker, I grab it from the shelf just as a voice cuts through the quiet.

"Hello?"

I freeze with my hand still in the locker.

I know that voice.

Correction: I *hate* that voice.

Molly.

Of course, it's her. The bane of my existence.

Figures she'd be the one here.

Who knows what she's doing, but she's always around.

There are soft footsteps as she approaches, pausing just shy of my locker.

"Oh, it's you."

I pivot where I'm standing and face her. "Hex."

"For crying out loud, can you stop calling me this? It's been a year. Get over it. I know I did."

Easy for her to say.

That day changed my whole trajectory on this team.

Now, all everyone sees is a player. An idiot. A reckless teammate who can't be relied on, and then a night like tonight happens, and lo and behold, I prove them right, even though the truth is far from what they all think.

Not that anyone cares to find that shit out.

"Great," I mutter, gently pocketing the photo. "Just what I needed. What are you even doing here, *Hex*?"

"I left something here last night." She shrugs, probably enjoying my misery.

We both stare at each other, silent for a moment.

"Well?" I make a shooing motion. "Don't you have something better to do? Another life to ruin?"

To say we don't get along after what happened would be an understatement. In the beginning, she tried to make nice, offering a water bottle after practice or an extra pack of grip tape. But I made it clear what I think of her backstabbing ass.

And from there, it spiraled out of control. We finally tore off the gloves. Now, there's no conversation we can't turn into a fight. No stone either of us will leave unturned.

She steps into my path, waiting for me to slam my locker shut before she speaks again. "What's the excuse this time? Alarm didn't go off? Stuck in traffic? Did you forget you're a professional athlete?"

I grit my teeth, resisting the urge to snap back. "Not that it's any of your business, but I had a family emergency."

Her smirk fades, replaced by a look of mild surprise. "Oh."

"Yeah, oh."

"Is everything okay?"

I sigh because she's being genuine, and it makes me hate her a little less. Emphasis on little. "Just peachy. Now, if you'll excuse me—"

"You're still late," she points out, frowning.

I mock clap around her head, knowing it'll piss her off. "Wow. A-plus observation, Captain Obvious."

Our brief truce is gone.

In an instant, the fire returns to her eyes, and she's back to her snarky self.

Molly leans a hip against a locker, her brows pulled together in mock concern. "I mean, I'm sure the team will totally understand. It's not like you have a history of this or anything."

I let out a sharp breath, running a hand through my hair. "You really live for this, don't you?"

"What can I say?" She tilts her head, shrugging. "You're easy to mess with."

I shake my head and turn my back on her. I have no interest in dealing with her after the day I've had. Instead, I head out the door, determined to beeline straight to my car.

"Drive safe, Wilde," she calls after me, her words echoing in the empty room.

With my luck, Hex just cursed me, and I'll end up in the middle of a ten-car pileup by the end of the night.

Molly stays behind. She can lock up. Or maybe someone from the cleaning crew will.

Not my problem.

I storm into the parking lot, shoving my bag into the Mustang's trunk with more force than necessary. Sliding into the driver's seat, I place the key in the ignition and turn.

Nothing happens.

No big deal.

This happens.

It's an older Mustang. A classic. My first purchase after I signed with the team.

The only problem with it? Sometimes the ignition is temperamental. Like most beautiful girls in my life, she came with a temper.

"Come on," I mutter, love tapping the steering wheel.

I turn the key again, and the engine doesn't so much as sputter this time. It's obvious something is wrong, and my biggest fear comes true.

The battery is dead, and so am I.

I slam my hands against the steering wheel, leaning back against the headrest as my frustration boils over. Of course, the battery's dead. Because why wouldn't it be?

I'm fucked.

Unless . . .

Nope.

That's off the table. Never in a million years.

I palm my phone, debating whether to call someone for help. But who? I don't know anyone in Redville. Everyone I *do* know is on that flight, halfway to the next city, and I'd rather eat my stick shift than run back into the arena and beg Molly for a favor.

But I need to get to the game, and the flights are booked. I checked on my way here. Shit. Maybe I can rent a car in time. The hotel is not that far, only five and a half hours away. Close enough that Coach won't even miss me. As long as I'm there tomorrow . . .

I check all the rentals in the area. Nothing is available. Fuck.

In my periphery, I spot Molly strolling to her car, her key swinging around her finger on a chain.

With a groan, I drop my head back against the seat.

This day can't possibly get any worse.

But knowing my luck? It probably will.

chapter six

Molly

I'M HALFWAY OUT THE DOOR, MY COFFEE THERMOS IN HAND, when I spot Hudson Wilde stalking across the parking lot toward me.

Whatever he wants, I'm sure I won't like it.

"Hell no," I mutter, quickening my pace.

I don't have time for whatever brand of asshole he wants to introduce me to today.

"Molly," he calls out, his voice tinged with a hint of desperation.

I ignore him and keep walking. I parked across the lot in my assigned space, a solid distance from the arena. I don't know why I'm always the rule follower. No one's here. I could've parked right in front and wouldn't have to deal with the madman beelining for me.

Hudson cuts me off, his bag slung over one shoulder and his expression equal parts sheepish and determined. "I need a ride."

I blink, certain I've misheard him. "You what?"

"A ride," he repeats, shifting his weight awkwardly. "To the game."

My mouth is wide open.

I can't believe what this asshole just had the nerve to ask me. Finally, I shake myself out of the stupor. "You're joking, right?"

"Do I look like I'm joking?"

He doesn't. Not at all. But I can't entertain such a ridiculous request. I refuse to.

"Absolutely not."

"Molly."

I cross my arms over my chest, glaring at Hudson. "Oh, *now* I'm Molly."

I've never met someone quite like Hudson Wilde.

He's warped into the biggest jerk I know. Yes, I did him dirty. I should've backed him up last year. Pulled Coach aside and explain what happened in private. But then, Dane had to follow up on the incident and blow everything out of proportion.

And I just . . . couldn't.

I couldn't let Dane find out.

One thing would lead to another, and he'd unravel every secret I've tried so hard to keep for ten years.

Hudson bats his lashes as if that'll change anything. "Pretty please?"

"Hudson"—I cross my arms—"I don't even like being in the same room with you. What makes you think I'd spend five hours in a car with you?"

He runs a hand through his hair, clearly trying to keep his frustration in check. "Look, I don't exactly have options here. My car's dead, and I missed the plane. I'll pay for gas or whatever. Just help me out."

I take a long sip of my coffee, pretending to mull it over. "Hmm. Let me think . . . No."

"Molly—"

"Nope." I turn on my heel and head toward my car.

"I'll be quiet the whole ride," he calls after me. "You won't even know I'm there."

"That's the dream," I retort, not bothering to look back.

beautiful collide

I'm halfway there when I feel my phone vibrate. I pull it out of my pocket. It's Dane.

Dane: Give him a ride.

"Seriously?" I hiss, spinning around to face Hudson. "You went to my brother?"

"What? Can't hear you. You're too far away." His voice carries a mocking tone as he cups a hand to his ear.

He's such an ass.

My phone buzzes again.

Dane: Please, Molly.

I groan, my jaw clenching as I read the message again, hoping I've misunderstood.

Me: Tell him to take a bus.

Dane: Molly.

I can practically hear the warning in his tone, and it grates on my nerves.

Dane: I can always fire you and ask my new assistant to drive him . . .

Of course. Dane fires me five to six times a week. He's under the impression that I'm only working for him out of guilt and that I'd be happier pursuing my own interests. Sure, he has a point. A tiny one. Practically microscopic, if you ask me.

At the end of the day, I need to stick with Dane.

He gave up his life for me.

It's only fair.

And that's why I refuse to accept his firing.

Me: As if you could actually fire me.

Dane: Don't tempt me.

Dane: Just drive him. Please.

Me: Fine. But you owe me hazard pay.

Dane: Thanks.

I can hear Hudson's footsteps crunching the gravel behind me. As much as I don't want to because I know I'm not ready to see his smug face, I have no choice but to turn and look at him. He's almost here, and I'm not okay with him behind me.

I pivot sharply. "What are you doing?"

"Getting a ride," he says nonchalantly, shoving his hands into his pockets.

"I can't believe you ratted me out to my brother."

"I didn't rat you out." He shrugs, his lips twitching into a smirk.

"Yeah. Okay. I'll bite. What did you do?"

"I asked for help, and Dane offered you up on a platter." He pulls his phone from his pocket again, holding it up.

"No way."

"Here. See for yourself." He lifts his phone until it's dangling in my face, his smirk deepening.

And true to his words . . . there, clear as day, it says:

Dane: Ask Molly. I'm sure she would be happy to help.

Bastard.

I clench my jaw, my fingers curling into fists at my sides. Although driving Hudson is the last thing I want to do right now, I can't say no.

Not now. Not when my brother—the guy who basically saved my life without even really knowing it—just freaking told him to ask me.

I shove his phone out of my face and readjust my bag over my shoulder, my glare sharp enough to cut glass. "Get in the car."

His brows lift in surprise. "Just like that?"

"You heard me," I snap, unlocking the doors. "Apparently, I'm your chauffeur now. We need to leave. Now. The Weather Channel mentioned a crazy storm later tonight, and I really don't want to have to drive in that."

"I'm ready whenever you are," Hudson says, his voice annoyingly cheerful.

"And your car?" I gesture to the beautiful car that won't take him anywhere.

"Guess I have no choice but to leave her." He sighs, glancing back at it. "I can't afford to be late."

"Says the guy who missed the plane because he was already late," I mutter, raising an eyebrow.

"That was beyond my control."

"Sure."

He looks at me like he wants to say something—maybe fire an insult at me, or perhaps something else. I can't place the look in his eyes. Other than exhaustion, he looks dead to the world with hollow, dark bags under his eyes.

"I can drive," he offers, his voice softer now.

"Um, this isn't the 1920s, Wilde." I tilt my head, narrowing my eyes at him. "Women are capable of driving."

"I never said you weren't capable." His lips quirk up into a teasing grin. "Jeez. Did you wake up on the wrong side of the bed . . . again?"

"Seriously? Are you really insulting me after asking for a favor?"

His eyes widen as if it's finally dawning on him that I do not, in fact, need to give him a lift.

I raise my brow, tapping my foot impatiently. "Well?"

"Nope." He holds up his hands in surrender. "You drive. I'm tired anyway."

"Long night?"

"You can say that," he mutters, running a hand through his disheveled hair.

"Eh." I give him a pointed look. "Is this your way of saying you were up all night with God knows who doing God knows what?"

"You, of all people, should know that getting laid isn't the reason I'm ever late," he says with a smirk that doesn't quite reach his eyes.

"Why would I know that?" My tone is sharp. Defensive.

Of course, I know I was in the wrong for the way we started off. So, no, I don't hate Hudson for being mad at me for last year. It's everything that's come *after* that I have no tolerance for.

He doesn't need to argue with me every chance he gets. We

could make peace. Have a truce. Agree to ignore each other whenever possible.

But I suppose neither of us can help ourselves.

At least, that's what it seems like.

This time, it's Hudson who lifts his brow. The closet. It always circles back to the damn closet.

"This again." I hop into the driver's seat, sparing him a glance as he dumps his bag in the back seat and slams the door shut. "I told you I'm sorry. You don't need to keep—"

"I didn't say anything. It's your guilt that did."

I roll my eyes. "Just get in the car."

He hops into the passenger seat beside me.

My lungs puff out, and then I exhale. This is going to be a long five hours.

We aren't even out of the parking lot before my hand collides with his while reaching for the radio.

His fingers beat me to it, and he changes the station.

"What do you think you're doing?" I snap, glancing at him.

He settles in his seat. "Everyone knows the passenger works the radio."

"Really? Everyone?"

"It's like Road Trip 101."

"This isn't a road trip. We aren't friends, and you don't get to pick the music."

"Real question. Is it just me, or are you always this crabby?" he teases in a light tone.

I continue to look forward, not giving him the satisfaction of a glance in his direction. "It's just you."

From the corner of my eye, I see his hand playfully clutch his chest. "Ouch, I'm wounded."

"You'll live."

My mouth opens, and I'm about to say more, but I stop myself. Five hours is a long time to be stuck in the car with this man.

"Go on, say it," Hudson urges, his voice low.

"Say what?"

Now, I *do* glance in his direction as I slow the car down to a stop at the edge of the parking lot.

Damn, he's got a smug grin on his face. Too bad he's so hot. It would be much easier if he weren't.

"Unfortunately."

"I never said that."

"You wanted to."

I did.

The truth is, I don't hate him. Not really. I hate that he saw me at my weakest moment. He's a daily reminder that the scared girl I thought I left behind is still very much a part of me.

I'm better now. The panic attacks don't occur regularly like they did right after my parents died when I was a girl.

They stopped soon after Dane stepped in and signed me up for therapy. He never knew I got them, let alone why I would. Before that day in the closet, I thought I was doing better, but every now and then, they do come back.

And every time I look at Hudson Wilde, he reminds me of that pesky fact.

The silence in the car is thick and uncomfortable as we pull out of the lot. I keep my eyes firmly on the road, my grip on the wheel tight.

"This wasn't my first choice, you know," Hudson says after a few minutes.

"Yeah, well, it wasn't mine either," I snap, my tone icy.

He leans back in his seat, crossing his arms. "You always this pleasant, or is it just me?"

"Oh, it's just you," I reply sweetly. "You bring out the best in me."

He lets out a dry laugh. "Well, that's mutual."

"How about we just don't talk?" I suggest, my voice tight.

"Sounds like a plan," Hudson responds, reaching forward to adjust the volume. "I'm going to nap. Wake me if you need me."

Good.

Great.

The tension simmers just beneath the surface. But when he goes quiet, and the only sound is the pitter-patter of the raindrops, I miss the company.

Any company.

Because now I'm just alone in my thoughts.

And that's a scary place to be.

I had another panic attack last week. At Dane's place. The wind slammed the door shut behind me as I raided his pantry, and I almost outed myself in front of my brother. I've been diligently avoiding him since, which hasn't been easy, given that I'm his assistant.

At the next light, Hudson clears his throat. "Thanks for doing this. Even if it's under duress."

"Don't thank me," I mutter. "Thank Dane. He's the one who insisted. If it were up to me, you'd be on a bus."

"I will. Right after I thank him for all the other wonderful things he's done for me this week, like letting me get railed in the hip during practice."

Despite myself, a small laugh escapes me, and I bite my lip to stifle it.

"Was that a laugh?"

"No," I say quickly, glaring at the road.

Hudson relaxes against the leather with a smug grin. "Sounded like a laugh."

"You're delusional."

"And you're bad at hiding when you think I'm funny."

I shake my head, refusing to give him the satisfaction of a response.

We've barely made it to the freeway, and I'm ready to toss him and his duffel bag to the curb.

chapter seven

Molly

IT FEELS LIKE AN ETERNITY HAS PASSED SINCE WE STARTED driving. Occasionally, Hudson will shift in his seat or mess with the vents, breaking the monotony of the road. Other than that, it's been completely silent for three hours. Two more to go.

Already, I've run out of ways to silently hate Hudson, so I've started focusing on the hum of the tires against the pavement and counting mile markers to pass the time. We couldn't agree on a radio station or playlist, so music is not even playing.

The rain pounds on my windshield.

I glance at the clock on the dashboard, debating whether it's worth stopping for coffee. Before I can decide, the shrill wail of a siren cuts through the car like a knife.

"What the hell—" I startle, gripping the wheel tighter.

Hudson sits up straighter, his head tilting as he listens. "Tornado sirens."

My stomach twists into a knot. Freaking *tornado* sirens. My foot eases off the gas as dread pools in my chest.

Dane. My thoughts fly to him immediately. Did their plane land safely? Are they already at the hotel? What if—

No. Stop. They flew. They're fine.

The flight from Redville isn't too long, and since the team left before us, they're definitely already there. So there's nothing to worry about.

I exhale sharply, gripping the wheel harder to ground myself, my knuckles white.

Okay, it's fine. It's all fine.

But then the realization slams into me—*I'm* not fine.

Tornado sirens mean one thing—there's a tornado nearby. And I'm driving straight into it.

Panic bubbles up, clawing at my throat. My breaths come faster, and the edges of my vision start to blur.

"Relax," Hudson says, his voice maddeningly calm.

I glare at him, incredulous. "Relax? Are you serious? There's a tornado out there, Hudson."

"I'm aware," he informs me, pulling his phone out of his pocket.

He doesn't even look worried. He's so infuriatingly composed that I want to scream.

My cell phone starts blaring with a warning, adding to the chaos.

My heart pounds faster. "What should we do?"

Hudson shrugs, his brow furrowing. "Depends on where it's on the ground."

I shoot him a quick look, frustration bubbling up. "Can you check where it's on the ground?"

"Will do."

Another alert blares from my phone.

He's taking too long to search.

"What are you doing?" I snap, my hands tightening on the wheel.

Hudson's fingers fly across his screen. "Looking up the nearest safe spot."

"How are you so calm?" I demand, my voice trembling.

He shrugs, glancing out the window. "Panicking won't make the tornado go away. Plus, it's not my first time dealing with one of these."

"Great," I mutter, my heart pounding. "Glad you're an expert."

He ignores my sarcasm. "Take the next exit."

"What?"

"Take the exit," he repeats, more firmly this time. "There's an old gas station about five miles off the freeway. It's got a decent structure. We'll be safer there than on the road."

I hesitate, my instincts screaming to keep going. To outrun whatever storm is coming. But the logical part of me knows he's right. You can't outrun a tornado.

"Fine," I finally relent, gripping the wheel and steering toward the exit.

I hate to admit it, but I'm glad he came with me on the drive. I would've freaked out had I been alone and maybe even kept driving through the tornado.

He continues scrolling on his phone. "We're not too far out."

I keep my eyes on the road, but out of the corner of my eye, I'm glued to Hudson's movements.

The sirens wail louder in the distance. The sky around us is dark and ominous, like a scene out of a bad horror movie. The storm grows louder with each passing second, its presence heavy and oppressive.

My hands grip the steering wheel tighter until my knuckles ache, and I veer off the highway. I don't need to know where the storm is hitting to know I don't want to be driving seventy miles per hour when it does.

Because it's not a question of *if*—it's a question of *when*.

The sky has already darkened to an unsettling shade. Lightning cracks in the distance, a stark contrast against the blackened clouds. The wind hammers against the car, shoving it in bursts that feel like we're being tugged by invisible hands.

Other than the storm and the sirens, the road to the gas station is eerily quiet, the sky growing darker with each passing minute. The sirens blare in the distance, a constant reminder of how precarious this situation is.

Hudson is still infuriatingly calm, guiding me with quiet directions as we approach the station. His steady tone chips away at the panic clawing at my chest.

"There," he says, pointing at a run-down building up ahead.

The gas station looks like it's been abandoned for years. The paint on the building is faded and cracked, and some od the windows are boarded up.

Hudson shoves his phone into his pocket, the picture of relaxed. "This looks promising."

"Seriously? Are we looking at the same place?"

"Got any better options?"

"I mean, no. But this place looks like it belongs in *The Texas Chainsaw Massacre*."

"The only other choice is starring in *Twister*, and not in an epic Glen Powell sort of way."

"I feel like you're more Bill Paxton."

"While I loved that man, I'd end up being the random guy nobody remembers—the one who gets sucked into a tornado before anyone learns his name. So come on. Let's go."

I park as close to the entrance as possible and hesitate. "Are you sure it's safe?"

Hudson is already out of the car before I can unbuckle my seat belt. "It's safer than out here." He tosses open my door and holds out a hand, motioning for me to hurry up. "Come on."

"I'm fine," I snap, brushing past him as I climb out.

"Sure you are," he mutters, following close.

The moment I step outside, I'm drenched. The wind batters me so hard I stagger.

Without asking, Hudson snatches my hand and drags me toward the building. "Let's go."

beautiful collide

He sprints toward the door, and I follow, struggling to keep up.

Luckily, the door is glass, which should be easy to break into. Hudson seems to think the same thing as he grabs something from the ground and bashes the glass above the knob.

I watch as he pulls his sleeve over his hand, then reaches in to turn the deadbolt. A second later, the door creaks open, and we dash inside.

The air in the gas station is stale and musty, thick with neglect. I wrinkle my nose. "This place is disgusting."

"It's not the Ritz." Hudson walks farther into the building, using his phone's flashlight to guide him. "But it'll do."

The stench of oil clings to the surface and tickles my nose. This is bad.

Stop that thought.

Just because it smells doesn't mean we're in danger. We're safe, for now—or at least safe from the rain and wind.

I cross my arms, leaning against the counter as he checks the back rooms. My pulse is still racing, but I can feel it starting to slow. His calm demeanor infuriates me, though I can't deny that it's also grounding.

He reappears a moment later, brushing cobwebs off his jacket. "No basement, but the walls are solid. We'll be fine here."

I nod, swallowing hard. "Okay."

"You good?" His gaze softens just enough to make me uncomfortable.

"Yeah." I look away. "I'm fine."

I don't believe my own words.

I stare at the tiles instead, willing the storm to go away.

A scraping noise catches my attention. I glance over to find Hudson dragging furniture toward the door, forming a makeshift barricade.

As if that'll stop a tornado.

The space is small, and there's nowhere to hide—or at least, I don't think there is. Hudson already confirmed there's no basement.

The lights are off, and the interior feels suffocating and eerie. Wrapping my arms around myself, I try to stop trembling, but the blaring sirens in the distance make it impossible.

I start to pace back and forth. Nervous energy winning over.

"Will you stop that?" Hudson grunts, nodding toward me. "You're gonna wear a hole in the floor."

"Sorry, Hudson, I didn't realize my existential crisis bothered you." I whip my soaked hair off my shoulders. Beads of water spray my face.

"There she is." He turns to look at me. "The real you. Aren't you tired of pretending to be perfect all the time?"

"Perfect? You don't even like me, so why would you care what I am?"

"True," he admits with a shrug. "But your brother would kill me if I let you spiral into whatever this is." His gaze softens, just barely. "So maybe . . . don't?"

The wind chooses that moment to howl louder, shaking the windows. My chest feels tight. Like the pressure building inside me mimics the pressure of the storm raging outside.

Each breath comes faster. Shallower.

I can't pull in enough air.

I can't breathe.

I'm dying.

"Stop it."

Hudson's smirk fades. "Molly?"

My knees buckle slightly, and I reach for a shelf for support.

"I can't—I can't breathe," I choke out. "What if it's not enough? What if—"

He shakes his head. "Stop that thought right there. It *will* be."

I can barely hear him over the sound of my own pulse.

"We're okay. I've got you."

My breath hitches as I look up at him.

My body trembles harder, the fear overwhelming me. "I think I'm dying—"

Hudson crosses the room in two long strides, grabbing me by my shoulders.

"Hey, hey, look at me." His voice is low, steady, more commanding than comforting. "You're not dying. You're panicking. Big difference."

My eyes lock on his. "You don't get it—"

"Then make me get it." He tilts his head. "What do you need?"

"Distraction," I say too quickly. "Just . . . something. Anything."

Hudson hesitates for a second, his brow furrowing. "Anything, huh?"

Before I can react, he pulls me into his arms.

I want to push away, to protest, but with my head against his chest, I can hear his heartbeat. Its steady rhythm calms me.

He doesn't wait for me to respond. Hudson dips his head, and his lips brush against mine with just enough pressure to make it obvious he's waiting to see how I'll react. On instinct, I freeze for a beat.

"What are you doing?" I whisper against his mouth.

"Distracting you." His voice sounds rough. His lips hover over mine, so close that I can feel the heat radiating from him. "Unless you want me to stop?"

My breath hitches in my chest, and adrenaline surges through my veins.

"You're an idiot," I mutter, but I'm crazy enough that I don't pull away.

"Probably," he agrees. Then he kisses me again, harder this time, like he's claiming something.

His hands slide up to cup my face, rough palms anchoring me to the here and now.

Not letting me get lost in the storm raging outside.

I clutch the front of his damp shirt. Despite some wet spots the soft cotton is still warm under my touch.

The kiss grounds me.

His lips are firm yet gentle, a perfect balance that steadies me.

Everything fades away.

I forget the storm. Forget where I am. *Forget myself.*

The world stops on its axis.

It narrows to this singular moment...

His mouth on mine, the taste of rain lingering on his lips, the way his hand cups the back of my neck like he's afraid I might disappear.

I lean into him.

I need this.

Need him.

I don't want to think about the storm, the mistakes, the fears. *Not right now.*

But then, just as quickly as the moment takes over, a flicker of doubt creeps in.

What happens when this ends? When the storm passes? The thought makes my stomach twist, but I shove it aside.

Not now. Not yet.

For now, I let myself sink deeper into the kiss, clinging to him like he's the calm in the middle of my storm.

For now, I let myself feel. For now, I let myself forget.

When we finally break apart, we're both breathing hard.

I stare at him. "That was—"

"Effective?" he answers for me, his lips quirking into a cocky grin.

I push him back. "A mistake."

My cheeks feel flushed, and I'm happy for the darkness.

He chuckles. Smug bastard.

"Sure, Molly. Keep telling yourself that."

chapter eight

Hudson

WELL, FUCK.

I don't know what that was, but I want it again.

Twenty-four hours a day.

But this isn't the time or placc.

"Come on." I brush damp strands of hair from Molly's face. "You should sit."

She nods and pulls back, her movements stiff. "Okay. Where?"

I shrug off my jacket, shake off the droplets clinging to the nylon material, and spread it on the floor. "Here."

Molly hesitates, glancing at the filthy floor barely covered by my jacket.

She bites her lip. "Hudson, it's fine. I don't need—"

"Molly." I soften my voice as I gently guide her toward the makeshift seat. "Just sit. You're shaking."

She slinks down, pulling her knees to her chest and wrapping her arms around them.

I start to step away. "I'll be right back."

Her head snaps up, her wide eyes locking on mine. "Where are you going?"

"To look for stuff," I reply, scanning the dimly lit aisles.

"Stuff?" She scrunches her nose. "Vague much."

"Yeah, well, I might not find anything, so it's best to be vague. I'm just looking for anything I can find." My answer sucks, but it's the truth. Who knows if I'll find anything useful, so I don't want to give her false hope.

I take a few steps and spot a flashlight on a nearby shelf.

Bingo.

If this works, I won't have to drain my phone's battery.

I carry it over to her and place it in her outstretched palm.

Molly turns it over, trying to switch it on, but it doesn't work. Well, that sucks, and now I look like an idiot.

She moves to hand it back, but I shake my head. "Keep it. You don't know if you'll need it."

She raises an eyebrow. "Why would I need a dead flashlight?"

"For protection," I reply with a shrug.

She hugs the flashlight to her chest. "Um. From who?"

"I don't know. Maybe an animal."

Her lips twitch, and she wants to laugh. "You think that if a wolf breaks in, I'll be able to use this?"

My lips tip into a smirk. "You never know. He could be a very hungry one."

Molly laughs. It sounds shaky, like she can't help but do it, but she's still afraid. "So, now, I have to worry about a wolf, a tornado, and let's be real, this place is straight out of a serial killer movie. So yeah . . . that, too."

"Yep. Have fun with that."

I start to walk away from where she's sitting.

My footsteps tap the tile floor, echoing in the space as I explore the aisles, running my fingers along the dusty shelves.

This place is surprisingly well-stocked. Something tells me it's only been closed for a few months—maybe a year. That also means some of this food might still be good.

I rummage through the items and grin when I find what I'm looking for.

"Bingo," I mutter under my breath.

Food.

The shelves are pretty bare, but there are a few cans of lord knows what. I keep going, bending down to see what type of candy bars I can find. The plastic is dusty, but some of these might do the trick.

I see chips, too, and grab them as well.

"I found Twinkies." I wave a pack in the air.

These things could survive a nuclear war.

Molly jumps up from where she's sitting, ready to take some of the food out of my hands. "Pass. I'm not that desperate."

"Could've fooled me," I shoot back.

"Funny," she mutters just loud enough for me to hear her.

If it were lighter out, I would bet my last snack she also rolled her eyes at me.

The only thing I can see is that she's watching me.

I head back to her, pulling my phone from my pocket and switching on its flashlight. The beam cuts through the gloom as I stand beside her.

"What else did you bring?" she asks.

"Not much. It was slim pickings."

Her brow furrows. "How do you know it's good?"

I grin. "Because everyone knows these babies will last through an apocalypse."

I place the Twinkie in her hand, watching as her fingers trace the wrapper.

Molly stares at it, then raises an eyebrow at me. "So you actually did get Twinkies? I thought you were messing with me."

I nod. "Of course, I did. I never mess around when it comes

to Twinkies or Girl Scout cookies, but unfortunately, we are all out of those."

"You're fired."

"I got chips, though. But we should check the dates on those."

"And not on the Twinkies?" she asks, her lips quirking up slightly.

"Everyone knows Twinkies don't go bad."

"That's BS," she says, shaking her head.

"Guess we'll find out." I tear open the wrapper and hold it out to her. "Ladies first."

She crosses her arms, leaning back against the wall. "No. I insist you go first since you found it."

I narrow my eyes. "Basically, you want to see if I die first?"

"Yeah."

"Real nice, Hex," I mutter before taking a bite.

It's just as good as I remember it to be. I haven't had one of these since I was a kid.

I grin, chewing dramatically. "Yum . . ."

She rolls her eyes and starts to eat, a small smile tugging at her lips.

Side by side, we eat in silence. Things feel normal—or as normal as they can be when you're sitting on the floor of an abandoned gas station eating Twinkies during a tornado.

But then the building shakes, and Molly flinches, her body tense.

There's a very good chance the windows will shatter. Hopefully, the glass is tempered, but from here, I can't tell, and I certainly won't be getting up to check.

That would require leaving Molly alone.

Speaking of Molly, she stiffens beside me, glancing up at the ceiling.

There's an ominous feeling in the air as the night sky illuminates with a fresh crack of lightning, and the entire building shudders again.

"Oh my God."

"Relax. Everything will be fine—"

As if Mother Nature has a sick sense of humor, a deafening crack cuts me off as if to challenge me. Molly jerks so hard, I'm afraid she's going to hurt herself if she doesn't calm down.

I set aside the Twinkies and move closer. "Molly."

"I don't want to die here," she blurts out.

"You're not going to," I respond firmly.

"No." She shakes her head. "I don't mean just the tornado. I mean . . . like this. Trapped in this shitty gas station with you."

"Ouch." I press a hand to my chest in mock pain, but I need her feisty attitude right now. That's how she'll push away the fear. "I don't think I've ever been so flattered."

"You're impossible."

"Yet here we are." I lean in. "What are you gonna do about it?"

All of a sudden, she grabs my shirt, yanks me down to her level, and kisses me.

It's not a gentle kiss. It's hard. And passionate.

It's hate and want. Fear and survival.

Raw and unpolished.

Driven by adrenaline and something else.

Defiance.

I can't help but smirk against her lips. "I thought this was a mistake."

"Fuck the mistake. Just make me forget."

I let my thumb trace the delicate line of her neck before leaning down and capturing her lips again.

With my other hand, I cup the back of her neck, pulling us closer until no space exists between us.

She clings to me, her fingers fisted in my shirt like she's afraid I'll let her go.

I won't.

Not now, at least.

After a few more passes of my tongue, I finally pull back, breaking the kiss.

Her lips are swollen, her breath coming in shallow gasps, and for a moment, I can't bring myself to look away. Damn. She's beautiful like this—flushed, dazed, and completely in the moment.

I swallow hard before reaching my hand out to tuck a loose strand of hair behind her ear.

It's such a small gesture, but it feels bigger, and I'm not sure how to feel about it. "Are you okay?"

She nods.

My hand lingers on her back for another second. *I should step back.* I should say something clever, something that breaks the tension.

I grin and do just that. "Good to know."

"What?"

I wink. "That Twinkies get you all hot and bothered."

"Shut up." Molly scoffs, but I know by the raspy pitch of her voice that she isn't upset.

I lean forward, almost touching her lips again. "Make me."

She does.

She kisses me again, tangling her fingers in my damp hair.

I don't hesitate to kiss her back, tilting my head down to deepen it.

From there, I wrap my arms around her waist, bracketing her body to mine.

Lost in the moment, she doesn't notice the storm, or how the wind howls, or how the entire building seems to shake around us. She only notices me, and that's exactly what I want.

My hands roam. Hers do, too, wild and unrelenting. They pull my shirt up until her small hands connect with my skin.

When the kiss ends, I rest my forehead on hers.

"So," I breathe out. "Am I still impossible?"

"Yes," she murmurs, brushing her lips against mine again like she can't get enough. "But I'm starting to see the appeal."

I chuckle. "Good. Because I don't think you're done with me yet."

I kiss down her jaw, trailing my lips against her skin.

Our breaths come fast and ragged in the dark store. I push her gently against the wall, hands roaming over her curves. Molly arches into me with a soft gasp.

"We shouldn't," she whispers, even as she tugs my shirt over my head.

"Probably not," I agree, helping her shed her own top.

But we're both too far gone to stop now. The fear and adrenaline have ignited something primal between us. My lips crash back onto hers as I lift her, her legs wrapping around my waist.

I carry Molly down the darkened aisles, but it's not easy. With each step I take, she trails hot kisses along my neck.

She's driving me wild.

My body feels like it's on fire.

"Wait," she breathes, tickling my skin. "Do you have a condom?"

I groan. "Fuck, I don't. Wait . . . maybe there's one here."

There better be one because I need this woman more than I need air to breathe.

I scan the shelves.

She must think I'm nuts, but I'm desperate. My cock is already straining painfully against my jeans.

"There." She points at a small display of condoms.

"Thank fuck."

She laughs at my outburst, which is fine by me, but she won't be laughing once I'm inside her.

I grab a pack, trying and failing to tear it open with my teeth. Molly takes the foil packet and rips it open, then reaches down between us.

She fumbles with my belt buckle as I kiss along her collarbone.

Thunder booms outside, but we barely notice.

We're both lost in the moment.

I hiss as she takes my cock in her hand and slowly rolls the condom on.

"Fuck, Molly," I growl.

I press her against the nearest shelf and capture her lips in a searing kiss.

She moans into my mouth as I push her panties aside and slide a finger through her folds. She's already so wet for me. I circle her clit with my thumb as I ease a finger inside her tight pussy.

"Hudson, please," she whimpers. "I need you now."

I carry her to the checkout counter, setting her on the edge.

I slide her jeans down her legs, trailing kisses in their wake.

Molly threads her fingers through my hair, guiding me where she wants me most.

I oblige.

When I finally push into her, we both groan at the sensation. I set a steady rhythm, gripping her hips. Molly meets me thrust for thrust, nails raking down my back.

"Harder," she demands, making me chuckle.

I comply, driving into her at a punishing pace.

The rickety counter creaks beneath us, but neither of us care.

The only thing that matters is being inside her.

I thrust deeper into her, and a groan escapes both of our mouths.

Too good.

She feels too good.

She's so fucking tight I can barely breathe.

Nothing in my life has ever felt like this.

If we die here tonight, at least I'll die having found heaven.

Molly's head falls back as she nears her peak. I kiss along the column of her throat, feeling her pulse race beneath my lips.

We tumble over the edge together, crying out as waves of pleasure crash over us.

There's nothing but bliss.

No storm. No danger. Just us.

chapter nine

Molly

SOFT LIGHT SPILLS INTO THE ROOM, MAKING ME BLINK.
   Where am I?

For a second, I can't remember anything. Last night feels like a fever dream. But then I do remember.

All of it.

A smile spreads over my face.

That was unexpected.

Blinking fast, I open my eyes wider and take in my surroundings. In the light of the day, this place is worse than I imagined. It's dirty and looks like it's been vacant for weeks, if not months. Dust and grime cling to everything.

I'm still curled up against Hudson, his chest acting as a pillow. It's tempting to fall back asleep and nestle into his comfort, but he has a game to play, and I have a client to cater to.

I sit up quickly, rubbing my eyes.

What time is it?

I reach to where I put my phone last night.

The battery is almost dead, but at least I have enough juice to see it's six in the morning.

We need to get on the road if we want to make sure no one finds out that Hudson didn't make it to Kentucky.

Still on the ground, Hudson is fast asleep, his head lying on his shirt as a pillow.

His jaw is slackened, his expression peaceful.

Even now, he's better looking than anyone I have ever seen. Meanwhile, I most likely look like death.

My gaze skims over Hudson's lips, and butterflies swarm in my belly as I replay flashes of all that happened last night.

Didn't see that coming, but *lord*, was it exactly what I needed.

I need to freshen up before he wakes.

Now that I actually care about his opinion.

How the hell did that happen?

I can't have him seeing me like this.

With a quick pass through the aisles, I find what I'm looking for—a travel toothbrush with toothpaste.

Then I head to the bathroom. It looks different than it did last night, with only a phone flashlight as a light.

It's dirty, with a film of dust caked on the cracked mirror. The sink isn't much better. It's barely functioning, so I bypass water when I brush my teeth and just spit the toothpaste out, vowing to find a bottle of water later.

Washing my hands, I finally study my reflection in the mirror. My cheeks look flushed, and my lips puffy.

Damn. I look well fucked.

Stop.

No thoughts like that, or I'll be beet red by the time he sees me.

Finally, I head back out and find Hudson up. He's standing near the counter, his back to me, holding his phone to his ear.

I freeze just out of sight, not wanting to interrupt him.

"Yeah, I'm good," he says, laughing lightly. "Don't worry about me. It was just a boring night in some random hotel. Totally fine."

Hotel?

At his words, my heart tightens in my chest.

"You always worry too much," he continues. Now, his voice lowers into a playful tone, dripping with affection. "I promise I'm fine. I'll see you soon, okay? Love you, too."

My mouth drops open as my pulse thunders in my veins.

Ground, open up, and kill me now.

How stupid can I be?

So stupid because, apparently, this asshole has a girlfriend.

But, of course, he does.

Why wouldn't he?

He sucks, after all. I knew this from the moment we met, and I caught him staring at my ass.

And you're the idiot who fell for his act.

Hook, line, and sinker.

I will myself to move, but I'm frozen in place as Hudson hangs up and slides the phone back into his pocket.

A few seconds pass before he turns around.

It feels like I'm punched in the stomach when our gazes meet, and his damn lips curve up into an easy grin.

Bastard.

Again, as I said before . . . Hudson Wilde sucks.

"You're ready?" He picks up his discarded jacket from the tiles. "We should get out of here."

I don't answer.

How can I?

First off, I swear there are marbles in my throat. Second, I have no desire to look like an idiot. He can go fuck himself.

Instead, I turn around and walk toward the door; jaw clenched, knuckles clenched, *everything* clenched. I might not say anything, but lord, am I feeling it.

As I push open the heavy glass door, the hinges squeal. The

early morning air is crisp, but it does nothing to cool the fire burning inside me.

I hear Hudson's footsteps behind me, but I don't slow down.

Unfortunately, his height allows him to quickly fall into step with me.

He slows at my side. "What's up with you?"

"Nothing." I cross my arms at my chest, my fingers digging into the sides of my ribs.

"Right," he responds like he doesn't believe me. Good. I don't care. "You look like someone kicked your ca—"

I stop abruptly, spinning to face him. "Can't you ever shut up?"

He blinks, caught off guard. "Wow."

"Yep. Wow," I snap before I turn back and walk toward my car, the only sound coming from the crunching of the wet gravel under my feet.

Hudson groans, speeding to catch up to my almost run. "Well, clearly, I did something. You gonna tell me what?"

"Nope."

His steps falter, but I don't look. "What the hell is wrong with you?"

I let out a bitter laugh, still refusing to look at him. Cheaters don't deserve answers.

Hudson is quiet before he coughs. "Is this about last night?"

Now, I do pivot to look at him.

I jab a finger into his chest. "You're just—you're so full of yourself."

His lips quirk. "Oh, so it *is* about last night."

My stomach churns. "Don't flatter yourself."

"You know . . ." He starts to respond, then stops. His jaw locks tightly for a minute. "If you regret it, you can just say so. This whole tantrum is exhausting."

"*You're* exhausting," I fire back.

I have more to say, so much more, but nothing comes out even though I open my mouth.

No matter how hot it was, last night was a mistake. I'm better off just getting in the car and leaving all of this where it belongs. In the past.

"Let's go. You're already late."

"Whatever you say, Hex."

chapter ten

Hudson

THE ROOM IS DARK EXCEPT FOR THE FAINT GLOW OF THE CITY lights spilling through the blinds. I stare at the ceiling, replaying every moment from last night, knowing I won't fall asleep anytime soon.

The game today should've been a distraction, but even as I tore down the ice, I couldn't shake her. *Molly*.

What was *that* this morning?

I press the heels of my palms into my eyes, groaning. God, what the hell happened at that gas station?

The memory rushes back in pieces. The storm pounding against the walls. The way she looked at me, half terrified, half something else entirely. And the way I caved, touching her like I couldn't stop myself, kissing her like the world was ending.

Because it felt like it might.

For a moment, when all we could hear was the storm pounding on the shoddy roof, all I could think was—we could die tonight, and I might never get the chance to touch her like I've always wanted to.

That's the thing about Molly Sinclair.

As much as I hate her—and I do . . . *a lot*—I like her, too.

She's funny, whip-smart, and cares about everyone (but me).

The truth is, she's hard not to like.

And then there was the following morning. The ice-cold, dismissive version of Molly I've grown wary of this past year. I hopped off the phone with my mom, relieved that I had managed to convince her that I hadn't spent the night in danger from that storm, when Molly barreled out of the bathroom like a demon.

She wouldn't even meet my eyes as she climbed into the driver's seat and peeled out of the station *without* me.

At the edge of the lot, just before she turned onto the road, she finally pulled to a stop and snapped, "Get in or don't."

Of course, I did.

I wouldn't put it past her to make me walk to the game.

But we spent the entire ride in silence.

I replayed that moment a thousand times today. Even during the game. Her tone, her distance, the way she acted like last night never happened.

It shouldn't bother me.

Hell, if anything, I should be relieved.

We hate each other, right? She's infuriating, constantly pushing my buttons, and I've been more than happy to give it back to her. That's our dynamic. That's how it's supposed to be.

But it does bother me.

I shift on the bed, raking a hand through my hair.

Molly Sinclair is a problem I don't know how to solve.

She's smart. *Too smart sometimes*, with a tongue sharper than a blade.

She's got a wit that keeps me on my toes, throwing punches I didn't see coming and making me laugh when I don't want to.

She's funny. And hot.

God, she's so hot.

Not just in the obvious, I-can't-stop-staring-at-your-ass kind of way. Though, let's be honest, there's that, too. The way she carries herself, with this fiery determination, makes you think she could take on the entire world if she wanted to.

She intrigues me, and I hate it.

I've been with a few girls here and there, and none of them have ever done this to me. They're easy. Predictable. I know what to expect from them, and I know how to leave before things get messy.

But Molly?

She's anything but easy or predictable.

She's chaos.

And for some reason, I can't stop thinking about her.

My phone buzzes on the nightstand, snapping me out of my thoughts. I grab it, squinting at the screen.

Mason: Wilde, where were you this morning? Waiting for the tornado to carry you here?

Of course, the team caught wind of how Molly and I holed up in the gas station (minus the sex), and they haven't stopped reminding me since.

Aiden: Late again? Shocker.

Dane: Do we need to chip you like a lost dog, Wilde?

I groan, scrolling through the avalanche of messages. The team group chat is relentless.

Mason: Seriously, though, how can one person always be late? Do you have a clock allergy or something?

Aiden: Coach is gonna have your ass if you don't fix this pattern, dude.

Dane: Fixing it would require effort. Doubt he's capable.

My fingers hover over the keyboard, debating whether to reply. What's the point? Anything I say will just fuel the fire. Instead, I toss my phone onto the bed and let out a frustrated sigh.

I close my eyes, but the image of Molly in the gas station flashes behind my lids. The way she kissed me, how she'd melted against me before pulling away the following morning like none of it mattered.

And maybe it doesn't matter. Perhaps it shouldn't.

But I can't shake the thought that it felt like it did for a few minutes last night.

And that terrifies me.

SEASON THREE

chapter eleven

Hudson

THE ARENA IS STILL QUIET SINCE THE DOORS AREN'T OFFICIALLY open to the public. A small crowd hangs out by the front entrance, but it doesn't affect me since I'm driving to the back.

I pull my car past the security checkpoint and toward the team parking lot. It looks like I'm one of the last to arrive. This is not a surprise, considering my life always goes to hell this time of year. My family needs me more in the fall, which affects my schedule.

At least the sky is clear this year, and there's no tornado in sight.

Just as I'm about to pull into my spot, a very familiar car beats me to it, parking exactly where I was supposed to go.

Hex.

Of course, it's her.

Ever since that night at the gas station, it feels like she's everywhere. At the rink. At events. And unfortunately, in my dreams.

What the hell is she doing in my spot?

I sit frozen, watching as she bounces out of her car with an extra pep in her step. She leans back in, grabs her bag, and starts walking.

I roll down my window. "Seriously, Hex?"

She doesn't seem to hear me. More likely, she's ignoring me.

I take my foot off the brake and pull forward, looking for another spot. But, as I'd already guessed, most of the close spaces are taken. After driving all the way to the end of the aisle, I finally find an open spot and take it.

I dash out of the car, rushing to make it inside.

Molly is about twenty feet ahead of me. If I sprint, she can let me in, and I won't have to hunt for my key card. She's fumbling with her bag as she approaches the players' entrance, pulling out her badge to unlock the door.

As she swings it open, I shout, "Hold the door for me!"

Still far away, I know full well I have no idea where my card is.

"Sorry, I'm in a rush," she shouts back, letting the door close behind her.

My jaw drops. Is this girl for real?

Jogging to the door, I grab the handle, but it's locked. No surprise there.

Where is my key card?

I rummage through my stuff and—shockingly—find nothing. I bang on the door.

No response.

I bang again.

Still nothing.

The back door usually has a guard who can let me in, but with my luck, no one is stationed there today.

My life is a comedy of errors. Why did I think the start of the season would be any different?

It's always like this.

Ever since my first day with Hex.

I sigh. Of course, this is how things would start. It's only the first week of the season, and I'm already screwing up. It's her fault. It always is. And now I have to find another way inside.

I start walking around the building, hoping to bump into

beautiful collide

someone who can let me in. The place is eerily quiet for this time of day. What the hell is going on?

I check every door I pass, but they're all locked—and not staffed.

By the time someone shows up, I'll officially be late. And I already know how Coach will react.

In the opening game of the season, Wolfe missed a critical pass during the third period against the Renegades. A textbook one-timer setup—perfectly placed by me, obviously, which made the miss even worse.

Coach Roberts didn't even wait for the play to finish before pacing behind the bench, his jaw clenching so hard I thought he might crack a tooth.

"Wolfe," he bellowed the second Wolfe skated back to the bench. The poor guy hadn't even caught his breath yet. "What the hell was that?"

"Sorry, Coach," Wolfe mumbled, barely audible over the crowd noise. "I didn't see it in time—"

Coach froze. He blinked slowly, like he was making sure he heard correctly. Then he exploded.

"Didn't see it? Didn't see it?" he roared, gesturing so wildly I thought he might knock over the water cooler. "It was right there! That puck was practically gift-wrapped and tied with a bow, and you—what? You blinked? Decided to take a mid-game nap?"

Wolfe's face turned red, and he opened his mouth to explain, but Coach wasn't done.

He jabbed a finger toward the ice. "That puck was so big, I thought it might be a goddamn meteor! How do you miss that?"

Mason, barely holding back a laugh, tried to chime in. "Coach, it was just—"

"Don't start with me, Mason," Coach snapped, pointing a finger at him. "If I hear one more word about 'it was just,' I'll have the whole team out here doing suicides until Christmas!"

That shut Mason up fast. Wolfe, meanwhile, tried to disappear into his gear. But Coach wasn't done.

"Wolfe, you're on the bench for the rest of the game. And after the game, we're staying late. Because clearly, you need a crash course in seeing the puck! Should we bring in an optometrist? Maybe invest in a telescope?"

Wolfe just nodded, his face redder than the goal light. He spent the rest of the game stapled to the bench.

The next day, Coach made us all come in on our day off to run drills while he shouted things like, "You see that puck? Don't blink, don't sneeze, and definitely don't pull a Wolfe!"

I grimace at the memory, my pace quickening. Wolfe has been in the doghouse ever since, and I'm not about to join him.

Last year, despite a literal tornado, I made it to the game with time to spare, and Coach never found out just how late I was. But today, with no excuses or disasters, I'm screwed.

I grab my phone and call Aiden.

Voicemail.

Next, Mason.

Same. They're probably in a meeting, and Coach would kill them if they answered.

Fine. Group chat it is.

Hudson: Someone help me.

Dane: What trouble did you get into this time?

Mason: This is getting ridiculous. You realize this happens every year, right?

I want to say yes, that it's all Molly's fault, but something tells me that won't go over well with Dane.

While I consider him a friend, he barely tolerates me. The man is so grumpy, he makes a Monday morning meeting feel like a vacation.

Hudson: Yes, I'm aware this is becoming an unfortunate habit.

Hudson: Has Coach noticed I'm missing yet?

Mason: What do you think?

Hudson: Fuck.

beautiful collide

Mason: Fuck is right. Where are you?

Hudson: Honestly, I have no clue.

Mason: The fuck?

Hudson: Somewhere between the players' entrance and hell.

Aiden: None of this is helpful.

Hudson: I left my key card, have no way in, and need help.

Mason: . . .

Hudson: You're not helping.

Dane: Maybe if you gave us an actual location, we could help.

Hudson: Glad to see the grump has entered the chat.

Dane has left the conversation.

Hudson: Oops.

Aiden: Why do you do this, man?

Hudson: Because it's too easy.

Hudson: So . . . is someone going to help me?

Aiden: No.

Aiden has left the conversation.

Hudson: Mason?

Mason: You're on your own.

Mason has left the conversation.

I type out a sad-face emoji but realize there's no one left to send it to.

Ouch.

Fine. I'll just head to the front of the arena. Someone will see me. Shit, I can't have that. Pulling my hoodie up, I hope the glasses-and-hoodie disguise works.

With my luck?

I doubt it.

chapter twelve

Molly

O KAY, MAYBE I'M AN ASSHOLE, BUT I REALLY COULDN'T WAIT for him. He was fully on the other side of the parking lot. If I had stopped, I'd have been late, and Dane needed his tape.

I mean, granted, he probably could have borrowed tape from someone else, but whatever, Hudson doesn't need to know that . . .

And the truth is, he deserves it.

He's a menace. A cheater.

And the worst part is a piece of me bigger than I want to admit, secretly likes Hudson Wilde. There I said it, sue me. Maybe I don't like him; perhaps I'm just jealous. I'm envious of the fact that he can be so unburdened by his past that he can have fun.

I wish I could be like that, and I find that every time I see him smile, I want to cry. Because deep down inside, I'm constantly pretending.

I pretend to be happy and put together when I'm a mess.

"Molly." My brother's voice is sharp and commanding.

I turn, finding Dane striding over to me with his usual

beautiful collide

no-nonsense expression. His brow is furrowed like he has the weight of the world on his shoulders.

"What?" I ask, crossing my arms.

"I need a favor." He stops in front of me.

My eyebrows rise. "Depends on what it is."

"You won't like it."

"Dear brother, I'll be fine. This is my job."

Dane sighs, pinching the bridge of his nose. "Don't say I didn't warn you."

"Now I'm intrigued." I lean against the wall. "I'm not fired again, am I?"

He fixes me with a serious look. "I need you to go find Hudson and let him in. Apparently, he got himself locked out."

Shit.

My stomach twists, but I force myself to stay calm. If Dane found out this was my fault . . . well, let's just say it wouldn't end well.

Well, that's if I let him fire me.

I wrinkle my nose, hoping to cover the flicker of guilt. "Why me?"

"Let's be honest." His voice dips. "He's probably wandering around outside like an idiot, and someone needs to let him in before Coach notices."

"That didn't answer my question." I narrow my eyes. "Why me?"

"Because I asked you," he says flatly, giving me that familiar older brother glare that says he won't take no for an answer. "And because you're fired if you don't."

"You don't pay me enough." I push off the wall.

Dane smirks. "Don't I know it."

With a long-drawn-out exhale, I turn to walk back to the arena's exit.

It's like a maze to get here, through long hallways, but apparently, rescuing Hudson is now my job.

He's rescued you.

I make my way to the side entrance, glancing outside the large windows. It's a beautiful day, so different from last year.

Don't think about last year, girl.

Too late.

My cheeks feel warm. Dammit. Why did he have to be so talented with his . . . ?

Nope.

Not going there.

Do not think about Hudson and how skilled he was. Of his touch.

Think of something else.

Dirty sock.

Chest hair.

A mullet.

Much better.

When I'm standing in front of the door, I push it open and head outside. I start to walk a few feet when I see a crowd of people. They look like they're having fun, all laughing and milling about.

One day, maybe I'll have that.

But for real, not just hanging with the team and pretending.

I pass the group, and as soon as I do, I spot him.

Hudson is pacing, his head tilted down, typing on his phone.

No one else notices him, which makes sense since his hoodie is pulled up. He doesn't look like a star hockey player.

He looks more like a sulky teen.

One who's been grounded and can't go to the party of the century. I'm about to get him when a group of people crosses my path.

The man in the group makes my stomach flip. At first, I think my mind is playing tricks on me. It has to be, right? There's no way he's here. But as I blink and stare harder, the figure becomes unmistakable.

It can't be *him*.

I tilt my head down. Don't see me. Please don't see me.

My chest tightens, and the air seems to grow heavier around me. The walls feel like they're closing in, and I instinctively back up into the corner of the lobby. He's here. He's really here.

My first instinct is to run, but my legs won't move. My second is to hide, but he's already walking this way, his eyes scanning the crowd.

Oh my God.

A group of teenage girls near the entrance are chatting loudly, and suddenly, I have an idea. A terrible, wonderful, reckless idea.

"It's Hudson Wilde!" I yell, my voice cutting through the noise.

Every head in the area snaps in my direction, and before I can think twice, I point toward the doors where Hudson stands, blissfully unaware of what's about to happen.

"It's Hudson Wilde!" I yell again, louder this time, and the crowd of girls erupts like I've thrown gasoline on a fire.

They don't hesitate.

In seconds, they're stampeding toward him, squealing his name and waving their phones in the air.

Hudson's head jerks up, his expression going from relaxed to panicked in a heartbeat. "What the—"

"Hudson! Hudson, over here!" one of the girls yells, and the rest of the group surges forward, their excitement turning into a full-blown mob.

I press myself further into the corner, watching the crowd swallow Hudson. A wave of guilt flickers through me, but it's quickly smothered by relief because *he* is nowhere to be seen.

Five minutes later, the entrance doors fly open, and Coach Robert storms outside with two members of the team's security staff in tow.

"Wilde!" he bellows, his voice loud enough to make everyone freeze.

The mob parts just enough for me to see Hudson, who looks thoroughly disheveled and more than a little pissed.

"Coach, I didn't—" Hudson starts, but Coach cuts him off.

"I don't want to hear it! Get inside, now!"

That isn't at all what I wanted to happen. I just wanted to be left alone.

Hudson glares at the crowd of girls, his gaze darting around like he's searching for the person who caused this chaos.

I duck further into the shadows, holding my breath.

As the doors close behind Hudson and the security team, I finally exhale, my pulse still racing. He's gone, and for the first time since I spotted him, I feel like I can breathe again.

I glance toward the entrance one last time before slipping away, my heart heavy with guilt. I owe Hudson for this. Big time.

But for now, I'm just grateful to be safe.

chapter thirteen

Hudson

Mason: 😂😂😂 "HUUUUDSONNNNN WIIIIILDEEEE!!!"

Hudson: Shut up.

Aiden: Did you survive? Should we send a search party or just put you on a milk carton?

Dane: Rookie move, Wilde. Getting stampeded by a bunch of teenagers? Come on.

Hudson: I don't want to talk about it.

Mason: Nah, we're absolutely talking about it.

Dane: You're lucky I didn't see it in real time. I'd still be laughing.

Hudson: You guys are the worst.

Mason: What did you expect, man? You were late. AGAIN. You basically asked for it.

Hudson: I WASN'T LATE.

Dane: My guy, you missed warm-ups. You're always late. It's basically your only personality trait at this point.

Mason: Wilde Time™. It's a thing.

Hudson: IT WASN'T MY FAULT.

Mason: It never is. 😄

Aiden: Yet it always happens.

Mason: He got tackled by teenagers. Literal children. That's what he gets.

Aiden: He's a public safety hazard.

Hudson: I hate all of you.

Mason: Did they at least chant your name?

Dane: Doubt it.

Aiden: Probably why he's still breathing. He'd enjoy that too much.

Hudson: Can someone remind me why I hang out with you guys?

Dane: Because we keep you humble. And alive.

Mason: Barely alive after today. 😄

Hudson: I'm muting this chat.

Aiden: Admit it, you love us.

Hudson: I'm blocking all of you.

Dane: Sure, you are. Just don't be late again, or we're putting you in a helmet cam next time.

Mason: Omg. A Hudson Wilde highlight reel of shame. I'll edit it.

Aiden: 10/10 content.

Hudson: I actually hate you.

chapter fourteen

Hudson

I FIND HER NEAR THE TEAM'S LOUNGE, SCROLLING THROUGH HER phone like nothing happened. Like she didn't just unleash the kind of chaos usually reserved for a Black Friday sale.

"Molly," I call out, my voice sharp enough to make her flinch.

She glances up, the picture of pure innocence. "Oh, hey, Hudson. You good?"

"Am I good?" My voice rises. "You unleashed a freaking stampede on me."

Her eyebrows furrow, and she tilts her head like she has no idea what I'm talking about. "I have no clue what's got you so hot and bothered."

"Don't play dumb, Hex," I snap. "I saw the security footage."

Her mouth falls open, her brows shooting up. "You looked at the security footage?"

"Yeah, I did," I retort, stepping closer. "Why wouldn't I when someone decided to yell my name in a crowd full of teenagers and send them charging after me like I'm Justin freakin' Bieber?"

"That's unhinged." She crosses her arms at her chest. "Who even does that?"

"Someone who just got trampled by a mob, that's who." I throw my hands in the air. "What is wrong with you?"

"Oh, please." She rolls her eyes. "It was just a bunch of teenagers. You're being a little dramatic for someone who gets body-checked for a living."

Before I can respond, Dane appears from around the corner, his face twisted into a scowl. "What did you say, sis?" He lifts a brow. "You think I let anyone body check Hudson? I'm the best enforcer this team's ever had."

Molly scrunches her nose. "What a fragile male ego. I'm disappointed in you, brother. Relax."

"Relax?" he repeats, stepping closer. "Do you know how hard I work to keep this team safe?"

"Oh, we all know," Mason chimes in from the couch, grinning as he leans back with a soda. "Big, scary Dane, always protecting his precious forwards."

"Shut up, Mason," Dane snaps, his glare cutting through the room.

Mason shrugs, unfazed. "Hey, I'm just saying, maybe if you'd been there earlier, you could've saved Hudson's ass from the teenage stampede."

The room erupts in laughter, and even I can't help but chuckle despite my frustration.

"Why am I always the one getting roasted?" I shake my head.

"Because you make it too easy," Aiden calls from across the room.

Where the hell did he come from?

Jeez. Is this Fuck with Hudson Day?

When the laughter dies down, I turn back to Molly, my tone softer, but it's still obvious that I'm disappointed. "Look, I get that you hate me. That's fine. But you didn't have to do this."

beautiful collide

"I don't hate you," she says way too quickly, her expression shifting. "I just—"

"You don't?" I interrupt, raising an eyebrow. "Because it sure feels like it. Every time we make even the slightest bit of progress, you do something to ruin it."

Her mouth opens, but no words come out.

She looks like a fish out of water struggling to breathe.

"I wish we could've been on better footing." I drop my voice, admitting something I don't want to admit. "But you're so determined to keep things the way they've always been. You won't even give us a chance to be something . . . better."

Her eyes soften, and for a moment, I think she might say something real. Something honest.

But instead, she crosses her arms again and looks away. "You're overreacting. It was just a few teenage fans. You're fine."

The disappointment in my chest deepens, but I force a tight smile. "Yeah, sure. Just a few teenage fans."

With that, I turn and walk away, leaving her standing there.

Let her think she won this one. I have bigger things to focus on.

chapter fifteen

Hudson

THE SAINTS LOCKER ROOM CONTINUES TO BUZZ FROM OUR WIN. The energy is electric, the kind of high you can't fake. There's nothing like coming off a big game, knowing you left it all on the ice. My legs ache, and my hands are sore, but I'm grinning like an idiot.

We're unstoppable.

What a game.

I could tell Coach was watching me, so I played like my life depended on it, and in truth, it did.

The team needed a win, and we got it.

Thank fuck.

The bar is packed when we get there, filled with fans who probably got word that we'd be celebrating here. Cheers erupt when we walk in, and Mason starts hamming it up immediately, bowing like he just won an Oscar.

"Relax, man," I mutter, elbowing him. "You're gonna pull something."

"You love it," he declares, grinning as he makes his way to the bar.

The heavy door slams shut behind me. Once inside, my eyes adjust to the dim lighting.

The music isn't too loud, which is why we picked this place. It's quieter than most places around here.

I follow Mason, soaking in the vibe. This is my kind of night. I have a good feeling about this year. The team is solid.

Nothing can ruin this. Not even Molly Sinclair, who I spot across the room before I've even had my first drink.

She's leaning against the bar, talking to the bartender, her arms crossed and her face set in that signature Molly scowl. With my post-win high, even she can't bring me down.

I don't know why, but seeing her here sends a thrill coursing through me. Maybe it's the adrenaline still pumping through my veins. Or perhaps it's because I know nothing she could say tonight will bring me down.

Feeling smug as hell, I grab my drink and make my way over.

Her sharp green eyes flick to me as I approach, and she lifts her drink in a mock salute.

I smirk, closing the distance between us with an arched brow. "And what are you drinking to?"

"Our anniversary." Her tone is dry before she takes another sip.

I laugh, shaking my head at her. "I'm surprised you're celebrating it."

She tilts her chin up, her lips twitching with amusement. "Who says I'm celebrating? Maybe I'm commiserating."

My hands lift in mock defeat. "Ouch."

"Just keeping it real."

Before I can reply, Mason steps up beside us, clapping me on the back. "Hudson, you're late as always."

"I carpooled with you," I deadpan.

He shrugs. "I've never met a traffic jam before I met you."

I roll my eyes, shooting a glance at Molly. "I guess . . . I'm hexed."

Molly raises an unimpressed eyebrow, her mouth quirking up in a wry smile. "Not everyone can be skilled in being punctual."

"Or maybe it's something else," I retort, narrowing my eyes at her.

Mason's gaze bounces between us, his brow lifting in curiosity. "What did I miss?"

"Nothing," Molly says too quickly, her voice a little too steady.

Mason catches on immediately, his lips curving into a knowing grin.

He turns to me with an easy nod. "Good game, man."

"You too," I reply, shaking off Molly's jab as best I can.

From beside me, I hear Molly's quiet laugh, and I swivel to face her. Her smirk is maddening, and it only grows when she sees my expression.

"What's so funny?" I ask, my tone clipped.

She waves a hand lazily, rolling her eyes. "Just you two, patting each other on the backs and telling each other how amazing you are. It's adorable."

"Well—"

"Barf," she interrupts, holding up her martini glass like a shield. "If you say you're amazing, I'll throw up."

"We kind of are amazing," I say, smirking despite myself.

Molly leans forward slightly, her expression unamused. "Were you watching the same game as me?" she deadpans.

My grin fades. "What's that supposed to mean?"

She turns to Mason, gesturing toward him with her drink. "I mean, Mason here was tight. He didn't let one puck past him. On the other hand, you are lucky my brother's got your back, and Slate is so skilled."

"Did you not see my goal?" I ask, sliding up beside her. "Pretty sure they'll be talking about it for weeks."

Her gaze flicks to mine, unimpressed. "You mean the one that bounced off your shin guard? Real skill there, Wilde."

I grin, unbothered. "Hey, a goal's a goal."

She snorts, turning back to her drink. "If you say so."

"Don't be jealous, Hex," I tease, leaning closer so only she can hear. "It's not a good look on you."

She whips her head around, narrowing her eyes. "Jealous? Of what? Watching you stumble around the ice like a baby deer? Please."

My grin falters for a split second, but I recover quickly. "Stumble? I had three assists tonight, Sinclair. That's hardly stumbling."

"Oh, congratulations," she says, her tone dripping with mockery. "Maybe next time you'll even manage to score."

The dig lands harder than I expect, and before I can stop myself, I fire back. "Maybe next time you'll manage to do something other than hang around the rink like some kind of . . . glorified babysitter."

Her eyes widen, and I immediately regret the words.

"Molly, I didn't mean—"

"Save it." She cuts me off, her voice sharp enough to draw blood. "You're too busy being the team's golden boy to even realize how gross you are."

"Gross?" I repeat, my voice rising.

"Yes," she says, her tone icy. "You strut around like you're God's gift to hockey and women, and it's disgusting."

Her words hit me like a slap. For a second, I'm too stunned to respond. Then anger flares, hot and unrelenting.

"Fine," I snap. "If you think I'm such a player, maybe I should act like it."

She blinks, her expression flickering with something I can't quite place. But before she can respond, I turn on my heel and make my way back to the team.

"Ladies," I say, sliding up beside Mason and gesturing toward a group of blonde fans practically drooling over us. "Why don't you join us for a drink?"

The blondes giggle and eagerly follow, and within minutes, we're all seated at a table with rounds of tequila shots being poured.

"You're in a mood," Mason says, raising an eyebrow at me as he downs his shot.

"Just celebrating," I reply, forcing a grin.

But my eyes keep darting back to the bar, where Molly still

stands. Her gaze flicks to our table for a moment before she turns away, her jaw tight.

Good. Let her be annoyed. Let her see what it feels like to be brushed off, dismissed, and ignored.

The night spirals quickly from there. The blondes cling to us, laughing too loudly at every joke Mason makes, and I'm leaning into it hard, playing the part of the charming playboy Molly accused me of being even though I couldn't be more disinterested in any of them.

But the more I play it up, the worse I feel. The tequila burns, but it doesn't dull the nagging ache in my chest.

And then it happens.

Molly storms across the room, her expression stormy as hell. She grabs my arm, pushing me back with more strength than I thought she had.

"Move," she snaps, her voice low but furious, though she went out of her way to get in my way.

"Molly—"

"Don't." Her tone vibrates with anger. "Just stay out of my way."

And with that, she storms out of the bar, leaving me standing there like an idiot.

The table is silent for a moment before Mason lets out a low whistle. "Damn, Wilde. What the hell did you do this time?"

I don't answer. I can't.

Because for all the anger simmering in my chest, all I can think about is the way she looked at me before she left. Like I wasn't worth her time.

And in an instant, the post-win high comes crashing down.

SEASON FOUR

chapter sixteen

Hudson

THE ELEVATOR DOORS SLIDE OPEN, AND I STEP INTO THE LOBBY of the local TV studio I've been summoned to.

I rake a hand through my still damp hair. *Great first impression, Hudson.*

You are totally nailing it. Nothing screams professionalism like looking like you just took a dive in a pool.

It would have been smarter to have showered earlier, but apparently, I'm destined to never be on time.

Case in point: this morning.

I was halfway through my breakfast, mid-bite of my bagel, to be exact, when it hit me. My interview wasn't at ten a.m., it was at nine.

Who schedules an interview at nine in the morning? Psychopaths, that's who.

First of all, whoever scheduled the interview at such an ungodly hour should be arrested.

Second, again . . . Actually, there is no second. Who schedules an interview this early? The sheer cruelty of this crime speaks for itself.

I barely had time to drink coffee.

So, yeah, my hair is wet, but at least I'm here. Maybe thirty minutes late, but better late than never. Time is subjective, anyway, right? Einstein said so.

It's just a small slipup. No big deal.

Except for the fact that Molly Sinclair is going to be here. Fabulous.

Now, I'll never live it down. It makes sense, though, since her being here is probably why I'm late.

Her being my hex and all.

When she's around, bad things happen. Like my alarm not going off or my sense of time deciding to take a vacation. *All her fault.*

I round the corner and head toward the waiting area.

Sure enough, there she is.

She stands at the far wall, back leaning against it. Phone clenched in her hand.

It's really a shame she hates me because that night in the run-down gas station will forever go down as the best sex I've ever had. Not that I'd ever tell her that. She'd probably laugh, tell me to keep dreaming, and then bring it up in every argument for the rest of eternity.

She looks good today too. Oh, who am I kidding? She looks good every day. It would be nice if she could tone it down a little bit for my sanity. As is, I'd be willing to put all the fucked-up shit aside just to feel her come on my dick again.

For a brief second, I allow myself to take her in. Her long brown hair sweeps past her shoulders in bouncy waves, and her soft features are highlighted by a touch of makeup.

A natural beauty.

The kind that makes me forget that she hates my guts until she opens her mouth, and I have no choice but to remember.

It's like the world is out to get me because she chooses this exact minute—when I'm practically undressing her with my eyes—to look up and catch me.

Her jaw locks, and she narrows her eyes. "What?" she mouths.

Great, I'm busted. Fan-fucking-tastic. Can't wait to hear what she has to say.

Guess we know how Molly's mood is today.

Ironically, I've watched when she hasn't seen me watching, and she's practically the life of the party.

Always smiling. Always laughing. It's infuriating.

But when she's near me? Nope. It's Hate on Hudson Day.

"Nothing."

She fixes her gaze on me with a glare so icy it could create a larger rink.

"You know, I did you a favor again."

"How do you figure?" Because clearly, I've missed this riveting tale of martyrdom.

"Who do you think took your spot when you decided yet again to be late?"

"If you remember correctly, it hasn't always been my fault I've been late."

"Whatever."

"Can't you just say . . . morning, and then I'd say the same?" I smile broadly, and she practically snarls back. "I can tell you missed me on your trip."

"I didn't. I enjoyed Europe immensely. I did miss Cassidy, but you? Nope."

"Harsh." I look around the room, then lift my wrist to check the time.

"Oh, I'm sorry. Are we keeping you? More pressing plans? 'Cause the way I see it, Dane saved your ass by coming in early."

"It's not the end of the world. Dane was already here, right?"

"You screwed my schedule. It's hard enough getting Dane to work after he sent me away all summer. He's extra grumpy these days, probably because of the new intern, Josie, poor girl, but that's neither here nor there. The point is—"

"Oh, is there a point? I thought you were just rambling." This earns me "the look."

If looks could kill, I'd be dead.

"There's a point."

"And that is . . . ?"

She throws her hands in the air. "I forget."

"Maybe Josie. Have you met her? She's ho—"

"Don't even go there. I don't want to sic human resources on you. Actually . . ."

"I missed you when you were on your Euro tour. I can already tell this season's going to be fun."

"No, it's not."

"Again, have you seen the new girl?"

"Hudson."

"Relax, Hex, not for me. But something tells me she might be right up your brother's alley. I might talk to Coach and see if you could work for me, so Josie can help Dane a little longer." I wink. "If you know what I mean."

Molly's jaw locks. Her mouth opens and shuts, and it makes me grin.

I walk closer to her, leaning down slightly so only she can hear me. "You know, it's kind of refreshing. For once, you're the one who looks a little . . . what's the word? Incompetent."

Her eyes flash, a mix of fury and something else—something more dangerous. Possibly murder, but we'll see.

"Screw you, Hudson."

"Any day, Hex. Just name the time and the place. I'd love a redo."

Her cheeks flush, and she takes a step back, her composure snapping back into place like a shield.

"You are not worth it." Her ice-cold voice stabs me in the chest. I watch as she goes. I won this round, yet it feels bittersweet.

Even though I've provoked her, I don't enjoy hurting her. It's just better than the alternative. That's dangerous territory because I'm already in too deep.

chapter seventeen

Molly

"YOU'RE FIRING ME AGAIN?" I CROSS MY ARMS AND GLARE AT Dane from across his kitchen table.

He shrugs, leaning back in his chair with that same infuriating calm he always uses to deliver bad news. "You need to find something for yourself, Moll. You can't keep running your life around me."

I roll my eyes, clenching my coffee mug tighter. "And you think firing me is the solution? I have a secret for you; it's not. You've tried this before, and it didn't stick."

"Yeah, because you refused to stay fired." He raises an eyebrow, clearly unimpressed with my resistance. "This time, I mean it. You're out."

"Oh, please." I scoff, setting my mug down with a loud clank. "What are you going to do without me? Forget your schedule? Wear mismatched socks to practice? You wouldn't survive a week."

"That's what Mason's for," Dane counters, smirking.

"Mason can't even remember what day it is, let alone manage your life," I fire back. For a second, he's silent. He knows I'm right.

He might want me gone, not for any other reason but his desire to have me live my own life, but without me, he's a mess. Or at least that's what I tell myself.

Running his life is easier than having to deal with my own.

Dane sighs, pinching the bridge of his nose. "You're impossible, you know that?"

"No, I'm indispensable," I correct, narrowing my eyes. "And you know it."

He shakes his head, but I can see the small smile tugging at his lips. "Fine. If you won't let me fire you, I'm loaning you out for the day."

I blink, confused. What is he talking about? "Loaning me out? What the hell does that even mean?"

"You're going to help Hudson," Dane says casually like this is a perfectly normal suggestion.

"What?" I nearly choke on my own breath. "Hudson? Hudson Wilde? That's a no. You will not be giving me to anyone. Why on earth would I do that?"

"Because he's got an endorsement interview today, and if there's one thing Hudson's terrible at—besides being on time—it's interviews." Dane leans forward. "Plus his agent can't be there and he needs someone to keep him on track. Which is where you come in."

"Me?" I ask, incredulous.

"Yes." Dane shrugs again. "You're the best at what you do."

I stare at him, waiting for the punchline because this can't actually be real. No way would my brother do this to me, but when none comes, I throw my hands up in exasperation. "Unbelievable. You're loaning me out like some used bowling shoe."

"Bowling shoes don't have your charm," Dane says, smirking again.

I slump back in my chair before letting out an exasperated groan. "I can't believe this."

"Believe it," Dane says, standing and grabbing his keys. "Hudson will pick you up at noon. Be nice."

"Nice?" I scoff. "To Hudson? Have you met me?"

"Just try." Dane gives me a pointed look. "And don't kill each other. Please."

By the time Hudson pulls up outside my apartment in his Mustang, I'm still pissed about Dane's ridiculous plan.

Can I disown him?

No.

He's all you have.

As I climb into the passenger seat, Hudson gives me one of his signature smirks.

Damn him.

Why does he have to be so good-looking? "Well, well, look who's slumming it with the likes of me today."

"Shut up and drive," I mutter, slamming the door.

"Oh, this is going to be fun." He grins wide as he shifts the car into gear.

"If by fun, you mean one torture session shy of the last circle of hell, then yeah."

He slams on the brakes. "What is your fucking problem?"

"My *fucking problem* is that I hate cheaters."

He arches a brow. "Okay?"

"Okay?" I repeat. "Okay!"

"Yeah. Okay." He shrugs. "What does that have to do with me?"

I toss my hands up. "You're exhibit fucking A, Hudson."

"Excuse me?"

"That night. Of the tornado. We had sex, and the following morning, I heard you whisper to some chick that you love her." I pivot in the cold leather seat. "You're such an asshole."

"What in the world are you talking abo—*Oh.*" He snorts. The snort turns into a laugh, which turns into a full-blown boisterous attack.

"It's not funny."

"It really is."

"I don't find cheating a laughing matter."

"That's great because I didn't cheat. I was talking to my mom. She calls me every time I travel to a game to make sure I get there safely."

I scoff. "That's a convenient excuse."

"It's not an excuse," he insists.

"Sure, it isn't."

I believe him slightly less than a puppy with crumbs all over his snout.

Sure, Buddy. You didn't sneak into the cookie jar.

He shakes his head. "If I'm such a playboy, how could I have a girlfriend? Aren't playboys notoriously commitment adverse?"

I shut up. He has a point.

I acknowledge it with a begrudging huff. "Fine."

"That sounds suspiciously close to an apology."

"Whatever."

I cross my arms and glare out the window, determined to get through this day without strangling him.

It probably won't happen, but here's to hoping.

chapter eighteen

Hudson

MAN, THIS IS BAD.

I shouldn't have even come. I knew this wasn't a good fit for me, pun intended, since I'm sitting across from the suits running Secure Condoms.

The room smells like cheap cologne and desperation. My agent is about to get a piece of my mind, but I need to get through today first.

I've been in plenty of awkward meetings, but this one takes the cake.

Someone says something, but I can't focus on what they're saying. Something about "target audiences" and "brand synergy," but all I can think about is the woman sitting next to me.

Molly Sinclair.

She's dressed in a tailored blazer and skirt, her hair pulled back into some sort of elegant twist. She looks like she walked straight out of a boardroom and into my personal hell. Professional, poised, and completely unimpressed by everything happening around her.

Of course, she's annoyed to be here—loaned out like some favor to help me.

I get it.

But she's here.

And despite the fact that she's probably plotting my demise, I'm grateful. More than she will ever know.

Her presence makes the whole situation a little more bearable.

A little less humiliating.

Not much, but enough that I'm still sitting here.

Which is saying something, considering the fact that I'm at a condom company endorsement meeting.

It's not that I'm not one for safe sex—of course I am—but to be the face . . . ? Yeah, no.

I would never be able to face my mother again.

"Now, Hudson," one of the suits says, leaning forward with a grin that makes my skin crawl. "Your . . . reputation precedes you."

I glance at Molly, who raises an eyebrow but stays silent. *And here it goes.*

The moment they pitch me as the party boy everyone thinks I am because I've never wanted to correct anyone.

"Right," I say, forcing a smile. "Happy to hear that."

"And that's exactly why we want you to be the face of our new campaign," the suit continues. "You're young, you're handsome, and you're known for being a bit of a . . . ladies' man."

Despite knowing this was coming, my jaw still tightens. Yet, I manage to keep my expression neutral. This again.

"We're thinking something edgy," another suit chimes in. "Like 'Hudson Wilde: Scoring on and off the ice.'"

I blink, stunned into silence. Did he actually just say that? Molly shifts beside me, her posture stiffening. Yeah, he did.

"And," the first suit adds, "we'd like to lean into your 'bad boy' image. Maybe even some tongue-in-cheek ads about—"

"No," Molly says abruptly.

The entire room turns to look at her, including me.

beautiful collide

"Excuse me?" one of the suits says, his tone confused.

"I said no," Molly repeats, her voice calm but firm. "Hudson is an athlete, not a punchline. If you want him to represent your brand, you'll focus on his accomplishments on the ice, not some fabricated reputation you're trying to exploit."

The room goes silent.

A pin could drop, and you'd hear it right now.

I stare at her, shocked. Molly Sinclair, the woman who has made it her life's mission to torment me, is . . . defending me?

If I could discreetly pinch myself right now, I would, but since I can't, I sit motionless and stunned instead.

"Ms. Sinclair," one of the suits begins, his tone condescending, "we believe this campaign is exactly what Hudson's image needs."

"No," she says again, her eyes narrowing. "What Hudson needs is to be taken seriously. He's not some one-dimensional stereotype you can slap on a billboard. He's an athlete. And a damn good one at that."

My chest tightens at her words. Damn. Who knew Molly had it in her to defend me like this? I've always known she's smart and passionate . . . but fuck.

The suits exchange uneasy glances, clearly unsure of how to respond.

Molly leans back in her chair, crossing her legs and fixing them with a pointed stare. "If you're not interested in showcasing Hudson's talent and professionalism, then we're not interested in this deal. Thank you for your time."

She stands, grabs her bag, and turns to me. "Hudson, let's go."

I blink, still processing what just happened, but her tone leaves no room for argument. I follow her out of the conference room, trying to keep up with her long, determined strides.

We step outside into the cool October air, and she spins on her heel to face me, her expression unreadable. It takes me a second to shake myself out of the stupor I'm in, and when I do finally come to, I grin at her while nodding.

"Don't say it," she warns, holding up a hand.

"Say what?" My smirk deepens.

"Whatever sarcastic, infuriating thing you're thinking right now."

I lean against the side of the building. "You know, for someone who hates my guts, you just defended me like a pro in there."

Her eyes narrow. "Don't let it go to your head."

"Too late," I say, unable to help the laugh that escapes me. "Seriously, though . . . thanks. That was unexpected."

She crosses her arms, her gaze softening slightly. "You're welcome. Someone had to step in, and clearly, your agent isn't showing up for you."

"Yeah, he's a good guy, but well, he's got bigger fish to fry," I mutter, running a hand through my hair.

She raises an eyebrow. "That doesn't mean you deserve to be treated like that."

"A part of it's my own fault. I don't give him much to work with."

"That's not true. You do. You deserve better than this, Hudson. You're a damn good player. Remember that."

I tilt my head, studying her. "You know, Hex, you're kind of amazing when you're not plotting my downfall."

"Don't push it," she says, but there's a faint smile tugging at her lips.

I can't help it—I grin back at her. For the first time in a long time, I feel like someone's in my corner.

And damn if it doesn't make me like her even more.

I can't help grinning like an idiot. Molly freaking Sinclair just walked into a roomful of sleazy marketing execs and turned the whole thing upside down. *For me.*

And now we're standing outside the building, her arms crossed and her scowl firmly in place, but I know I saw it—that little smile she tried to hide back there.

"Come on, Hex," I say. "Admit it. You like me."

Her eyes narrow, and she takes a deliberate step back like she wants to get as far away from this conversation as humanly possible. "I just defended you because I didn't want to sit through another second of that train wreck. Don't get it twisted."

"Defended me like a damn hero." My grin widens. "If I didn't know any better, I'd think you were starting to like having me around."

"Wrong." She rolls her eyes.

"Oh, come on." I step away from the wall, prowling closer to her. "You were incredible in there, and you know it. If I didn't already think you were hot, that whole taking-no-bullshit act might've done it for me."

She blinks at me, her face going blank for half a second before she recovers with a disgusted look that's almost theatrical. "Ew," she says, wrinkling her nose. "You're gross."

"Am I?" I tease, tilting my head.

"Yes," she says firmly. "And don't you forget it."

I take another step closer, grinning down at her. "You're standing awfully close for someone who finds me so gross."

"You're the one moving. Not me." Her eyes flash, and she steps back to prove her point, holding up a hand to stop me. "Just because I defended you in there doesn't mean I've forgotten what an insufferable, cocky, perpetually late pain in my ass you are."

"Don't forget charming," I add, smirking.

"Gross," she repeats, spinning on her heel and heading toward the parking lot.

I follow, unable to wipe the grin off my face. "You know, most people would say thank you after a compliment."

"Most people don't get their compliments from walking red flags," she shoots back over her shoulder.

I laugh, jogging to catch up with her. "Red's a good color on me, don't you think?"

She stops abruptly, turning to glare at me. "If you say one more word, I'm stealing your keys and leaving you here to figure out your own ride back to the rink."

I hold my hands up in surrender, still grinning. "Noted."

The drive back is quieter than I expected, but every time I glance at her, I catch that little crease in her brow and how her lips press together like she's holding back something biting.

She can pretend all she wants, but I know I've gotten under her skin.

And if I'm being honest? She's gotten under mine, too.

chapter nineteen

Molly
Six Months Later
The Playoffs

THERE IS NO QUESTION THAT I LOVE MY BROTHER, BUT BEING his assistant isn't actually the dream job I would make it out to be.

Honestly, it's not bad, and I happily do it—he did give up his life for me—but recently, I have felt like I'm not needed anymore.

It's not like I don't understand. Of course, I do. But that doesn't make it any easier.

Dane's life has stabilized since meeting Josie and mine . . . hasn't. Watching him thrive should feel like a victory. Instead, it feels like someone pulled the rug out from under me.

It's a weird feeling to have, and I don't like it.

For so many years, I've been by his side, silently paying off the imagined debt I had to him. He never demanded this, nor did he even know that's why I did it, but now am I even needed?

Josie does most of the things I used to do, and a good manager could handle the rest.

Where does that leave me? My job, taking care of Dane, has been my identity for years. Now the job doesn't feel like my own.

I feel disposable.

It feels like my life is spiraling out of control, and I'm not sure where my place in the world is.

If I'm not Dane's assistant, who am I?

It's a question I've been too scared to ask myself for years. Still too scared to ask.

I'm so used to managing the chaos of Dane's life that now that there is no "chaos," I'm not sure what to do.

Laptop in hand, I take a seat on the bench that faces the practice rink. Later tonight, we'll be flying out for the first game of round one of the playoffs.

I'm currently working on answering Dane's emails.

What can I say? It's a glamorous life.

It's quiet at this time of day. The players haven't arrived yet, and while I usually work in the office, I love the crisp smell of the ice. Something about it is so comforting.

The sharp, cold air.

The faint scent of something sweet and earthy.

I've spent most of my life close to a rink, so much so it now smells like home.

Peering down onto my screen, I start to go through each email one by one. Public appearance requests, emails from his bank, and even fan mail.

After about twenty emails and no clue how much time has passed, I hear the telltale signs of skates cutting across fresh ice.

I tilt my head and look to see who's here this early and already on the ice.

The second I spot who it is, my cheeks warm despite the cold.

Hudson Wilde skates freely, without a care in the world or if

I'm watching. He looks all serious and broody and in an annoyingly typical way, hot as hell.

Of course, it's him. Who else would show up *early*, the man who never shows up *early*? Well, there goes my morning.

It's about to get more complicated. Maybe I did something wrong in a past life. That's the only answer to this insanity. My luck is shit. Hudson might be right about my nickname.

Hockey players shouldn't be as hot as Hudson. It's truly not fair.

My job and life would be easier if they—he—weren't.

I need to get out of here before he notices me, but obviously, I'm already too late because the bastard chooses this exact minute to glance up.

Oh, perfect. Eye contact. There go my plans to avoid this exact situation.

"Enjoying the show?" He skates closer to where I'm sitting.

I shake my head. "Not even watching."

"Me thinks you're lying, Hex."

And there it is, just as I thought, my damn nickname. As if I need another reminder.

I close my computer. Knowing me, I'll probably accidentally break it with how enraged this man makes me, so it's smarter to just put it away now. I'll finish my work elsewhere.

"I'm not."

He smirks. The man enjoys pissing me off way too much.

"Then why haven't you blinked since you noticed me?"

I blow out my breath. "Wow. Cocky much?"

"You know it." He winks.

My head shakes. "It's really not a good character trait."

"Well, it can be added to my long list of shortcomings you must think I have."

"If it walks like a duc—"

"Quack." He smiles.

"You're a toddler."

"I might be, but at least I learned a few lessons in pre-k. You, however, didn't."

"Will you ever get over it? I said I'm sorry. I don't even know why you're so upset. You're doing amazing."

"Despite the consequences."

"What consequences? Oh no. A few years ago, you got benched from one game."

"My first, Hex. My first game, and Coach has never given me a chance since. Why do you think I'm here so goddamn early every day? Why do you think I practice so much—"

"Because you like hockey."

"'Cause I want to be taken seriously."

My mouth opens and shuts. All words have died on my tongue. There is a rawness in his voice I don't expect, and for a brief second, I feel guilty.

"Well, maybe if you stopped being a man wh—"

"Watch yourself."

"What? You're a player. It's not like it's up for discussion."

"Am I, though? Or is it just the role I fell into because of you?"

He skates closer, looking at me in a way that brings a chill down my spine. Almost arctic.

This is a different look for him. It's not cocky. It's darker.

All these years, I knew I hurt him, but he always seemed okay, so it never dawned on me that there might be more hiding under his perfect exterior.

"Careful, Hex. Keep staring at me, and your brother might start to wonder."

"There's nothing to wonder about."

"Hey, what's going on over there?" My brother's voice booms, and I turn my head to see him stepping out onto the ice. "You good, Moll?"

Relief floods through me. Saved by Dane.

I give my brother a sugary-sweet smile, then I turn it toward Hudson. He absolutely does not deserve it, but maybe . . . No.

He doesn't deserve it.

Best to stay far away from Hudson Wilde. That man is not good for my health.

chapter twenty

Molly

"ARE YOU KIDDING ME?" THE WORDS WERE MEANT TO BE ONLY for me, but of course, my damn mouth opened and said them out loud, and now everyone on the chartered plane might have heard me. Despite my high-pitched tone, it doesn't appear that anyone heard me. Well, anyone other than the idiot sitting beside the only empty seat on the plane.

I can't complain, though, because family is not allowed to travel with the team, but since I work for my brother Dane—and when need be, the team—they make an exception for me, so complaining about my seat most likely won't be well received.

I continue to peer around the small plane. It's not exactly spacious in here. It feels more like an oversized minivan than a luxury flight. Sometimes, the chartered planes are nice, but this one is lacking. Especially the passenger sitting next to the seat where I'm supposed to sit.

My life is a cosmic joke.

Of course, this would happen. Of all the open seats on the

plane, the universe has chosen this one for me. *Well played.* I obviously sinned in a past life.

No way am I riding five minutes next to this man, let alone two hours.

"You planning on standing there all day? I'm pretty sure the pilots won't take off unless you're strapped in."

I ignore him as I continue to search for another seat. There must be another option. Maybe someone who doesn't make my blood boil every time he breathes.

"There's none." Hudson's voice cuts through my inner rambling.

"How do you know?" I practically snarl at him. *Easy there, killer.*

"'Cause I looked."

Of course, he did.

I roll my eyes. "Maybe someone will switch with me."

"Am I that bad, Hex?" He drops his chin, giving me his best wounded-puppy-dog face. A lesser woman might crumple. I am not that woman.

"Stop calling me that," I hiss.

"Nope."

The nickname. Always. Years later, and it still feels like nails on a chalkboard. All because of one mistake years ago.

And well, maybe a few times after too.

I'll never live any of it down.

I thought that he'd be too busy being the team playboy to even give a fuck about me, but I was wrong.

That coupled with what happened the following year, and well, the next . . .

Every season starts the same way. I think it's going to be different, yet here we are.

Rinse, wash, repeat.

Instead, one small lie has grown fucking tentacles. The truth is, none of the shit I did even hurt him.

The man has sponsors and a new woman every day.

The man is the biggest player I have ever met.

He might hate me, but really, we're all better off.

Letting out a sigh, I admit defeat. Guess this seat will have to do. Lucky me.

It won't be that bad. I'm sure Hudson will be busy, and I'll listen to my earphones. I plop down in the seat and pull open my bag that's now on my lap.

My fingers start to riffle through all the crap I have in there.

Receipts I don't need, gum wrappers, a notebook I forgot I owned, and oh my God, what is this—a candy bar? Who knows how old it is. This bag really is a black hole.

"Damn, maybe I should call you Mary Poppins."

I turn to look at Hudson, my brow lifting in question.

"You know, because your bag has all sorts of crazy shit in there. Do you have a lamp?"

Now, it's my turn to roll my eyes. "No, I don't have a lamp."

"You sure? Have you checked? I bet you do." He grins. That grin—dangerous and disarming. It's no wonder half the women in this city fall at his feet. However, I'm not one of them. But if I'm being honest, if he wasn't such a pain in the ass, I might fall for it. But unfortunately for him, I'm not interested. Not that I think he is.

With my free hand, I pull the opening wider and bend my head farther down to peer inside.

"Find whatever you're looking for yet?" he asks from beside me, his gaze practically burning a hole in my side. I wish he'd just mind his own business and leave me alone. Or is that asking too much? Maybe this is my karma—having to put up with his sarcastic quips as my penance.

"Do you ever stop?" I snap, frustration bubbling over.

"No. Not really. Especially when it does what I hope it will," he replies, a smirk playing on his lips.

"And that is?" I counter, raising an eyebrow.

"Drive you crazy," he says, leaning back with a triumphant grin.

beautiful collide

"Hasn't it been long enough? I get it, you hate me, but seriously. Grow up," I shoot back, crossing my arms defiantly.

"What fun would that be?" he retorts, amusement dancing in his eyes.

Why does he always look like he's having the time of his life, even when he's being the worst? It's infuriating.

"A lot," I deadpan, my expression unyielding.

I pivot my body away from him, trying my best to tune him out. The man is like a gnat—persistent, annoying, and impossible to ignore.

I can't find my earphones, which doesn't bode well for this flight.

If this were a normal flight, we would have the little free headphones the flight attendant passes out, but since this isn't a far trip, the team chartered an older, smaller plane that apparently doesn't have entertainment.

Of course. Because when it rains, it pours.

"Can't find whatever you're looking for?"

"Not that it's any of your business, but no."

"That sucks. What to do? What to do?" he asks himself.

As if I don't know his plan is to drive me up the wall. Hudson leans forward, and I brace for verbal impact.

By coincidence, the plane's wheels start to move.

As the plane bounces down the runway, the sound is loud enough that maybe I won't need the headphones.

Just as the wheels lift and the plane takes flight, he finds what he's looking for, pivoting to me, headphones in his hand.

"Don't say I didn't do anything for you . . . twice."

His words carry a mix of smugness and truth, and I hate him for it.

Once up in the air, I'm hopeful the flight will go by fast. If I remember correctly, it's only two hours, so that's not too bad.

Two hours. Just one hundred and twenty minutes of pure torture. Totally survivable. *Yeah, probably not.*

Not much is worse than being stuck next to Hudson for the flight. A flight with turbulence would make it worse.

The seats aren't too cramped, so at least I have that going for me, but the thing is, Hudson is larger than life.

His presence suffocates in the worst and most distracting way possible.

Cramped seats? Annoying. But even a few hours squeezed into a tiny airplane seat, elbow to elbow with my archnemesis? *Still too much.* This has to be my personal hell.

Now that the plane is at a cruising altitude, I settle into my seat.

From the corner of my eye, I see Hudson recline his. He doesn't go all the way, which surprises me. He goes just far enough back to be comfortable but not far enough to bother whichever of his teammates sits behind him.

It's a small thing, barely worth noticing, but it feels intentional. Thoughtful, even. It throws me off.

It's oddly sweet. Although I don't want to admit that.

I move my body again. I'm not one to lean back, but I'm not comfortable.

My back is on fire. It feels stiff, and my nerves are frayed.

And why won't the tension in my shoulders go away?

I'm really a mess. Maybe I'll do what he did. Recline my seat just a little bit.

I reach my hand out and press the button, the back of my seat moving a few inches before I stop.

"Are you inspired by me?"

"Um, no," I murmur.

The words come out clipped and way too defensive. Why do I always feel like I've walked right into a trap whenever I talk to him?

"Then why did you move your seat like mine?" he says, trying to bite back a smirk.

I roll my eyes. "Oh, sorry, are you the only person allowed to recline?"

"No, but I'm the only one to do the half recline." He points around the plane. "Most are full recline or no recline." I want to knock the smug look off his face. He's impossible. He's acting like he invented the concept of reclining.

I try to tune him out, distracting myself by looking at pictures on my phone. My lips spread as I see a picture of Josie and Dane.

"They're cute." I hear from beside me.

I nod. "They are."

"Do you think you'll keep working for him?"

I turn to face Hudson, my brows furrowing. "Why wouldn't I?"

"I just figured—"

"That Josie would handle it? Hardly."

"No. I just thought—"

"And herein lies the problem, Wilde, you thought."

His jaw stiffens, and my stomach tightens. Why do I always do this? Speak first, think later.

It's like I have no control over myself. A reflex.

Maybe I went too far. Perhaps I shouldn't be so mean to him.

An uncomfortable silence stretches between us.

Reaching into my bag, I pull out my Kindle and try to focus on the book I've been reading, but the harder I try to read, the more hyperaware I am of the fact that he's placed his arm on the armrest between us.

Despite trying not to think about it, I can't stop.

A part of me wonders if he'll touch me.

The thought shouldn't even cross my mind. It's a ridiculous thought.

Yet . . .

My heart pounds heavily in my chest.

Do I want him to?

No.

I don't.

I should move my arm, right? From the corner of my eye, I peek over at him. While I might be freaking out, he seems calm and collected.

Serene.

Bastard.

How am I so affected by him, yet he isn't bothered?

As if he can hear my thoughts, he opens his eyes and catches me staring. Of course, he does.

Again, cosmic joke. I'm the hex, after all.

"You good?" he asks.

"Yeah, why?"

"Well, you're staring."

I shake my head. "No, I'm not. I'm reading." I lift my Kindle in the air as if to say "see."

His eyes narrow as he looks from my Kindle to my eyes.

"And what are you reading?"

I blink, snapping my gaze back to my book. Shit. *What am I reading again?* My brain goes blank. Probably because of him. No, it can't be that. It's probably because it's been weeks since I opened this thing. I've been so busy that I haven't had time. Yeah, that's the reason. Not his proximity. "Oh. Um, it's a mystery novel."

Hudson raises an eyebrow. "Really? For some reason, I don't believe you."

"What does that mean?"

"I see you with something lighter. You seem like a hopeless romantic."

My mouth drops open, and he laughs. "Really?"

"Nah, Hex. You probably don't have a romantic bone in your body." His words hurt. They shouldn't. I know they shouldn't, but they do. I don't let on, though.

Instead, I try to think about a witty rebuttal when an announcement begins to crackle overhead.

Something about turbulence.

I instinctively tighten my grip on the armrest. Flying is on my list of things I don't love. Which, I guess, in the grand scheme of things that I'm scared of, would be considered a good thing, but still, when I'm up in the air and the plane starts to bump, I forget this isn't one of my fears.

Just as I'm about to put my Kindle away, the plane gives a harsh jolt, and my device falls to the floor.

I'm about to reach for it when the turbulence becomes more violent, and my heart pounds furiously in my chest.

It's fine. I'm fine. This is normal.

Turbulence is normal.

I inhale deeply. Fuck. I hate this.

Deep down, I know flying is safe. Statistically safer than driving. But when the plane bumps and shakes, all my rational thoughts leave the building, and I can't stop the intrusive ones that wage war inside me.

What if something is wrong?

What if the pilots aren't telling us?

What if this is it? What if I die sitting next to Hudson? No. Stop. This is ridiculous.

You aren't dying.

My pulse accelerates. Blood pounds through my veins at a rate that probably could cause a heart attack.

I'm lost in my thoughts of *what-if* when Hudson shifts.

Hudson.

Goddammit.

Why does it always have to be him? He is the one person in the world I don't want to see me unraveling. Yet this man is always around when I'm having a panic attack.

I need to rein it in, but even as I think these words, I know it's impossible. When I go down the path, it's hard to push away my thoughts.

Then I feel it. His fingers brush against mine on the armrest.

Despite my efforts to be unaffected, my skin tingles at the contact. *Traitor.*

I freeze, glancing down at where our hands now touch.

His hand now fully covers mine.

I tilt my head up until my gaze meets his.

Locked in a stare, neither of us speaks.

The plane continues to shake uncontrollably.

His hand tightens around me. His fingers softly caress my skin.

"We're okay," he finally says. "Just breathe."

His voice is calm and steady—a lifeline in the chaos.

I try to inhale, my head dropping to look at the floor. I'm trying desperately to calm down, but as the plane drops, I'm not sure I can.

His fingers continue to circle, but this time, his free hand reaches out and touches my chin. "Don't look away from me."

I obey.

When I meet his stare, I feel anchored to the world. It makes no sense, but his blue eyes seem to hold me hostage, and as he looks at me, I regulate my breathing.

"I've got you. I won't let anything happen to you."

And like in the closet and the gas station . . . for some reason, I believe him.

chapter twenty-one

Molly

THE FAINT HUM OF SKATES ON THE ICE FILLS THE RINK AS I stand on the sidelines, pretending to scroll through my phone. Really, I'm watching Hudson.

Not because I want to, of course. It's purely circumstantial. He's been on fire today, weaving through drills like the puck is his bitch.

We're back home after a two-game loss, and the guys are practicing for the next game tomorrow. They need to win this next one.

Even Dane gave him a fist bump after some crazy play I have never seen before, which is saying something.

It's annoying, really. No one should be that good at hockey, and that's infuriating.

I sigh and tuck my phone into my pocket, shifting my focus to the clipboard in my hand.

Dane asked me to update some sponsor scheduling for the week, which is why I'm here in the first place.

Definitely not because I want to see Hudson Wilde in action.

"Hex."

Speak of the devil.

I glance up to find Hudson skating toward me, his helmet pushed back enough to reveal that stupidly perfect smirk of his. He pulls to a stop at the boards, resting his gloved hands on the top rail.

"What do you want, Wilde?" I ask, narrowing my eyes. Contrary to my words, my tone is light. I can't help but be thankful for his help yesterday.

Instead of answering, he removes his glove and reaches into his skate—pulling out a small white card. He slips it through the gap in the boards, holding it out to me.

"What's this?" I ask, reluctantly taking the card.

"Just read it," he says, his tone surprisingly serious.

I glance down at the card, half expecting some sort of dumb prank or an invitation to another tequila-fueled disaster. Instead, my heart stumbles as I take in the text.

Dr. Karen Aldridge
Licensed Therapist
Specializing in Anxiety, PTSD, and Trauma Therapy

I stare at the card, my chest tightening.

"Is this a joke?" I ask, my voice sharper than I intended.

"Nope," Hudson says casually, leaning a little closer. "She's good. Helped a couple of my teammates when they were going through stuff."

I glance up at him, still holding the card between my fingers like it might burn me. "And you thought you'd just . . . slip this to me?"

His expression softens, and for a moment, I see something in his eyes that makes my throat tighten even more. Concern.

"You don't have to call her," he says, his voice low enough that no one else can hear. "I just thought . . ." He hesitates, scratching the back of his neck. "After last night, you might want someone to talk to."

The memory of the flight from last week rushes back—Hudson

quietly guiding me through a panic attack on the plane, keeping everyone else oblivious while he talked me down.

It was . . . kind. Too kind. And now, this card feels like it's carrying more weight than I can handle.

"You're unbelievable," I say, my voice shaking. "What, you think you're my savior now? That you get to fix me?"

Hudson frowns. "That's not what this is."

"Then what is it, Hudson?" I snap, waving the card in front of him. "Because from where I'm standing, it looks a lot like you butting into my business."

"It's not about butting in," he says, his tone calm but firm. "It's about helping. You don't have to do everything alone, Molly."

"I've been fine alone," I shove the card back through the gap in the boards and watch as it falls onto the ice. "For years."

"Have you?" he asks, I meet his stare again. His gaze is piercing.

The question feels like a slap, and I take an involuntary step back. "You don't know anything about me."

"I know enough," he says, his voice softening. "I know you're strong as hell. But strength doesn't mean ignoring what's hurting you."

Heat rises in my chest, my defenses flaring. "Don't you dare lecture me on strength."

"I'm not lecturing," he says, holding his hands up. "I'm just saying it's okay to ask for help. It doesn't make you weak."

"Thanks for the therapy session, Dr. Wilde," I snap, my voice dripping with sarcasm. "Now, how about you mind your own damn business?"

His jaw tightens, but he doesn't back down. "I can't do that, Molly. Not when I see you struggling."

"I'm not struggling," I yell, the words echoing louder than I intended.

Several players glance over, their curiosity obvious, but Hudson waves them off, keeping his focus on me.

"You're right," he says, lowering his voice. "You're not struggling. You're surviving. But don't you think you deserve better than that?"

The question cuts deeper than I'm prepared for, and my hands clench into fists at my sides.

"I didn't ask for your help," I say, my voice trembling with a mix of anger and something I don't want to name.

"I know," he says quietly. "But that doesn't mean you don't need it."

I turn away, needing to put distance between us before the tears threatening to spill actually do. "You don't know what you're talking about."

"I do, Molly," he says, his voice following me as I walk away. "And whether you believe it or not, I just want to see you happy."

His words hang in the air, but I don't stop. I can't. Because if I do, I might actually have to confront the truth in them.

And that's something I'm not ready for.

chapter twenty-two

Hudson

Dane: Boys. Bar tonight.

Aiden: I'm in.

Mason: I'll come if Hudson comes.

Hudson: Pass.

Mason: What?

Aiden: Excuse me?

Dane: You okay, Wilde? That sounded like a no.

Mason: A no to the bar? Is he sick?

Aiden: Do we need to send a wellness check?

Mason: Bro, blink twice if you're being held hostage.

Hudson: I'm not being held hostage. I just don't feel like going out.

Dane: Who are you, and what have you done with Hudson Wilde?

Aiden: You're the one who drags us to the bar after every win.

Mason: Exactly. Last week you said, and I quote, "It's a crime to waste a post-win buzz. And we just won two in a row."

Hudson: I said that?

Aiden: Yes. Very passionately.

Dane: Hudson, seriously. What's going on? You hiding something?

Mason: Are you sick? Hurt? In love???

Hudson: I'm fine.

Aiden: Liar.

Mason: Definitely in love. Only a girl could make Hudson say no to a bar.

Hudson: I'm not in love.

Mason: I forgot you don't fall in love.

Dane: So what's the excuse?

Hudson: Maybe I just want a quiet night in for once.

Mason: A quiet night in??? Who even are you right now?

Aiden: Is this what retirement looks like?

Dane: Pathetic.

Hudson: Can't a guy take a break?

Mason: No. Not when that guy is you.

Aiden: We're coming to drag you out of the house.

Mason: Put on deodorant. We're on our way. I don't need you stinking up my car.

Hudson: I'm locking the doors.

Mason: You say that like I don't know where your spare key is.

Hudson: . . .

Dane: I'll bring the car around. You're done fighting this, man.

Aiden: Resistance is futile.

Hudson: Fine. You guys are relentless.

Mason: That's what teammates are for. Now get ready.

beautiful collide

Aiden: Wear something nice. Mason and I are putting you on Tinder if you're this mopey.

Hudson: I hate all of you.

Dane: See you in 20, Wilde.

Mason: Don't forget your hairbrush.

chapter twenty-three

Hudson

THE BAR IS LOUD.

It's also the last place I want to be. Nature of the beast, though. This is who they expect.

It doesn't matter who I really am or what I want. This is the persona I've taken on. The space around me is filled with laughter and clinking glasses.

This was my idea. It's what's expected.

Has been ever since I became a Redville Saint.

The fun guy.

The player.

The titles are exhausting, and I hate it. But it's easier than letting anyone in.

The good news is I can at least grab a drink and escape for a moment. The bad news is the conversations that will most likely be flung at me, which I don't want to partake in.

I navigate through the crowd, and for a moment, I feel relief as no one approaches me.

beautiful collide

Until I collide with something. Scrap that. Someone.

"Watch where you're going," a feminine voice snaps. I don't even need to look down to see who I ran into.

I do, though.

Molly steps back and glares up at me.

Okay, I might have overstepped when I gave her that card. But I hate the idea of someone struggling alone.

"Seriously, Wilde. Do you ever pay attention?"

"Me? Are you kidding?" I cross my arms at my chest and lower my head to gesture to her phone in her hand, the screen still lit up from the texts.

"Maybe if you weren't staring at your phone, you'd see what's in front of you," I fire back.

"You're blaming this on me?"

"Changing the truth is what you do, Hex." There is no question this is residual anger from the other day.

"Wow. You're a jerk."

I nod. "That I am. But at least I'm not a liar."

"Aren't you?"

I raise an eyebrow. "Not that I can remember. Tell me, Hex, what did I lie about?"

"Stop calling me that. It's a ridiculous name."

"It's been years. Don't you realize the name stays? Plus, is it really that far-fetched? Everything goes wrong when you're around."

"Can you just go?"

"Me? You can go."

"Find your flavor of the night already, and do us all a favor." Her voice drips with distaste.

My back goes ramrod straight. "You think you know me, but you don't."

"'Cause you aren't a player."

I throw my hands up. "You know what? You aren't worth it. Throw your walls up. Lie. I don't have time for this shit."

"Walls? What the hell do you know about my walls?" she shoots back, her voice rising over the noise.

My jaw tightens for a moment, the tension hanging thick in the air between us. "I know more than you pretend I do."

Her expression stiffens, a flicker of something crossing over her face. "Fine. I'll go."

For a heartbeat, everything seems to fade away, and I can once again see her all those years ago. A part of me wants to pull her close and ask her what haunts her.

But I decide to let it go and let her walk away.

chapter twenty-four

Molly

IT'S GAME DAY.

Today is game five.

And we need to win.

I have a bunch of stuff to do before the boys get on the ice, but first, I need a cup of coffee.

Grabbing my phone out of my bag, I fire off a text to Dane and Josie.

> **Me:** Anyone want to meet me for coffee? Apparently, there's a new coffee shop attached to the hotel.
>
> **Josie:** No can do, but Dane said he'd meet you.
>
> **Dane:** Give me ten minutes.
>
> **Molly:** See you soon.

Grabbing my jean jacket off the chair in my hotel room, I head toward the hall.

I have a few minutes, as I'm early, a habit I have grown accustomed to since working for my brother, so I decide to take the stairs.

Stairs are a safer bet when you don't love enclosed spaces.

Swinging the door open, I step inside the stairwell and start my descent.

The sound of my shoes clinking the concrete echoes around me. Since my room is only on the fifth floor, it doesn't take me too long to make it to the ground level. Climbing back up won't be as fun, but at least I'll be caffeinated. It will be my workout for the day.

I throw the door open and head into the small hallway before entering the lobby and making my way out the front door.

The coffee shop is attached to the hotel, but the entrance is outside.

It's brisk today despite it being early May. The weather hasn't decided to be cooperative.

It's only a few steps before I stand in front of the door. A tiny bell jingles as I pull it open.

As soon as I'm inside, my eyes scan the space. A small line has formed in front of the register, but none of the people here are my brother.

Oh, well, I guess I'll just order. He'll be here eventually.

I walk over to the register. The couple in front of me steps out of the way as soon as they order, and I take their place.

I order our coffees and stand off to the side, my patience wearing thin.

Clutching two steaming cups, I shift my weight from one foot to the other, trying to push down my annoyance.

It's not like Dane to be late, so something must have happened.

I let out a sigh and continue to peer around the room, when my eyes land on *him*.

The person who haunts my waking thoughts and my dreams. In equal measure.

My opposing feelings for him give me whiplash.

Sometimes, I want to thank him.

Other times, I wish he never existed.

beautiful collide

Dramatic, sure. But Hudson Wilde elicits strong feelings from me. Most often, bad ones.

Sometimes, apparently, homicidal ones.

Why does he have to be so damn handsome?

With that rugged look and a dusting of hair on his face, he looks like he would fit in better out on the land riding a horse than on the ice, but lord, is he good on skates.

With tousled, dirty-blond hair and a sharp jawline, he should come with a warning label.

I'd rather deal with a dozen over-caffeinated idiots than one cocky and annoying hockey player who's great in bed.

And the worst part . . . he's the only man who's made me come.

So, yeah, I hate him.

And it's just my luck to bump into him. Maybe he's right. Perhaps I am the hex. As I try to escape, he notices me and crosses the space to intercept me.

Of course, I want no part in that, so I move faster, but when I do, my foot snags on the carpet runner, and like in slow motion, my cup slips from my grasp.

And, of course, Hudson, being Hudson, is already beside me, trying to once again be the hero.

Joke's on him because it's already falling.

Time slows to a turtle's pace as I watch it tumble, coffee splattering all over Hudson's white Henley.

He jumps back, his hands flying to pull his shirt away from his body.

"Fuck, that hurts." He continues to fumble with his shirt until he eventually goes to lift it. He apparently remembers that he has nothing underneath because the moment his perfect washboard abs are in plain view, he drops the soaked material back down.

"Great, just great," I mutter, eyes wide.

I'll never hear the end of this. I'm sure he'll figure out a way to attach this moment to my nickname.

Clumsy Hex or something stupid.

Hudson looks me up and down, his mouth twitching into a smirk as the hot liquid drips down his once white shirt. "Nice aim."

"I've been practicing for years."

"I bet you have."

I take a step to the right.

"What? Abandoning me so soon?"

"I'm getting you napkins, dick." I reach out and fumble for napkins from the nearby stand.

"Wow, dick? Aren't I the victim?"

"Victim of what? An accident."

"If you say so."

"I do. I didn't mean to. You're just so . . . distracting."

He raises an eyebrow, amusement dancing in his eyes. "Distracting? Interesting choice of words."

"I have a few choice words I would say." I reach forward and start to blot the fabric.

"I should charge you for the dry cleaning." He leans in closer as I continue to wipe.

"Good luck with that. Dane doesn't pay me enough." My heart races. I shouldn't be touching him. Being this close to him is dangerous too. Even though he's not my favorite person, I can admit that he smells like heaven this close-up. Like pine on a warm summer day. It's intoxicating.

Needing to escape, I take the soaked napkin and toss it in the trash.

"Well, I'm sorry. Didn't mean to spill on you, no matter what you believe."

"Oh, I believe you." A playful grin breaks through the sarcasm.

I dry my hands on my jeans, feeling the familiar heat rise in my cheeks.

We stand there, the air lighter than usual. It feels like something has shifted.

Just then, my brother appears with a look of confusion as he takes in the scene in front of him. He's most likely curious about why Hudson and I are talking.

"What's going on?" he asks, eyeing Hudson's coffee-stained shirt.

"Nothing," I say too fast.

Dane looks from me to Hudson, his gaze drifting down to Hudson's saturated shirt.

"A cup of coffee attacked me," Hudson explains.

"Is that so?"

"Yep, you know me; I'm always dropping stuff." He covers for me, which is downright shocking. If he spilled a cup of coffee on me, I'm not sure I'd pretend otherwise. *Not true. You would.*

"Funny, I thought you were known for the opposite."

"Well, only on the ice."

"Right," my brother replies. "Let's hope that's it. And you aren't bothering my sister about something." He lifts a brow.

"Nope. All good here."

"If you say so."

"Well, on that note, I have to be going."

chapter twenty-five

Hudson

"You don't have to go," Dane says, stepping closer. His words might tell me not to leave, but his face begs me to behave.

I take a step back. "Something tells me my presence isn't wanted."

I glance over at Molly, who has suddenly become very interested in her shoes. No one can call her subtle.

Dane's gaze bounces between us. "You know it wouldn't be unheard of for you to . . . I don't know, get along."

Molly snorts. "Yeah, I don't think so."

"Wanting to kill each other is apparently more our speed," I respond.

"Come on, guys. Is it really that hard? I never understood why you hated each other. It's not like anything happened?" If only he knew how much he didn't know about her. Not that I know a lot, but it's obvious she's holding back on him.

She finally lifts her head from where it was angled, looking at the floor. Her expression tries to appear neutral, but in my opinion, I don't know who she thinks she's fooling. It's written as clear as day on her features that there is a story there.

"It would be pretty hard," I say, cutting the tension.

Dane inclines his head, leveling me with a stare that would frighten most men. Not me, of course, but most. "Seriously, Wilde, are you making a dick joke at my sister?"

I hold up my hands in mock innocence. "Not this time." But I can't help when my lips split into a grin. "But it is tempting."

Dane's eyes narrow. "Seriously."

"He's easy to want to kill, isn't he?" Molly mutters.

"That's neither here nor there." The way Dane looks at his sister while he says this makes me want to laugh. He's got the dad scolding face reserved for a kid who just painted the walls with peanut butter and is attempting to lick it off.

"I'm funny. Admit it, Dane."

"That you're easy to kill. Sure, I'll admit it. But seriously, just get along. For my sake, at least."

I tilt my head toward Molly. "How about it?"

She lets out a long-drawn-out breath, dipping her head like she's considering it. "Sure, Dane, I'll get right on it. Hell, maybe we can take up a hobby together." She meets my stare. "How do you feel about crocheting? We can make matching scarfs."

"I've always been interested in making my own clothes. Maybe we should make something for Dane to wear."

"That's a fabulous idea." Her lip tips up. "See, look at that. Your plan is already working." She smirks at Dane.

"I think his color is pink."

"Fuchsia?"

"Yeah. Maybe with canary yellow."

Dane ignores me and instead glares at us both. "For fuck's sake. You guys are driving everyone insane."

Molly throws her hands up. "Fine."

"Fine," I agree, leaning forward and allowing my lips to tip up into a smile. Molly rolls her eyes instantly.

"What are you smirking about?"

"Me? Smirking?"

She throws her hands up. "I give up. Dane, he's intolerable."

"Who? Me?" I put a hand to my chest, feigning shock.

"Yes. You. Even now, that damn smirk. Jeez, Hudson, grow up."

"Grow up? Hell, why would I do that? We should make it more interesting."

She narrows her eyes. "Yeah, and how are we going to do that?"

"How about a bet?" I grin like a fool. No way will she be able to resist.

She raises an eyebrow. She knows she's walking into a trap. I can practically see her brain working, weighing out whether she'll play along.

She'll do it.

No way she's saying no.

It's not in her nature to back down from a challenge.

"If you can go through the rest of the playoffs without arguing with me, I'll stop annoying you." God, I'm a smug bastard. But this will be so worth it.

"Yeah, sure."

"Nope. Scout's honor." I place my hand on my chest.

She snorts. "No way you're a Boy Scout."

"You don't know me. Maybe I am."

"Fine." She leans in slightly. "Let's say you can actually do that. What happens if I lose?" she asks.

I shrug. "I'll get back to you."

"Nah, that's BS." She points a slender finger at me. "No way am I agreeing to these terms."

"Afraid you can't be nice for a few weeks? Wow, Moll, that's concerning."

Dane, who's silently been watching us like a tennis match, suddenly speaks up. "I'm going to have to agree with Hudson. Even though ninety percent of the time he talks out of his ass, he's making sense this time."

"I'm wounded, Sinclair."

"No, you're not." He laughs.

"Yeah, I'm not." But my words don't match how I feel. All of this, it's all a fucking facade, and they don't even see it. The jokes and the banter are a hell of a lot easier than admitting how I truly feel.

I extend my hand. "Do we have a deal?"

She eyes me carefully before sighing. "Sure. Whatever."

chapter twenty-six

Molly

THE MOMENT HUDSON WALKS OUT OF THE COFFEE SHOP, I LET out the breath I've been holding.

Another thing that happens instantly is that the tension swirling around the room immediately drops.

It vanishes completely.

Or so I think before I pivot to turn to look at Dane.

My brother's "Dad Mode" has been activated. It's easy to tell when he falls back into his parental role by the way he stands, arms crossed over his chest, and how his expression locks on to me, the one I have been known to love and hate in equal measure.

"You okay?" His voice is lower than normal. Great. He's concerned.

I force a smile, one I hope looks more convincing than it feels. "Of course. Why wouldn't I be?"

The lie rolls off my tongue so easily that I almost believe it myself.

Almost believe that my anxiety hasn't gotten worse over the past few months.

But inside, my stomach twists.

My chest feels tight.

My head screams . . . *liar*.

I'm not okay. I haven't been okay in months. Ever since I saw *him*, things have been . . . bad. He's gone now. You're okay. But I'm not.

The panic attacks are back with a vengeance, clawing at me when I least expect them. Some nights, I'll wake up gasping for air, my heart pounding like I'd just sprinted a mile.

Other times, I find I'm afraid to walk into rooms.

To be alone.

To fly.

Anything where I question my control.

If I feel out of control, it feels like I'll suffocate.

I know that fear is just a mirage. It disappears if you have the courage to walk through it, but knowing it's an illusion doesn't help. . .

Honestly, it only makes it worse.

But no way am I about to dump this all on Dane.

He's already been through so much in life.

I won't add my mess to his.

"If you're sure." He doesn't sound convinced, but he doesn't push. That's not Dane's style. He's more the grumpy, brooding type.

Instead, he gestures to the small coffee table by the window. "Sit. Let's have coffee before the chaos starts. I'll have to head to the arena soon and still need to do a few things."

"Anything I can help with?"

"Nope. Josie's helping."

At the mention of his girlfriend, Josie, my back tightens. It's not because I don't like her. Actually, it's the opposite—I love her. It's just because with her in his life, does he really need me?

I nod, moving toward the table, then sliding into one of the chairs.

My coffee is still warm when I take a sip.

Dane sits across from me, watching me a little too closely. I know that look. He's trying to figure out what's wrong with me.

"You've been pulling a lot of late nights," he says casually like he isn't trying to pry.

"I've been busy." I shrug, lifting the mug back to my lips. The coffee isn't the best. It's not awful—but it's stronger than I like. "Someone has to keep your life from imploding."

He snorts. "I could hire someone else, you know. Someone who insists on taking their vacation time."

"I went to Europe last summer."

"Only 'cause I forced you."

I roll my eyes. "Well, you can try to replace me." I smirk. "But good luck finding someone who'll juggle your schedule, deal with your sponsors, and pick up your dry cleaning without strangling you."

Dane laughs, and for a second, the tension eases. "Fair point. You're irreplaceable, I guess."

"Obviously." I lean back in my chair, keeping my voice light even as my chest tightens again. *Don't let him see it. Don't let him know.*

Dane studies me, his brow furrowing slightly. "You know you don't have to do everything, right? You could take a break. Breathe for a bit."

His words make me flinch, but I cover it quickly with a sip of coffee. "I'm fine," I respond, a little sharper than I mean to. "Really, Dane. I'm good. You don't need to worry about me."

He hesitates, his gaze lingering on me like he isn't sure whether to believe me. But after a long pause, he nods. "Okay. But if you need anything, you'll tell me, right?"

"Of course," I lie again.

I'm going to hell.

The last thing he needs to know is that I'm barely keeping it together. He'll ask too many questions.

It's easier this way.

Much easier.

He finally smiles, easy and wide. Something he's been doing more and more since he met Josie. "Good. Because I was thinking about adding social media to your to-do list."

I laugh. "Finally. Did Josie convince you?"

"Um." He leans back. "Yeah, I'm sure you'll love the job too. Josie had a great pitch of all the fantastic posts you can make." He rolls his eyes before continuing. "She painted a pretty picture."

"Such as?"

"She said you could write 'Dane Sinclair: Hockey's Golden Boy—or Just a Guy Who Can't Remember His Passwords?'"

Despite myself, I laugh, shaking my head. "Please, tell me Josie didn't come up with that."

"She didn't. I just forgot what she said and tried to shoot from the hip. I failed."

"You'd be lost without me, brother."

"Probably," he admits with a laugh of his own.

For a second, it feels normal. The laughter and the teasing almost make me believe that everything will be fine.

But deep down, I know better. I'm not okay. Not really. But as long as Dane believes I am, I can keep pretending.

chapter twenty-seven

Molly

I GRIP THE EDGE OF MY SEAT, FEIGNING INTEREST IN THE GAME. If anyone were looking, they'd probably ask what's wrong since my knuckles are white from the pressure.

Luckily for me, Josie and Cassidy are way too interested in watching what their men are doing to have any idea I'm currently in the middle of having an existential crisis.

I can't even blame the game for my stress because, let's be real, it has nothing to do with it. My tension has nothing to do with the scoreboard or how the guys play. It doesn't even have to do with the fact that Dane just finally got out of the penalty box. Nope. Not at all.

"You okay over there?" Cassidy's voice cuts through my thoughts. *Damn.* Now, I have to play it cool because I don't want the girls to know what my problem is.

My problem is Hudson. *Obviously.* Or better yet, the fact that I can't stop watching him.

He really is the bane of my existence and the reason for this ridiculous bet I've trapped myself in.

I grit my teeth together as my eyes track him on the ice. I tell myself it's not because I want to. It's just because I'm hoping for him to mess up. Like trip over his skate or send the puck sailing into his own goal.

Something I can mentally frame as proof he isn't perfect.

I would live for the moment when he does.

But I'm full of shit.

Absolutely pathetically full of shit.

Because deep down, I know that's not why I'm watching.

I can't tear my eyes away from him because he is perfect.

Obnoxiously so.

The way he moves with such stupid, effortless grace. It's infuriating.

How he commands the ice—like he belongs there and owns it—is annoying as hell.

A ridiculous thought flies through my head. *How many women here are undressing him?* Not me, of course. Never me.

Someone needs to put me out of my misery because I really shouldn't be watching him like a pathetic schoolgirl with a crush on her bully . . . except for some reason, I feel like maybe I'm the bully in this situation.

He's the good-natured, hot jock. I'm pretty sure I've seen this movie before. He ends up with the quirky artist with a heart of gold, which is not me.

Also, why am I thinking about this?

Oh, yeah, I know, because Hudson is the kind of guy who makes it impossible not to notice him, even when you really, really want to ignore him. So, yeah, now I'm sitting daydreaming about him. Great. Just great.

What. The. Fuck.

No.

He's none of these things.

I hate him.

What is wrong with me? A lot, that's what. Because even in my own inner monologue, the person who should be the villain—is the good one.

No. I need to snap out of this. He's insufferable. Obnoxious. Infuriating.

Then why are you still staring at him?

Nope. I'm not gawking. I'm taunting. Yeah, that's it.

The damn stupid bet.

I agreed to be on my best behavior, but that doesn't mean I have to make it easy on him.

This is a loophole I can live in. I won't break the rules, but I can bend the hell out of them.

Maybe I can't argue with him in public, but I can goad him.

Hudson skates past the bench, his focus seemingly on the puck as the Saints set up for a power play. He doesn't even glance my way, but as he coasts by, his glove comes up just enough for me to catch it.

My jaw drops.

No. That's not what I think it is. It's hard to tell because of the thickness of the glove, but it looks like one of his fingers is sticking up more than the others.

Oh, he wouldn't. Except, of course, he would.

That has got to be his middle finger.

The bastard just discreetly gave me the middle finger.

I blink, caught between shock and admiration for how brazen he is.

If only I had thought of that. Sure, he probably wouldn't see it because he's supposed to be playing, but obviously, since he just did it to me, maybe he would have.

Nope. You're better than cheap moves like that.

Anyway, this might mean I win. Someone had to have seen it. I whip my head toward where Dane is skating. Surely, he saw that, right?

beautiful collide

I can't catch a break. Unlike Hudson, he's too engrossed in the game.

I turn my head to Josie. Maybe she saw it. She can vouch for me.

No luck there either.

She's watching my brother like the lovesick fool she is, totally oblivious.

Cassidy?

Unless the picture she's currently taking is of Hudson, which it's not, she doesn't have the evidence I need.

I'm alone in my outrage, which makes it burn hotter. I clench my fists, my nails biting into my palms.

The nerve. The audacity.

The pure, unfiltered chaos this man brings into my life with every breath he takes.

He's totally going to find a way to be smug about this later.

The worst part is I have to bite my tongue when he does. The bet has officially become the most infuriating thing I've ever agreed to.

I will not be the one to lose the bet.

The man is diabolical.

He knew exactly what he was doing, and I can practically feel him smirking through the glass.

By the time the Saints win in overtime, I'm about ready to explode. The moment the buzzer sounds, I slip past the throng of celebrating fans and head for the hallway near the locker rooms.

I need air. Not that stale arena air full of sweat and melted ice, but air where Hudson isn't occupying my thoughts like an uninvited guest who refuses to leave.

Since the guys aren't out yet, I pace back and forth, my heels clicking against the floor. Despite the door being closed, I can still hear the muffled cheers of the team inside.

Hopefully, they aren't in there too long. I'd like to speak with my brother and find a way to pull Hudson aside and whisper-shout at him.

Okay, mostly yell. The whisper part is negotiable.

After five minutes, the door swings open, and Hudson appears, his hair damp and his black thermal untucked as he laughs. He's with Mason and hasn't spotted me yet.

The sight of him—relaxed, cocky, like he doesn't have a care in the world—only stokes the fire inside me.

After he finishes chuckling at whatever Mason said, he tilts his head up and notices me. Instantly, his lips spread into a smirk.

Oh, there it is. The smirk that makes me want to punch him and . . . do other things I refuse to acknowledge. *Won't go there.*

While I know he's not surprised to see me here because I work for Dane, he knows he's the reason I'm here tonight. His antics.

"Molly," he drawls, stopping in his place. "To what do I owe the honor?"

His tone is pure mischief, and it takes every ounce of my willpower not to throw anything at him.

And there it is. That smug grin that makes my blood boil.

He knows why I'm here, and the worst part is that he's enjoying this. He lives for moments like this—to push, to bait, to see how far he can go before I snap.

I'm about to answer with something biting, something that will wipe that smirk off his face, when Dane strolls out of the locker room behind him, grinning like he's on top of the world.

"You coming out tonight?" Dane asks, his excitement so palpable it's hard not to smile back.

"You're going out? Willingly?" I tease, narrowing my eyes at him.

"Yeah."

I reach out, pressing my palm to his forehead like I'm checking for a fever. "Who are you, and what did you do to my brother?"

"It's called love, Molly." I don't even need to look at Hudson to know he's enjoying this.

beautiful collide

Dane snaps his gaze to Hudson, his brow arching. "Careful, Hudson. That could be construed as sarcasm."

Hudson lifts his hands in mock surrender, his grin never wavering. "Nothing sarcastic here. You're in love, and when someone's in love, they change."

I can feel the words bubbling up inside me—sharp, sarcastic comebacks just begging to be unleashed. But I promised. I promised to play nice, and the effort of holding it in is physically painful. My teeth sink into my cheek to keep them in.

Hudson, of course, notices. He raises an eyebrow, clearly amused. He knows exactly what I'm doing and why, and the smug satisfaction in his eyes is almost unbearable.

He crosses his arms, leaning against the doorframe, his lips twitching as if he's waiting for me to crack.

Dane looks back and forth between us, clearly missing the subtext but clocking the tension. "Looks like you guys are following through with the bet. I'm proud of you both."

"Guess we're just full of surprises. Right, Hudson?" I manage, my voice tight and my smile strained.

Dane laughs, clapping Hudson on the back. "Good."

Watching Dane like this—light, happy, so completely different from the way he used to be—my anger dissipates.

This is what I've been hoping for, working for, this version of him.

I love it. It makes all the chaos and Hudson-related nonsense almost worth it. Almost.

Dane glances at me. "What's it going to be? You coming?"

"I'll catch up," I reply, forcing my voice to stay even. "I need a minute."

"Cool." He gives me a quick hug before heading down the hall, his strides confident and carefree.

The second Dane disappears around the corner, I whirl on Hudson, grabbing the front of his shirt and yanking him into the hallway.

"You think you're cute, don't you?" I whisper-shout, my voice low but furious.

"I am cute," he replies without hesitation. *Annoying jerk.*

I inhale deeply, trying to keep my composure. "You know what I mean."

He scrunches his nose, tilting his head like he's genuinely puzzled. "Do I? I kind of think I don't."

I step closer, narrowing my eyes as I whisper, "You flipped me off."

His grin doesn't falter for even a second. "Did I? Or were you just looking for reasons to be mad at me? Because it's hard to flip someone off while wearing hockey gloves. You, of all people, should know how bulky they are. I think you're making this up just to win the bet."

"You're such a—"

"Careful." He leans down just enough to bring us eye to eye. "Wouldn't want to break our little deal, would you? That'd be embarrassing."

My jaw locks so hard it's a miracle my teeth don't crack. The worst part is he's right. If I snap, I lose. And Hudson, the king of arrogance, would never let me live it down.

I glare at him, my whole body vibrating with restrained fury. "You're insufferable."

"Yet here you are," he counters, stepping around me with infuriating ease. He gives me a cocky wink as he walks away, his voice trailing him. "See you at the bar, Hex."

He whistles as he goes, like he doesn't have a single care in the world.

My fists clench at my sides, and I vow—right then and there—that I will win this bet if it's the last thing I do. Hudson Wilde may have the upper hand tonight, but he has no idea who he's dealing with.

He thinks he's clever and untouchable, but this isn't over. Not even close.

chapter twenty-eight

Molly

WITH THE FIRST ROUND OF THE PLAYOFF OVER, IT'S NICE TO have this little break even if it's only for a day.

Of all the events we do as a team, this is by far my favorite.

Not because I'm particularly social or love standing around with players who constantly test my patience.

No, it's because there are puppies.

Dozens of adorable, squishy, barking puppies.

My heart doesn't stand a chance.

I love dogs.

Dogs are the greatest thing that has happened to all of humankind.

Honestly, if I was given a choice, I'd adopt every dog, start a compound, and live there happily for the rest of my life.

Unfortunately, logistically, that's not an option, so instead, I take part in fun events like this. Helping dogs in need get adopted.

A few feet away, I hear a commotion and turn to look in that direction. The makeshift stage buzzes with activity, and in the background is my favorite sound—the sound of puppies barking. I try to keep a straight face, but every time one of them lets out a yip or trips over its own paws, my resolve crumbles a little more.

Heaven.

This must be what heaven is.

Except for a few pesky details. Like the press. Cameras flash as the dogs run around and play.

I want to scoop one up and run off into the sunset, but instead, I stand near the edge of where we've set up for today's event, trying to look like I'm in control. The truth? I'm already plotting which of these pups I'd adopt if I could.

From the corner of my eye, I see my brother. He's shaking his head as Josie approaches him, cradling the cutest labradoodle I've ever seen.

"Good luck," I call to him, fighting the urge to laugh.

"Thanks," he mutters back, knowing full well that if Josie wants this puppy, it's already a done deal.

"But first, before any adoption can take place, there's a little matter of a photo shoot," I remind him.

"I'm not doing it," Dane grunts.

"Tell that to your girl. She signed you up," I say, biting back a grin.

"I'm keeping my shirt on."

"No, you're not." Josie bounces closer, still holding the puppy.

"Hellfire . . ."

"Don't hellfire me, Mr. Grump. We will raise triple the money for these dogs." She lifts the dog, her eyes practically glowing with mischief. "Please."

"Fine," Dane sighs, trudging off toward the photographer. The labradoodle wags its tail enthusiastically, oblivious to Dane's suffering.

I watch them walk away, but my attention is drawn elsewhere.

Of course, it's Hudson.

He's dead center in the photo shoot, shirtless, holding a Maltese puppy like it's the Cup. His grin is so annoyingly perfect that it practically blinds me. And if how handsome he is isn't enough, he starts to nuzzle the dog.

Goddamn.

My ovaries are in full revolt. This is not fair.

No man this hot should hold a puppy. It's basically cheating.

Next to him is Mason, the team's second-in-command for attention-seeking antics. He's striking a pose with a squirming beagle, laughing every time the puppy licks his face. The crowd loves it. They love them. Cameras flash as fans cheer and whistle.

If I roll my eyes any harder, they'd be in the back of my skull.

I shouldn't be surprised. This is what Hudson does, after all.

Always the life of the party. He's always front and center, soaking up every ounce of attention like he was born for it.

I turn to distance myself from him and find Dane still holding the puppy as if it's radioactive.

"Can't I just write a check?" he asks Josie, who's now shaking her head at him with an exaggerated pout.

"He wants us to adopt him." Oh, she's laying it on thick, bottom lip puffed out and all.

"The team should adopt him," Hudson says, his voice way too close for my liking.

Of course, he's here. He's always here. Like a shadow I can't escape.

"I don't think that will work; he needs an owner," Josie says sweetly. "Like us."

"It's not going to be us," Dane responds flatly.

Josie pouts harder.

"Since Molly and I are besties now, we can adopt him," Hudson announces with that infuriatingly chipper tone of his.

I pivot so fast that I nearly fall over. "What?"

Has the man lost his mind? Does he ever think before he speaks?

"It's a great idea, right?" His voice is sugary sweet, and his grin is so wide I want to smack it off his face.

Damn bet. Seeing as everyone from the team is here—and they're all officially in on the bet—I plaster on my fakest smile, aware of the watchful eyes.

"Maybe. Seeing you with a dog would be a highlight of my life." I move closer, lowering my voice so only he can hear. "Watching you clean up shit, that is."

He throws his head back in a boisterous laugh. "I think it's a done deal."

Hudson leans in close, his voice a low murmur, sending heat prickling along my neck. "I know you want to kill me."

"Guess I owe Mason twenty bucks. I bet you'd break before the end of the event," Dane chimes in, smirking.

Hudson leans down so only I can hear. "Double or nothing, I make you snap before dinner?"

I open my mouth, ready to fire back, when I catch sight of the photographer stepping in front of us. The last thing I need is photographic evidence of me losing my temper.

"I need you guys closer," the photographer says.

Hudson obeys immediately. "Perfect. Almost there."

Before I can react, Hudson wraps me in his arms, smooshing the Maltese puppy between us.

The warmth of his chest seeps into me, and for half a second, I forget to be annoyed. The camera flashes, the puppy wiggles, and for just a moment, I feel something dangerously close to contentment.

I smile broadly, mustering the fakest one I have inside me. But for a moment, as the camera flashes and in the warmth of his arms, I almost smile for real.

Almost.

A small part of me wonders what it would be like to have a dog. The unconditional love, the companionship . . . but then reality sets in. There is a "no pets allowed" rule in my apartment. Not even a goldfish. If I want unconditional love, I'll have to get it elsewhere.

Or in my case . . .

Never.

chapter twenty-nine

Molly

D INNER BEFORE A HOCKEY GAME IS ALWAYS CHAOTIC.
Dinner with the Redville Saints before game one of the eastern conference semifinals is something else.

It's loud. It's ridiculous. And apparently, it's now my personal hell.

Like tonight, it's like I'm trapped in a bad 1990s sitcom, and I'm the punchline.

When I walk into the room, I make a beeline to sit as far from Hudson as possible. I don't even look at him, knowing his smirk is probably locked and loaded.

Of course, the whole team has different plans.

Those plans are to drive me crazy and, most likely, win the side bets they all made.

I stop dead in my tracks when Mason laughs loud enough to draw attention from the entire room. That's never a good sign.

From the way Mason is laughing like a damn hyena, he's up to something, and it doesn't take me long to figure out what when he makes a sweeping gesture toward the seat beside Hudson.

The only empty seat.

I glance around, hoping for some miraculous alternative, but nope—every other chair is taken. This is a setup. A cruel, calculated setup.

My feet are weighted to the floor and refuse to move.

"Right there, Molly," Mason announces this time. "That's your seat." It's said in a way that the whole team can hear.

My face burns, but I keep it together. I will not give them the satisfaction of seeing me sweat.

"Actually, I was going to—"

"Sorry, there are no other seats unless you aren't eating with us." Mason, ever the troublemaker, flashes a wicked grin. "Dane said it would be okay."

I shoot my brother a glare across the table, but Dane just shrugs, barely looking up from his phone. "It's part of the truce," he mutters, clearly more interested in whatever's on his screen than my impending misery.

Traitor.

Hudson is already in the seat, leaning back in his chair, one arm draped over the backrest like he owns the place.

His smirk is so wide he looks like he belongs in the movie *Smile*. "Don't worry, Hex. I won't bite," he whispers for only me to hear.

The double meaning in his voice makes my stomach do an unwanted flip. *Damn him.*

"Whatever," I mutter as I slide into the chair beside him.

The table is way too small, clearly designed for "intimate" dinners—which this is absolutely not. The second I sit, my knee bumps into Hudson's under the table. Of course, he doesn't move it.

I press my lips together.

Great. Just great.

He's way too close to me. I can feel his arm and his thigh.

beautiful collide

I try not to focus on it, but my traitorous brain has other plans. Images I've tried to bury resurface: his hands, his touch, the way his voice dips when he's being serious.

I close my eyes, willing the thoughts away. But the moment Hudson's fingers brush against my bare thigh, I nearly choke on my own breath. It's like he can read my mind, and he's weaponizing it against me.

I cough uncontrollably.

"You okay?" Hudson asks, his voice so innocent it could win awards.

"Yes," I groan back because I'm not. I'm annoyed, flustered, and horny. Not a good combination.

The entire table turns to watch, grinning like they're all in on some inside joke. Mason and Aiden exchange a look, and I know exactly what it means: they're betting on how long I'll last before snapping.

"No way you're winning," Aiden says, raising an eyebrow at Mason.

"Fifteen minutes, I'm telling you," Mason replies, leaning forward like this is the most important conversation of his life.

They're *all* betting on us. I figured Mason would, but everyone? *Jeez.*

This is low, even for them.

Hudson picks up his menu, smirk still firmly in place as he tilts it toward me. "What do you think, Molly? Want to share?"

I clench my jaw, forcing a tight smile. "How about I order something spicy, and you stay far away from it?"

Mason snorts. "I think it's going to happen. I can feel it," he tells Aiden in a half-whisper that might as well be a shout.

Hudson leans in, and I brace myself for whatever ridiculous thing he's about to say. "We can share a Twinkie."

I practically spit but manage to just choke instead.

"You okay?" His voice drips with faux concern.

"Yes."

"Was it something I said?"

My nails dig into my palm as I fight the urge to throttle him.

The server arrives just in time to take orders, and I use the menu as a shield to avoid Hudson's smug face.

As we wait for the food to arrive, I play on my phone, scrolling through videos and hoping no one bothers me.

I'm surprised when the food arrives only a few minutes later, but I welcome it because the faster we eat, the faster I can leave.

A few seconds later, the table is covered in steaming dishes that look like something out of a foodie's dream. My plate is loaded with spicy pasta and vibrant red sauce. Hudson's meal, of course, looks annoyingly perfect—a rare steak with roasted vegetables arranged like artwork.

I focus on eating, trying to lose myself in the familiar comfort of food. But even that's impossible with Hudson sitting so close. Every time his fork clinks against his plate or his knee brushes mine, it's like a jolt to my system.

Hudson's body is way too close to mine through the whole meal, and I'm hyperaware of all his moves.

Even the way he chews somehow gets under my skin.

He doesn't make noise. Or slurp. There's no jaw clicking. He actually has great manners. Can he do anything wrong?

Why does he have to look so good doing the most mundane things? It's infuriating.

The pasta is amazing, spicy enough yet not too spicy that it burns my lips.

For a brief few minutes, I manage to tune out the chaos around me. But it doesn't last.

After I'm done eating, it becomes harder. Hudson doesn't stop leaning closer, doesn't stop smirking like he knows exactly what he's doing to me.

When the server finally clears the last of the plates, I let out a sigh of relief. Dinner is almost done, and I made it.

"Tonight's been . . . educational," Mason says once the server is out of the room.

Hudson raises an eyebrow. "Educational?"

Mason grins. "Yep, tonight we learned that Molly has the patience of a saint. I'd never be able to sit next to you for this long. Not without killing you at least."

Aiden nods. "I had money on Molly lasting thirty minutes."

"I'm surprised you all didn't already know that I'm a saint," I fire back.

"Hardly," Hudson mutters, just loud enough for me to hear.

There's something in his tone, though—a softness buried under the teasing. It lingers, tugging at memories I'd rather leave buried.

A knowing tone.

One that tells of past secrets and future promises.

chapter thirty

Molly

D AMN, IT'S COLD IN HERE.

Cold enough to make me regret not grabbing my coat.

My arms are wrapped around myself as I hustle down the aisle, scanning the rows for Josie.

The game is already underway, and the tension in the arena is palpable.

The cheers, the whistles, the booming voice of the announcer—this place is nuts.

I spot Josie waving at me with her signature sunny smile, an empty seat beside her.

"Took you long enough." She rolls her eyes sarcastically as I slide into the chair.

"What happened to the sweet Josie I've come to love?" I shoot back, placing my hands on my legs and rubbing them, trying to stop the chill seeping through my leggings.

"Your brother happened. Now I'm the grump."

"Doubtful."

beautiful collide

She giggles, the sound warm and light. "But seriously. It's not like you to be late."

"Had a few last-minute errands."

That's a lie. The truth? I spent too long trying to talk myself into coming. Too long trying to shake the mental image of Hudson Wilde out of my head. The man has taken up way too much real estate in my brain lately, and it's starting to piss me off.

My upper body shivers.

Doesn't matter that I'm used to freezing arenas; today, it feels worse. Maybe because my defenses are already frayed. Perhaps because I spent half the afternoon convincing myself that Hudson isn't worth the mental energy I keep wasting on him.

The cause of my issues, the one and only Hudson.

Yep.

He's cocky, infuriating, and way too good-looking for his own good. And I hate that my mind keeps replaying the sound of his voice, smooth and deep, like it was meant for late-night secrets.

Stop.

Nope.

I hate Hudson.

I hate everything he stands for because he's a man-whore ass who is cocky.

Yet here I am, thinking about him instead of focusing on the game.

The blaring horn shakes me out of my thoughts. I pivot my body and focus back on the game.

The rink is a blur of motion, players darting back and forth, skates slicing the ice, the puck zipping like a black bullet between sticks. The buzz in the crowd is electric, pulling me into the moment whether I want it to or not.

Hockey is one of my only good memories as a kid—watching Dane play.

To this day, I can't help but smile whenever I'm in the crowd.

The action around me has me on the edge of my seat, eyes locked on the rink.

I watch as the puck skids across the ice.

My breath lodges in my throat as it bounces from one player to the next.

Hudson is out there, moving like a predator. He skates along the blue line, his body low and his stick ready as Aiden passes it to Wolfe, who passes it back to Aiden.

Aiden then pushes the puck forward, weaving around a defender before dishing it to Hudson, who takes off like a rocket. The defenders close in on him, but he doesn't falter. Instead, he keeps his head up, scanning the ice like he's five steps ahead of everyone else.

With a quick deke, Hudson threads the puck through a defender's legs and passes it back to Aiden, who's already waiting. Aiden doesn't even pause, sending it right back to Hudson as he cuts toward the goal.

It's like they're reading each other's minds, the kind of connection you don't see often. The crowd roars as Hudson shoulders past another defender, his speed and control making it look effortless.

Despite telling myself not to look, I can't help it. I'm instantly drawn to him.

My gaze finds him—number 17.

His jersey clings to his broad shoulders, his movements sharp and calculated. He's mesmerizing, and I hate that I notice.

I should be watching my brother, but instead, I'm riveted by Hudson Wilde.

He's fast, darting down the ice like he's untouchable. Every stride is smooth and powerful, like he was born for this.

I can't help but admire him.

His control and precision speak of years of practice.

But it's more than that. There's a fire in the way he plays, a hunger that sets him apart. He doesn't just skate; he dominates.

But it's more than just his speed. It's the way he sees the ice, the way he moves like he already knows how this play will end.

"He's good," Josie says from beside me.

"He is. Too bad he's an ass."

"You still hate him, I see. Despite playing nice?"

"It's not about hating him. I'm indifferent to him."

"Sure seems that way," she retorts, and I turn my gaze away from the rink to look at her.

She's smirking, her expression pure mischief. I want to argue, but I know it'll only make her smugger.

She's adorably cute in a sunshiny way. And perfect for my grumpy-as-all-sin brother.

I'm about to say something when the crowd around us erupts.

Needing to know what's happening, I turn back to face the game.

Hudson has the puck. He pushes off a defender and powers toward the net.

As if my body has a mind of its own, I lean forward, placing my hands on the edge of my seat.

"Yep, just as I thought," Josie says from beside me.

"Shh." I shoo her off. "This has nothing to do with Hudson. I just love hockey."

"Sure you do."

Hudson pulls his stick back, and for a brief second, the world stands still.

Everything in me clenches, caught between wanting to see him succeed and wanting him to miss just so I can wipe that smug grin off his face later.

My heart pounds frantically in my chest. Waiting. Watching. Wishing.

The puck rockets off his stick.

Time slows as it sails through the air, cutting toward the top corner of the net.

Go in.

In a flash of black, the puck darts in the air, zooming past the goalie's glove.

Before I realize what's happening, I'm on my feet, cheering with the crowd.

I forget everything—our bet, his smirk, the way he drives me insane. All I see is his skill, his brilliance. He might be a bastard, but he's beautiful on the ice.

chapter thirty-one

Hudson

Mom: Guess what, birthday boy! 🎉 🎂

Anna: Oh no. What now?

Dad: We're coming to visit you for your birthday!

Mom: Flights are booked, bags are almost packed.

Anna: "Almost packed"?? Mom, we're staying for, like, ten seconds.

Mom: It's called being prepared, Anna. Not that your brother will read this.

Dad: He's probably asleep. Needs his beauty rest.

Anna: Extra beauty sleep. Lord knows he needs it.

Mom: Be nice, Anna.

Anna: I am being nice. I didn't even mention his hair.

Mom: Leave his hair alone.

Anna: I can't. It looks like a bird rolled around in it.

Dad: That's a sign of character.

Anna: Sure, Dad. Character.

Mom: Has anyone heard from Hudson? He's been suspiciously quiet.

Anna: He's either napping or pretending not to see this so he can act surprised later.

Dad: Or he's eating. That boy's appetite is a sport of its own.

Mom: True. Hockey burns a lot of calories.

Anna: So does sleeping.

Mom: Hudson, are you alive?

Anna: Are you being held against your will?

Anna: Do you guys think we'll get a ransom note?

chapter thirty-two

Hudson

A FEW DAYS LATER, AND WITH TWO MORE WINS UNDER MY belt, I wake to a familiar smell.

It smells like my childhood home.

Which is weird since I'm not there. I'm in Redville in my bed.

But still, that doesn't stop the fragrant smell of sweet, buttery, delicious food from hitting me in the gut.

Wait, maybe I'm still asleep.

I keep my eyes shut.

Refusing to allow myself to wake from this phenomenal dream.

I wonder if the biscuits will taste as good as they do in real life. Despite not wanting to, my eyes pop open. Curiosity killed the cat, after all.

Wait.

That smell is real.

The sounds coming from my kitchen are most likely real too.

The clinking of pots and slamming of drawers don't usually end up in a dream. A nightmare, maybe.

Early morning sunlight streams in through the drapes, and I know it's time to get up and see what's going on.

Once dressed, I head downstairs.

The full smell hits me before I even make it down the stairs. I take another step and hear laughter—my mom's laughter.

I jog down the last few steps. Standing in my kitchen are my parents and younger sister, Anna. My mom is flipping pancakes, Dad fiddles with the coffee maker like he's never made himself coffee, probably never has, and Anna—who's a troublemaker like me—is eating whipped cream straight out of the can.

"My darling birthday boy," my mom squeals when she sees me.

"What are you guys doing here?"

"I thought that part was obvious. We're making you a birthday breakfast."

"It looks like only you are." I gesture to my sister and dad. "Anna looks like she's about to get high on whippets, and Dad, well, Dad already looks high."

"Um. Okay. I guess happy birthday," Anna says, barely acknowledging me.

My mom places the spatula down and comes up and hugs me.

"Wow, you're all really here."

"We are," my dad says.

"Why?"

"We didn't want you to spend your birthday alone."

Anna nods enthusiastically, still holding the whipped cream can. "Yep."

I blink and stare at the counter. This must be a dream. I missed my family, and here they are. On top of that, my gaze fixes on the towering stack of pancakes and crispy bacon sitting in the middle of the table. My family came here and made me breakfast.

"You didn't have to do this," I whisper.

My mom waves me off. "Of course, we did. It's tradition."

But it hasn't been. Not for a while. *Not since I left home.*

beautiful collide

I rub the back of my neck, glancing around the room. The sight of my family standing in my kitchen makes my chest tighten.

This is what I miss.

I clear my throat and try to lighten the moment. "How did you get here? I don't want you spending money to see me."

My dad gives me a pointed look. "Hudson, we're not discussing that."

"Seriously," I press, walking over to lean against the island counter. "Let me reimburse you. I'll cover the tickets, the hotel, whatever. Just say the word."

My mom shoots me a look over her shoulder that says *stop*, all while continuing to flip another pancake. "We've been over this. We don't need your money."

"Yeah," Anna chimes in, licking whipped cream off her finger. "We're good. Chill."

I cross my arms over my chest. "You don't have to do this, you know. I want to help."

My mom turns around, her expression soft but firm. "We know you do. And we appreciate it. But I promise we're good."

I open my mouth to argue but stop.

There's no point, and when my mom drops a plate of pancakes in front of me, the smell alone is enough to shut me up.

I take a bite, and like always, it's delicious. After I swallow, I put the fork down.

"Will you guys come to the game? I'll get you tickets."

"Yes, we'd love that," my dad says.

Thank fuck, because I didn't want to fight with them today. They don't come here often. Money is tight, and they always refuse my help. While they don't have much, they have always given me so much more. I just wish they would let me repay them for that. Small steps. I'll take the win on the hockey tickets. Maybe next time, I can give more.

chapter thirty-three

Molly

TONIGHT IS A BIG NIGHT.

The boys need to win this game to take a commanding lead in this series.

I'm excited and nervous, and it's not just about the game. Seeing Hudson always makes my tummy feel weird.

I purposely arrived late so I wouldn't bump into him before they got on the ice. With quick steps, I head to my seat. I wonder if Josie and Cassidy will be here. Sometimes they sit with the hockey wives, but not often. Granted, none of them are married yet, but they practically are.

I think they sit by me because they feel bad and don't want to leave me alone.

Fine by me.

Tonight, the seats reserved for us are extra-filled.

There are some faces I've never seen before standing about, trying to figure out where to sit.

"Excuse me, dear," the older man says.

beautiful collide

He's standing next to an older woman and a younger girl, probably in her late teens. The parents seem overwhelmed. The pretty young blonde is too busy taking selfies on her phone to notice.

"Yes?" I move closer to them. The woman is petite and has a warm, welcoming smile. She holds her purse close to her chest like she's afraid someone will steal it.

"I was wondering if you can tell me where our seats are?" the woman says. "We're not exactly sure where we're supposed to sit."

"Of course," I answer. "Let me see your tickets."

The young girl hands me her phone, where the tickets are. It makes sense; her parents give off boomer vibes. I look at her phone and see the seat number.

I gesture to the seat right behind me, a row back. "You're right there."

"Oh, thank you so much," the man says, his voice tinged with relief. "We've never been to a game before."

I smile and wait for them to sit before turning around to talk to them.

"Is there anything else you need? I'll be happy to help."

"I think we're good," the woman answers.

"Speak for yourself. I want food." The young girl cuts in. "I just can't leave these two." She rolls her eyes. "They're boomers," she whispers to me.

I can't help but laugh. "I can grab it for you," I offer without thinking.

"We couldn't ask you to do that," the woman protests.

"Sure, we can, Mom. She offered." The teen turns to me. "Think you can get me a hot dog? Oh, maybe a pretzel . . . shit, how do I pick?"

"Anna, we don't talk like that."

"Whatever, Mom. You let Hudson talk like that."

Hudson?

She couldn't mean my Hudson.

He's not your Hudson. He's not your anything.

The woman I now know as Hudson's mom turns toward me. "We can't ask you to get us food."

"You're not asking," I say with a smile. "I'm offering. It's no trouble."

She smiles broadly, and I head out to grab the Wildes some snacks.

A few minutes later, I return with two hot dogs, a bag of popcorn, and sodas.

"You're so sweet," Hudson's mom says. "Thank you, dear."

"It's nothing." I take my seat. "Enjoy the game."

The game starts, and it's as if Hudson is playing even better than usual. His parents cheer, and I can't help but cheer for him too.

"He's so talented, isn't he?" His dad beams as he points at Hudson. "Always has been since he was a kid."

"He's . . . an incredible player. Really gifted." Despite my issues with him, he is one of the best players on the team.

My heart aches in my chest. The love they feel.

I wish I had this. Sure, I have Dane, but this is different. My mom did love me, but every year that passes, I forget that love. It's so clear how much they love Hudson, flaws and all. My eyes fill with tears.

The end of the game comes with a Saints victory. Instead of leaving right away, I stay behind, not wanting his family to get lost. When the crowd thins out, they make no move to leave, still buzzing from the win.

"Want me to take you to Hudson?"

"Oh, no, that's okay. He's meeting us at dinner. Do you know Hudson?"

"I do. I actually work for the team, well, not the team. My brother, Dane, is a Saint."

"You're Molly?" his mom asks.

I smile. "I am."

"Hudson has spoken of you. It's lovely to meet you. I'm Mary."

"It's nice to meet you."

beautiful collide

What has Hudson said about me? Something tells me nothing bad since she's still being nice to me.

"Thank you so much for your help tonight. You didn't have to, but we're so grateful."

I smile, tucking my hands into the pockets of my coat. "It was my pleasure. Really."

"I'm Hudson's dad, David. We're heading to dinner to celebrate his birthday. Would you like to join us? We'd love to have you."

His birthday?

How did I not know it was his birthday?

Do any of the players know?

I hesitate for a second. My heart tugs in two directions. Spending more time with Hudson's parents, who are so sweet and not interfering. Or spending time with Hudson. But the part of me that wants to be part of this moment a little longer wins out.

"I'd love to."

chapter thirty-four

Hudson

DINNER WITH MY PARENTS IS A CHERRY ON TOP FOR TONIGHT'S killer win. I open the door to the restaurant where I'm meeting them. It's a cozy Italian restaurant close to my house. The type of place that makes you feel at home, even when you're not.

We haven't had dinner together in ages. This is long overdue.

When I step inside, the scent of roasted garlic and fresh bread greets me. I scan the room for my family.

The place is packed and warm.

Almost too warm.

Soft candlelight bounces off the red-checkered tablecloths, and the faint hum of conversation blends with Sinatra playing in the background.

I don't notice my family at first through the crowd, but then they come into focus.

Mom and Dad are looking at a menu, and Anna is scrolling on her phone. Surprise, surprise. At least she's consistent. Anna and her phone are basically a package deal at this point.

I can't help the stupid grin that eclipses my face.

Then I see *her*.

My lips thin.

Why is *she* here?

Molly. My little Hex.

The woman who has haunted my thoughts for years sits at the table, chatting animatedly with my mom. She laughs softly at something my dad says. Her entire demeanor is relaxed, so unlike when she's with me.

I love her for this.

I hate her for this.

And, deep down, I know I'm screwed because she looks like she belongs here with them. With the people I care about most.

It's as if we have a thread tethering us because Molly looks up and catches my eye. Our gazes tangle. It's like a dance—almost. She doesn't look away, and I don't either. The space between us crackles with something unspoken, something I can't name but feel all the same.

Her green eyes are cool and unreadable.

A million questions blur in my head.

What is she thinking?

Does she know the chaos she stirs just by being here?

Is she trying to figure me out the way I'm always trying to figure her out?

Is she as frustrated by this invisible thread between us as I am?

I force myself to walk, crossing the room to go sit with my family. Each step closer is a step closer to her orbit, where I'm sure I'll get burned. Why the fuck can I not resist the pull?

When I arrive, I lean down and kiss my mom on the cheek.

"Hey, guys." I pull back and look toward Molly. "Molly?"

"Oh, Molly helped us so much at the game," my mom gushes, smiling up at me. "She showed us to our seats, got us food, and even helped us find the car. Isn't that sweet?"

"Very." I slowly slide into the empty seat across from Molly, staring at her as I do.

Did she know who they were when she did?

It's as clear as day that my mom adores her. At this rate, she'll be in the family Christmas photo by next week.

What the hell did I miss during this game?

I look back at Molly, still wondering how this all happened. It's as surprising as me winning an award for punctuality.

She meets my stare, never flinching, and smiles brightly. "Your parents are amazing. I see where you get it."

I hesitate, half expecting her to follow it up with a dig. Instead, she just keeps smiling at me like she means it. Weird.

Finally, I bite. "Get what?"

Molly blinks innocently at me. "Your personality and kindness."

Oh-kay.

Not what I expected.

Am I hallucinating? Did someone replace Molly with her nicer, less terrifying twin?

My mom lets out a little sigh of what can only be described as pure happiness. It's over. I'm fucked. Mom might adopt Molly on the spot. Then I'll hit the news headlines with a new scandal. The hockey player who screwed his sister.

Molly reaches across the table and squeezes Mom's hand. Mom hasn't paid a lick of attention to either Dad or Anna. She must've had a hard time choosing her seat—sit next to Molly and bask in her "greatness" up close or sit across from Molly and see her in all her glory.

Molly merely tilts her head, all innocence.

What is this girl up to?

I narrow my eyes slightly, doubt settling.

"Um. Are we talking about Hudson?" Anna chimes in.

Great, now I have *both* of them ganging up on me. It's two against one, and I'm a goalie without pads. Fantastic.

"Yup." Molly casts a glance my way. "Hudson."

beautiful collide

I don't understand what's happening. Anna gave Molly a way to attack me, but she didn't. No one here knows about the bet. It would be the perfect moment for her to take me down without her brother or anyone on the team ever knowing.

I'm waiting for the punchline, but it's not coming. This is uncharted territory.

It's unsettling. Like catching Coach Robert smile.

Lost in my thoughts, I only pick up bits and pieces of the conversation taking place. From what I *do* manage to hear, Molly is basically making me sound like the next Gretzky. I feel like a deer staring down a hunter. Any second now, she'll pull the trigger.

My dad beams at her words. "We're so proud of him. He's worked so hard to get here."

"Absolutely," Molly agrees, smiling warmly.

She's never nice to me. Never. Is this reverse psychology? Am I supposed to insult her back?

It feels like I'm in a fever dream. Like I've wandered into an alternate reality where Molly Sinclair is my biggest fan. Or maybe I'm on a hidden camera show where everyone's in on the joke except me.

The whole meal is a blur. She spends appetizers raving about my playing style, the main course ranting about how the Saints need to bump up my salary ASAP, and dessert bellowing about the media's antics.

If this is Molly's way of catching me off guard, it's working.

I'm officially off-balance.

It can't possibly be real, but when my parents get up to leave, I hang back, needing to know why. Why she's doing this. Why the Molly I know—the one who could slice me in two with her words—has suddenly turned into my biggest cheerleader.

As soon as my family is out of earshot, I block her path to the exit, my voice low. "All right, Hex. What's your game here?"

Molly tilts her head, her smile softening into something I can't quite read. "Maybe I just wanted to be nice for a change."

I snort. "You? Nice? Forgive me if I'm not buying it."

Her smile doesn't falter, but her eyes narrow just a fraction. "Maybe you should try it sometime. Being nice might actually suit you."

And there it is.

A spark of the Molly I know. The Molly who doesn't just push my buttons but installs new ones just to press them.

I sit back, crossing my arms. "If this is you being nice, I think I liked you better when you were mean."

I don't mean it, though. I'm just . . . uncomfortable. Like I'm stuck in limbo, unsure how to process the past ninety minutes. I feel like I've missed some pivotal moment when Molly decided she doesn't actually hate me.

And if I'm really being honest, I want to know how—so I can do it again. Over and over.

You are so fucked, Wilde.

"Duly noted," Molly says, securing her bag over her shoulder. "Next time, I'll let your mom know all about how you chewed out that poor referee last week."

"Wait—what?" I start, but she's already halfway out the door, leaving me sitting there, stunned and—dammit—grinning like an idiot.

Because, for all her jabs, I can't help but like that she keeps me guessing.

Molly takes the long way, weaving through crowds because she's too short to notice the exit on the other end. I take that door and round to the front, where I wait for her to make her way outside the place, my back against the brick wall.

When she finally bursts through the door, she spots me, and a scowl immediately forms on her lips.

I move to stand in front of her. "Seriously, Hex. What was that?"

Molly arches an eyebrow. "What was what?"

beautiful collide

The woman doesn't even realize what she's done to me. That I'm practically glitching inside, trying to figure out her endgame.

Maybe this is her latest tactic—kill me with kindness and watch me squirm.

"You. Being nice. Praising me like I'm some kind of saint." I throw my hands up, frustrated. "What's your angle?"

Molly takes a deep breath. She opens her mouth, closes it, and then shakes her head, starting up again. "You wouldn't understand."

I don't budge. "Try me."

She looks down. "I always wanted parents like yours. I just wanted to be part of a family for a minute."

It feels like a slap in the face. I'm stunned. Taken completely off guard. For once, I can't think of a single thing to say. She's knocked the wind out of me.

"They're so proud of you." Her gaze drifts down to her hands. To where's she's twisting her fingers together. "So supportive."

I stare at her, her soft words doing something unfamiliar to me. "They're my parents," I say like it's the most obvious thing in the world. "That's their job."

Her laugh is soft and bitter. "Not everyone's parents got that memo."

The words are quiet, but they pack a punch.

I fumble for something to say, anything to fill the silence stretching between us. "Molly, I—"

"Don't." She finally lifts her gaze to mine. Her eyes are hard, guarded. "Don't say something you think I want to hear. I'm not looking for pity."

"It's not pity," I say quickly. Too quickly.

I don't know much about how she or Dane grew up, but it's obvious now that something happened. Sure, I knew she didn't have parents, and her brother raised her, but something about her words suggests there's more to it.

She raises an eyebrow, her mouth pulling into a humorless smile. "Of course it isn't."

The air between us feels heavy. Suffocating. My chest tightens at her words, the casual cruelty she's wielding against herself.

"You don't have to talk about it," I say softly, stepping closer.

"No, I don't," she agrees, her voice sharper now. "But maybe I wanted to, just this once, sit at a table with people who don't look at me like I'm broken. Who don't expect me to be the strong one all the damn time."

I blink, the vulnerability in her words cutting deeper than any insult she's ever thrown my way. "Molly . . ."

"Forget it." She shakes her head. "I shouldn't have said anything."

She moves to step around me, but I reach out, my hand lightly brushing her arm.

"Hey." My voice is firm but gentle. "You don't have to forget it. You don't have to do any of this alone."

Just talk to me, I want to scream. *Tell me.*

It's a stupid thought. One I have no business thinking. We don't even like each other. Not really . . . right?

Her eyes flick to my hand and back to my face.

Something soft crosses her expression, but then it's gone, replaced by the familiar steel I know so well. "I've been doing it alone for years. I'm fine."

"Yeah, you are. But that doesn't mean you have to be."

She pulls away, taking a step back and crossing her arms over her chest. "Why do you even care, Hudson?"

The question catches me off guard. I don't have an answer.

Finally, I say, "Because you're not as unbreakable as you think you are."

Her jaw tightens, and I think she's going to throw another verbal dagger at me. Instead, she just shakes her head, muttering something under her breath before walking away.

I let her go, my hands clenching at my sides as I watch her retreating form.

She stops just shy of the parking lot, twisting to face me. "Hudson?"

"Yeah?"

"It's beautiful, Hudson. How much your parents love you. How proud they are of you." Molly closes her eyes, sucking in a breath. "I could see it on their faces every time they talked about you."

Stop talking.

Keep talking.

But the more she talks, the more the guilt needles into me. My parents deserve so much more than they accept. And *Molly*. She deserves all the love I've ever felt, too.

"Your parents are everything I ever wished for growing up." Molly glances down. She looks up at me then, her expression unreadable. "I couldn't take that away from you."

There are people around us close enough to hear and a big enough gap that we have to raise our voices to be heard. Anyone could eavesdrop. But neither of us cares. We're too caught up in each other. This moment when, somehow, we became the only people who understand each other.

I close my eyes, unsure what to say, and settle for a simple, "They're the best."

It's the truth.

The beautiful, tragic truth.

Silence stretches between us, but it isn't uncomfortable. It's . . . different. Like we're standing on the precipice of something big. Something neither of us fully understands but doesn't want to walk away from.

"I mean it. I've always wanted parents like yours." A wistful smile graces her lips. "I just wanted to be part of a family for a minute."

Her words hang in the air, raw and unguarded.

She's breaking my fucking heart.

A sudden laugh bubbles out of her, and she shakes her head.

"I have no idea how this got so serious. Thank you for the dinner, Hudson. I enjoyed it."

"Thanks for tonight." I clear my throat. "It means a lot."

For all the tension in that conversation, I know one thing for certain: Molly Sinclair is a storm, and I'm already caught in her path.

And that truce?

It feels real.

chapter thirty-five

Hudson

Mason: Guys. I figured out our retirement plan.

Aiden: I don't wanna know.

Dane: Is it illegal?

Mason: I'm serious. It's a game. I call it: Where's Hudson?

Mason: It's like Where's Waldo, except instead of tracking down a hipster with no fashion sense, we're tracking down a train wreck with no fashion sense. I'm trademarking it as we speak.

Aiden: For real. Dude is Houdini. Where did he even go after the game last night?

Dane: Probably busy "reflecting on his life choices." (Source: The Redville Post this morning. Hudson, you should probably have a libel lawyer on retainer at this point.)

Mason: Oh, he was reflecting all right. You should've seen him at the bar after I dragged his sorry ass there.

Dane: Do tell. 👀

Aiden: Story time. 🍿

Mason: The man was flustered. Red as a tomato. Muttering into his beer like the world personally wronged him.

Dane: Are we talking about the same guy?

Mason: Four drinks in, and he kept moaning, "Why is the world so cruel?" Like some tragic Shakespearean hero.

Dane: 😂 Was he crying into his drink?

Mason: He looked like he wanted to. Almost spilled tequila on my shoes when he dramatically sighed.

Hudson: Are you all done?

Dane: Nope. Mason, any more details?

Mason: Oh, just that at one point, he mumbled something about "hexes" and "torture."

Aiden: Hexes? As in witchcraft?

Dane: Should we be concerned? I'll ask the cleaning crew to hide their broomsticks.

Hudson: I hate all of you.

Mason: Bro, the world might be cruel, but we will always be crueler. <3

Hudson: You're all dead to me.

Mason: 😘 Love you, too, big guy.

Hudson: [Attachment: Middle finger selfie]

Dane: Frame it. Hang it in the locker room.

Aiden: New team logo.

Mason: 😂 Cry harder, Shakespeare.

chapter thirty-six

Hudson

I'M ALONE.

Mom, Dad, and Anna took off this morning while I slept in, a little hungover. Mason dragged me to get drinks last night after Molly and I parted, and I regret it now.

My head pounds like someone brought a drumline into the arena. The headache reverberates in my skull.

The overhead lights in the practice arena are way too bright, like they're punishing me for my poor life choices.

I can feel every inch of yesterday's beers sloshing around as I skate, my legs heavier than usual. Even the sound of skates slicing the ice feels sharper today.

Mason, of course, skates circles around me like he didn't put back just as much tequila.

Asshole.

I usually like time at home in Redville. Especially since my family came to visit. But not today. Not after last night.

After Molly.

The conversation keeps replaying in my head like a highlight reel.

Her voice, so calm but raw, when she admitted her past. How hard it was to grow up without a family.

And then, the way she looked at me—not with her usual sharpness, but with something softer, something that made me feel like she was showing me a piece of herself she doesn't share with anyone.

It rattled me more than I care to admit.

I didn't know what to say then, and I still don't now.

I like being on the road when I feel this way. It helps.

I should pay attention to everyone on the ice around me, but I can't. Instead, I'm paying attention to her. Molly.

A part of me wants to hold on to my animosity toward her, but a bigger part knows I got rid of it years ago.

Now, it's just a habit.

When Coach blows his whistle, I'm off the ice faster than ever before.

"What's the rush, Wilde?" Mason calls out, skating past me with a smirk. "Hot date with your mom?"

I forgot to tell him my parents left this morning. Fucker.

"Probably late for his nap," Aiden chimes in.

Dane snorts from across the rink. "Or maybe he's just trying to keep up his streak of Coach's most hated player. You're not supposed to make it so obvious you want to leave, doofus."

"Shut up," I call over my shoulder, ignoring the chorus of laughter that follows me. "At least I'm not last, Mason."

"Touché," Mason fires back. "Don't pull anything while sprinting off the ice, Grandpa."

I ignore the rest of their hollers and catcalls.

I want to find Molly.

I *need* to.

I change quickly, throwing my gear on the floor for the

beautiful collide

equipment manager to figure out. Once I'm back in my street clothes, I head out in search of her.

I move through the maze of the practice arena, checking every spot I can think of.

Weight room? Empty.

Seating area? Dead quiet.

I make my way through the halls that wind behind the rink, the sound of my footsteps bouncing off the concrete walls.

Each corner I turn, I expect to see her, but she's nowhere to be found.

It's ridiculous how much my chest tightens with every empty hallway.

The last time I saw her, she looked . . . off. Not herself.

And something about that pulls at me.

I stop in my tracks when I find her, silent as I take in the sight of her. She's standing near the far wall, one hand braced against it like she's holding herself steady.

Her hair, usually tucked neatly out of her face, falls loose around her shoulders.

The sleeves of her Saints hoodie are rolled up like she's trying to fight off a wave of nerves.

There's tension in her frame—her shoulders tight, her breathing just a little too quick.

Yet, even now, something about her stops me cold. Her sharp edges and soft curves all tangled into one.

We're on the far side of the arena, farthest from the locker room. Right in front of a closet . . . *like the one we first met in*.

Molly looks like she's caught somewhere between here and somewhere else entirely.

Her face is pale, her usual confidence nowhere to be seen. She's fidgeting, her fingers twisting together in a way that makes her look . . . small. Vulnerable.

Her gaze darts around.

There's almost panic in her eyes.

"Hey," I say softly, stepping closer to where she is. "You okay?"

I move carefully, like I'm approaching a skittish animal—slow and steady, trying not to make any sudden movements.

Molly's breath hitches, and I realize I scared her. Something I seem to do a lot of, though not on purpose.

And every single time, it leaves this hollow, twisting feeling in my gut. Like I'm the reason she's looking over her shoulder, and I hate it.

I hate that I'm a part of the fear she's carrying.

I wonder what's upset her, and then I notice she's staring at the closet door. Is it the memory of the panic attacks? I have no business wondering, but I do.

I don't know why I'm always curious when it comes to Molly Sinclair, but I am.

Fucking sue me.

Of course, I remember all the times I've seen her like this, but I figured it got better. Obviously, it hasn't. In fact, it feels worse. Bigger.

I've spent so many years avoiding her, trying my damnedest not to pay attention, but maybe the panic attacks never went away.

Or did something trigger her today?

"I can't," she whispers to herself, her voice trembling.

"You can't what?"

She tips her chin to the door. "Go in there."

"I'm here." I take another step forward. "I'll make sure you're okay."

She pivots her upper body to look at me. Her head shakes. Tears begin to well in her eyes. I want to reach out and hold her.

But I don't want to push.

Who knows if touching her will set her off or calm her?

I need to tread carefully.

"Why are you being so nice to me?" Her voice is a mix of confusion and vulnerability. "After everything that's happened?"

Neither of us brings up yesterday. When shit got too real.

It's like some unspoken agreement.

Maybe we'll *never* bring it up, but it doesn't change the fact that it happened. It happened, and we can't undo it, and I will never look at Molly Sinclair the same.

And hopefully, she's done looking at me the same way she has the past few years.

"Believe it or not," I reply, my voice steady, "despite all the rumors, I'm actually a nice guy."

She huffs out a breath, not quite a laugh, but close enough. "Nice guys don't torment their teammate's sister until a bet makes them stop."

I wince, shoving my hands into my pockets. "Touché. But for the record, you've tormented me right back, so let's call it even."

Molly doesn't respond right away. Her eyes drift back to the closet door, and I can see the way she's bracing herself—like just looking at it takes more strength than she wants to admit.

"What happened, Molly?" I ask softly. "Why can't you go in there?"

Her fingers twitch where they hang at her sides like she's fighting the urge to fidget.

She doesn't look at me when she speaks. "It's stupid."

"It's not stupid," I say immediately, my voice firm but gentle. "If it was stupid, you wouldn't look like you're about to bolt."

She swallows, her throat working hard.

For a second, I think she's going to shut down completely.

But then she speaks.

"When I was a kid . . ." She stops, shaking her head as if trying to get rid of the words before they're out. "No. Never mind."

I take another step closer. Carefully. Slowly.

"When you were a kid . . . what?"

Her gaze flickers to me, her walls starting to crack just a little. Then she shakes her head again, and the moment is over. "Never mind."

My jaw tightens, the words hitting me harder than I expect.

"You can tell me. I won't judge. I won't even say anything else if you don't want me to."

Her eyes snap to mine, sharp and guarded again. "Don't bother trying to pry. Others have tried and failed."

"Fine. You don't have to tell me," I reply, holding her gaze. "I'm saying . . . I get it."

She blinks, caught off guard. "What do you mean, you get it? I haven't even told you what *it* is."

"I mean, I get why you can't go in there. Why it feels like you're drowning just looking at it. You're not crazy, and you're not weak for feeling like this."

She stares at me for a beat, like she's trying to decide whether she believes me. Then her voice drops to almost a whisper. "I hate it."

"Hate what?"

"This," she says, gesturing vaguely to the door. "How one stupid door can still make me feel like I'm thirteen years old all over again. How I can't . . . I can't get over it. Not really."

Thirteen?

Fucking. Thirteen.

I don't know what she means by this, but I'm horrified for her. Furious that someone hurt her. And angry with Dane for letting it happen.

You don't know that, I tell myself, forcing a breath out. *Don't make stupid assumptions.*

"You don't have to get over it," I tell Molly softly. "Sometimes things stick with you, no matter how strong you are."

Her eyes narrow, like she doesn't believe me. "Easy for you to say. You're not afraid of anything."

"That's not true."

She scoffs. "Oh, please. You fight guys twice your size for a living."

"Yeah," I admit. "But that's different. On the ice, I'm in control. I know what to expect. But fear? Real fear? It's not something you just 'get over.' It's something you learn to face one small step at a time."

She's quiet, processing my words.

"Look," I continue, trying to keep my tone light but honest, "you don't have to go in there right now. Or ever, if you don't want to. But if you do . . . I'll be here. I'll stand right next to you. I won't let anything happen to you."

Molly's gaze softens, and for the first time, I see something in her expression that looks like trust. "Why do you care?"

The question catches me off guard, but I answer honestly. "Because I do."

I don't know if she'll believe me.

Especially with our background.

But I mean it.

We can fight, we can argue, we can hate each other to the core, but I'll still care. You can't hate someone without caring. Not that I ever really hated her. Even when she lied about the closet thing to Coach.

She must've had a reason.

Molly looks down again, biting her lip like she's trying to keep her emotions in check. "You're annoying, you know that?"

I grin faintly. "Yeah, I've been told." I pause a beat. "By you. Repeatedly."

A tiny laugh shakes her shoulders.

She returns my smile, tucking a strand of hair behind her ear.

A long silence stretches between us, but it's not heavy this time. It's . . . different.

Finally, she lets out a shaky breath. "Just . . . give me a minute, okay?"

"Take all the time you need."

I step back a little, giving her space but not leaving. Not yet.

And as I watch her standing there staring at the closet door like it's a mountain she has to climb, I realize something I'm not ready to admit out loud.

Molly Sinclair is stronger than she thinks.

And I'll stand here as long as it takes for her to see it, too.

Her gaze softens, but the fear is still there, clouding her expression as she stares at the closet door again.

"I'm scared," she finally admits. "I'm scared of small, enclosed spaces. I'm scared of losing control."

The emotion in her voice hits me in the stomach like a gut punch. She's not throwing up walls or masking it with sarcasm.

It's just her—bare, honest, and vulnerable in a way that I don't think anyone else gets to see.

"Then don't go in," I say quietly.

"I have to."

Her words are resolute, but her voice trembles just slightly.

I move closer to her until we both stand in front of the large door. The air feels charged, like the space between us is holding its breath.

"What do you need from here?" I ask, my voice as gentle as I can make it.

"Dane needed something."

I glance at the door, then back at her. "Why don't you tell me what he needs, and I'll grab it for you?"

She looks at me, her green eyes sharp but soft around the edges, like she can't quite figure me out. "While I appreciate that, I have to get over this."

It's not just stubbornness in her tone. It's determination.

And God, it guts me.

She's standing in front of something that clearly terrifies her, and still, she's ready to face it. That takes more courage than most people ever find.

"Has it been bad this whole time?" I ask. Needing to know if I was too self-absorbed to notice. If I missed something so *big*.

"No."

Her answer is short, but the silence that follows says more

than she does. I don't move, waiting—giving her the space to say more if she wants to.

Finally, she exhales a shaky breath, her hands clenching at her sides.

"It comes and goes. I've been better for a while, but lately . . ." Her gaze flicks to the door, then back to the floor. "Lately, it's been creeping back. Little by little."

I nod, even though she's not looking at me. "You're here now. That's what matters."

Her lips twitch, almost like she wants to smile, but it doesn't quite land. "You make it sound so simple."

"It can be," I say quietly. "You don't have to conquer everything at once. You can start small. Just one step at a time."

She glances at me then, and for a second, the vulnerability in her eyes sucks the breath out of me. "And what if I can't?"

"You can," I say without hesitation. "I know you can."

She looks away again, and I watch as her shoulders rise and fall with another shaky breath. "Why are you so sure?"

Because you're the strongest person I've ever met.

Because I've watched you handle things no one else could.

Because even when you're scared, you don't stop moving forward.

But I don't say any of that.

Instead, I shrug lightly, trying to keep my tone easy. "Because I'm always right."

That earns me a faint laugh—a real one this time. The weight in the air lifts just a little.

"You're insufferable," she mutters, but there's no heat behind it.

I grin. "You'd miss me if I wasn't."

Her lips press together, but I see the way her shoulders relax, even just slightly. She glances back at the door, her expression tightening again, but this time, something is different about it—like she's steeling herself, bracing for the fight.

"Ready when you are," I say softly.

She doesn't answer right away, but she nods, just barely. And as she moves closer to that door, I stay beside her, ready to catch her if she falls.

I watch as she takes a tiny, almost imperceptible step forward. Then she steps back, groaning at herself.

I offer her my hand. "Focus on me. You don't have to go in there."

"I do."

"Then I'll go in there with you."

She hesitates, and my eyes search hers.

All while never breaking our gaze, she takes my offered hand. Her soft fingers brush against mine.

"One step at a time," I remind her, guiding her toward the door as I open it.

I can feel her shaking, the tension radiating off her. Each step is a battle, but like the tough girl Molly is, she does it.

Together, inside the utility room, I switch the light on, making sure to leave the door wide open.

"I swear, it wasn't always this bad." Her voice is quiet, almost apologetic.

"You don't have to talk about it, Molly," I reply, glancing at her.

"But I feel like I owe you something." Her gaze drops to the floor, her fingers fidgeting with the hem of her sleeve.

"You don't owe me anything."

She exhales sharply, brushing her hair back with a trembling hand. "I feel like I'm losing control. And I hate it. Things that used to scare me and didn't for a while are back. Irrational fears."

"Such as?"

"Closed spaces."

"That I figured."

"Heights. Sometimes."

"Like flying?" I ask, tilting my head slightly.

"No, that was a fear of losing control." She shakes her head, her lips pressing into a thin line. "I mean like heights, when I have no control."

"Got it."

I don't really understand, but I don't want her to stop talking, so I don't chance it by asking her to explain.

"And so much more I don't even know where to begin." Her voice cracks slightly, and she turns away from me.

"I understand," I say softly.

I don't. Not really.

But if she's talking, I'll listen.

"I lied when I said it's creeping back little by little. It's *storming* in, and I can't stop it," she admits, her tone heavy with frustration.

"Maybe you should—"

"No. I'm fine. I'll get through it. I did before." Her voice is final, resolute, the kind of tone that closes a door.

I nod, not wanting to set her off again. Whatever is triggering these bouts of panic, I don't want to make it worse.

Molly steps away from me, rummaging through a bin on the shelf. Her movements are quick and almost frantic. She shakes her head, clearly not finding what she's looking for.

Then she stops, her back stiffening as she looks up.

Right then and there, I know that what she needs is too high for her.

Moving to where she stands, I reach out, grabbing the box just out of reach, high enough that she would have needed a ladder if I weren't with her.

"Let me."

Her mouth opens as if to object, but then it shuts.

Once I bring down the box to her level, she rummages through it and grabs two bottles of skate polish, then nods at me when she's done.

I place it back on the top shelf and turn to face her.

Her chin is tilted down, and I reach out and place my hand under her chin, making her meet my stare.

"Thank you," she whispers.

My fingers trail across her jaw.

I want to kiss her.

I want to forget everything between us.

I close the space between us, my heart pounding louder than any words I could say. There's been nothing—absolutely nothing—I've wanted more than this.

I hesitate for a fraction of a second, watching her, searching for any sign she'll pull away.

But she doesn't.

Her chest rises and falls, her lips parting like she's waiting for me, too.

That's all it takes.

I tilt my head, bending down, and crash my mouth to hers. It's not soft or sweet—it's heat and hunger, a collision we've been building toward for far too long.

She meets me halfway, her hands gripping the front of my shirt like she needs something to hold on to. The second her lips part, I deepen the kiss, tasting her, swallowing the small sound she makes as her tongue moves with mine.

We kiss like the moment might disappear.

Like we're afraid to let go.

It's urgent and messy and all-consuming, a fire neither of us can put out.

My hands find her waist, pulling her closer until nothing is between us, just the heat of her body pressed against mine. Her fingers move to my neck, threading through my hair and bringing me in deeper.

I'm completely lost in her. Lost in the way she kisses me like she's been waiting for this as long as I have.

Like we're both making up for wasted time.

I don't know how long we stay like that, tangled up in each other, but eventually, we slow, the desperate edge easing just slightly. My lips linger against hers, softer now, savoring her.

When we finally break apart, we're both breathing hard, the silence between us thick and electric. She takes a small step back, her hands sliding away, her gaze darting downward like she's suddenly unsure of herself.

I stay still, watching her, trying to catch my breath. My heart continues to hammer, and I can feel the ghost of her kiss everywhere—on my lips, on my skin.

She steps back; her gaze darting downward.

"We shouldn't . . ." Her voice is shaky.

"Bullshit." I shake my head, resolute. "We should."

"My brother . . ." Her words are barely above a whisper.

"What about him?" I lean closer, searching her face for answers.

"He can't know."

"Molly, you're a grown woman. He—"

"He can't know," she repeats sharply, stepping farther away, her hands wrapping protectively around herself.

I reach out instinctively, but she's already out of my reach.

"I have to go." Her voice is distant, her eyes avoiding mine.

I open my mouth to say something, to stop her, but before I can, she's already moving toward the door.

Then she's gone.

A mirage fading into the distance, leaving nothing but silence in her wake.

Like she never happened.

chapter thirty-seven

Molly

THERE IS NO WAY I'LL BE ABLE TO AVOID HUDSON TODAY.

We're back in the practice arena, which means more chances to bump into him.

If it weren't for our next fundraiser we are already planning, I would have told Dane I needed to take a few days off. But with the event looming, I can't afford not to be present.

The worst part? Hudson will be here.

Because, of course, Hudson wants to be more involved in team philanthropy.

To drive me crazy.

Stop.

Just because he makes my brain mush doesn't mean he's a bad person.

I put Hudson in a box that he doesn't belong in.

I know this.

He knows this.

But in my defense—

Oh, shut it, Molly. You fucked up. Just admit it.
Fine.
I fucked up.

I shouldn't have judged Hudson before I got to know him, I shouldn't have taken out my personal issues on him, and I shouldn't have lied all those years ago because I'm a chicken who's too afraid to tell her brother about what happened during that period he wasn't in my life.

I speed walk through the doors of the arena and head straight for the back office I've been using to coordinate Dane's donations to the event.

"Molly," one of the staff greets me before leaving me alone in here, a box of empty balloons tucked under her arm.

The medium-sized room is bigger than a closet but smaller than a conference room.

But somehow, even its extra square footage feels suffocating.

The walls are painted a dull beige, the kind that absorbs light instead of reflecting it. A small, cluttered desk is shoved into one corner, a filing cabinet in the other, and a long granite counter stretches across the back wall.

It's not cramped, not really.

At least, I tell myself that.

Still, the air feels thick, like the walls are slowly creeping closer with every second I stand here. I leave the door open, needing the illusion of space—of an escape route. Closing it would feel like letting the past swallow me whole.

I didn't lie when I told Hudson it's storming back with a vengeance.

I can't help but groan, heading to the table and gripping its edge. "Why are you like this, Molly?"

My thoughts are a mess. Tangled up tightly like a web of yarn that can't be unknotted.

What the hell am I going to do?

And not just about my annoying attraction to Hudson.

But also with Dane.

It's obvious that my role needs to change.

Working for him is no longer necessary.

He's okay.

And doesn't need me.

And that's okay.

Then why does it hurt so badly?

"It wouldn't be abandoning your brother," I try to convince myself. "You'll still be in his life to bug him. He would never let you out of his sight anyway."

My eyes well with tears.

Why does everything have to be so damn complicated?

I've spent so much of my life the past few years trying to repay the debt to Dane. Without that purpose, what will I do? Do I even have hobbies? Likes and dislikes?

Who am I?

Who is Molly Sinclair?

I don't even know.

"Pathetic." I shake my head. "You're pathetic, Molly."

The faint sound of the door creaking has my heart racing.

I left it partly ajar, but there's no mistaking that this isn't a gust of wind. Someone is here, and I'm on the verge of tears.

Real smooth, Molly.

Footsteps echo behind me.

The thing is, I don't even need to turn around to know it's him. It's like my body knows before my brain does. My shoulders stiffen, my heart picks up speed, and a familiar heat blooms low in my chest.

The footsteps aren't heavy, but they carry a confidence that could only belong to *him*. Hudson Wilde moves like he owns every room he walks into, even when he doesn't. Even when he shouldn't.

It's infuriating.

Even if my spidey senses weren't tingling, the closer he gets, the surer I am, thanks to the scent of his familiar cologne wafting in the air.

"Molly." His voice carries his usual teasing tone.

I don't answer.

I keep my eyes trained forward on the wall in front of me.

There's a small crack in the paint.

I should tell someone to touch that up.

Maybe if I don't look at him, he'll go away.

But of course, that won't happen.

He's made it his lifelong mission to break down my walls.

The scary part is, he would if I let him.

"You're avoiding me again," he says as he steps closer.

I let out a sigh, finally turning to face him.

Damn.

I shouldn't have done that.

The man is freshly showered. His dirty-blond hair looks brown as the water still clings to each strand. Droplets of water drip down his face.

He showered fast.

Or maybe he took a page out of Slate's playbook and dunked his head. It doesn't matter because this man should be illegal. He should one hundred percent come with a warning label.

It's unfair—actually *unfair*—how good he looks without even trying.

The ends of his hair curl slightly where they're still damp, making him look just this side of boyish. Except nothing about the rest of him is boyish.

His jaw is sharp, dusted with just enough stubble to make him look rugged. A single droplet trails down his neck, disappearing beneath the collar of his T-shirt.

My gaze dips lower without permission, taking in the way the shirt clings to his broad shoulders and chest, still damp enough to hint at the hard lines of muscle underneath.

And just like that, my mouth goes dry.

My heart stumbles, and heat creeps up the back of my neck like it's trying to expose me. It's maddening, really, the way my pulse betrays me every time he's within a ten-foot radius.

Hudson Wilde isn't just handsome—he's infuriatingly, stupidly hot.

And right now, standing there like he just stepped out of a cologne ad, he's every bit the kind of trouble I don't need.

"I'm not avoiding you." I plant a hand on my hip, feigning confidence. "I'm just . . . busy."

Hudson's lips twitch, a hint of disbelief flickering across his face. "Busy, huh?"

"Yep." I pop the *p*.

He arches a brow, his expression equal parts amused and skeptical.

"All right, I'll bite." He tilts his head, that infuriating smirk tugging at his mouth. "What's got you sooo busy you can't spare two minutes to talk to me?"

"What do you want, Hudson?" I snap, sharper than I mean to.

The words land heavy, and regret churns in my stomach. He hasn't done anything to deserve this. Not today, anyway.

We had a moment that's been on a constant loop in my brain. I'm wound up too tight, and it's spilling out the wrong way.

Hudson crosses his arms, but nothing about it is defensive. If anything, he looks more relaxed—more determined.

"I want you to stop running." His calm, steady voice dares me to argue.

"I'm not running."

His gaze pins me. "We both know you are."

"I can't help it," I admit before I can stop myself. My voice is smaller now, faltering.

"Why?"

The quiet word cuts through me like a blade.

I swallow hard, looking anywhere but at him. "I don't know."

"You act like this—us—is a bad thing."

"Maybe it is," I whisper, biting my lip hard enough to hurt.

My fists curl at my sides.

Hudson's jaw tightens, his expression hardening just slightly.

"Do you actually believe that?" His voice lowers, steady but sharp. "Or is this about your brother?"

The mention of Dane punches through my armor like a wrecking ball. My stomach twists painfully.

I could say yes.

I could tell Hudson that Dane would never trust him, that he's too protective, too stubborn. And while that's true, it's not all of it.

The bigger part?

That's on me.

It's about the fear gripping me, the fear of what could happen if I let someone in.

"You wouldn't understand," I murmur, my voice barely audible.

"Try me." He steps closer, the teasing gone from his tone. Now, it's gentle but unrelenting.

"It's not that simple." I shake my head, wishing I could shake away the truth.

"It can be."

"I'm not sure I can," I choke out, my voice cracking under the weight of it all.

"Hex." The way he says my name—steady, unflinching—hits me straight in the chest.

Like a quiet challenge.

Like he's daring me to keep lying to him.

I look up, and for one stupid moment, I let myself feel it. The pull between us. The way the air thickens when we're too close. The way his eyes—blue and unwavering—make me feel seen and exposed all at once.

But then reality slams into me like a tidal wave.

Dane would never understand.

And Hudson? I don't trust myself to let him in.

Not when the stakes feel this high.

"I can't," I whisper, stepping back. The space between us grows, but it doesn't feel like enough. "I can't do this."

Hudson doesn't move for a long second. He just watches me, his expression unreadable, and then he nods once.

"For now," he says quietly, his voice carrying a weight I don't want to unpack.

Then he turns and walks away, leaving me there.

Leaving me with the unshakable feeling that this isn't over.

Because it isn't.

Not even close.

chapter thirty-eight

Molly

Cassidy: Brunch at the diner. Be there or be ten pounds lighter but ultimately unhappy without cinnamon rolls.

Josie: I'm in.

Molly: Can't. Busy.

Cassidy: Busy doing what? Avoiding us or avoiding Hudson?

Molly: 😞 Avoiding you two, obviously.

Josie: Lies. We're delightful.

Cassidy: I'm offended. Personally. Deeply.

Josie: Truly. This feels like a breakup.

Molly: You two are so dramatic. I'm actually working.

Cassidy: Oh, right. Working . . .

Josie: Working hard not to think about Hudson Wilde.

Molly: *Throws phone out window.*

Josie: Denial isn't just a river in Egypt.

Molly: You promised to stop bothering me about Hudson.

Cassidy: Correction: We promised not to bother you about Hudson AT LUNCH.

Josie: Technically, this is a group chat. So. Loophole.

Molly: I hate both of you.

Cassidy: You don't. You hate that we're right.

Josie: And that we know things. Important things.

Molly: What things?

Cassidy: Like how you and Hudson disappeared together the day after he binge drank with Mason.

Molly: OMG. Drop it.

Josie: And that you haven't been able to look him in the eye since. • •

Cassidy: Curious. Very curious.

Molly: *Adds Josie and Cassidy to my block list.*

Cassidy: We're unblockable. Like cockroaches.

Josie: Or glitter. You'll never get rid of us.

Molly: Fine. I'll go to lunch if you swear on your lives not to mention him.

Cassidy: Deal.

Josie: Sworn. No Hudson talk.

Molly: If either of you so much as hint about him, I'm leaving.

Cassidy: We'll be angels.

Josie: I'll polish my halo and everything.

Molly: I'm serious.

Cassidy: Molly. When have we ever broken a promise?

Molly: . . .

Josie: . . .

Molly: Why do I feel like I'm walking into a trap?

Cassidy: Because you are. Cinnamon rolls at noon, babe. Don't be late.

Josie: We'll save you a seat. But not a cinnamon roll. There are limits to my kindness.

Molly: I'm going to regret this.

Cassidy: Probably. But we're worth it. 📸

chapter thirty-nine

Molly

THE SMALL DINER I LIKE TO GO TO WITH THE GIRLS IS WARM and cozy.

It feels straight out of a Hallmark movie, with mismatched chairs that look like they've been collected from garage sales over the years, checkered tablecloths, and a waitstaff that calls us "hon."

The walls are lined with old photos—black-and-white snapshots of the town's history mixed with colorful prints of flowers and hand-lettered signs with cheesy sayings.

Come hungry, leave happy.

Coffee: A hug in a mug.

I sit across from Josie and Cassidy, picking at my fries while the two of them debate milkshake flavors.

"You have to try the chocolate peanut butter," Cassidy insists, her dark hair pulled into a sleek ponytail. "It's life-changing."

Josie wrinkles her pert nose. "I'm a purist. Strawberry or nothing." She looks over at me, waiting for my input on the matter, her blond curls bouncing as she tilts her head. "Molly? Thoughts?"

I push my fries into a small pile. "On what?"

Cassidy smirks, leaning forward and placing her elbows on the table. "On whether or not you're capable of focusing when Hudson Wilde isn't in the room."

I blink, heat rising into my cheeks.

Shit. I'm totally blushing.

Play it cool, Molly.

I arch a single brow. "Excuse me?"

Josie laughs, propping her chin on her hand. "She's got a point, you know. You've been weirdly quiet today. Suspiciously quiet."

I grab my soda for something to do. "I'm just tired."

Damn, girl, you just answered that way too quickly.

Act casual.

"Mm-hmm." Cassidy's knowing smile grows as she leans back in her chair. "Tired because you've been spending all your energy trying not to strangle Hudson every time he opens his mouth?"

Hearing his name makes me scowl.

I'm already wound so tight. I can't escape this when I'm alone with my own thoughts. I don't need this with them, too.

This is supposed to be a Hudson-free lunch, and they just . . .

Shit. I fell right into the trap.

"Exactly." Josie giggles, shoulder-bumping Cassidy. "Look at her face."

I sigh, feigning boredom. "Nothing is going on. Just the usual hatred and mutual loathing. You know, the cornerstone of any healthy working relationship."

Josie snorts, twirling her straw between her fingers. "You sure about that? Because Dane mentioned something about you two not fighting as much lately."

I stiffen. "Dane doesn't know what he's talking about."

Cassidy raises an eyebrow. "So it's a coincidence that every time the team teases Hudson about you, he doesn't snap back? Or that you've actually been tolerable in the same room?"

"Yes, it's a coincidence. Plus, neither of us wants to lose the bet," I say firmly. *Take that. One point to the home team.* "And I have no idea what you're implying, but you're wrong. So wrong."

Josie and Cassidy exchange a look; twin smirks spreading across their faces.

"You're totally lying." Josie grins. "I know it. She knows it. Hell, the server probably knows it."

"Whatever you think you know, you don't." I point a fry at them for emphasis. "Nothing is going on between Hudson and me. Nothing except mutual disgust and an endless desire to avoid each other whenever possible."

Cassidy snorts, and since she was sipping her water, it's not pretty. "Right. Yet at the charity event, you two looked downright cozy holding those puppies together."

"That wasn't cozy. That was forced proximity," I grit out, but my stomach gets butterflies at the memory.

Dammit to hell.

Josie's expression softens. "Molly, you can tell us, you know. We're not going to judge you."

"There's nothing to tell," I insist, before shoving another fry in my mouth and looking away.

Josie and Cassidy are mind readers.

I can't give them an inch.

Cassidy taps her fingers against the table, watching me closely. "You're not denying that something's changed, though."

I roll my eyes. "If anything's changed, it's that I'm too tired to waste energy fighting him. That's it."

"Uh-huh. Sure. Because that totally explains why you've been blushing like crazy every time his name comes up."

"I am not blushing."

"You are. And for the record? If something is happening with you and Hudson, you should just admit it." Cassidy shrugs. "I think you'd be good for him."

"Good for him? Are you kidding me? He's an egotistical, smug, insufferable—"

"Hot," Josie adds helpfully.

"Nightmare," I finish, glaring at Josie.

Cassidy grins. "Hot nightmare, though."

My hands lift to cover my face. "Why do I even eat lunch with you two?"

"Because we're fun," Josie says brightly. "And because we're right."

"You're not right."

"Keep telling yourself that, Molly. But we're not blind." Cassidy steals a fry off my plate. "Something's going on. And when you're ready to admit it, we'll be here."

Damn Cassidy.

Always the voice of reason.

I shake my head as the two of them continue to laugh, but as much as I want to brush off their teasing, their words stick with me, leaving a nagging question I don't want to answer.

What is going on between Hudson and me?

chapter forty

Hudson

THE CROWD IS DEAFENING TONIGHT.

Even though it's an away game, a sea of screaming fans wave Redville Saints flags and chant my name.

I skate across the ice, adrenaline coursing through my veins. I've been in the zone all night—every pass, every play, every shot landing exactly where they needed to go.

And now, with the clock winding down and the fact that we are ahead by three, I know the game is in the bag.

The puck drops into the offensive zone, and I charge forward, my skates cutting sharply into the ice. Aiden sends a perfect pass my way, and I don't hesitate to snap the puck toward the goal. It sails past the goalie's glove, slamming into the back of the net.

The arena erupts into complete chaos.

I raise my arms, roaring triumphantly as my teammates swarm me, slamming their sticks against my pads and shouting in celebration. The final buzzer sounds, and it's official.

We won.

Once we break away, I head out to leave the ice, grinning so hard my cheeks hurt.

This is the best.

I love this feeling.

The electricity in the air. The roar of the crowd.

Best. Feeling. Ever.

Once we're in the locker room, the party starts.

Someone dumps a bucket of water on my head—ice-cold water.

Aiden sprays champagne onto Mason, who retaliates by dumping a cooler of ice water over him.

I shake off the water clinging to my hair and look up. Dane leans against the wall, shaking his head with a rare smile.

"You're welcome, boys," I call out, smirking as I peel off my gloves.

Mason rolls his eyes, grinning. "Oh, we're supposed to thank you for doing your job now?"

Aiden laughs, slapping me on the back. "Let him take the win. The guy's been on fire all night."

"Damn right," I say.

Dane snorts. "You're unbearable when you're like this."

"Yet," I reply, grabbing a bottle of water and chugging half of it, "you love me anyway."

Everyone loses their shit.

The guys roar with laughter, and even though I should be celebrating, I can't help but wonder where Molly is.

It's a compulsion.

The need to seek her out is all-consuming. I try to stop myself, but I can't.

When did I become so obsessed with her?

After the charity event?

Dinner with my family?

Most likely, it's everything in between. All the little moments.

In the past, I would have ignored this voice telling me to go find her, but I can't stop myself any longer. I don't know what's happening to me.

I don't recognize this version of me.

I step outside the locker room, not able to hold back another second. It's much quieter out here. Everyone is too busy celebrating inside.

A small crowd has formed, but it's nothing like what's going on inside. I start to make my way through the people milling about.

Luckily, no one stops me as I head to seek her out. I find her relatively fast. She's standing at the far end of the hallway, leaning against the wall, scrolling through her phone.

"Anything interesting on that thing?" I ask once I'm near.

She doesn't look up, but her lip twitches. "Just some story about a hotshot scoring a goal."

"Oh, really?" I can't help the cocky grin pulling at the edges of my lips. I *am* a hotshot. Glad she knows it. "And who is this hotshot?"

"No one you know, Wilde."

Although her words are sarcastic, there's no hate in her voice. Unlike back then, her barbs are light and airy.

I don't answer.

Instead, I take her wrist and gently tug her down the hallway, away from the prying eyes of the media and staff. I don't need another *Redville Post* headline accusing me of debauchery.

"What are you doing?" Molly stumbles slightly as she tries to keep up with me. "Where are we going? Someone might see us."

"No one's looking, Hex."

I make a left and head down one of the back hallways, then I turn another corner. This place is a maze, but right now, I welcome it.

In the corner, outside a closet, is a stack of crates holding equipment.

I glance around, confirming we're alone. "This will have to do."

She furrows her brows. "What will have to do?"

beautiful collide

I maneuver us so we're hidden out of sight.

Once we're blocked by the walls, I turn to face her. "I can't stop thinking about you."

Her eyes widen at my admission, she looks stunned.

Her lips twitch into a grin.

Reckless Molly is coming out to play.

Molly flips her hair over her shoulder. "Let me get this straight . . . you just won your game, and you're thinking about me?"

"Yeah." I move closer, my fingers toying with the edge of her shirt. "That's right."

Molly opens her mouth, most likely to fire back a witty rebuttal, but whatever she's about to say dies on her lips the moment I cup her cheeks and bring my mouth to hers.

The kiss isn't soft or gentle.

It's filled with want and desire. Fueled by weeks—*years*—of tension.

Molly's fingers clutch the front of my shirt, pulling me closer yet pushing me away at the same time.

This woman is one big contradiction.

But as long as she kisses me back, I don't care.

She freezes for half a second.

A sound penetrates my ears. Footsteps, maybe. But I don't care. I'm lost in this woman. All that matters is how she feels. How she tastes. The world could implode, and I wouldn't fucking care.

"Hudson?" It's Mason. The fucker has the worst timing on the planet. "You back here?"

Shit.

Molly jerks back like she's been electrocuted.

Her hands press against my chest to create space between us, but I don't budge. Her breath hitches, and for a split second, she looks as rattled as I feel.

I don't let her get far.

I cage her in without thinking, one hand braced against the wall beside her, the other curling loosely around her waist.

My heart slams in my chest, hammering against my ribs like it's trying to escape.

I look down at Molly. Her eyes are wide, and her cheeks are flush, pink streaking up from her neck to the tips of her ears.

I'd be lying if I said I didn't want to kiss her again, Mason be damned.

She sucks in a breath, her chest rising and falling against mine. Her lips are still parted, still red. *Still mine.*

I lift my finger to my mouth to signal for her to be quiet.

She shoots me a look, her brows furrowed like I'm somehow the one to blame for this chaos. Her gaze darts around the room, scanning for an escape route, but there's nowhere to go.

I dip my head down until my lips brush the shell of her ear. Close enough that my words don't carry, and I feel her shiver. "Relax, Hex."

"This is a disaster."

"I know." I smirk, the corner of my mouth twitching. "We didn't even get to the best part."

She tries and fails to glare at me, her eyes narrowing, but her cheeks still flushed. "Not what I was talking about."

"Was it?"

"You're impossible," she whispers, her tone still breathless from the kiss.

"Yet you kissed me back," I say with a grin, dropping my voice just enough to make her blush harder.

Before she can snap back, Mason's voice echoes closer, loud and annoyed. "Hudson, come on, man." He sounds like he's shouting into the void—unaware I'm here but banking on the slim chance that I can somehow hear him. "Coach wants us to talk to the media. You don't want to keep him waiting."

Shit.

That is one thing I can't afford to do.

Mason continues to shout the same thing over, his voice growing further away this time. I can imagine him dipping from room to room, sweeping the place for me. Not for nothing, he's a killer friend.

I sigh, stepping back from Molly, but I don't let go of her gaze. She's still standing there, her lips slightly parted, her cheeks flushed, and I'm not sure which one of us looks more wrecked.

My eyes locked on hers. "We'll finish this later."

"You wish," she retorts, but the words lack heat. Her gaze betrays her, lingering just a little too long on my mouth before darting away.

I grin, tilting my head as I take another step back like I'm giving her space, but we both know it's not enough. "Keep telling yourself that."

She scoffs, crossing her arms like she's trying to regain some kind of upper hand, but I don't miss the way she swallows hard.

Mason's voice echoes one last time, distant now. "Hudson Whatever-The-Fuck-Your-Middle-Name-Is Wilde. If you're screwing around somewhere, Coach is gonna bench your ass."

I shoot Molly one last look, a silent promise hanging in the air between us.

We will *finish this.*

It's just a question of when.

And judging by the way her eyes flick to mine and hold there for just a second longer, she knows it, too.

chapter forty-one

Molly

Unknown Number sent an attachment.

[Link: "Hudson Wilde—Hockey God or Hockey Legend? Why Not Both?"]

Unknown Number: Thought you'd like to read this. Since you're my #1 fan.

Molly: Who is this?

Unknown Number: You're joking.

Molly: Sorry, new phone. Lost all my IMPORTANT contacts.

Unknown Number: You've had the same phone since I met you.

Molly: 💀 ♀ I don't save numbers of men who annoy me for a living.

Unknown Number: That's a lie. I annoy you recreationally. I don't even get paid for it.

Molly: That's unfortunate for you.

Unknown Number: You're telling me. I'd be a billionaire by now.

Molly: Congrats on the article, though. Truly. You must be so humble about it.

Unknown Number: Humility is for people who AREN'T described as a hockey god. I'm just embracing the truth.

Molly: Right, because your ego clearly needed a boost.

Unknown Number: I'm here to inspire. It's practically a public service.

Molly: You should put that on your résumé. "Hockey god, legend, and part-time philanthropist dedicated to fixing overpopulation by annoying innocent victims to death."

Unknown Number: Don't forget "bringer of joy" and "man of the people."

Molly: Man of the people?????? Who are these people? And are you sure they don't live inside your head?

Unknown Number: My fans. The same ones who chant my name. Don't act like you haven't heard it.

Molly: Oh, I hear it. It's hard not to when they're chanting it at decibels that could shatter glass.

Unknown Number: It's the sound of greatness, Hex. You'll get used to it.

Molly: I'll put in earplugs.

Unknown Number: Still won't drown me out. I'm unforgettable.

Molly: Unbearable is the word you're looking for.

Unknown Number: Close enough. So . . . you saving this number yet?

Molly: Nah. I'll just keep calling you "Who is this?" It feels right.

Unknown Number: Unbelievable. I'll have you know that I've been described as a god AND a legend. Yet you're treating me like a scam caller.

Molly: Honestly, you do give scammer vibes.

Unknown Number: Keep talking to me like this and I'm billing you for my therapy.

Molly: Oh, please, you love it.

Unknown Number: . . .

Molly: We both know you have a degradation kink. Why else would you still talk to me after four years of being thoroughly roasted?

Unknown Number: Shut up and save my number, Hex. You'll need it when you decide you can't resist me anymore.

Molly: Don't hold your breath, Wilde.

Unknown Number: I'll wait. You're worth it.

Molly: Nice try.

Unknown Number: So that's a no on saving the number?

Molly: Hard pass.

Unknown Number: Unreal.

Molly: Go read your article again, Hockey God. Maybe it'll comfort you.

Unknown Number: Don't worry. I'll send you more tomorrow. Can't let you forget me.

chapter forty-two

Molly

Who is this? sent an attachment.

[Link: Hudson Wilde: Best Right Wing of the Century.]

Who is this?: Your daily dose <3

Molly: [Screenshot of their messages with the name "Who is this?" circled in red.]

Who is this?: *Unreal.*

chapter forty-three

Molly

I STIR MY COFFEE, MY GAZE TRAINED ON THE SWIRLING CREAM as if it holds the answers to the question, but really, I can't stop thinking about the kiss from two nights ago.

Even now, as Hudson sits diagonally across the table from me, I feel my cheeks warm. His presence is larger than life and impossible to ignore.

The air between us feels like it's charged with electricity, but ironically, neither of us has said anything to each other.

Well, he made a "Hudson" joke when I walked in, and I grunted in response. And earlier, when he managed to pull me aside, he tried to convince me to change his name on my phone from "Who is this?"

Our friends are eating the tension up. Especially with how awkward we are.

That is annoying because there's currently a huge elephant in the room with us, which is the memory of a crazy-ass, impulsive kiss that defied all logic. One I can't forget.

Cassidy taps her fingers on the diner's sticky table. "What's up with you this morning, Molly?"

I tilt my head in her direction and find that she's staring intently at me, nose scrunched. "Just tired."

I force myself to smile, lifting my coffee to take a sip. The moment I do, I want to curse my stupidity, because, lord, it's hot.

"Tired of losing the bet?" Mason quips, smirking over his Bloody Mary.

My stomach drops.

What does he mean by that?

Does he know about Hudson and me?

Maybe he *did* see us together after the game.

No.

That doesn't make any sense. Losing the bet means I've been mean to Hudson, so kissing him is the opposite, right?

I dart my gaze to Hudson, who doesn't seem bothered by what's transpiring. He just sits there, without a care in the world, casually flipping through the menu.

Must be nice.

Me, on the other hand?

It feels like I've stepped out onto a stage naked.

"You know what you want?" Dane asks me.

For a second, I don't understand what he's asking, but then I remember the menu in my hand.

Duh, Molly.

I glance down at it and immediately regret it.

As if the tension in the room isn't already enough.

I could cut it with a knife. But the world is out to get me because this damn menu—I blush at the options.

I want to crawl back into my bed and ask for a do-over.

Whoever named the dishes at this restaurant was clearly in a mood.

And that mood?

Horny.

Very horny.

The options are absurd.

The Morning Wood—a loaded breakfast sandwich.

The Thirst Trap—a mimosa flight.

Buns and Sausage—self-explanatory and mortifying.

Please, universe, let the ground open up and swallow me because I can't possibly order one of these right now.

I clear my throat, scanning the menu for something—anything—that doesn't sound like a dirty joke. "Uh, I'll just have the . . . Sunrise Bowl."

"God, you're boring," Mason mutters, earning a glare from Dane. Gotta love my protective brother. Mason smirks. "I'll have some Morning Wood."

Idiot.

"What about you, Hudson?" Cassidy asks, grinning. "Let me guess. Buns and Sausage?"

I nearly choke on my coffee, and of course, Hudson doesn't miss a beat, setting down his menu with a smirk that is way too condescending for this ungodly hour of the morning.

"Tempting," he says, his eyes flicking toward me. "But I think I'll go with Mason. The Morning Wood. Sounds . . . filling."

Mason snorts.

Dane groans.

And me?

I set my cup down way too hard, causing the coffee to spill. "You're all children."

Cool it, Molly.

It's so obvious how little chill I have right now.

Hudson shrugs. "I didn't name the menu."

But the damn smile on his face tells me he's loving every cursed minute of this breakfast, which leads me to my question.

I pop a brow up. "Who picked this restaurant?"

"Why, that would be me," Hudson responds.

Bastard.

He totally did this on purpose. That's it. I'm leaving him as *Who is this?* for all of eternity.

Pulling my gaze from him, I focus back on my coffee. I'm sure I'm blushing. My cheeks feel like they're on fire.

Hopefully, no one notices.

But this man does something to me.

I can't explain it, but I feel like a live wire when he's around.

"Okay, what's going on?" Dane asks suddenly, his voice cutting through the chatter.

I freeze. "What are you talking about?"

Dane gestures back and forth between Hudson and me. "You're both acting weird."

"I have no idea what you're talking about," Hudson answers, but his tone doesn't match his words.

Smug bastard.

Great. Just great.

The man practically just confirmed something is up with us.

He might as well just hold up a sign that says we kissed again. Again.

Man, if my brother finds out . . .

I don't even want to think about that. Dane thinks Hudson is the biggest player in the world. He will not be okay with something happening between us.

"Nothing is up," I snap.

"Did Hudson do something, Moll?" Dane turns to Hudson, his entire face darkening the way it does when he's about to make an opposing player regret they've ever been born. "What the fuck did you do, dick?"

Hudson opens his mouth to speak, but Dane cuts him off.

"Obviously, you lost the bet." He jabs a finger in Hudson's direction. "Did you upset my sister?"

All eyes on the table focus on me.

I try not to shrink in my chair.

"He didn't do anything," I say way too quickly. With a pitch way too high.

Way to be obvious.

Hudson leans back in his chair, looking annoyingly calm. "Yeah, we're good. No bets broken."

And that's that.

The server comes over, saving me. I make a mental note to give her the biggest tip I can afford later.

We all place our orders with varying degrees of mortification and amusement. I'm hopeful Dane has dropped the subject. That this is the distraction I need to be able to change the conversation.

No such luck.

As soon as the server leaves, Mason points a finger at me and then quickly at Hudson.

"You're both lying." Mason slams his palms onto the table. "Spill. Who lost?"

"Neither of us," I insist, knuckles turning white on my mug.

"Whatever you say . . . but you're both being weird." Cassidy narrows her eyes and looks at Hudson. "Although that's not saying much for you, since you're normally weird."

"Maybe you've all forgotten what normal looks like," Hudson counters smoothly, his smirk still firmly in place.

Mason grins, leaning forward. "Okay, but we doubled down on bets, so I need to know who's winning. I have twenty bucks and a potholder collection riding on Molly."

Josie bursts out laughing. "A potholder collection? Are you serious?"

"Dead serious," Mason replies, unfazed by how ridiculous this all sounds.

"Dane said he'd wash my car if Hudson loses," Cassidy adds, grinning. "So I'm kind of rooting for him to crack first."

I glare at my brother. "Neither of us cracked."

Dane crosses his arms, eyeing us suspiciously. "You're sure? Because you're acting like you did after that time Hudson got a

beautiful collide

ride from you to the game. Like you can't even look at each other. Like you hate each other."

Well, we *did* hate each other.

But that was different.

I avoided him back then because I hated him.

I'm avoiding him now because I don't trust myself not to climb him like a flagpole.

Josie grins, her eyes darting between us. "I think they're acting like the opposite of hate."

I scowl. "What's that supposed to mean?"

Josie shrugs innocently. "Just saying. The tension is palpable."

Hudson chuckles, the sound grating on my last nerve.

Then why do you feel tingly down there?

Fine. His laugh is hot.

He's still annoying.

"Palpable, huh?" Hudson is like the cat who ate the canary. "Interesting choice of words."

Does this man ever shut up?

He's just making it worse.

I shoot him a warning glare, all while trying to remain calm despite my heart pounding in my chest.

"Well"—Cassidy leans back with a smirk—"I guess we'll just have to keep an eye on you two."

Great.

Just great.

chapter forty-four

Hudson

THE NIGHT IS EERILY QUIET; THE HUM OF THE CITY MUTED THIS high up. I lean against the doorframe to the rooftop of the hotel where the team is staying, staring at the figure sitting underneath the stars.

I might not see her face, but I'd know her anywhere.

She's haunted my thoughts for longer than I care to admit.

I watch her for a minute, sitting up against the low wall, knees pulled up, face tilted up to the sky.

She shouldn't be up here.

Hell, I shouldn't be either.

But something brought me here, and I have to believe it's her. It's almost like I'm stuck in her gravitational pull, and even if I tried, I'd never escape it.

Who are you trying to kid? You've never really tried.

For a hot second, I pretended I didn't care about her.

That lasted all of two seconds.

I let the world think I was losing myself in an endless bevy of women, but it was all bullshit. None of that shit was real. The only thing that was real is that the very first time I saw Molly Sinclair, I was obsessed.

I move from where I'm perched, desperate for a closer look, needing to see her face.

When she comes into focus, she practically takes my breath away. She looks so different right now. Not her usual sarcastic self. There's nothing combative about her.

She looks serene. Peaceful.

I want to be with her.

I stumble from the revelation.

I don't care what her brother says, or what anyone says . . . I want Molly, and I'm going to do everything in my power to have her.

I step out of the shadows, my boots crunching softly on the graveled rooftop. This place definitely isn't safe, but if she's here, then I'm here.

Molly glances over her shoulder. It might be dark out, but even from here, under the black sky that blankets us from above, I can tell her expression looks wary.

I take another step out until a small light from the neighboring building lights the space. Her head whips in my direction.

It's not bright out, but clearly, it's enough for her to realize it's me. Her eyes widen before a smile tugs at her lips.

"Can I help you?" Her voice carries over the cool night.

"Just out here to get some air."

"Well, this roof is taken."

Despite her words, I can tell from her light, airy tone that she's happy to see me.

I lift my hands in mock surrender. "Didn't know I'd be crashing your stargazing party."

"It was supposed to be a party for one." She arches a brow, turning back to the sky. "Or at least that's how it was advertised."

I bite back a grin. "You should get your money back."

I make my way over to where she's sitting and plop down beside her, tilting my head up to match her.

The stars are clearer here than I expected, but I guess it makes sense since this building is higher than the rest of the area.

For a few moments, we sit in silence. The tension is sharp, but not in a bad way. Almost exciting.

After brunch today, I wasn't sure how she would react. But as I sit beside her, I know she doesn't regret the kiss. That doesn't mean I'll make it easier on her. That's not who we are, after all.

Being assholes to each other is practically our love language, or I think that's the term Anna uses when she talks about boys she likes.

"You're avoiding me," I finally say, cutting through the silence as I tilt my head down to look at her again.

Molly glances at me, her lips pressing into a thin line. "I'm not avoiding you, Wilde." I give her a pointed look, and she smiles. "Fine. I'm avoiding you. But it's because I needed to think."

"Think about what?"

She exhales deeply. "Don't play dumb. You know what I was thinking about."

"The kiss," I say, my voice dropping low.

"Oh, jeez." She scrunches her nose. "Can you not say it like that?"

"Say it like what?" I use the same tone, knowing it'll press her buttons.

"Like you're trying to seduce me."

I wiggle my brows at her. "But aren't I?"

She doesn't answer, and I wonder if she plans to just stop speaking for the night.

But then she breaks the silence. "After today, who knows?"

"I'm playing the game I'm expected to play," I answer vaguely.

She furrows her brows. "What's that supposed to mean?"

I sigh. "People expect a certain version of me. That's all."

It's the same stupid story. The reputation I never asked for but ended up wearing anyway. What did Dane say again?

Hudson Wilde: the star that plays on and off the ice?

It didn't matter what I said or how I acted. People had already made up their minds.

After that showdown in the hallway, word got out. The first time someone accused me of being a womanizer, I tried to laugh it off.

Then, when the rumors spread outside the arena, I fought against it.

I told them they were wrong.

I told them I wasn't that guy.

But no one believed me.

The truth didn't matter because the lie was more interesting.

Eventually, I stopped fighting it.

If they would paint me as the villain, I figured I'd give them what they wanted. I played the role they'd written for me—the smirking, careless, bad boy with a revolving door of women.

But the truth is, it never felt right.

I wasn't proud of it. It's not who I am, and it never was.

But the more I let people believe it, the more I felt like I'd buried the real me so deep, he'd never come back.

Molly bites her lower lip, sparing me a glance. "And that's not who you are?"

I shake my head, no longer staring at the stars. "No."

She shifts slightly, resting her chin on her knees, turning to face me fully. Her voice softens. "Then why pretend?"

I sigh, deciding to answer her honestly. "Because no one cares to see past the facade."

"That's not true, Hudson."

"So . . . you do?"

She doesn't answer.

I let out a bitter laugh, the sound empty and sharp. "Exactly."

The silence that follows stretches, and it's not a comfortable one. She opens her mouth like she wants to say something—maybe defend herself, maybe argue—but she closes it just as quickly.

I lean back, staring at the night sky again, the stars a blur I can't focus on. "You know, it's easier that way."

"For everyone else," she points out.

"Maybe." I close my eyes, letting the wind lap at my cheeks. "They get to keep their neat little story about me. No one has to bother looking for more. And eventually . . ." I pause, forcing out a humorless laugh. "You start wondering if they're right. If maybe you *are* just the bad guy they say you are."

Molly's quiet before she murmurs, "You're not."

The words are so soft I almost don't hear them. I glance over at her. For the first time tonight, she's finally looking at me. *Really* looking at me. Studying me.

Staring deep into my soul.

For a second, I think maybe she does see past it. Maybe she sees me.

And then, she looks away.

Of course, she does.

I shake my head, my voice low. "Doesn't matter if I'm not. People love their lies."

Molly doesn't argue this time. She just stays quiet, watching the stars, and for some reason, that silence hurts more than if she'd disagreed.

"I'm so fucking sorry, Hudson."

Her words catch me off guard.

I tear my eyes away from the stars, peering down at her. "For what?"

"I did this to you. I gave you this reputation. And back then, when I tried to apologize, I never did it sincerely."

I move to speak, but she holds up a hand.

"Let me get this out. Please. It's long overdue." She straightens, her eyes locked on mine. "I know that I ruined your reputation the first day we met. I tried to tell myself it didn't matter, but it obviously did, and I'm so fucking sorry that I did it, that I can't tell you *why* I did it, and that I haven't given you the genuine apology you deserve until now."

"You did," I point out, trying to make her feel better. I can't help but want to stop the tears welling in her eyes. "You apologized a few days later. I didn't let you."

"Yeah, well, I didn't try hard enough. And to be honest, I didn't mean it like I do now. Now that I know you better. Now that . . ." She sucks in a breath, closing her eyes. "Now that I'm willing to admit I want to know you better. So tell me. Please. What's going on with you?"

When she looks at me like that—so fucking sincere that I want to bottle up that gaze and keep it with me when life gets dark—I can't help but spill.

I sigh, leaning back on my hands. "It's just been . . . a lot lately. Between hockey and everything else, sometimes I feel like I can't keep up."

"Everything else?" Her tone drops.

For a second, I hesitate to speak. No one's asked me anything like this before. Not even Mom.

Not how I'm feeling, nor what's going on in my life.

It's been so long since someone has genuinely asked. Sure, I've had bullshit interviews with the media, but that was all superficial. Vultures hunting for a soundbite.

Molly is genuine and real, and fuck, it's addictive.

A part of me doesn't want to talk. Just wants to keep my walls up. To be the fun, carefree Hudson everyone expects me to be.

But then I feel her hand on mine, and it spurs me to talk.

"My family, they own a farm." I sigh, feeling lighter as the words finally escape me. "It's a small operation, but it's been in the family for generations. My dad's getting older, and the farm's not doing great. They're close to losing it."

Molly turns to me, surprise flickering across her face. "I didn't know that."

"Why would you?" I shrug before looking down to stare at the gravel under my boot. "I don't talk about it much. But it's why I'm late to things sometimes—helping out on the farm. Especially during harvest."

"You help them?"

"I do." I shrug. "Sometimes it's small things, other times bigger. I do whatever needs doing."

"Shouldn't your parents have hired help for that?"

"They should." I nod. My throat feels tight. "And they could, if they'd just let me help them out financially. But they won't. They're stubborn and refuse to take my money."

"Why?"

"They say they don't want me solving their problems just because I'm making good money now." I shake my head, frustration welling in my chest. "It's pride. It's stupid fucking pride."

"Or maybe it's guilt."

I freeze, more than a little surprised I never considered that. "What do you mean?"

"When Dane got custody of me, I felt weird asking for things. Stupid things. A toothbrush, shampoo, socks." She laughs, but it's a bitter laugh, full of regret. "I didn't even let him buy me pads. I just felt like . . . he worked so hard for the money, he put in so many hours, and I didn't want to be his burden."

"He would never see you as a burden," I promise her.

"I know that. Well, sometimes I do. Other times . . . not so much." She shakes her head. "Anyway. It wasn't pride. It was *guilt*. Pride is standing tall and saying you don't need help. Guilt is curling in on yourself because you know you do, but you're too afraid to accept it."

It strikes me that it means something that she's sharing this.

Molly has walls taller than Mount Everest. She doesn't let anyone in. But to make me feel better, she's sharing a piece of herself she never does.

A realization hits me in the chest.

beautiful collide

Molly is the calm I need.

She's quiet.

I keep my eyes trained on her until she meets my gaze. Her eyes search mine.

"Just food for thought," she says, sheepish. She rubs the back of her neck. "From what I know of your parents. So, since they don't let you pay for help, you help them yourself, right?"

"Yeah." I run a hand through my hair, accepting the lifeline she gave me. "It's not enough, though. And it kills me to see them struggling when I could help."

Molly doesn't respond right away.

Instead, she looks back at the stars. "They're lucky to have you, you know. Not everyone would stick around and help like that."

I laugh, but the sound lacks humor. "They're the best people I know. I couldn't not help. They've given me everything, and they ask for nothing in return. That's just who they are."

Her hand squeezes mine. "That's . . . really amazing, Hudson. I mean it."

My chest feels tight.

This is Molly.

The real Molly.

There's no sarcasm. No hate.

She's just . . . *her*.

I flip my hand over, linking our fingers together, testing the waters. "Thanks."

She doesn't pull away. Our hands laced together, we fall into another silence, but this time, it isn't awkward. It feels almost natural. Like the tension between us all day has finally faded away.

I tilt my head back, my gaze fixing on the stars. "You ever think about how small we are? Compared to all of this?"

Molly chuckles softly. "What, are you getting philosophical now?"

I grin. "Maybe."

She shrugs. "Makes sense, it's the stars. They do that to people."

Her voice is soft, almost wistful.

For a second, I forget how to breathe.

The moonlight casts a glow across her face, catching on her cheekbones, her nose, and the soft curve of her lips. I swear the girl could make a guy forget his own name.

I shift closer, just slightly, but it's enough to catch her attention. She glances at me, her eyes darker than usual in the low light.

Something shifts in the air between us.

"Why are you looking at me like that?" she whispers, her voice barely audible.

"Like what?" I ask, even though I know exactly what she's talking about.

"Like I'm—" She swallows, her words catching in her throat.

"Like you're everything," I finish for her.

Her lips part, her breath hitching, and I don't wait for her to argue or deflect or push me away. I lean in, closing the space between us slowly, giving her time to stop me if she wants to. But she doesn't.

Instead, she leans in, too.

When my mouth finally brushes against hers, it's soft at first—tentative. But then she presses closer, her hands tangling in my shirt, and I lose every ounce of self-control I thought I had.

I cup her face in my hands, deepening the kiss, pouring every unspoken thing into it—every fight we've had, every tense fucking moment, every single time I've wanted this and told myself I couldn't.

Her fingers curl into my chest, and I don't even have it in me to be embarrassed by how fast my heart beats.

The world fades around us.

There's no sky, no stars, no sound.

Just her.

Just us.

The kiss grows frantic. Hungry.

Like we're both trying to devour the years we've spent avoiding this, denying this.

Her hands tug at my shirt, her nails scraping against my skin, and I'm gone. Absolutely fucking gone.

My fingers skim down her back, gripping and pulling her closer because there's no such thing as close enough. I feel her everywhere—her lips on mine, her breath mingling with mine, the heat of her skin beneath my palms.

We yank at each other's clothes, blindly tugging at any fabric we can get a hold of. It's a blur of hands, lips, and teeth, and I swear, something tears—her shirt or mine. We toss them aside like they've offended us.

And then we're crashing back together, kissing, biting, and claiming each other's lips. Her hands roam all over me—my chest, my back, my cock.

"Touch me, Hex. Get me nice and ready." She grips my hardness at the base, tugging upward, drawing a groan for me. "I need to fuck you."

"Here?"

"Yes, Hex, do you have a problem with that?" Her lips tip into a sexy smirk. "That's what I thought. Remove your pants."

She inhales before moving her hands to the waist of her leggings. "Now your top. I want to taste every inch of you before I fuck your sweet pussy."

It might be dark, but as she strips bare for me, laying her clothes in a neat pile on the ground, I take her in.

She's gorgeous.

The dim light casts a soft shadow over her, giving me enough light to see her perky tits. It's her nipples that have me licking my lips.

Her small hand grasps my dick and runs it from root to tip, getting me nice and ready for her.

"Since I don't want either of us to fuck up our knees on the gravel, I'm going to need you to bend over, Hex. Hands on the wall."

She hurries to follow my orders, and fuck, if that doesn't make me harder.

I reach into my back pocket to grab a condom and waste no time slipping it on.

Stepping up behind her, I run my hands over her ass, dipping lower and lower until I run my fingers through her drenched folds.

"I love how wet you get for me."

I slide a finger into her, and she moans as her head rolls back while I stroke and tease her G-spot.

But I'm not a generous man right now. She'll get her turn, but not before I'm inside her.

Pulling my finger out, I quickly replace it with my cock, resting the tip right outside her pussy. She wiggles back, which makes me laugh.

"Ahh, is my little Hex impatient?"

"Stop talking, Wilde, and fuck me."

"Is that what you need? And here I thought you were out here to stargaze."

She wiggles back again, and I swirl my hips, my cock tracing her damp skin but still not entering.

A groan escapes her mouth. "Tell me . . . how bad do you want me."

"Bad enough to ignore this is a bad idea."

"Oh, is that so?"

"Yep." She pops the *p*, full of attitude, and it only makes me smile.

"Very well." I pull my dick away.

"What the hell?" She turns over her shoulder.

"Tell me you want me."

She bites her lip.

"Tell me."

"I want you," she admits in a whisper.

"Not good enough. Tell me you want me to fill you with my cock."

beautiful collide

Her eyes widen, and her mouth stays shut.

"Beg me, Hex."

She doesn't speak, but I can see the words all over her features. From the way her eyes are glassy to the way her body trembles beneath me. We both know damn well she wants to be fucked.

"Fuck me, Wilde, please."

"Not what I asked you to say, but it will have to do."

I push forward, and the tip of my dick slips inside her.

A moan escapes her, and I move another inch in.

With every move I make, I feed her pussy more of my cock.

Finally, when I can't take it anymore, I drive my whole length within her, loving how her muscles pulsate around me.

I start to thrust faster, harder, deeper.

The city sounds are all around us, but it isn't loud enough up here to drown out the sound of our bodies slapping together.

"Just like that. So good."

"Are you going to come?" I ask, reaching around and finding her clit. "Now, be a good girl and give me what I want."

I drive into her again.

"Oh God," she moans, so I pick up my pace.

My thrusts are now punishing as I furiously rub her clit. "I'm coming," she pants as her pussy tightens, and my balls do the same.

"Good girl, come all over my cock." And she does, tightening so hard around my dick I almost see stars. I'm quick to follow her over the edge.

Afterward, I place my shirt down on the gravel, and we sit together on the rooftop, the cool night air brushing against our skin. Molly's head rests against my shoulder, her breathing soft and steady.

I tilt my head, pressing a kiss to the top of her head. "You good?"

She hums, her voice sleepy and content. "I could go again. Give me fifteen minutes."

"Isn't that supposed to be my line?" I chuckle softly, running my fingers through her hair.

"Yeah," she says, turning slightly to look up at me. Her face is suddenly serious. "You know that . . ." She winces, stopping.

"That Dane can't know," I finish for her.

I expected this.

"Are you okay with that?" Her face is etched with hesitation, like she's waiting for me to argue or walk away.

But I don't.

I can't.

"Yes," I finally say.

Because the truth is, I don't want to live another lie—*not again*.

I've spent years pretending to be someone I'm not, building walls and hiding behind them. But right now, all I can think about is her.

I want Molly Sinclair.

So if keeping this a secret means I get to have her—even if it's just for a little while—I'll play the game.

I'll take the lie as long as I get her.

chapter forty-five

Molly

Who is this? sent an attachment.

[Link: Hudson Wilde: True contender for MVP.]

Molly: Who is this?

Who is this?: . . .

Who is this?: Come on. Still?

Who is this?: At least change it to Greatest Hockey Player to Ever Live.

Molly: ☹ Someone's humble.

Who is this?: I'd like to be, but then the media wrote that. Not my fault I'm a contender for greatness.

Molly: You're a contender for being insufferable, that's for sure.

Who is this?: Admit it. You read the whole thing.

Molly: I skimmed.

Who is this?: You definitely read the whole thing. Bet you even bookmarked it.

Molly: You're delusional.

Who is this?: I'm also undefeated. Add that to the article.

Molly: Undefeated in what? Overinflating your ego?

Who is this?: In making you think about me.

Molly: 😒You're one comment away from being blocked.

Who is this?: Joke's on you. You'll miss me when I'm gone.

Molly: I'll take my chances.

Who is this?: Just save my number already, Hex. I'm getting offended.

Molly: Fine. I'll save it.

Who is this?: Wow. This is progress. I'm honored.

Molly: [Screenshot of Hudson saved as Hockey Pest #2.]

Hockey Pest #2: Unbelievable.

Molly: It feels right.

Hockey Pest #2: I hate you.

Molly: No, you don't.

Hockey Pest #2: . . . Shut up.

Molly: Blocked.

Hockey Pest #2: Liar.

Hockey Pest #2: Wait. If I'm Hockey Pest #2, who's Hockey Pest #1?

chapter forty-six

Hudson

I KNOW I SHOULD BE CELEBRATING, AND IF YOU ASK MY teammates, they'll say it's my second home, but really, bars aren't my thing.

Sure, they're great to drown out your sorrows. To hide from the real world and the problems you have.

But in truth, I find them too loud, too crowded, and full of way too many people I have no interest in getting to know.

I'm fucking tired.

Tired of pretending I don't give a shit.

Tired of acting like an ass, so Molly won't know that she affects me.

And after last night, I hope I don't have to anymore.

To be honest, I'd much rather have stayed in the hotel and had a round two of the rooftop—this time on a bed instead of the gravelly roof I had to make do with.

One day, we're going to have sex like normal people.

But for now, I'm just going to remember how she felt wrapped around my dick and try not to get too annoyed as people interrupt my night out with my team.

Fans don't usually bother me. I'm okay signing autographs and taking pictures. But it's when they think I owe them a part of myself that I have a problem.

I get that it's partially my fault. I let them think I was accessible, but now I'm not.

Which is why I'm sitting at a high-top table near the back of the room, drinking a watered-down glass of tequila.

Mason is speaking.

I'm not listening.

As if he can hear my inner thoughts, he calls me out. "Dick, are you even listening?"

"No."

At least I'm honest.

My attention drifts toward the bar, where a cluster of people stands laughing, clinking glasses, and having the time of their lives.

And then, I see her.

Molly.

She's wearing a little black dress, the kind designed to ruin a man. It hugs every curve, stops just above her knees, and leaves her shoulders bare, her skin glowing under the low lights of the bar.

Her long brown hair cascades in loose waves down her back, a few strands falling forward, brushing against her collarbone.

She's laughing at something someone said, the sound soft and light; her lips curved into a mysterious smile.

I feel like I've been sucker punched.

It's ridiculous, really. I've seen Molly Sinclair a thousand times before, and I know better than to let her get to me.

But tonight? She's different.

Or maybe it's me who's different.

Either way, the sight of her—confident, stunning, and oblivious to her effect on me—hits me like a freight train.

My chest tightens, my pulse quickening as my gaze travels back to the way the dress dips at the small of her back, subtle but lethal. She shifts, reaching for a drink, and the movement is enough to send my thoughts spiraling.

She's beautiful, and worse, she makes me *feel*.

And I hate that.

I hate how easily she can knock me off balance, how seeing her smile in that stupid dress makes me want to walk over and pull her out of this crowd to have her to myself.

I'm screwed.

This is bullshit.

Yeah, I agreed to this. I said I was okay with not acknowledging each other tonight when she texted me that Dane was coming, but fuck, this is a lot harder than I thought.

She stands near the center of the group, making my pulse race in that dress.

Damn, she looks good.

Like a goddess sent down from heaven to torture me.

"You got it bad."

I barely register Mason's words.

When I do, I tear my gaze away from Molly. "What?"

"Dane might be stupid enough not to see the way you look at his sister, but I do." He knocks back the rest of his drink. "You want her, dude."

"Nah." I shake my head, trying to play it off, replacing my tequila with a new beer bottle. "It's not like that."

But my voice sounds off. Too casual. Too forced.

Mason squints at me like he's reading a damn book, and my chest tightens.

Shit.

My heart pounds in my ears, drowning out the noise of the bar. He can't know. No way. Molly would kill me.

If Mason has figured it out, it's only a matter of time before it gets back to Dane—and I don't even want to entertain that nightmare.

My grip tightens around the beer bottle in my hand as I try to keep my face neutral, but my thoughts are spiraling.

How the hell did he catch on?

I've been careful.

We've been careful.

No stolen glances in front of the team. No brushing hands, no sneaking out of rooms together. Nothing. Well, other than that time in the hall.

But I swear he didn't see us.

Yet here Mason is, acting like he's got front-row seats to my unraveling.

If Mason tells Molly I've slipped up—even a little—she'll lose it. She'll panic. She'll think this whole thing is blowing up in our faces, and then what?

She'll end it.

She'll shut me out faster than I can blink, and this thing between us—whatever it is—will be over.

The thought of it makes me feel like I've taken a slap shot to the chest.

I can't let that happen.

I *won't* let that happen.

I force out a laugh, trying to sell the lie better this time. "Mason, you've had one too many, man. You're seeing things."

Mason doesn't buy it. He never does. He just smirks knowingly, leaning back in his chair like he's got all the time in the world.

"You keep telling yourself that," he says, drumming his fingers on the table.

I don't respond and just take a long pull of my drink, trying not to let him see that he's hit a nerve.

Because he has.

And if he knows, if he even suspects . . . I'm totally screwed.

"Fine." A smug smirk graces Mason's lips. The fucker just won't let it go. "Then tell me what it's like."

"We barely tolerate each other."

"You keep telling yourself that."

I ignore him, lifting my drink to my mouth and closing my eyes for a brief second.

"Hmm . . ." Mason says in that asshole tone of his. "Then you won't mind that some guy is hitting on her."

My eyelids fly open. "What?"

"Oh, and it's not just some guy. It's Hayes from the Colts."

My stomach twists as I take in the sight in front of me.

It's just as Mason said.

Hayes, the center for the Colts, is talking to Molly, and worse, she's eating that shit up. Her head is thrown back as she laughs at whatever he says.

I place my drink down with a thud.

Mason pats my chest, pushing me back a little. "Easy there, killer."

"I'm fine."

"Breathe."

I might need to breathe because my knuckles are now white.

Mason's voice cuts through my spiraling thoughts. "You're not even listening, are you?"

I blink, tearing my gaze away from Molly. "What?"

Mason smirks. "You're two seconds away from chucking that glass across the room. Let's try this again . . . what's going on with you and Molly?"

"Don't be ridiculous. I wouldn't waste good beer."

"It's watered-down shit, and we both know it."

He does have a point.

I turn my attention back to Molly. Hayes leans in, and his hand brushes Molly's arm. Even from here, I can see her stiffen.

"Calm down, Wilde." Mason keeps his hand planted on my torso like he's afraid I'll launch myself over there if he lets go. "Molly is a grown girl. She can handle herself."

"Where the hell is Dane?" My voice is sharper than I intended, and my eyes lock on Hayes like I could set him on fire just by staring.

"Again. Molly can take care of herself," Mason repeats, but there's a hint of caution in his tone now. He knows me well enough to hear the edge in my voice.

I grit my teeth, watching Hayes get even closer, leaning in like he owns the air she's breathing. I can see Molly's shoulders go rigid, her lips pulling into a tight, polite smile she barely holds in place.

It's the look she wears when she's enduring something she hates.

My fists curl so tight that my knuckles scream in protest.

Don't do it. Don't do it.

Mason's hand presses firmer against me, probably feeling the tension rolling off me like a thundercloud.

"Hudson," he warns under his breath.

He has a point.

Molly's feisty as hell. She'd be pissed if I interfered. She's handled worse, I'm sure. If she catches me storming over there, she'll probably bite my head off before Hayes even gets the chance to process what's happening.

Not to mention, the press will have a field day if they catch wind of this.

I exhale a shaky breath, willing myself to calm down, to let it go—

And then that bastard touches her waist.

My blood boils.

My vision goes red.

That's it.

Mason's hand is no longer enough to stop me.

I shrug him off and stalk across the bar, the pounding of my feet matching the rapid beat of my heart. Every muscle in my body is taut, coiled like a spring about to snap.

"Hudson," Mason hisses from behind me, but his voice fades into the background.

It's just Hayes and me now.

And he has no idea what's about to hit him.

Mason sighs, giving up. "Well, shit. This is gonna be good."

Once I'm done kicking Hayes's ass, Mason is up next.

It doesn't take me long to reach them, and by the time I get there, Molly is already trying to step away. The polite smile she's throwing at the center is the fuck-off smile Molly reserves for people she thinks are assholes. Present company included most of the time.

Luckily, she no longer looks at me this way.

The asshole doesn't seem to notice the signals Molly throws out because his hand is still on her.

"Hey," I say, my voice low and even, the kind of calm that usually comes before a fight.

The guy turns, looking me up and down.

His expression shifts when he recognizes me. "What do you want, Wilde?"

I ignore him, my attention on Molly. "Everything okay here?"

Molly blinks before meeting my stare. "Fine."

"You sure you're fine, or is he giving you a problem?" I gesture to Hayes.

He frowns, clearly annoyed now. "What's your problem, man? We're just talking."

"Talking doesn't involve touching unless you were invited," I tell him.

The guy bristles but takes a step back. "Should be a fun game tomorrow."

It would be so easy to clock him right now. To swing and catch him right on the cheek.

I force myself to take a deep breath.

Mom would kill you if you made headlines for this.

She might, the devil on my shoulder starts, but she also might reward you when you tell her you did it for Molly.

"Hudson," Molly warns.

Fine.

I glare at Hayes, getting in his face. "I'll see you tomorrow on the ice."

Both of us have made our intentions very clear. We'll finish this in the rink.

When the douchebag walks away, Molly glares at me. "I didn't ask for your help."

"Didn't need to," I shoot back.

Molly hesitates, almost like she's torn by how to act, but finally, her posture relaxes. "Thanks, I guess."

"You're welcome."

I step closer, bending down so only she can hear. "I know you said this is how it has to be, but know this: I'm going to change your mind."

Then I pull back and walk away, leaving her with that parting gift.

chapter forty-seven

Hudson

The rink is alive with noise. The crowd roars as the guys and I skate out for warm-ups. I tighten my jaw as I survey the players on the Colts.

My eyes find Hayes immediately.

He's such a douche. Skating like he owns the ice.

Spoiler alert: he doesn't.

I do.

He needs to be knocked down a peg.

Lucky for him, I'm up for the job.

I can't get the image out of my head—Hayes leaning in too close to Molly, his hand brushing her waist. Molly's polite but stiff smile, her annoyance evident to anyone paying attention.

The image is burned in my brain, fueling my anger.

I clench my hands. I'm ready to fight.

Thirty minutes later, the game begins.

Right off the bat, it's fast and physical.

We score, and then they score.

My frustration is at an all-time high every time Hayes is near, which is often. I focus on playing, though, trying desperately not to let him goad me.

That's what he wants to do, after all. He wants to get into my head. Fuck with me, and then, in turn, throw me off my game.

I don't let it happen.

Well, that is, until the third period.

The puck is still in play. I chase it down the boards. My focus is razor-sharp as I speed across the ice.

Out of nowhere, Hayes blindsides me with an elbow to the head, knocking me down. Pain shoots through me as I scramble to get back up on my feet.

The whistle blows for a penalty.

Fuck this.

I don't hesitate to charge him. Dropping my gloves, I close the distance. Hayes swings first, but I dodge it easily. Pulling back my arm, I punch, my fist connecting squarely with Hayes's jaw. Hayes staggers.

The whistle blows and blows and blows.

I grin at his bleeding lips. "Not smiling now, dick."

All around me, I hear the crowd erupt into chaos.

They love this shit, and I'm about to give them the show of a lifetime.

I land another punch, but it's not long before arms pull me back. Looking over my shoulder, I see Dane.

The deafening chants from the crowd are a mix of cheers and boos.

My chest heaves as I glare at Hayes, who is currently being dragged to the bench by his own teammates, a hand pressed to his jaw.

At least I wiped the smug-ass grin off his face.

That thought alone makes me smile.

I'm escorted to the penalty box.

Coach is pissed.

Oh, well. No one touches my little Hex but me.

"Wilde," Coach barks as I slump onto the bench, peeling off my helmet. "What the hell was that?"

I don't answer.

Instead, I stare straight ahead.

Coach wants me to feel bad.

Fuck that.

I have shit to feel bad for. Hayes had it coming.

Even with the scuffle, the game ends in a victory.

I head to the locker room, still fuming and amped up.

Once inside, Mason throws an arm around me, clapping me on the shoulder. "Nice punch."

"How about maybe save it for after the game next time, huh?" It's Dane who speaks this time. "*The Redville Post* hates when they don't have an exclusive, and I just bought their stock."

I laugh, shaking my head. "Yeah, sure, asshole."

I have a feeling that he'd encourage me if he knew why I punched Hayes. Then he'd punch me himself for catching the feels for his sister.

As if he heard my thoughts, Mason leans in, his voice dropping. "You finally ready to admit it?"

"Admit what?"

"You know what," he deadpans.

I don't reply.

But Mason, being the persistent dick that he is, isn't ready to drop it. "Come on, you can't tell me this isn't about Molly—"

"It's not." I sidestep him and head for the showers.

I need to fucking cool off.

A few minutes later, the hot water pounds down on my shoulders.

It helps loosen the tension from the game, but it doesn't stop the voice that keeps screaming in my head that Mason is right.

This has everything to do with Molly.

Obviously.

By the time I'm ready to leave, I'm fucking exhausted and can't wait to relax. I love flying home after a game. Nothing like sleeping in your own bed. I have no desire to party or celebrate, and for the first time in a long time, I'm not going to.

I'm done being the guy everyone expects me to be.

As I approach the plane, my phone vibrates in my pocket. I pull it out and glance at the screen.

A message from Molly.

Molly: Thanks for kicking his ass for me.

I shake my head and laugh.

Hudson: He had it coming.

Three dots appear, and I wait for her reply.

Molly: But next time, try not to get benched over me. It's not worth the risk. Dane is insufferable when he loses.

My lips spread into a smile.

Hudson: No promises.

As I pocket my phone, any remaining tension slips away. Whatever this thing is between us, it might not be simple . . . But I want to try.

chapter forty-eight

BREAKING NEWS
"Wild Brawl: Hudson Wilde Throws First Punch in Finals Showdown"

By: Taylor Davis

The tension between Redville Saints right wing Hudson Wilde and Colts defenseman Hayes Anderson reached a boiling point game at game two of the eastern conference finals last night, leading to a brutal fight that had fans on their feet and referees scrambling to break it up.

The clash began early in the third period after a hard hit near the boards that left tempers flaring. Replays show Wilde throwing a killer punch, sending Hayes stumbling. Blood on the ice, furious shouts, and a deafening roar from the crowd set the scene for what may go down as one of the most talked-about fights of the season.

Wilde was given a five-minute penalty for fighting, with Hayes earning the same.

Despite his time in the box, Wilde returned to the ice with a vengeance, assisting on a critical third-period goal that secured the Saints win.

Wilde's response was characteristically vague when asked about the fight postgame: *"Sometimes, you've got to stand your ground."*

Fan Comments:

@Saints4Life: Hudson Wilde is a LEGEND. Did you SEE that punch? Hayes had no idea what hit him.

@HockeyChick99: I swear Hudson looked like he wanted to murder Hayes. Never seen him so furious. Blood on the ice, man. 10/10 entertainment.

@ColtsForever: Hudson Wilde threw the first punch, as usual. Typical thug move. Should've been ejected.

@RedHotFan: Not condoning fighting, but . . . did y'all notice how wild Hudson looked? Like, eyes blazing, pure rage. • •

@HockeyDad47: I don't let my kids watch fights, but even I was on my feet for that one. Wilde doesn't play around.

@SpilledTeaSports: Rumor has it there's beef between Hayes and Hudson off the ice. What's the story, boys?. • •

@RedvilleRiot: "Sometimes you've got to stand your ground." Translation: don't mess with Hudson Wilde.

chapter forty-nine

Hudson

IT'S BEEN DAYS SINCE THE FIGHT, AND I'M LOSING MY FUCKING mind.

I've been trying to keep it cool. No fights.

Apparently, the media relations team doesn't want my face plastered everywhere.

Don't cause trouble.

Easier said than done.

It hasn't been easy to ignore Hayes. Every game he's in my face. It's a pain in the ass, but I have no choice.

My life is boring as hell. I practice, play and stay home.

My walls are closing in. The TV, my phone, even my fridge—it all feels like it's mocking me.

And knowing Hayes is still walking around without a permanent scratch on his smug face? It makes my blood boil all over again.

But then, there's Molly.

She's been slipping over late at night when no one's watching.

We've been sneaking around for a while now, and somehow, it's the only thing keeping me sane.

Tonight, she shows up with a bag of takeout and a glare that could make a lesser man crumple.

"You're a moron, you know that?" she says, dropping the bag on my counter.

I smirk, leaning against the doorway. "Nice to see you, too, Hex."

She rolls her eyes, shrugging out of her jacket and tossing it over a chair. She's wearing one of those fitted sweaters that clings in all the right places, and I have to bite back a comment that'll only piss her off.

"Seriously, Hudson," she continues, unpacking the food. "What were you thinking? Fighting Hayes?"

"What was I thinking?" I repeat, crossing my arms. "I was thinking that prick had it coming."

She shoots me a look, sharp and unimpressed. "You risked the playoffs, your team's chance, because Hayes looked at me funny?"

"Funny?" I scoff, my temper flaring. "He didn't just look at you, Molly. He was all over you."

"And I handled it," she says, her tone firm.

"Not fast enough," I mutter under my breath.

"What was that?" she asks, narrowing her eyes.

"Nothing," I say quickly, grabbing a pair of chopsticks from the counter. "Let's eat before the food gets cold."

We sit on the couch, eating in comfortable silence for a while. She curls her legs under her, looking far too relaxed for someone who's spent the past five minutes yelling at me.

"You're lucky no one knows why you fought him," she says eventually, breaking the quiet.

"Yeah, well, if they did, I'd be in even deeper shit," I admit, leaning back against the cushions.

Her gaze flicks to mine, something softening in her expression. "You really didn't have to do that, you know."

"Maybe not." I shrug. "But I wanted to."

She shakes her head, but a hint of a smile tugs at her lips. "You're impossible."

"You say that like it's a bad thing."

"It is."

"Is it?" I ask, leaning closer, my voice dropping lower.

Her breath hitches, and I swear her cheeks flush, but she quickly schools her expression. "Stop looking at me like that."

"Like what?"

"Like you're about to kiss me," she says, her tone a mix of exasperation and something else entirely.

"And if I was?"

She opens her mouth to respond, but whatever comeback she has dies on her lips as I lean in and kiss her.

It starts slow, soft even, but it doesn't stay that way for long. Her fingers tangle in my hair, pulling me closer, and I swear the world outside this apartment ceases to exist. No noise, no people, no team, no past.

It's just her. Just the taste of her lips, the warmth of her skin, and the way she matches me beat for beat like she's been waiting for this as long as I have.

The second her hands slide up to tangle in my hair, something snaps. A current rushes between us, hot and electric, and I lose any hope of taking this slow.

I deepen the kiss, angling her face as I press closer, my hands trailing down to her waist, anchoring her against me.

Her lips part, a soft gasp escaping her, and it's all the permission I need. The kiss turns desperate. Her fingers tug at my hair, and it's like a shot of adrenaline driving me to pull her closer and feel every inch of her against me.

By the time we finally pull apart, my chest is heaving, and her breathing is uneven. Her lips are slightly swollen, her cheeks flushed.

I take a moment to just stare at her, trying to memorize the way she looks right now.

"You're still a moron," she mutters, her voice breathy.

"Yeah." I grin. "But I'm your moron."

She groans, shoving me back against the cushions. "You're impossible."

"Yet you're still here," I point out, laughing.

She doesn't reply, but the faint smile on her lips is enough to tell me I'm not entirely wrong.

chapter fifty

Hudson

Hudson: I'm officially out of jail. Thank fuck we won this round. Coach says I'm free to roam the world again.

Molly: Did you have to do someone a "favor," or did they let you out for good behavior?

Hudson: No favor. Just my natural charm and undeniable greatness.

Molly: Ah, so they finally gave up trying to fix you.

Hudson: Or they realized they can't hold me back. I'm like a majestic bird, Hex. You can't cage this.

Molly: More like a stubborn pigeon that keeps wandering into traffic.

Hudson: A majestic pigeon, thank you very much.

Molly: Sure, Wilde. Congrats on being a free man again. Try not to embarrass yourself in public this time.

Hudson: Who, me? Never. I'm a role model now.

Molly: That's horrifying.

Hudson: You're just jealous.

Molly: Keep telling yourself that, jailbird.

Hudson: 🐦

Molly: What is that?

Hudson: A pigeon. For accuracy.

Molly: 😂 You're impossible.

Hudson: Hmm . . . yet you keep texting me back.

Molly: It's called charity work.

Hudson: Admit it, you'd miss me if I ever went to real jail.

Molly: I'd survive.

Hudson: Liar.

Molly: 🙄 Whatever. Don't do anything stupid.

Hudson: Can't make any promises.

chapter fifty-one

Hudson

IT'S BEEN A LONG TWO WEEKS, AND MY MIND IS A MESS.

Tomorrow's the championship game. The culmination of everything we've worked for all season.

The hotel room is quiet. The only sound is the hum of the air conditioner and the occasional muffled laugh from the hallway. I'm lying on the bed, staring at the ceiling, trying to will myself to sleep.

It's not working.

I should feel confident.

I should feel ready.

But instead, my brain won't stop running through every possible scenario—the good, the bad, and the downright catastrophic.

A soft knock on the door startles me out of my spiral.

I glance over, my pulse kicking up. Only one person would knock that way.

"Molly," I say quietly, opening the door just enough to see her standing there.

She's in sweatpants and an oversized hoodie, her hair loose around her shoulders.

"Can I come in?" she asks, her voice barely above a whisper.

I step aside, holding the door open. "You know this is probably against a hundred rules, right?"

She shrugs, slipping past me. "You're not exactly a rule follower, Wilde."

"Fair point," I say, shutting the door behind her.

She walks into the room like she's been here a hundred times before, her presence instantly grounding me.

"Couldn't sleep?" she asks, perching on the edge of the bed.

"Something like that," I admit, sitting down beside her.

She studies me, her sharp green eyes missing nothing. "You're nervous."

"Am not," I say automatically, leaning back on my hands.

"You're a terrible liar," she counters, crossing her arms.

I exhale heavily, running a hand through my hair. "Fine. Maybe I'm a little nervous."

She raises an eyebrow, clearly not buying it.

"Okay, a lot nervous," I amend, leaning forward and resting my elbows on my knees. "It's the championship, Molly. Everything's riding on tomorrow. What if I screw it up?"

"You won't," she says, her tone so steady it makes me believe her, if only for a moment.

"You don't know that," I mutter, shaking my head.

"I do," she says firmly. "You've worked your ass off for this, Hudson. You're not going to screw it up."

Her confidence in me is almost overwhelming. I glance at her, the knot in my chest loosening just a fraction. "What if I don't know how to turn my brain off?"

She tilts her head. "What can I do to help?"

I can't help the grin that tugs at my lips. "I can think of a few ways," I say, my voice dipping into something lower, something teasing.

She rolls her eyes, but the faint blush on her cheeks gives her away. "I'm being serious, Hudson."

"So am I," I reply, leaning closer.

She gives me a look, but she doesn't pull away. Instead, she shifts, her legs brushing against mine. "You want me to distract you?"

"Wouldn't hurt," I say, smirking.

She narrows her eyes at me, then slowly, deliberately, she straddles my lap.

My breath catches as her hands rest on my shoulders, her touch warm and familiar.

"Like this?" she asks, her voice soft but with an edge of mischief.

"Perfect," I murmur, my hands settling on her waist.

She leans in, her lips brushing against mine in a kiss that starts slow and sweet but quickly deepens. Her fingers thread through my hair, and for the first time all night, my mind goes blissfully quiet.

She pulls back slightly, her forehead resting against mine. "Feeling better?"

"Much," I whisper, my grip tightening on her waist.

She smiles, and it's the kind of smile that makes me think, just for a second, that maybe everything really will be okay.

For the rest of the night, I don't think about the game, the pressure, or the noise waiting for me tomorrow.

There's only her.

And it's enough.

More than enough.

chapter fifty-two

Hudson

Molly: Good luck today, Wilde.

Hudson: Wow. Encouragement? From you? Did hell freeze over?

Molly: Don't get used to it. I just don't want to hear you whine later if you lose.

Hudson: If I lose? Hex, please. I'm a sure thing.

I'm not, but I don't let myself freak out over it. I know she's kidding with her attitude. The woman helped me out last night. Calmed the storm inside me and didn't leave until she was one hundred percent sure of it.

Molly: 😠 You're pacing, aren't you?

Hudson: No.

Molly: You're totally pacing.

Hudson: How do you even know that?

Molly: Because you get cockier when you're nervous.

Hudson: I'm not nervous.

Molly: Hudson.

beautiful collide

Hudson: Okay, fine. Maybe I'm pacing a little. Happy?

Molly: You'll be fine. You always are.

Hudson: Yeah?

Molly: Yeah. You're Hudson Wilde. The hockey god, remember?

Hudson: You're really bad at hating me.

Molly: I still do.

Hudson: You're kind of a softy when you want to be.

Molly: Delete that thought immediately.

Hudson: Too late. It's burned into my brain.

Molly: 😐

Molly: Look, just breathe, okay? You're good at this. The best, probably. I know you don't need to hear it from me, but in case you do . . . You've got this.

Hudson: . . .

Hudson: Thanks, Hex.

Molly: Don't make it weird.

Hudson: Too late. I'm gonna dedicate my first goal to you.

Molly: If you do, I'll never speak to you again.

Hudson: You're obsessed with me, so we both know that's not true.

Molly: Focus on the game, Wilde.

Hudson: I will.

Hudson: Thanks for grounding me, Hex.

Molly: Someone has to. Now go win a championship, or I'll never let you live it down.

Hudson: Yes, ma'am. For you, anything.

chapter fifty-three

Hudson

M Y ENTIRE BODY HUMS WITH ADRENALINE, BUT MY FOCUS IS razor-sharp.

Whoever wins this game wins the Cup.

The noise inside the arena is deafening. The crowd roars with excitement. My lungs burn, and my heart pounds.

Focus.

You've trained for this. Don't screw it up.

I take a deep breath, steadying myself against any doubt that can creep in.

It's complete chaos. But it's also what I live for.

This is the moment. Make it count.

The puck drops into play, and everyone explodes into motion. I tear down the ice after Aiden. He's ahead of me, skating like his life depends on it, and in all fairness, it does because the Vegas Aces defenders are also hot on his tail.

"Here," I shout as I cut toward the net.

Aiden glances back, and with a flick of his wrist, sends the puck flying toward me. I receive the pass, and then I'm off, weaving past the Aces defender and firing it back to Aiden.

There's no time to think and no place for error. We have practiced our whole lives for this moment.

Aiden doesn't hesitate. He pulls back and takes the shot. The goalie reaches out, but he's not fast enough.

The light flashes red.

The horn blares.

Holy fucking shit. Did we just—

And for a second, everything goes silent in my head.

Then everything comes rushing back as the crowd erupts.

We did it.

Again.

Holy fuck. We did.

Back-to-back. Holy shit. This is real.

I skate over to Aiden and grab him. "Hell, yeah!"

Everyone rushes together to celebrate. All my teammates.

I'm soon surrounded by a rush of hugs and shouts.

It's a beautiful thing.

I see Mason and throw my arms around him, and then I find Dane, who actually smiles this year.

Dane's happiness hits me harder than I expect. He's a different person these days. Seeing him like this makes this victory even sweeter.

From there, everything is a blur.

Once in the locker room, it's complete chaos.

"Back-to-back. Feels like I'm never gonna stop smiling," Mason says, grinning ear to ear. I can't help but laugh because I feel the same way. The only thing that will make this better is seeing Molly.

Soon.

Not soon enough.

Because as much as I'm desperate to be with her, I still have team business.

The press.

Here we go. Plaster on a smile.

The faster you get this done with, the sooner you get to Molly.

Like vultures waiting for their kill, they swarm to us, all hungry for our story.

Cameras flash. Then microphones are shoved in our faces.

"Wilde! Over here," one of them shouts.

I sigh. It's the nature of the beast, sure, and Coach will expect me to play nice, but I really want to escape.

Mason, on the other hand, is eating it up. Dane hides. Aiden is indifferent. Me? I'm itching to leave.

"Hudson, how does it feel to win back-to-back Cups so early in your career?"

Give them what they want so I can get the hell out of here.

"Amazing." I force a smile. "It's what we worked all season for. Every game. Every practice . . . it all led to this."

"Can you walk us through that final play, Aiden?"

I step back, letting Aiden step forward. "It was a great team effort. One that we'll celebrate tonight, and then we get back to work."

And that's Aiden Slate—totally avoiding a question yet appeasing the audience all at the same time. *Fucking legend.*

The rest of the questions are muffled by the sound of our celebration. I answer them like I'm on autopilot.

When the reporters finally leave, Mason strides up to me, a silly as fuck grin on his face.

"You ready to hit the bar after this?" he asks.

"Absol—" I'm about to respond when Mason sprays me with champagne.

Ass.

I wipe the liquid off my face, then head to the showers. I'm ready to leave and get this party started. Coach wanted us to talk to the press, and we did. I answered all their questions—but now I'm ready to find her.

Molly.

Since we hooked up again, I've wanted to claim her, but seeing as Molly wants to keep this a secret, I have no choice. So, while I want to celebrate, it sucks that I can't be with her in public.

An hour later, the whole team heads out to hit up a club.

The energy is insane. Music pounds through my body as I head to the VIP area.

Once there, Mason and I go shot for shot. I might be having a great time, but my eyes keep searching her out.

The alcohol burns, but it doesn't dull the edge. If anything, it sharpens my focus to find Molly.

Then I see her.

The sight of her stops me cold.

She's near the back of the room, talking to Cassidy and Josie. She's dressed for sin—a tiny black dress—one I want to rip off her. She's gorgeous. A siren. I'd gladly sail to my death for a chance with her.

People come and go, but for me, she's the only person in the room.

She doesn't see me at first, but that's fine. It gives me a moment to stare unnoticed.

I watch her laugh, and I'm jealous.

Jealous that I can't be the one making her laugh in public, that I can't just walk up to her and claim her the way I want to.

I put my drink down and weave through the crowd. When I'm only a few feet away, our gaze locks.

Her eyes widen when she sees me, but she recovers quickly, arching a brow and putting on the playful facade I've come to know recently.

She makes my heart race faster than a game.

"Hex." I lean in so she can hear me.

She raises an eyebrow, her lips curving into a smirk. "Wilde." Her tone is playful, but there's something else there, something softer, something she doesn't show often, and I feel blessed she's choosing to show it to me.

I grin, eating up the last remaining space between us. "You celebrating with me tonight?"

"I'm here, aren't I?" she teases, but her heavy gaze pulls me in. It feels like we're the only people in the room.

I reach for her hand, brushing my fingers against hers. It's subtle enough not to draw attention. "You know what I mean, Molly."

"I do, but how?"

"Come with me." I tug her away from the main room and into a back alcove hidden from any prying eyes. She hesitates for half a second before stepping into the darkness with me.

"I've been thinking about you all night," I admit.

Molly looks up at me, her eyes searching my face. "You just won the Cup, and you're thinking about me?"

"Yeah." I brush a strand of hair behind her ear. "Because none of this feels complete until I'm with you."

Her breath hitches, and for a second, neither of us moves. Then, slowly, she leans in, and her lips brush against mine.

Everything fades away. It's just us.

chapter fifty-four

Molly

IT'S DIMLY LIT BACK HERE. EVERYTHING IS HAZY, CAUSING MY eyes to have a hard time adjusting to how dark it is.

It's almost too dark, but maybe that's fitting for what this is.

It's funny that I'm not afraid.

Usually, I would be.

Darkness and isolation terrify me, but not now. Not here. Not with him. *Never with him.*

The little girl inside me wants to cry out in fear, but the grown Molly, wrapped up in Hudson's arms as he whispers, *he misses me*, is okay.

I'm more than okay, actually. I'm excited because despite being tucked away in a shadowy pocket far from prying eyes, I'm here with Hudson. How does he make everything feel so safe yet dangerous at the same time?

After a few more seconds, we separate, and Hudson steps back, leaning casually against the wall. He crosses his arms at his chest, and his black T-shirt clings to him in all the right places.

The sight of him makes my heart race. He's a shot of coffee to my system. A live wire ready to explode.

"Took you long enough to get here tonight." His trademark smirk tugs at the corner of his mouth. There it is. That stupid, cocky smirk should annoy me, but somehow, it only makes me want him more.

"I've been here the whole time. You just couldn't find me." I shrug.

"Damn, Hex. You always have to make things difficult." Despite his words, I can hear the humor in his voice.

Difficult? Who's he kidding? He loves the chase. And we both know it.

"Do you know how hard it is to sneak away without Cassidy and Josie interrogating me?" I fire back, loving the playful banter Hudson and I are known for.

Hudson pushes back off the wall, stepping closer. The dim light from the main part of the club illuminates his face. He's smiling down at me in a way that quickens my pulse. This man does crazy things to me. Makes me feel alive and like anything is possible.

Like I'm the only person in the world for him.

"It's worth it, though." His hand brushes against mine, and it sends a shiver up my spine.

Such a small gesture, yet it has the ability to turn me into mush.

How does he do that? It's just a touch, but it sets my entire body on fire.

I lean into his warmth, wanting desperately to close any distance between us. When I feel the heat of his body against mine, a sigh escapes my mouth. "It is."

"Then why are we sneaking around?" he asks, his voice low and, if I'm not mistaken, sad.

I wish I had an answer. But I don't. Other than to say Dane. I'm not sure how Dane would respond, but in truth, I'm not ready to find out. I don't want to ruin this, whatever this is with Hudson, so if that means keeping us in our bubble a little longer, so be it.

I shrug. "Because if Dane finds out, he'll kill you." My answer is matter-of-fact, but it's the truth. Murder wouldn't be off the table for Dane.

Sucks.

If Dane is one thing, it's protective.

Too protective. Sometimes, it feels like I'll always be the little sister he had to save.

Even now that I'm an adult, he still takes his role as my guardian very seriously. "Also, let's not kid ourselves. It's not just Dane." I roll my eyes despite the fact that he can't see it since I'm pressed against his chest. "It's the whole team. They'd never let us live it down."

"True," he concedes with a laugh. "But you like sneaking around. Admit it." His voice dips into a teasing whisper.

Do I?

Or do I just tell myself that's the best alternative?

I bite my lip, fighting back a laugh. "Maybe I just don't want to be alone, and you're the best option."

"Mason or Wolfe aren't up to your standards?" He chuckles. I love the sound. It makes me feel warm inside.

No one else comes close to you, Hudson.

Not even close.

His hands tighten around my waist, pulling me flush against his body. I can feel the hard contours of every muscle he has. Everything in the club fades away. It's just us at this moment.

This.

This is why I can't stay away.

"Fuck, I want you so bad right now," Hudson groans.

"Who knew you were into that kind of thing."

"With you, I'm into anything I can get."

It shouldn't be normal for my heart to beat this fast. If someone put a heart monitor on me, they'd probably think I ran a marathon when, in truth, Hudson makes me feel this way.

The touch of his fingers under my jaw, as he tilts my head up to meet his gaze, makes my breath catch.

Once I'm looking at him, he brushes a strand of loose hair from my face. His touch is light, and it lingers until goose bumps break out against my skin.

Just as he leans in to kiss me again, something vibrates between us.

Hudson's phone.

Mason: Where the fuck did you go?

Mason: Come on, man. We're supposed to be celebrating.

"Better get back, or he will never stop," he mutters, stepping back reluctantly. "Mason is such a cockblock."

I hate how much I miss him already, and he hasn't even gone.

I nod, trying to mask the pang of frustration in my chest. "Go. Before they send a search party."

"He would." He shakes his head, his gaze lingering on me. He's not ready to leave me. Good that it's not just me. I'm not ready for him to leave either.

"This isn't over." He leans forward, brushing his lips over mine. I open for him, sweeping my tongue against his. I melt into his body, savoring the feeling, knowing it will end soon. When he finally does pull back, a groan escapes my mouth.

I want to say *no, don't leave me*, but I don't. As much as I want to be with him, I'm not ready to give up my control to him. My walls need to stay up. I can't let him in, even if I want to. *Even if I need to.*

The movement of his body pulls me out of my thoughts. "I have to go." His voice is soft and resigned. He doesn't want to go. It should make me feel better to know I'm not the only one who hates this and is confused, but it doesn't.

I nod. "Have fun with Mason."

"I won't," he responds. I expect a laugh, but when none comes, I see he's not joking. He won't. I narrow my eyes. He's serious that he won't have fun without me. His answer shocks me, but at the same time, it does make sense. What I'm starting to realize is that Hudson is not who I thought he was.

I wait a few beats before stepping out of the alcove, forcing my expression into something neutral as I make my way back to the VIP section. No one seems to have noticed I was gone, and I slip into my seat, plastering on a smile like nothing happened.

The night stretches on, but I can't stop noticing how easy it is for everyone else. Josie is curled up in Dane's lap, laughing at something Mason said, her arm draped over his shoulders like it belongs there. Cassidy leans into Aiden, her fingers casually tracing patterns on his knee as they talk.

It looks effortless. Comfortable.

And it makes me wonder—what would it be like if Hudson and I didn't have to sneak off to shadowy corners or keep our touches fleeting and hidden? If we could just be together like everyone else.

Would it feel easier? Harder? I don't know. All I know is that this—stolen moments and fleeting touches—is exhausting. It's draining me more than I expected.

As if on cue, Hudson passes by me again, heading toward the bar.

His hand skims mine for the briefest second, the touch so subtle I'm almost certain I've made it up. But when he looks back at me, I know I didn't.

My breath catches in my lungs.

How does he do this to me?

Why does he take my breath away?

I exhale, sinking deeper into my seat, my gaze following him even as he disappears into the crowd.

For now, this is what we have. Stolen moments. Fleeting touches.

It's not perfect. It's barely enough.

But it's enough to keep me here. At least for now.

chapter fifty-five

Hudson

THANK FUCK.

It's finally time to leave, and not a moment too soon.

As the night winds down and the celebration comes to an end, Mason is still itching to continue the night.

Of course he is.

Mason—the fucker—has enough energy to power a small city, and right now, his life's mission is dragging me along for the ride.

It's the last thing I want to do.

Yet the man is relentless.

Don't get me started on the guilt trip he's throwing my way. I should be earning hotel points by now.

But, man, is he laying it on thick. I guess since everyone else already left, I'm his only option. Which is bullshit, because there are nineteen other guys who I'm sure would be more than happy to party with him.

Why the hell am I the unlucky one?

I trail Mason as he strolls out of the exit, and with each step, I try to think of a way to get out of it.

There's only one place I want to be, and it's not taking shots with Mason's drunk ass. It's alone with Molly.

I shove my hands deep into my pockets and continue to head out of the club and into the main area of the casino of the hotel we are staying at.

It's complete sensory overload right now. The flashing lights. Chiming slot machines. Usually, I'd take it all in stride. Hell, a few years ago, I'd be right there with Mason, looking to continue the festivities, but right now, it feels like a distraction that's keeping me from where I really want to be.

Speaking of Mason, the idiot is really making an ass of himself. From the corner of my eye, I see what he's up to, and all I can say is . . .

Wow.

Either he's the biggest idiot in the world, or he's drunker than I realized. As he walks through the casino, he's attempting some sort of dance move—if you can call it that—and failing miserably.

I cringe as he flails his arms and swivels his hips, and don't even get me started on the crowd he's amassing.

A crowd is forming and not in a good way. One woman has her cell phone trained on him, and it looks like she's deciding whether she's going to film him and send it to TMZ or call security.

I walk right past him because shit, I don't need to be photographed with him. It's bad enough Coach thinks I'm a moron. I can't imagine what he would do if the press got embarrassing pictures of me.

"Where're you going, Wilde?"

I halt my steps, turning around to look at him.

When I do, I can't help but laugh. The man looks like an idiot. He has his button-down shirt over his head like a bandanna, and now he's just in an undershirt. I'm half expecting him to grab a stick and start a limbo line.

As bad as this is, I should consider him lucky because I'm not sure the hotel would look fondly at him if he were bare chested walking through the slot machines.

"We're calling it a night, Goodie."

Mason mutters something under his breath, but doesn't respond loud enough for me to hear.

"Come on, the elevator is this way." I walk over to him like he's a cow I'm corralling. It takes far too long to get to the elevator and even longer to walk Mason to his room.

When he finally stumbles through his door, I don't even wait for a goodbye or a thank you. Instead, I shake my head and hope he doesn't choke on his own tongue tonight.

That shit's on him.

A better man would tuck him in and make sure he doesn't die, but alas, I'm not that nice of a guy.

I stand outside his room for a brief second, and when no sound is heard, I head to my own room.

An idea strikes me when I'm standing outside my door. I turn the knob, push it open, and then close it right away.

Why did I do this? So if Dane, whose room is right next to mine, happens to be listening, he thinks I'm home.

I'm not going home, though.

Nope. I have somewhere else I have to be.

More pressing matters.

Molly.

She's the only thing I've been able to think about since the final buzzer, and I'm done waiting.

I move quietly down the hallway, pausing when I hear a noise. I turn around to see if anyone I know is coming, but it's nothing. Nobody is coming. Good.

Taking a steadying breath, I make my way to the far end of the hall and stop in front of Molly's door. I knock lightly, glancing over my shoulder to make sure no one is around.

My heart might beat out of my chest as I wait for her to answer.

Even though I saw her earlier, this feels exciting. Sneaking around, knowing her brother might catch us, adds a layer of thrill that I can't ignore.

The door opens just a crack, and there she is. Her face is barely visible. Only a faint glow of the hallway lights illuminates her face.

"Took you long enough," she whispers, stepping aside to let me in.

The corners of her mouth twitch, and my chest tightens at the sight.

She really is perfect. A dream come true in her oversized sweatshirt that falls on her bare thighs.

Fuck, she's stunning.

Tempting.

And mine. *Or at least she should be.* All in good time.

I grin as I slip inside, the door clicking shut behind me. "Had to make sure Mason didn't die. It's a hard job, but someone had to do it. Plus, I had to make sure Dane was sleeping. Dane would kill me if he knew I was sneaking into your room."

She rolls her eyes, crossing her arms. "I'm not a teenager sneaking boys into my parents' house, Hudson."

"No," I tease, stepping closer, "but you're the girl who could ruin me with one word to her brother. That makes you kind of dangerous, Hex."

"Good." A small smile tugs at her lips. "Keeps you on your toes." Her voice is light, but I can hear the edge to it. There's a challenge in the way she talks.

The room is dimly lit, music playing softly from her phone. On the table by the couch sits a bottle of champagne and two glasses, the setup casual but thoughtful.

"Are you trying to seduce me?" I pick up the bottle, lifting it in the air.

"Figured you might need one more drink to celebrate." She flops onto the couch with an easy grin.

Hell yeah, I do. How did I ever get so lucky?

Tilting the bottle so that it doesn't spray, I pop the cork. Of course it doesn't go smoothly. Why would it?

Champagne sprays out everywhere, drenching my hand and the floor.

I wipe my hand on my pants, and Molly claps, mocking me. "Look at you, full of surprises."

"Don't act so impressed." I pour us each a glass. "We both know I'm the whole package."

She snorts into her glass. "You're a package, all right."

"I have a package, you mean?"

"Hmm." She crinkles her nose. "That's not at all what I said."

"Ouch."

She rolls her eyes. "Fine. You have a big package. Happy?"

"Yes. Immensely."

She starts to laugh, and the sound makes me laugh harder. All the tension melts away at seeing her happy. Being with Molly like this makes everything feel easier.

Champagne continues to flow, and at some point, she puts on a playlist of songs, and I find myself pulling her off the couch.

"Dance with me," I say, holding out a hand.

"You've had too much to drink," she teases, but her hand slides into mine anyway.

"And you haven't had enough," I counter, twirling her around the room.

Her unrestrained and carefree smile is brighter than the sun. She's so different from the first time we met. She's peaceful when she's with me. The knowledge of that hits me square in the chest.

Seeing her like this feels like a privilege, one I promise myself not to take lightly.

I don't care how clumsy my moves are or if the room spins a little when we move, all I care about is watching her at this moment. Soaking up these moments with her. Seeing her like this—with me . . . it's better than any moment in my life.

beautiful collide

When the song slows, so do we. Her hands linger on my shoulders, and I slide mine to her waist, pulling her closer.

"You know . . ." I brush my lips against her neck. "I think this is the happiest I've ever been."

Her body stiffens in my arms. "You don't mean that."

"I do," I say with conviction, meaning every word. "Out there, on the ice, with the team—it's amazing. But this? Being here with you? That's something else."

She doesn't respond. Instead, she tilts her head up, moves to be on tiptoes, and brushes her lips to mine. The kiss sends my heart racing all over again, and it's not from adrenaline. It's her.

The kiss becomes more heated, my chest heaving by the time she pulls away from me.

"I need you." Her voice sounds raspy, desperate, and she pulls me closer, her hands grasping at the zipper of my pants and pulling it down.

Molly is never this forward, but I welcome it as she grabs my cock from inside my pants and frees me from the tight confines of my briefs. Once I'm fully exposed to her, she strokes me from root to tip.

A drop of cum beads on the tip of my dick, and she does something I don't expect. Her finger swipes over the liquid, and she raises her hand to her mouth and licks her finger.

Holy shit.

If that's not enough to have my excitement in overdrive, Molly drops to her knees.

"Fuck," I groan as she takes me in her mouth, and all my words are lost.

Holy shit, does this feel good.

Molly is apparently an expert with her tongue.

She slides it up and down my shaft, making sure to run it up the vein in my dick before swirling it over the crown.

My legs almost buckle beneath me as she pushes forward, my cock now hitting the back of her throat.

Placing my hands on the back of her head, I start to fuck her throat in earnest. Her small hands grab my ass as I do. Nothing in the world has ever felt this good. The way her throat contracts every time I push farther in makes stars burst in my eyes.

I'm going to come if I don't stop. Which is something I want to do, but not in her mouth. I want to see my cum drip out of her freshly fucked pussy.

I pull back with a pop, my wet dick hard and ready for more.

"Get naked, and then I want you on the bed, Hex."

She follows my commands, stripping her dress off and getting naked on the bed.

"Spread your legs. Let me see you."

A soft blush colors her face, but she does what I ask, spreading her knees apart until her pussy is on full display.

"Fuck," I groan, taking my dick in my hand and stroking myself. "You look good enough to eat." So I do. I pull her parted legs, making it so she's almost hanging off the bed, then I drop to the floor and bury myself in her cunt.

I devour her.

Feed off her essence.

Lick and suck her clit until she's a quivering mess, her desire dripping down her thighs.

"I need to fuck you. Need to feel this wet pussy clinging to my dick as you come."

"So fuck me already."

I press myself against her heat.

"Condom?"

"No. I'm on the pill."

Fuck yeah.

Despite seeing how wet she is, it's got nothing on how it feels to rub my crown over her drenched skin. I swirl the head over her clit, then at her entrance, collecting the moisture.

Her hips wiggle at the sensation, and I run myself down to where she needs me most. I can't wait to sink inside her, so I don't.

I slam into her hard and fast, and she gasps when I bottom out inside her.

A moan escapes her mouth, and I pull my dick out until the top hovers just outside of her. "Please, Wilde."

I swirl my head around her opening again, pushing just the tip in. Her greedy pussy quivers, trying to suck me in, but I don't let her. I just continue to torture her.

"Please what, Hex?"

"Please stop torturing me."

"Only if you watch us."

I meet her stare.

"What do you mean?"

"Watch as I fuck you. Watch as your greedy pussy takes my cock."

She lifts up onto her elbows and tilts her chin down to get a better view.

Once I know she can see, I let myself admire the sight too. I swirl my dick one more time and then push forward, loving the sight of her pussy lips spreading for my cock as I thrust all the way to the hilt, and I disappear inside her.

I pull back out, and when I do, my dick jerks at the sight of my gleaming, cream-covered cock.

"Hex. Do you see that?"

She nods, her mouth half open, and I thrust back in. This time, a gasp escapes.

I continue to fuck her like that.

Time stands still as her walls quiver around me.

She's close.

My balls tighten.

I'm closer.

My hand reaches down, and I find her clit rubbing it furiously.

She cries out.

Her walls tighten around me. I flick her clit harder and fuck her deeper until my balls feel so tight that I know I'm about to explode, and I do. My dick starts to jerk, cum spilling into her until I fill her up.

Our bodies tremble together as we both catch our breaths, but then reality sets in. I pull out, and she sighs as I do.

"Now what? Do you have to leave?" she asks, and I hate that I do. Unless we're ready to tell Dane about us. Seeing as she just asked the question, I don't think she's ready to tell him yet either.

"I really don't know, Hex."

And I don't. All I know is I don't want to leave yet. So maybe I won't. Perhaps we can keep the night going.

For just a little longer . . .

chapter fifty-six

Molly

Hudson: r u mrrriying me??

Molly: wat

Hudson: u. yes???

Molly: im litcherally next to you, stop texting me

Hudson: no bc ur far away. ur like. a whole 3 inches away.

Molly: u smell like tequila.

Hudson: u smell like mine.

Molly: what is hapening.

Hudson: ELVIS

Molly: elvis???

Hudson: THE GUY IN THE SPARKLY SUIT

Molly: wtf r u talking about

Hudson: his hair is so shiny

Molly: hudson focus

Hudson: FOCUS. yes or no

Molly: stop yelling at me

Hudson: ur not answeringggg

Molly: im THINKING

Hudson: thinking is for nerds. say yes.

Molly: why is ur face in my phone

Hudson: bc im ur hsbnddddiekao

chapter fifty-seven

Molly

MY HEAD POUNDS.

Is there a drumline competition in my head?

Nope. *It's just you drank too much, like an idiot.*

I lift my hands to my eyes and scrub away the remaining sleep. The movement makes me groan. *Ouch.*

Why does everything hurt?

As the world around me comes into focus, the sunlight streaming through the hotel curtains feels less like morning and more like a punishment, each ray stabbing at my already fragile senses. Even breathing too deeply makes me feel sick to my stomach, nausea rolling through me in fresh, horrifying waves.

What the hell happened last night?

I sit up slowly, clutching the sheets to my chest as the room tilts.

The faint smell of champagne lingers, mixed with something sweet—is that cake?

Did I eat cake last night?

My brain is a mess. Pure chaos as I try to think, but the raging hangover I currently have is making that impossible too.

Images, feelings, snippets of words . . . all of it slips away every time I try to remember. I rub my temples, willing the headache to go away so my memories will return.

Okay. Club. Dancing. Sneaking off into the alcove with Hudson. Kissing. Touching. Mason texting.

This is good. I remember the club.

Think.

What else happened?

I left.

Am I just hungover from the club?

No.

I drank more after.

Champagne in the room . . .

My stomach twists uncomfortably as the memories come back to me in flashes.

Hudson showed up at my door.

The bottle of champagne I gave him to open.

Why did I do that again? My headache definitely stems from that poor decision.

I was already drunk before my tongue even touched the bubbles . . .

Okay, what else can I remember?

Think.

His grin.

The kind of grin that spells trouble.

Laughing. I remember laughing so hard my belly hurt.

Music?

Okay, that one throws me for a loop. Did I really play music in my room?

I did, and we danced.

"Shit," I whisper, my eyes widening as a wave of scenes play out in my mind.

Hudson and I stumbled out of the hotel.

We were drunk.

Okay, but where did we go?

I remember we were still high on adrenaline from the Saints winning the Cup.

He threw his arm around me . . .

We weren't hiding. It felt as natural in the world to walk openly with him. Granted, it was the middle of the night, and everyone we knew was already asleep. Maybe that's why we felt so comfortable.

A flash of him beaming down at me, a smile so wide it was big enough to split the Vegas Strip.

A joke.

He made me laugh.

Then he said . . .

"You know—we should just get married. Solve all our problems in one shot."

I laughed, swatting at him like it was a joke. "Yeah, sure, Wilde. Great plan. Nothing could go wrong there."

We wandered the streets.

Neon lights flashed.

Crowds of people partied to all hours of the night.

We giggled like teenagers.

And then we saw it—oh God—an Elvis impersonator. A white chapel.

Hudson looked at me like I was the only person in the world.

"Oh my God."

I shake my head.

"No. No. No."

As if I were watching a movie in my mind, I see myself clear as day . . . A very drunk version of me, swaying and smiling as I say the words . . . *"I do."*

"Holy crap." My hands fly to my face as the final piece of the night slams into me like a freight train.

I jump out of bed, my heart pounding harder than my head as I stumble toward the mirror.

Wow. I look awful.

My reflection matches the outcome of my memories—hair a tangled mess, mascara smudged on my cheeks in a way that screams bad decisions, and a faint red mark on my neck suggesting... Holy shit, are they hickeys? Who gets hickeys anymore?

Me. *Apparently. I do.*

I raise my hand to see if it's not a hickey, but maybe just lipstick smudged when something glints in the morning sunlight.

Ground, please swallow me whole.

What the fuck is that?

My stomach flips as I glance down at my left hand. This has got to be a joke. The universe's cruelest joke because what I see on my hand makes my heart stop beating.

A simple silver band on my ring finger.

"No, no, no, no," I mutter, pacing the room as the memories play back in sharper detail now, each more horrifying than the last.

Hudson's crooked grin as Elvis asks him if he takes me to be his lawfully wedded wife.

Hudson saying yes.

My eyes close. Maybe if I don't open them, it won't be true.

But that's bullshit because I can now see it clear as day: Me saying yes.

I said yes.

What the hell was I thinking?

You weren't thinking. Not at all. Not even a little bit.

In a haze of booze and fits of laughs, I say *I do.*

I blame the champagne.

I blame Hudson's damn smirk. It needs a warning label. One shouldn't be held accountable for what they do when Hudson Wilde smirks at you. You're liable to accidentally get married. *By Elvis.*

I groan. The feeling of his fingers brushing against mine is currently living rent-free in my brain. The heat in his voice when he whispered, "You're mine now, Hex."

I bury my face in my hands. I never stood a chance against him. He's too damn enticing.

Maybe this isn't real.

Maybe this is a horrible alcohol-induced fever dream.

The ring.

If it's all a dream, how did the damn ring end up on my finger?

A pounding on my door snaps me out of my pity party.

I freeze, my heart lurching into my throat. Who the hell is here? Please, not Dane.

"Hex. I know you're in there."

Shit. This is worse than Dane being outside my door, so much worse.

"No, I'm not," I say low enough that I don't think he can hear me through the door.

"Really? Then who's talking?" Another knock. "Just open the door. Wouldn't want your brother to catch me."

Shit. He has a point.

Hopefully, he doesn't remember, and I won't die of embarrassment. Or maybe he'll tell me it was all a joke, and he was just messing with me. A fun prank.

But as I open the door, all my hopes and dreams crash and burn with two words.

"Morning, wife."

chapter fifty-eight

Hudson

THIS SHOULD BE FUN.

I lean against the doorframe, bracing for impact.

There's a good chance this won't go well.

Molly opens the door with a look of pure shock on her face. That and horror. Almost like she might throw something sharp at me, like a knife.

Yeah, she remembers last night.

"Morning, wife." I grin at her, and she meets my grin with a scowl. The face of someone ready to commit homicide.

It's funny.

While she looks like she wants to throttle me, all I can think of is just how much I want to kiss the shit out of her.

"You have got to be kidding me." She crosses her arms at her chest. "Please, for the love of God, tell me this isn't real."

I hold up my left hand, where the cheap silver band rests. "It's real." And I'm brave. Because there's a full risk she will kill me, but

beautiful collide

I still smile broader. "And legally binding, I might add. Pretty sure Elvis signed the paperwork."

Molly groans before dragging a hand down her face. "I hate you so much right now."

I take a step closer, my large frame invading her space.

She's cute when she's mad, and if looks could kill, I'd be currently reading my own obituary.

"Liar." I lean down and place a kiss on her head, then step around her and walk inside like I own the place. Bold move, since she's most likely currently plotting my demise.

It takes her a few seconds to shake herself out of the haze she's in.

"How the hell did this happen?" She crosses the space before plopping down on the couch.

"It started with you saying in the room, and I quote, '*You're so funny, Hudson. I'd totally marry you in Vegas.*'"

"Seriously. That was clearly a joke."

"Was it, though?" I drop down onto the chair perpendicular to the couch. "Because if I remember correctly, you were very excited about it."

"No, I wasn't." She glares at me.

"And then I said once we hit the Strip, '*You know, you're right. We should just get married. Solve all our problems in one shot.*'"

"That doesn't prove anything."

"I take it you don't want me to show you the video of you begging me to marry you, then?"

"I didn't do that."

I reach into my pocket and pull out my phone. She throws a pillow at me, but I'm too fast and deflect it.

"So that's a no, you don't want to see it?"

"Yeah. That's a no." Her jaw is locked so tight I'm afraid she might snap.

Honestly, I should probably stop while I'm ahead, but I never pretended to be smart.

"Calm down, Hex. It was all in good fun. It's not the end of the world."

She covers her face with her hands and groans again. "Why didn't you stop me?"

I shrug. "I tried. Sort of. Well, not really. Plus, you said you loved me."

Her hands drop from her face. "I did not say that."

"Fine, you didn't." I flash her my phone. "You sure you don't want me to play the recording?"

She lunges for me, but again, I'm too fast for her. I blame it on my stellar hockey reflexes. I pull her onto my lap, and she squirms, trying to break free from my grasp. "Relax. Don't fight it." I kiss her head again. "For what it's worth, you're a pretty great wife so far."

Her chest rises sharply, and she blows out a loud, frustrated breath, nostrils flaring and all.

"We've been married for less than twelve hours, Hudson."

"And it's been the best twelve hours of my life."

It might be a slight exaggeration, but not by much.

Molly's face grows serious. A storm is brewing behind her green eyes.

I finally let her go, and Molly sits on the edge of the couch, her shoulders stiff, her arms crossed tightly over her chest. She looks like she might fall apart if she lets herself go.

Shit.

Teasing is one thing, but I'd never want to hurt my little Hex.

How do I fix this?

I get up from my chair and sit beside her. Taking her hand in mine, I wait for my cue that she needs my help.

She doesn't speak, and I narrow my gaze, wondering if a panic attack is about to begin.

The quiet in the room feels thick with tension. I wait for her to do something, anything. I need her to lead me.

I don't want to fuck this up.

Usually, I'd make some dumb joke because that always has a

way of helping. But now, it feels like we're hanging off the side of a building, and I'm the one trying to save us both. *No pressure. Fuck, that's a lot of pressure.*

"I'm okay," she finally says. "I know you're waiting for me to break."

"You're not going to break. You're strong, Molly. The strongest woman I know."

She did hold her own in a room full of stuck-up suits who sold condoms for a living, so that has to stand for something. Most people would have crumbled, present company included, but not her.

"It's not me, it's you. When you're around—you have a way of calming me. Always."

Wait. What? Did she just say that? Did she really say I'm good for her? I want to reach out and touch her forehead to make sure she doesn't have a fever, but I refrain. Never know how she will react. The woman tends to give me whiplash, after all.

"Don't sell yourself short, Hex." She turns to face me and smiles. I squeeze her hand in mine. "If you're okay . . ."

"I am."

"Then I think we should talk about . . . our marriage."

Molly flinches, and I hate it. "Can we not say that word?"

I lean forward in the chair. "What should I call it? Our Vegas disaster? Or maybe one happy Elvis memory?"

From where she sits beside me, I catch a glimpse of a smile tugging at her lips. It's faint, like she's trying to fight it, but it's there.

"That's better," she says dryly.

Progress. I'll take it.

"All right, one happy Elvis memory, it is." One I have no intention of forgetting. "But seriously, we need to figure out what we're doing here."

She tilts her head up to the sky. "We're fixing it. And no one can know."

"Molly," I say softly, and she brings her head back down to meet my stare. "This isn't just on you, okay? I was there too. You might have made the joke about getting married, but I agreed. I'm the one who found Elvis. We both said 'I do' although, in hindsight, I'm not sure how we did that. The guy was ridiculous."

She blinks at me, her lips twitching like she's trying not to laugh.

"Oh, wow, admit it," I say, grinning now. "You want Elvis. It's the sideburns, isn't it? I just can't compete with face hair like that."

"Stop," she says, but her voice is calmer now.

I press on, leaning closer. "I knew it. You're a sucker for a man in a rhinestone jumpsuit. I'll see if I can borrow one for our next date."

That earns me a snort, and she finally meets my eyes. "You're impossible."

"Yet here you are. Married to me." I waggle my eyebrows.

Her fingers knot together on her lap. "Hudson, this isn't funny."

"You're right. It's not funny. It's just I don't know what to say. My default setting is humor." I take her hands, which are still locked, and place a kiss on her knuckles. "We'll figure it out. We just need a second to think about it, but I promise it will be okay."

"Why are you not freaking out?"

"I am freaking out," I admit. "I got married in Vegas. I'm the biggest joke in the NHL. If this gets leaked, I'm ruined, but freaking out isn't going to help us, is it?"

She bites her lip, her eyes darting away again. "I just . . . I don't want this to ruin everything we've built. This thing we have? It's more than a friendship, but not quite a relationship. I'm just not ready to hate you again."

"Then don't," I say firmly, reaching out to take her hands. She stiffens but doesn't pull away, so I keep going. "Look at me."

She hesitates, then finally lifts her gaze to mine.

"This doesn't ruin anything," I tell her. "You and me? Whatever we are? We're going to be okay. We won't go back to being enemies."

Her eyes widen slightly, and I can see the tension in her shoulders loosen just a fraction. "You promise?"

"I promise," I say, squeezing her hands for emphasis. "And we will get this sorted because let's be real here—being married to someone everyone thinks you hate is ridiculous. *Even for me.* And my standards for ridiculous are pretty high."

She laughs softly, and it's the most perfect sound in the world.

"So," I continue, keeping my tone light, "I think we should find a lawyer. Someone we trust. We'll get this annulled, and then we can figure out the rest. Together. Deal?"

Molly stares at me for a long moment, her expression unreadable. I can practically hear the wheels turning in her head, weighing every word I've said.

Finally, she nods. "Deal."

Her shoulders relax, and I can tell I've just brought her the relief she needs. I lean back and grin up at her. "See? That wasn't so hard."

She raises an eyebrow. "Speak for yourself. I'm still recovering from the trauma of hearing you say, 'Morning, wife.'"

I laugh, unable to help myself. "Come on, you've got to admit that was funny."

"I almost had a heart attack," Molly says, but there's a hint of a smile tugging at her lips again. "You almost killed me."

"Murder isn't my style." I shrug. "I'd charm you into submission first."

She rolls her eyes. "And I'd let you think you succeeded right before I hit you with a pillow."

"See? Everything is going to be okay."

"You're not bad, Wilde."

"Only the best for my wife," I say, winking.

Molly groans, shoving my shoulder. "Stop calling me that."

I let myself fall back on the couch dramatically. "Fine. Whatever you want. I won't say—Okay. I might. I'm starting to get used to it." It's true. I am. More than I should.

She leans over me, her face hovering above mine.

I forget how to breathe.

"Hudson," she says, her voice softer now. "Thank you."

"For what?"

"For . . . not making this harder than it has to be," she says. "For making me laugh, even when I don't want to. And for . . ." Her brow furrows slightly. "For not letting this ruin everything."

I reach up, tucking a strand of hair behind her ear. "Molly, you should know by now—nothing about you could ever ruin anything for me."

Her breath catches.

I think she's either going to cry or kiss me.

I pray for the latter. But then she pulls back, sitting up and clearing her throat. "Okay. So first thing when we're back in Redville, we find a lawyer, right?"

"Right." I sit up and hold out my hand for a shake. "It's a deal."

She stares at it, then rolls her eyes. "I'm not shaking on this."

"A kiss?"

Her big green eyes search mine, and I answer her silent plea by picking her up and walking us toward the bed.

Once I lay her on the bed, it doesn't take me long to undress her, seeing as she was already in a sleep tank and shorts. When she's fully naked on the bed, I remove my own clothes, and once naked, I crawl onto the bed, spreading her legs and lining myself up with her core.

I rub the head up and down her slit. I drag it slowly through her drenched skin.

"What are you doing?"

"Patience, Hex. I'm getting my dick nice and wet."

She reaches her hands up and covers her eyes at my crude words, and it makes me chuckle.

"Don't get shy on me now."

"I'm not."

"Oh, my sassy girl is back."

"Wilde."

"Yes."

"Shut up and fuck me already."

With one sharp thrust, I give her what she wants, silencing her with my mouth. I kiss her as I move inside her, filling her to the brink. Reaching my one arm around and under her, I lift her hips so I can get deeper.

Being inside her at this angle, this deep, is the best feeling in the world.

My head rolls back as I savor the moment.

It feels like we're the only people who exist. Nothing else matters but feeling her grip me tightly as she climbs toward her release.

After a beat, I begin to thrust again. Sliding my cock in and out of her.

"Fuck yeah, Hex. I love the way you take my cock." I groan. "So perfect."

She takes every inch like a champ, her pussy clamping down so tightly, I can barely breathe. She's like a vise around my cock, and I fucking love it.

Time ceases to matter when we're here, like this.

"Need more," she moans, and I reach my hand to where we are joined, placing my finger on her clit. I rub her in the same rhythm that I sink inside her, throwing her quickly over the edge. The moment her walls start to quiver around me, it throws me over the edge.

"I'm coming." And I do, my cock jerking inside her, her walls milking me dry.

After my dick stops twitching, I hesitate for a second before pulling out.

If I could do this every day, I will, and hopefully soon, I can.

For a second, we don't move.

"That was amazing."

"Well, since I'm pretty sure the Elvis marriage counts as binding until we officially annul it, we might as well keep doing this. Aren't you so happy you're stuck with me?"

Molly groans again, but this time, she's laughing as she does it. "God help me."

I stand and head to the bathroom, then grab a towel and run some water on it before returning and wiping her off.

She takes the towel from my hand. "You don't have to do that."

"I want to. I like taking care of you."

"For now," she says, but her tone has no bite.

I grin. "You adore me."

"Hardly," she shoots back, but she's smiling as she says it.

And for now, that's enough.

chapter fifty-nine

Molly

D**ID THAT JUST HAPPEN?**
We're back on the plane, and I can't believe how different things are now.

It's funny how much has changed since the beginning of the playoffs.

Back then, I didn't want to sit next to Hudson. Now, I'm praying he'll take the seat next to me.

The roar of jet engines fills the cabin as I settle into my seat on the chartered plane. I stare at every single person who walks on the plane and wonder . . . do they know?

They can't know. Right? Hudson and I have been ridiculously careful. Or at least, as careful as two impulsive idiots who got drunk and married in Vegas can be.

I'm overthinking. It's obvious I am, but I can't stop myself from doing it despite knowing I'm allowing my intrusive thoughts to have a field day.

No one here knows what happened in Vegas.

No one knows I'm married to Hudson Wilde.

Married.

The word still makes me queasy.

I married my brother's best friend.

Jeez, this sounds like a plotline for one of the romance novels Josie is always trying to convince me to read. I don't need to read them now. I'm living it, Elvis ceremony and all.

How is this my life?

It's fine. *Totally fine.*

Nothing to see here.

We'll get an annulment, and no one will ever have to know that Hudson and I managed to go from enemies to not to ... whatever this is in the span of one drunken, Elvis-fueled night.

"Wilde." Mason's voice booms across the cabin, interrupting my mental spiral. I glance up to see his trademark smirk as he gestures toward the seat beside mine. "Don't look so glum. There's an empty seat next to Molly. I was going to sit in it ... You're welcome."

Oh, come on, Mason. *I'm going to kill that man.* He has a way of making everything worse without even realizing he's doing it.

Making a mess of things might be his sixth sense.

Mason is too much to handle on a good day, but I'm still hungover and cranky from all that transpired in Vegas.

I blink, then glance at Hudson, who's strolling down the aisle behind Mason, looking about as relaxed as someone who was just told he won the lottery. His lips twitch into a grin when he sees me glaring at Mason.

"Really, Mason?" I ask, my voice sharper than I mean it to be. "Can't you just do everyone a favor and keep some thoughts to yourself?"

Mason shrugs as if he didn't just say something that annoyed me. "You guys are good now, so why shouldn't he sit next to you ... unless."

"We're fine," I grumble back. While I love Mason since he is one of my brother's best friends, I also loathe him right now.

He claps a hand on Hudson's shoulder and all but shoves him into the seat next to me. "Have fun, Hudson." The smug bastard smirks before looking at me. "It's on the bet contract," he jokes. "You learn how to read the fine print."

I'll show him where he can shove his "bet contract."

It's somewhere where the sun won't shine.

"I didn't sign anything," I deadpan, crossing my arms as Hudson drops into the seat.

"You didn't have to." Mason drops into the row across from us. "It's a verbal contract. Binding by law."

"Is that so?" I raise an eyebrow.

"Yup," Mason says, popping the *p*. "And just for fun, we've decided that anyone who loses the bet has to wear a crochet creation to the next charity event."

"What is this, summer camp? I must have missed the memo that you were a teen girl separated at birth from your sister."

"Anyone ever tell you you're funny, Moll?"

"Not often, Mason. Now, please tell me you're making this up. If not, I'm seriously worried about you."

"What do you think?" He raises an eyebrow.

Hudson leans back in his seat, placing his arm on the armrest beside mine. "I'd look hot in crochet."

"You would look like an idiot." I brush his arm off, pretending not to notice how warm it is.

"Careful," Hudson says in a low voice, just for me. "People might think you actually care about what I do."

"Meaning?"

"You care about my clothing choices? They might think you care."

"I do care," I whisper. The way he looks back at me makes my pulse quicken.

The way he makes me feel is unnerving. The way he makes my pulse race.

The problem isn't that I don't like him. It's how much I like him. And that's the scariest part. I don't trust myself with feeling like this. Don't trust myself not to fall for him.

I can't be with him. It would never work out. Just the thought of giving myself fully to someone like that has my mind unraveling.

I'd have to tell him everything . . .

I'm not ready for that.

He continues to smile down at me. How is he not completely unraveling like I am?

Maybe he's not as affected by you as you are by him.

Bullshit.

He is.

He's just stronger.

A few minutes later, the plane takes off, and I try to focus on anything other than the heat radiating off Hudson or the fact that Mason is watching us like a hawk. Of course, Mason is watching. The man lives for drama. He's practically a card-carrying member of BravoCon.

I pull out my phone, scrolling aimlessly through old pictures. I can feel Hudson's gaze on me.

"You're fidgeting," he says after a few minutes.

"I'm not fidgeting." My fingers stop moving, and I hold perfectly still to make a point.

"You're absolutely fidgeting." He leans closer. "I forgot you don't like flying. Is there anything I can do?"

I turn to face him, scrunching my nose. "No. It's not that. It's just after yesterday, I'm not sure I want to be trapped next to you for so many hours."

He grins. "Afraid you're going to want to join the mile-high club? Sorry, I'm so irresistible."

"Out of curiosity . . . is there a law against murdering someone at thirty thousand feet? Or is it like maritime law, where anything goes? Asking for a friend." I give him a sugary-sweet smile.

Before he can reply, Mason cuts in. "Hey, Wilde, wonder if you can help us out."

"What's up?"

And just like that, the focus is no longer on me, and I can breathe again.

"We were just talking about all your worst habits. Got anything you'd like to add?"

Hudson groans, tipping his head back against the seat. "Just how I wanted to spend the flight. Public humiliation courtesy of people I once considered friends."

"Oh, come on," Mason says, clearly enjoying himself. "This is all for Molly's benefit."

"I'm not following," Hudson says. "And truly, I'm not sure I even want to."

"You know, in case she ever has to do damage control for one of your PR disasters."

I freeze, my stomach flipping. Does Mason know? He couldn't possibly. No, he can't. He's just messing around. Stirring the pot. That's kind of his thing. Still, the way Hudson's eyes flick to mine for a split second makes me want to sink into my seat and vanish.

"All right." I can see Mason rubbing his hands together from the corner of my eye. "Let's start with the fact that Wilde cannot, for the life of him, remember to turn off lights. You could walk into his house at any hour, and I guarantee every single light is on."

"I like it when things are bright," Hudson says with a shrug.

"Electricity isn't cheap." I scoff.

"Especially if you care about the planet," Mason retorts, but I don't know who he's trying to kid. The irony is so thick, I could choke on it. I've been around Mason for years, and I have never in all the time I've worked for the team seen him do anything that would allude to the fact that he gives a lick about the environment. Hell, the man doesn't even recycle. I saw him throw a Coke can right in with the regular garbage, despite the bright blue bin begging for his trash. Who is he to tell Hudson how to save the planet? I don't respond with that, though, because I don't want Mason to think I'm defending Hudson.

I move closer to Hudson, leaning in for only him to hear. "Do you leave lights on?" I ask, arching an eyebrow.

"Maybe," he admits, a faint grin tugging at his lips. It's the kind of grin that screams, "Guilty, and what of it?"

"Maybe?" Mason says. "What about the time you left the lights on in the team bus and drained the battery?"

I turn toward Mason and narrow my eyes. "Why are you listening?"

"You were whispering, so I thought it might be important."

"So you decided to eavesdrop?"

"Obviously."

"Mind your own business, Mason," I fire back while rolling my eyes.

"That was one time," Hudson answers super late to the conversation.

I twist in my seat to face him. He looks exhausted but hot at the same time. This man is dangerous to my health.

"It was twice," Aiden chimes in from a row behind us.

Seriously? Is this a whole team convo? What's next, an intervention? Maybe someone will bust out a sign containing a chart of Hudson's shortcomings.

It's not such a bad idea now that I think about it. Maybe it will help me not fall into bed with him every time he looks at me.

Hudson groans, dragging a hand down his face. "Okay, fine. Twice. But in my defense, someone should've reminded me."

"That's not how responsibility works," I say, unable to hide my grin.

"See? Even Molly agrees." Mason cackles.

Hudson's eyes narrow at me. "Traitor. You're supposed to be on my side."

"Why would I ever be on your side?" I counter.

His grin returns as he mouths, "Because you secretly like me."

I snort, rolling my eyes. "Keep dreaming."

The roast of Hudson continues, with Mason and now Aiden

listing everything from Hudson's tendency to steal food off other people's plates to his questionable taste in music.

"I don't care what you say," Hudson says at one point. "Britney Spears's 'Toxic' is the best thing that came out of the 2000s."

"We're still in the 2000s, idiot," Aiden mutters.

Hudson crosses his arms in mock annoyance. "I stand by my answer."

"That's fine, as long as you don't start singing."

"Challenge accepted, Slate."

"That wasn't a challenge, Wilde. Shit, Goodie, if he starts singing, I'm holding you accountable."

"How is this my fault?" Mason asks.

"You started this shit." Aiden sighs.

By the time Hudson sings every song from Britney's catalog, I'm laughing so hard I can barely breathe. It's easy to forget the awkwardness of marrying my former archnemesis and let myself get swept up in the Redville Saints chaos and all their antics. These guys are like family, and when I'm with them, it's easy to pretend that everything will be okay.

But then Mason says something that makes my stomach drop. "Remember that time Wilde got caught sneaking out of that girl's apartment by her dad? What was her name again?"

I stiffen, my laughter dying instantly. Hudson's grin fades too, and his gaze darts to mine.

"That didn't happen," Hudson says firmly.

"Oh, come on," Mason says. "It totally did. You climbed out the window and landed in the rose bushes."

"I did not," Hudson insists, his voice tight now.

"Pretty sure you did," Wolfe chimes in. Where did he come from? I didn't even realize he could hear from where he's sitting.

"Guys," Hudson says sharply. "Drop it."

His tone is enough to shut them up, but the damage is already done. My mind is spinning, and I can feel Hudson's eyes on me like he's waiting for me to say something.

"Hex," he starts, his voice low, but I hold up a hand to stop him.

"Don't," I say quietly, staring straight ahead. "I don't want to hear it."

He sighs, leaning back in his seat. "It's not true," he says, his voice barely above a whisper.

I glance at him, my chest tightening. "I didn't ask."

"I know," he says, his expression unreadable. "But you deserve to know anyway."

Neither of us speaks, the noise of the plane filling the silence. I want to believe him. I do. But it's hard to reconcile the guy sitting next to me with the reputation that seems to follow him everywhere.

Finally, I take a deep breath, forcing myself to push the thoughts away. "You're lucky I don't keep a list of your worst habits," I mutter, trying to lighten the mood.

His grin returns, slow and easy. "You'd need a lot of paper."

By the time the plane begins its descent, the tension has eased again, and Mason is too busy arguing with Aiden about whether or not pineapple belongs on pizza to notice the awkwardness between Hudson and me.

As we taxi down the runway, Hudson leans closer, his voice low. "Hey."

I glance at him, raising an eyebrow. "What?"

"You okay?" he asks, his tone surprisingly gentle.

I nod, swallowing hard. "Yeah. Just . . . tired."

He studies me, then nods. "Me too."

For once, there's no teasing in his voice, no smirk tugging at his lips. Just honesty.

Which I appreciate, and somehow, I think maybe everything will be okay.

chapter sixty

Hudson

THIS IS THE LAST PLACE I THOUGHT I WOULD BE AFTER WINNING the Cup. But here I am, sitting in a lackluster office with horrible fluorescent lights that make my eyes twitch. Seriously, how do people work under these things? I feel like I'm in a bad crime movie.

The worst part? This is the third office I've been to in three days. Trying to find an attorney that is the right fit to "handle the situation" is much harder than I expected.

Also, I hate the word "situation." It makes everything sound like I'm in high school and just got caught sneaking out after curfew. I can practically hear my dad's stern voice telling me how much potential I have and how I will squander it.

Spoiler alert: I didn't.

Molly is currently sitting beside me.

Her hands are clasped tightly in her lap like she's afraid she might start gesturing wildly. That isn't alarming on its own, but the way her knee bounces makes me nervous. It's jerking so much that it causes the cheap and poorly made conference table to rattle.

Yeah, this place doesn't bode well for me. If the lawyer can't afford a sturdy table, how am I supposed to trust them with my divorce?

I press my foot against the leg of her chair to stop the shaking, but she shoots me a glare.

"What?" I whisper, knowing full well why she's shooting me a death stare.

"Nothing," she seethes back.

The third attorney in our pathetic attempt to find proper legal counsel is a balding man in a slightly too tight suit.

Again, I'm not at all impressed.

His tie is aggressively green as if he's trying to prove he has a personality despite his monotone voice. The only thing it's doing is making my eyes hurt. Like, I get it, you want me to think you're "cool." But I'm not buying it.

Here's the thing, I don't need this ridiculous man to have a personality. I just need him to know the law.

He adjusts his glasses, looking at the folder on the table between us like it contains the meaning of life. Spoiler alert: it doesn't. Unless the meaning of life involves regrettable decisions made while in Vegas.

"So," the attorney says, flipping a page for no apparent reason, "you're looking for help with . . . annulment matters?"

I glance at Molly, who is staring hard at the man like he's about to accuse us of something. She's about one glare away from standing up and abandoning this whole meeting.

I'm with you, Hex. This is bad.

We'd agreed not to spill too many details during this consultation. Not because we're embarrassed. *Okay, I'm not embarrassed.* Molly, on the other hand . . . but I digress, the issue is this guy doesn't exactly scream "trustworthy."

"Yes," Molly says curtly, her voice clipped.

The attorney nods, his face expressionless. Way to calm her nerves, buddy. Stellar bedside manner. Do they teach this in law school? "You mentioned it was a marriage that occurred . . . recently?"

I resist the urge to smirk. "You could say that."

"And you believe annulment is the best course of action?" He looks up at us for the first time.

Molly stiffens beside me; her knee starts to bounce again. Great. "Yes," she says too quickly for my liking.

I narrow my eyes at her and notice that her chest is rising and falling too quickly. She's about to have a panic attack. The thing is, people might think I'm the team clown, but I'm very good at reading people, especially Molly.

I clear my throat, stepping in before she does. "We just need someone who can handle it discreetly. No unnecessary questions, no leaks to TMZ."

The man's expression doesn't change, but there's a flicker of something in his eyes—curiosity, maybe? Or greed. Definitely not confidence. This isn't a good look for him.

"Of course." His tone is as bland as his office decor. This isn't going to work. No way can I put up with this man for however long it takes to get this annulled. "Discretion is a priority in cases like this."

"Great." I lean back in my chair. "So, hypothetically, if we hired you, how long would this process take?"

"That depends on the specifics." He folds his hands on the table. "The circumstances of the marriage, the jurisdiction where it occurred—"

"It was Vegas," Molly blurts, then immediately clamps her mouth shut like she's said too much. I bite back a laugh when her face turns cherry red.

The attorney arches an eyebrow. "Did you say Vegas?"

Despite how tightly I'm pressing my lips together, a small laugh leaks from my mouth. I turn my attention to Molly, who doesn't find this situation nearly as funny as I do. She looks like she wants to melt into the floor.

My stomach twists at her reaction. It's not like I thought she'd be thrilled about being married to me, but I also wish she didn't have such a bad reaction to being married to me. Sure, it's a mistake, but she doesn't have to act like it's the end of the world.

"Yeah." Never breaking her gaze, I lean forward. "Quickest weddings in the country. They're like drive-through burger joints but with vows."

Molly glares at me, her cheeks flushing.

Her eyes screaming, *shut up*.

"Right." The attorney scribbles something in his notes. I'd love to see what. Something tells me it's not favorable. Maybe he's taking notes for when he does decide to sell our story to the tabloids.

Well, technically, he can't do that.

Attorney client privilege. But I never paid him money . . . *is privilege still in place?*

I shake my head, pushing away the thoughts spiraling in my head.

"And how long ago did this . . . union take place?" At this point, I should have scheduled a root canal instead. That would have been more fun than this.

"A week," Molly mutters, barely audible.

This time, the attorney doesn't react, but I can see the faint twitch of his pen. "And you're certain annulment is the best course of action?"

"Yes," we both say at the same time, though Molly's answer is more forceful than mine.

"All right." He closes the folder, placing the pen down on the table beside it. "I'll need more information to proceed, but based on what you've told me so far, this should be a straightforward process."

Straightforward. Sure. Because nothing about this has been straightforward so far.

We leave the office half an hour later, and I don't have to even look at her to feel the tension. She's like a ticking time bomb, one that's ready to explode.

As we walk through the parking lot, she still doesn't break the silence.

She actually doesn't utter one single sound until we're both in the car, and even then, she just sits there with her arms crossed, staring out the windshield.

"Well," I say after a long silence, "that was a waste of time."

Molly turns to me, her eyes narrowing. "You think?" she deadpans.

Do I think? I still think getting a root canal would have been more pleasurable, but I hold back that answer.

"He wasn't that bad." I shrug. "I mean, he didn't offer us a Groupon for his services like the first guy. Or a BOGO like the second guy. As if I'd get hitched again by Elvis and need another annulment. What kind of man does he think I am?"

"I think it's kind of obvious, don't you think?" She lets out a sigh. "None of these lawyers inspire a lot of confidence."

I sit back in the driver's seat. "No, but at least this office didn't smell like burnt popcorn."

Molly slumps back in her seat. "I can't believe we're doing this again. I thought the third time would be the charm."

"Third time's never the charm," I say. "That's just something people say to make themselves feel better. Like 'love at first sight.' Or 'just the tip.'" I laugh.

She gives me a side-eye glare, but there's no real heat behind it. "You're not helping."

"Sure, I am," I say, flashing her my best grin. "I'm keeping things light. You'd be miserable without me."

"I'd be less annoyed without you." She's trying to sound angry, but I don't miss the faint smile tugging at her lips.

I laugh, starting the car. "All right, where to next? Do we find lawyer number four, or do we just wait for Elvis to call us and offer his legal expertise?"

Molly groans, covering her face with her hands. "I can't believe I'm stuck doing this with you."

"Hey, don't blame me," I say, pulling out of the parking lot. "You said yes, remember? This is a fifty-fifty partnership, Hex."

"Do you ever take anything seriously?"

"Sure." I glance at her quickly before focusing back on the road. "Like hockey. And my fantasy football league. And this weird little marriage we've got going on."

She lets out a sharp laugh. "It's not a marriage, Hudson."

"Technically, it is." I grin, and I'm sure if I were looking at her, I'd see my favorite scowl that she often gives me. "We've got the paperwork to prove it."

"Which we're trying to get rid of," she points out.

"Doesn't mean it's not real," I tease. "In fact, I think we might set a record for the shortest marriage in history."

Molly groans again, but this time it sounds like she's trying not to laugh. "We're not even close to the shortest marriage. Remember that celebrity couple who lasted fifty hours?"

"Ah, true," I say, nodding. "Then we'll have to settle for something more impressive. Like longest annulment process. At this rate, we're going to hit our one-month anniversary before we get this sorted."

"That's not funny," she says, and I sneak a glance at her and see her lips are twitching.

"It's a little funny," I counter. "I mean, think about it—if we keep this up, we might outlast my parents' marriage."

That gets her. Molly finally allows herself to laugh, her head falling back against the seat. "God, you're impossible."

"Yep," I say, grinning. "But you still married me."

"Remind me to never drink with you again."

"Noted," I say. "But for the record, you're the one who said, 'I do.'"

"One more word, and I'm calling the next lawyer by myself."

I remove my right hand from the steering wheel and mock surrender. "Fine. I'll behave."

"That'll be the day."

We drive in silence for a while.

The awkwardness from earlier fades away. It's strange—this whole mess should be unbearable, but somehow, being stuck in it with Molly makes it . . . tolerable.

Maybe even fun.

I glance at her out of the corner of my eye, watching as she absentmindedly taps her fingers against her knee. She catches me staring and raises an eyebrow.

"What?"

"Nothing," I say quickly, focusing back on the road.

She doesn't press, but I can feel her watching me for a moment longer before she turns back to the window.

Yeah, this whole situation is ridiculous.

But if I'm being honest with myself, I'm not in any rush to fix it.

Not yet, at least.

chapter sixty-one

Mason: Where the hell have you been, Wilde? You've been MIA.

Aiden: We haven't heard from you much. Not even texts. Did you join a cult? Blink twice if you need help.

Hudson: I'm alive. Thanks for the concern.

Mason: Barely. I've seen ghosts more social than you lately.

Dane: You guys want to hear something funny?

Aiden: Always.

Mason: Please, tell me Hudson did something embarrassing.

Dane: Oh, he did. I saw him yesterday, driving down Main Street. In a SUIT.

Mason: A suit??? Hudson Wilde? The guy who wears joggers to team dinners??

Aiden: Was it even him? Maybe it was his evil twin.

Hudson: I don't have an evil twin.

Mason: Nah, bro, YOU are the evil twin. What's with the suit? Job interview? You finally going corporate?

Aiden: He's certainly pissed Coach off enough to lose his job.

beautiful collide

Hudson: Very funny. It's none of your business.

Dane: Hudson in a suit is everyone's business. You looked like you were heading to a wedding or something.

Mason: A wedding? Hold up. Is there something you're not telling us?

Hudson: Relax. I wasn't at a wedding.

Aiden: Were you late for it? Because that tracks.

Hudson: I hate all of you.

Mason: Suspicious silence. Bro's definitely hiding something.

Dane: No doubt. Hudson Wilde wearing a suit on a random weekday? I don't buy it.

Aiden: Dude probably spilled coffee on his joggers and panicked.

Mason: Or he's secretly in the mob.

Hudson: I'm not in the mob. And I don't panic.

Dane: The suit begs to differ.

Mason: Be honest, are you in trouble? Did Mommy and Daddy finally punish you for all those times you broke curfew?

Hudson: You guys need hobbies.

Aiden: Bullying you is my hobby.

Dane: Ditto.

Mason: Answer the question: WHY THE SUIT, WILDE?

Hudson: You'll never know.

Dane: Sketchy.

Mason: Extremely sketchy. I'm googling "Hudson Wilde spotted in suit" to see if you made the news.

Hudson: Good luck with that. I'm not telling you anything.

Aiden: He's hiding something.

Mason: 100%. I'm adding this to the list of Hudson Mysteries.

Dane: We'll find out. We always do.

Hudson: Keep dreaming, boys.
Mason: Someone's butt hurt.
Hudson: I'm muting this chat.
Aiden: 😂 Guilty as hell.
Mason: This isn't over.

chapter sixty-two

Hudson

THE ICE FEELS LIKE HOME. IT'S WHERE I'M MYSELF.

For me, it's not about the fans. It's the game.

The sound of the puck sliding across the ice.

The scrape of blades as I skate.

The way everything disappears.

It's my therapy.

Especially when I'm just messing around with the guys, running drills.

We just laugh and fuck with each other.

There's no pressure today. No Coach barking orders at us. Just a few friends having a good time.

Mason's working on some sort of save that he's convinced will "blow everyone's mind" next season, but from where I'm standing, it mostly makes him look like a toddler learning how to walk. *A drunk one at that.*

I line up a puck at center ice, aiming for the top left corner of the net. I'm in the zone, my stick slicing the air as I prepare to take the shot, but then . . .

My attention drifts.

It's her.

She's up there, watching from the coaching box like she's working, even though today's session isn't remotely official, so she doesn't really need to be here.

Unless Dane asked her to take notes on Mason's "walking on ice" performance, which is doubtful, her presence is definitely a surprise.

Molly Sinclair is dressed casually today in jeans and a long-sleeved black shirt. Her legs are crossed, and she has her tablet balanced on her lap. She looks like she's analyzing every move we make, but I know better.

She's not working. She doesn't need to be here.

She's here for me.

Watching me.

Or at least that's what I hope.

"Hey, Wilde." Mason skates out from the net and heads my way. He jabs his stick lightly against the back of my knee.

"What?" I mutter, shoving him off as he skates into my space.

"Your girl's here." He smirks.

"Shut up, Goodie. She's not my girl." My tone lacks any real conviction, and Mason knows it.

Mason raises an eyebrow, clearly unimpressed with my lie. "Right. And I'm not the best goalie in the league. So you want to tell me the reason you're staring at her like a lovesick teen, then?"

I aim my stick to hit the puck, ignoring him. He skates back to the net, leaning on his stick, prepared to block my shot. "Seriously, just go talk to her. You're not exactly subtle, dude."

"I don't know what you're talking about." The words come out too fast. I want to cringe at how defensive I sound.

Mason snorts, shoving off the ice and skating in the opposite direction. "Sure, you don't."

I let out a long breath. My heart's pounding like I've been sprinting drills for an hour, but I know Mason's right. I'm not doing myself any favors by pretending I'm not aware of Molly sitting up there.

I skate toward the boards.

By the time I reach the coaching box, my pulse is doing double time. I have no plan. No reason to be here. I've spent years thinking I'm good at improvising, but somehow, every time Molly's involved, I feel like I'm seconds away from tripping over my own feet.

The door creaks as I step inside, and Molly looks up, startled.

"Hudson?" she says, her voice sharp with surprise. "What are you doing here? Shouldn't you be on the ice?"

I shrug, leaning casually against the wall. Or, at the very least, trying to look casual while it's blatantly obvious I came in here for her. I am regretting all my life choices at this very minute.

"Needed a break and wanted to check-in. Looked like you were working hard."

She narrows her eyes. "The coaching staff isn't here. What exactly are you checking on?"

"You," I say simply. She hasn't been herself lately. With every failed lawyer, I can feel her getting more and more anxious.

Her mouth opens like she's about to respond, but no words come out. Her cheeks start to flush. It's adorable how flustered she gets. She pulls her gaze away from me and looks back at her tablet, clearly trying to compose herself.

No one is buying the act, Hex. Just admit you're excited to see me.

"I'm fine," she says after a moment, but her voice is tight.

"Yeah, I can see that. You're working so hard up here. Really breaking a sweat."

"Someone has to." Her eyes are still on the screen, refusing to look at me. It's cute. It's as though she thinks I'll stop bothering her if she continues to ignore me.

Spoiler alert: It won't work.

I take a step closer, folding my arms. "Admit it. You just like watching me skate."

That makes her look up. "Excuse me?"

"You heard me," I taunt. "You're up here, watching me. And you're not even subtle about it."

"I'm working." She sits up straighter. "Not everything revolves around you, Hudson."

"Sure, it does." I take another step closer. "So, what's on the tablet? Practice stats?" I challenge. "Notes on my incredible performance today?"

Her lips press into a thin line, and she angles the screen away from me. "You're ridiculous."

"Yet," I say, leaning against the table beside her, "you're still here."

She rolls her eyes but can't fight the smile tugging at the corner of her mouth. "Don't you have something better to do? Like chasing pucks or falling on your face?"

"Funny," I say, tilting my head. "You didn't mention anything about me falling on my face. *In Vegas.*"

Her eyes widen, and her cheeks flush a deeper shade of pink. "Don't you dare."

I grin. "Don't I dare what? Remind you of the Elvis vows? Or the fact that you were a willing participant?"

"Hudson." She glances toward the glass window, most likely worried that someone might hear us. "We agreed not to talk about this in public."

"We're alone." I move in closer. "And I'm just saying, I think Elvis would be proud of us right now."

She groans, covering her face with her hands. "Why are you like this?"

"Charming? Irresistible? Devastatingly handsome?" I offer.

"Infuriating," she mumbles through her fingers.

I reach out, placing my hand on her shoulder. "Come on, Hex. Admit it. You like me. Just a little."

She reaches out, removing my hand. "You're insufferable."

"Which is basically the same as lovable," I point out.

She shakes her head, but her lip twitches. "You're impossible."

"Yet"—I lean close, my lips practically touching hers—"you married me."

Her breath catches, most likely trying to decide whether to punch me or kiss me.

"Hudson." Her voice catches me off guard.

"Yeah?" I raise an eyebrow.

"You need to go back to practice before Mason comes up here looking for you."

I shake my head. "He won't."

"And why's that?"

"Because he's too busy perfecting his drunk toddler move," I say, grinning.

Molly laughs, the sound light and unexpected, and everything else fades.

It's just us in this stupid little box, and I don't want to be anywhere else.

"You're impossible." She shakes her head.

"You already said that. Plus, it doesn't matter. You're stuck with me."

She inches her head back, the space between us growing. I don't like it and will need to remedy that. "For now."

"For now"—I reach my hand out, cradling her jaw—"but I don't mind."

"I don't mind either," she whispers, and just like that, I know I'm screwed.

With that settled, I pounce, pushing her back until she leans on her elbows, that way no one can see us, and then I make quick work of dropping down to the floor in front of her.

"What are you doing?" Her eyes are wide, full of shock.

My lips spread into a giant grin. "Tasting my wife."

I think she's going to say no, but instead, she shivers at my words.

Never an objection.

She lifts her ass, giving me ample space to remove her underwear.

Once they're off, I sit back and look at what's mine. Her pussy gleams back at me. Hot and wet and ready to come. Which she will, but only on my tongue today.

There's not enough time to fuck her right. But I still need to see her fall apart.

Molly Sinclair coming is my favorite sight. Making her come . . . my favorite pastime.

I lean forward, placing my hands on her thighs to keep them spread, then lift to place a kiss on her lips. She tastes like cherries and sin.

Her tongue swirls around mine. I kiss her once, twice, and on the third peck, I pull away, moving my mouth to her jaw.

With slow movements, I trail a line down her neck, dipping my tongue in the hollow before moving to her exposed collarbone.

Since she still has her shirt on, I drop down, positioning myself to continue my exploring. When my mouth meets her skin this time, my teeth graze her soft flesh.

It drifts up, getting closer and closer to where she wants me, but I don't go there. Instead, I trail kisses up and down her thigh.

Hands tug at my hair, and I look up to find Molly staring down at me, her eyes fiery with desire.

"Don't you dare pull away again." She groans as my tongue starts its descent in the opposite direction as she wants.

Her legs shake in protest. "Please."

"Patience." I lick my way back up, leaving goose bumps in my tongue's wake.

A groan escapes her mouth, but I still don't give her what she wants. "Has anyone ever told you that you're an asshole?"

"Wow, I didn't know you were so impatient, Hex." I chuckle against her skin.

I nip her thigh. Then I trace my tongue over her bare pussy lips, kissing the plump skin.

"Beg me to fuck you with my mouth."

"No."

I lean forward and blow on her swollen clit. Her whole body shudders. A primal moan escapes her lips.

I pull back. "Beg me, Molly."

I peer up, catching her glassy gaze, mouth open in pleasure as she silently begs me with her eyes to get her off.

When she shakes her head, I move closer, running my tongue from the bottom of her slit to the top.

"Tell me what you want. And I'll give it to you."

"Fuck me with your tongue."

"Good girl. Your wish is my command, wife."

And I do. My lips move up, kissing her clit once before sucking it into my mouth.

A primal moan escapes her as I swap off between licking and sucking.

My tongue moves lower, leaving her clit and finding her dripping wet hole. I dip my tongue inside until she's squirming against me, then I add a finger, replacing my tongue.

"Fuck, you're so tight."

My fingers push, curving upward to find her sweet spot, while my mouth latches back on to her clit.

"What I'd do to fuck you right here. Right now. Fuck. Your pussy is grasping my finger so tight. It's begging to be fucked by my cock."

"Just do it already," she groans, making me chuckle.

"Is that what you want? For me to fuck you?" I press a firm kiss to her again, nipping this time. Driving her crazy.

"You're all talk."

"And you're a needy little girl. But I'll shut you up." And with that, I return my mouth to her clit, pretending it's her mouth and kissing her until she's a mess.

"I'm coming."

And she does, on my tongue, just like I wanted.

Fuck, she's perfect.

And as I told her . . .

All mine.

And when she finally comes down from the high, I can't help but ask, "Would it be the worst thing to stay married to me?"

"No," she says sadly. "No, it would not."

chapter sixty-three

Hudson

IT'S PANDEMONIUM IN THE CONFERENCE ROOM.

The reporters maneuver for a good position in the room, causing chaos to erupt.

The flash of the cameras is nearly blinding.

We're here to discuss a new team fundraising campaign that we will be kicking off, but as usual, it's open season for these vultures.

For the past ten minutes, we've barely covered anything we prepared.

Instead, reporters have been firing off personal questions while we dodged them.

Everyone looks pissed, but I'm okay. Seeing as I've never had a good reputation, I'm used to it. The PR team has prepped me well. Smile. Joke. Deflect.

Basically, keep them entertained by my stellar personality.

Usually, it's easy. Today, though, there's a tightness in my chest I can't shake, and it's all because of Molly.

I glance down the line of my teammates, all sitting at the long table with me. Mason's leaning back in his chair, looking bored as hell.

Aiden's answering a question about his offseason training regimen with his usual calm professionalism. And Dane—is being grumpy.

I try to focus, but my mind keeps drifting back to Molly. It's been eight weeks since that fateful night in Vegas, eight weeks of looking for an attorney and finding them all lacking.

None of them have been right for us, so we've been sneaking around in the meantime, hoping this mess doesn't blow up in our faces.

"Hudson!" someone shouts my name, pulling me out of my thoughts. It's coming from a reporter at the far-right corner of the room. He's got brown hair and has a voice that looks too deep to be coming from him. He stares at me before speaking again. "Let's talk about your plans for next season. Do you think the Saints can pull off another Cup win?"

I flash a grin, leaning into the mic. "We've got a great team, great chemistry. If we stay focused, I think we've got a real shot."

Safe. Easy. Next question.

Another reporter chimes in, asking about the charity event the team just pledged to. Finally, a question that matters. *Took long enough.*

It's why we're all here, after all.

I let Mason take it, nodding along as he talks about the importance of giving back.

And then it happens. "Hudson, one more question."

The voice is calm, almost casual, but it makes every nerve in my body go on high alert. I glance at the reporter—an older guy with a sharp suit and a sharper smile. He adjusts his glasses, his gaze locking on to mine like a predator sizing up its prey.

"Can you tell us how married life is treating you?"

The room goes dead silent.

My lungs burn, and it feels hard to breathe. It's like the air has been sucked out of the room. Every reporter, every teammate, every PR staff member turns to me like I just grew a second head.

My heart slams against my rib cage, but I force my face to stay neutral, even as my mind races.

What the hell? How does he know?

Mason lets out a bark of laughter, breaking the tension. "Hudson? Married? Yeah, right. He can't even commit to a pizza topping."

A ripple of laughter moves through the room, but it's short-lived.

Fuck.

The reporter doesn't seem to be buying it. He keeps his eyes on me, his smirk widening.

"It's true, isn't it?" he presses. "You're married."

"Excuse me?" My voice sounds too tight. *Keep it together, Wilde.*

Don't give anything away.

"Let me rephrase," he says smoothly. "Is there any tension in the locker room now that you're married to a teammate's sister?"

The silence that follows is somehow louder than the laughter from before. Everyone in the room but the shithead asking the questions is frozen in place, staring at me like I've just confessed to a crime.

"What?" Dane's voice cuts through the quiet, sharp and demanding.

I open my mouth, but no words come out. My brain feels like it's short-circuiting. The reporter raises an eyebrow, clearly enjoying the chaos he's unleashed.

"So, Dane . . ." He turns his attention away from me and onto Dane. "Are you happy for your sister and Hudson?"

Dane blinks, his jaw tightening. He looks at me, then back at the reporter. "I—what—what the hell are you talking about?"

"All right, that's enough," our PR manager snaps, stepping

forward and cutting the reporter off. "This press conference is over. Thank you all for coming."

The room erupts into chaos again, but this time, it's worse than before.

Reporters are shouting questions, cameras are flashing, and I still can't get my brain to function.

Luckily for me, the PR team moves quickly, ushering us off the stage and into the hallway. Everyone is stunned into silence except for Mason, who mutters something I can't make out. Most likely, it's an obnoxious comment, and I'm happy I don't hear, because I'm sure I'd want to punch him. Something tells me that wouldn't bode well for me with Coach.

As soon as we're away from the press, Dane turns to me, his face a mixture of confusion and anger. "What the hell was that?"

I run a hand through my hair, my heart still racing. "Dane, I can explain—"

"Explain what?" he snaps. "That reporter just said you're married to my sister. My sister, for fuck's sake. Please tell me this isn't true."

My pulse quickens, and I feel like I've been punched in the gut.

The hallway feels too small, too loud, even though no one's talking but us. I glance at Mason and Aiden, who are both hovering a few feet away, clearly not sure if they should step in or stay out of it.

"Yeah," I say finally, my voice low. "It's true."

Dane's face goes blank for a second, like he can't quite process what I've just said, and then, like a veil of fog being lifted, the anger flares.

"You're fucking joking," he says, his voice sharp. "Shit. Please tell me you're joking."

"I'm not."

"You—" He cuts himself off, his fists clenching at his sides. "Are you out of your damn mind? Do you have any idea what you're doing? Molly is my sister."

"I know," I say, my voice steady even though my chest feels like it's caving in. "I know, Dane. And I'm sorry we didn't tell you sooner. But this—what Molly and I have—it's real."

"Real?" Dane scoffs. "You're a playboy, Hudson. You've never been serious about anyone in your life. Why the hell would I believe you're serious about her?"

"Because I am," I say firmly.

He laughs, but it's humorless. "You don't even know how to be serious, Hudson. You think everything's a joke. What happens when this gets old? When you get bored? What happens to Molly then?"

"Stop," I say, my voice sharp now. "You don't get to talk about her like she's some fling I'm going to toss aside. You don't know how I feel about her."

"Then tell me," he snaps. "Tell me why the hell I shouldn't be worried about my sister being tied to a guy who treats relationships like disposable coffee cups."

I take a deep breath, trying desperately not to snap. I want to yell at him, to defend myself, but I know that won't help. So I force myself to calm down, to find the words that will make him understand.

"Because she's not just some girl to me," I say finally. "Molly's . . . everything. She's smart and stubborn and funny. When I'm with her, nothing else matters. Everything fades away. The noise, the pressure, the bullshit—it doesn't matter. She's the only thing that matters."

Dane stares at me, his jaw tight, his eyes searching mine.

"I know my reputation," I continue. "I know what people think of me. And yeah, I've screwed up a lot in the past. But Molly? She makes me want to be better. I'd do anything to be the man she deserves. Fuck." I look up at the ceiling, trying to find the right thing to say, before looking back down to meet his stare again. "I'd bring down empires if it meant keeping her safe."

The words hang in the air, heavy and raw. Dane doesn't say

anything for a long moment, and I can't tell if he's processing or just deciding how hard he wants to punch me.

Finally, he exhales, shaking his head. "Why didn't you tell me?"

"We wanted to," I say. "But we didn't know how. And after Vegas . . . it just got more complicated."

"Vegas?" His eyes narrow.

Shit.

I wince. "Yeah. That's where . . . it happened."

Dane's face tightens, and I can see him putting the pieces together.

"You married her in Vegas," he says flatly.

"Yeah."

"And you didn't think I deserved to know?"

"We were going to tell you," I say. "We just . . . didn't want to do it like this."

Dane exhales sharply, running a hand through his hair. "Unbelievable."

"I'm sorry," I say, and I mean it. "But I swear to you, Dane, I care about Molly. More than anything. I'm not going to screw this up."

He's quiet as he continues to look at me, his expression unreadable. Finally, he nods, though it looks forced.

"You'd better not," he says quietly.

"I won't."

He doesn't respond. He just turns and walks away, leaving me standing in the hallway with the weight of everything still hanging over me.

This wasn't how I wanted him to find out.

But now that he knows, there's no turning back.

chapter sixty-four

BREAKING NEWS: Hudson Wilde Marries Teammate's Sister in Secret Vegas Ceremony

By: Erin Hart, Sports Insider

Hockey fans, brace yourselves—Redville Saints' star right wing, Hudson Wilde, has dropped a bombshell bigger than any game-winning goal. Reports surfaced this morning that Wilde, infamous for his "bad boy" reputation, secretly tied the knot in Las Vegas . . . and the bride? None other than Molly Sinclair, the younger sister of Wilde's teammate and Saints enforcer, Dane Sinclair.

When asked about the shocking news at today's press conference, Wilde declined to comment. The usually smug and quick-witted player looked uncharacteristically uncomfortable as cameras flashed and reporters pressed for answers. His only response: "Next question."

Speculation about the couple's relationship history—and Dane

Sinclair's reaction—has already taken over social media. With the Cup Finals still fresh in fans' minds, many wonder why the pair kept their relationship (and now marriage) under wraps.

Fan Comments:

@SaintsFanatic99: HUDSON WILDE??? MARRIED??? To DANE'S SISTER??? I NEED ANSWERS.

@HockeyGirlForever: I'm devastated. I'm in mourning. Hudson Wilde was supposed to marry me.

@WildeChild89: Honestly? Respect. Man scored on and off the ice. 🏆

@TeamSinclair: WAIT. Dane's sister?! Hudson's a dead man walking. I bet Dane's sharpening his skates right now.

@PuckLife23: Hudson Wilde, secret family man? Did not see that plot twist coming. My condolences to single girls everywhere.

@SportsSpill: The real question: How did Hudson Wilde—a man who can barely show up on time—pull this off?

@MollyFanClub: Okay. I just looked up her pics. Molly Sinclair is goals. Marry a pro athlete AND tame him? Iconic behavior.

chapter sixty-five

Hudson

I'M SITTING IN THE TEAM LOUNGE, STARING AT MY PHONE AS IT buzzes on the table in front of me.

I can't think straight.

My brain is actual mush.

Normally, I pride myself on being quick-witted and funny, but right now, I can barely form a sentence, let alone a joke.

My brain's been spinning since the press conference earlier. All I can think about is Dane's pissed-off face.

Honestly, in Dane's mind, I'm the worst thing that can ever happen to his sister.

It pisses me the fuck off, because none of that shit is true. I'm not a player. I'm an asshole. I let everyone think one way about me because it was easier, and now, I'm feeling the consequences of that decision, and it hurts.

Real bad.

Today has sucked.

Between Dane and the reporter's smug smirk, as he dropped the wife bomb, I can't catch a break.

Wife.

Shit. Every time I hear the word, I like it more and more. Something I can't admit to Molly.

I'm married. That word feels both ridiculous and . . . not so ridiculous when I think about the fact that it's to her.

It doesn't feel wrong.

I pinch the bridge of my nose, leaning back into the plush leather couch. The room is quiet, empty except for me and the sound of my phone vibrating against the wood.

How is it still ringing?

Can't they take a hint?

Welp, apparently not. Since it's ringing again. Now for the third time. Something tells me this is going to be a bad day.

Finally, when it's obvious the person isn't giving up, I grab the phone and glance at the screen.

It's my agent. What the hell does Travis want? Something tells me I already know.

I let it ring a few more times, not wanting to get reamed out again for my drunken Vegas antics.

It's bad enough that I lived through the press conference, and I really don't want to have part two.

"Travis," I say, trying to sound unfazed. "If this is about that reporter, I already got the PR lecture."

"Not about that," Travis says. His voice is lighter than I would expect for this type of situation. "Though I did get an earful from the team's PR team. Apparently, you and Dane are on media lockdown for a week?"

"Yeah," I mutter. "Lucky me."

"Good timing, actually," he says, his tone shifting. "It gives us a chance to talk about something big."

"Big?" I sit up a little. Now I'm curious.

"You've got an offer." His voice rises. I've heard him like this before, and it's usually followed by a substantial cash value.

"An offer? You mean like an endorsement?"

"That's right."

"Let me guess." I sigh, frustration bubbling up. "Another condom company? Oh, I got it, it's a new tequila company, and they want me to pose with their stuff? Or maybe it's an energy drink this time. Something to keep the 'bad boy' image alive."

Travis chuckles. "Not this time, Hudson. This one's different. It's a cereal brand."

I pause, my mind short-circuiting like an old computer that needs updating. "A cereal brand?"

"Yep. They want you to be the face of their new campaign."

I blink, trying to process this. "You mean like a BDSM cereal brand?"

"Nope."

"Are you messing with me?"

"Why would I mess with you about cereal?" Travis jokes before his voice becomes more serious. "Look, I know it sounds out of left field, but hear me out. This isn't just any cereal. It's family-oriented. Wholesome. They're looking for someone with a relatable image who can appeal to parents and kids."

Now it's my turn to burst out laughing.

This is absurd. "Travis, have you met me? Wholesome? I'm the guy who got caught in a nightclub fight last year. I've been on the cover of tabloids more times than I can count. I'm not exactly 'family-friendly.'"

"You *were* that guy." His tone has me sitting up straighter. "But now? Things are changing. People are talking about you in a whole new light after today's press conference. Married to a teammate's sister? That's gold, Hudson. I couldn't have planned this better if I tried."

"I'm not following."

"You're not just the bad boy anymore—you're a family man."

"Family man," I repeat, the words tasting foreign on my tongue.

"That's right," Travis says. "And that's why they want you. This cereal company sees an opportunity to reshape your image, to take you from reckless bachelor to someone parents can trust."

This is absurd.

He can't be serious.

My thoughts are spiraling with how ridiculous this is.

How is it even possible that he's not pulling my chain right now? There is no way a cereal company would want me.

The last time he called me for an endorsement deal, it was for a condom company. How can my "marriage" change my perceived persona so quickly?

Is it really that easy? That simple.

I don't respond right away because I can't.

I'm actually at a loss for words.

Family man.

It shouldn't be the furthest thing from reality since I did grow up in a close-knit home with strong family values, but I've been stuck with a reputation I didn't deserve for so long, a part of me believes I deserve to still be there.

I don't even know what that means for me yet. Sure, I'm married to Molly, but we're trying to get the marriage annulled.

"This is insane," I say finally.

"It's not," Travis counters. "It's smart. Look, Hudson, you've always been marketable, but you've been stuck in a niche—sex, booze, and bad decisions. Now you've got a chance to break out of that. Think of this as a reset button for your career. Sponsors love a redemption arc."

He makes a good point. They do love that . . . but for me? I'm not sure.

I glance out the window, the skyline of downtown Redville sprawling out beneath the setting sun.

"What's the offer?" I'm wondering if it's even worth contemplating.

"Seven figures," Travis says smoothly. "And that's just the starting point."

My head snaps back like I've been hit. "Seven figures? For cereal?"

"For cereal," he repeats. "They're serious, Hudson. They want you for commercials, social media campaigns, and maybe even some charity events with kids. You'd be their flagship ambassador."

"Damn." I let out a low whistle. "Seven figures."

That's a shit ton of money. That's the kind of money that will help . . . my family. *If they let me.*

"You still there?" Travis asks.

"Yeah." I swallow. "Just . . . processing."

"Look, I know this is a big shift," he says. "But you'd be stupid not to at least consider it. This is the kind of opportunity most players never get, Hudson. You'd be broadening your appeal and setting yourself up for long-term success, even after hockey."

All of this is nuts.

It's so far from the image I fell into, but maybe that's exactly what I need. I've lied for so long about who I am. Perhaps it's time I take down the walls and show the world the real me.

The one who loves his family and wants one of his own.

"I'll think about it," I say finally.

"That's all I'm asking," Travis says. "I'll send over the details. Take a look, talk it over with Molly—"

I cut him off. "She doesn't know about this yet. Hell, she doesn't even know about the press conference fallout. She's going to kill me when she finds out."

Travis laughs. "Good luck with that. But seriously, this is a good thing, Hudson. Don't overthink it. Call me when you're ready to move forward."

"Yeah, thanks, Travis."

I hang up and stare at my phone, the weight of the conversation settling over me.

Did that really just happen?

Did a cereal company just offer me a seven-figure endorsement deal?

I pinch the skin on my wrist. Nope, I'm not dreaming.

All of this is real, and the craziest part is that it all started with a drunken Vegas mistake.

A part of me wonders if that "mistake" is the best thing that has ever happened to me.

I leave the lounge and head to the parking lot, my thoughts still moving a mile a minute.

Molly told me before the press conference that she would meet me at my place. We haven't spoken since, and does she know?

Will she be pissed?

Of course, she will be.

I should regret this, but I don't. I don't regret the leak, and I don't regret the marriage, but what does that mean for the future?

Wholesome. Redemption. The words keep looping in my head, and for the first time, it doesn't feel like a joke.

I pull out my phone and open my messages.

Hudson: Hey. We need to talk.

I stare at the message before hitting send.

This marriage might've started as an accident, but it doesn't feel like one anymore.

Maybe it's exactly what I need.

chapter sixty-six

Molly

I WISH I COULD JUST TAKE A SICK DAY.

But no, instead of taking a nap like I want to, I'm working despite my throbbing headache.

Okay, maybe I'm not working, but I am checking emails.

I'm halfway through answering one when I hear a noise. I can't make out what it is, though, from where I'm sitting on the couch. It kind of reminds me of the chaos before a game, just not as loud. *And less swearing.*

Another series of shouts happens.

This is ridiculous already.

Either my neighbors are throwing an impromptu block party or it's the end of the world. Honestly, with how my life is going currently, either is a strong possibility.

I stand up from the couch and head for the window.

Once the blinds are pulled back, my eyes go wide.

Holy shit.

There are a few people there.

What the hell is going on?

Gas leak. There's got to be a gas leak, right?

Shit. Why didn't an alarm go off, and why am I still standing here?

I need to evacuate. But no . . . instead, I'm standing here because I most likely have a faulty monitor and will die.

Yeah, that sounds about right.

I am a *hex,* after all.

My eyes narrow. What is that? Are they holding something? Are those cameras?

Okay, so maybe the building isn't being evacuated.

Oh, I know, they must be filming a movie. In Redville. Yeah, I think not. The biggest celebrity we have here is Hudson Wilde, which says a lot. Typically, reporters don't follow hockey players around.

Wait, shit, are those reporters? No. That's ridiculous.

Please say they aren't.

Why would reporters be outside my building?

My stomach twists. What if it's me?

No. Totally not. That's ridiculous.

No one knows about Hudson and you.

It has to be something else.

My nose scrunches as I think.

I know some athletes live in the building, but no one who would garner this much attention.

Hmm.

Yeah, I doubt that's it. It's not like some star quarterback secretly moved in and decided to hold a press conference on the sidewalk.

My best guess would be a movie, but that doesn't make sense either. If it were someone really famous, like an actor, there would be more press than this. This looks more local.

What the hell is happening?

My chest tightens, and I step back from the window like they can see me from all the way up here.

beautiful collide

Not that they are looking for me, but still. No one wants to be the poor idiot caught on camera as collateral damage. Like the time my neighbor left her patio door open, and a raccoon destroyed her apartment. I wouldn't necessarily call that newsworthy, but here in Redville, it apparently was.

My phone buzzes on the counter, and I snatch it up, barely glancing at the screen before answering.

"Dane, if this is about—"

"Ms. Sinclair, don't go outside."

I double-check the number, realizing it's not Dane. It's Sean, one of the guys on the Saints security team. I've talked to him twice. Once when Dane first came to the team and didn't know which entrance to use. And another time when he got into a fender bender half a mile from the arena.

"Sean? What is going on?" I grip the phone tighter. Why can't I leave? Is there a murderer on the loose? That would explain the commotion. But not why Sean, of all people, called me.

"Take a breath, Sinclair," he reminds me, and for some reason, I listen, calming a bit. "Some reporter said something about you and Hudson—"

I freeze. "What about me and Hudson?"

"That you're married."

Married.

The word hits me like a slap in the face. My pulse spikes, and my hands become clammy around the phone.

I can't breathe. This makes no sense.

Did I hear that right?

"How—how would they even know that?" I stammer.

"I'm not sure."

"This doesn't make sense. How do they know?" I repeat more to myself than to him.

"I don't have any details. I just know your brother and Hudson spoke to the media team after the press conference, then asked me to secure your home. I'm out of town, but I'll be there with a team to guard the place in two hours if you can manage until then."

"Press conference." The words echo in my skull. "As in the press conference I skipped because of my headache? That press conference?"

"I suppose?" Of course, he wouldn't know. I don't talk to him. "Local reporters are all over the story. The team hasn't confirmed anything to them, but Hudson—"

"What did Hudson say?" I interrupt, my pulse racing.

"He didn't deny it. The PR team shut the conference down before he could say much, but it's too late. It's everywhere."

I sink onto the couch, my knees weak. *Married*. "It's everywhere? As in the internet? Social media?" This is awful.

"Ms. Sinclair, are you okay?" His voice is softer now.

I nod, even though he can't see me. "Yeah," I say, my voice hollow. "I'm fine."

"Or would you prefer if I call you Mrs. Wilde?"

Holy crap.

He's serious.

The severity of how my life is about to change hits me at once, and my knees buckle. I fall onto my couch, winded.

"Molly is fine." My voice is steadier than I feel. "I'll text you the security code to my apartment."

What I want to say is this is my problem, and I'll deal with it. That I need to learn to be strong, but I don't. Obviously, Dane and Hudson sent him my way.

God. Dane.

What is he thinking right now?

He must hate me.

There's a long pause on the other end of the line as I hear another car honk.

"Works for me. Molly." I hear his turn signal flick on. "Call me if you need anything. And don't talk to the press."

"I won't."

I end the call before he can say anything else.

I just stare blankly at the wall as the weight of everything sinks in. My mind races. *Married. Hudson. Reporters.* How did my life become this?

The questions they're going to ask, the judgment that's bound to follow—it's too much. Typically, reporters don't care too much about professional hockey players' private lives, but this isn't any hockey player. *It's Hudson Wilde.*

The press loves him and all the crazy antics he gets into, and now I'm one of them. Leave it to me to find the one hockey player with twenty-four-hour media coverage.

My phone buzzes again, and this time, it's a text from Hudson. *This day just keeps getting better.*

Hudson: By the looks of things, I'll assume you heard the news.

Molly: Yep.

Hudson: I'm coming over.

Molly: No.

Hudson: Too bad.

I groan, throwing my phone onto the couch. Of course, Hudson is coming over. He also probably thinks he can fix it with his signature charm and a well-placed smirk.

I barely have time to process what just happened before there's a knock on the door. Jeez, how fast did he drive? Or was he already on the way here? Unless it's not him and it's a reporter instead.

My heart leaps, and I scramble off the couch, peering through the peephole.

It's him. Duh. I knew this already.

Real smooth, Molly.

I fling the door open, and my heart starts to race.

There he is—Hudson Wilde in all his tall, obnoxiously sexy glory. He's trying to blend in—like he could ever do that—wearing a ball cap pulled low over his eyes and a leather jacket.

"Hey." His low and steady voice makes butterflies swarm in my belly.

"What are you doing here?" I cross my arms to keep my hands from shaking from the nerves of the day. Having my secret—our secret—out is a lot to handle. Now, what do we do?

"Saving you," he says simply, stepping inside and closing the door behind him.

I blink, caught off guard by his calmness. How can he be so at peace right now? I'm a hot mess, shaking like a leaf, barely able to function. "Saving me from what?" I play dumb. Maybe if I pretend it's not happening, it won't be.

"From the vultures downstairs," he says, nodding toward the window. "It's a madhouse out there."

"I noticed," I mutter, running a hand through my hair. "How did they even find out?"

"Good question." His jaw tightens. "But right now, the how doesn't matter. We just need to get you out of here."

"Out of here?" He stands tall in front of me, like a knight in shining armor, ready to rescue me. It makes my heart do stupid things *like hope*. "To where?"

"My place," he says, like it's the most obvious thing in the world.

"Isn't that going to be just as bad?" I ask.

"I have better security. Let's go."

I shake my head. "Hudson, I can't—"

"You can." His voice is firm. "Unless you want to stay here and deal with that."

He gestures toward the window, and I glance outside again. The crowd has grown, reporters fighting for a better position to get the shot. Their cameras are aimed at my building, at my apartment, to be exact. This is bad. My stomach flips, and I look back at Hudson, my resolve crumbling.

"Fine." I nod. I could pretend to be strong, but there's no point. I'm basically lost at sea, and he's offering me a life preserver. "But how are we supposed to get past them?"

beautiful collide

He grins, and for the first time since I noticed the crowd outside my window, I feel a flicker of something that isn't panic.

"Leave that to me." The damn smirk that makes me stupid appears on his face.

Head in the game, Molly. This is not the time to look at him like you want to—

"Stop looking at me like that, Hex. Or we'll give the reporters a real show." Welp. That does it. All impure thoughts are officially knocked out of my head.

"Let's just go." I roll my eyes, but there's no hate there. *Not anymore.*

Five minutes later, I'm standing in the hallway, wearing a hoodie and a pair of sunglasses he produced from his jacket pocket.

"This is your plan?" I ask, tugging the hoodie tighter around me.

"Trust me," he says, adjusting his cap. "I've dealt with the press enough to know how to dodge them. Just stay close and keep your head down."

"Great," I mutter. "I feel so reassured."

He rests a hand lightly on my back as he leads me toward the elevator. "Relax, Molly. I've got you."

It's tense in the elevator ride, and my heart is pounding by the time we reach the lobby. Hudson steps out first, scanning the crowd outside the glass doors before pulling me to his side.

"Ready?" His voice is so low I can barely hear him.

"No." I follow him anyway. I have no other choice, and the truth is, if I have to face the press, there is no one else I would feel comfortable doing it with. Not even Dane.

The moment we step outside, the reporters pounce.

"Hudson. Is it true you're married to Molly Sinclair?"

"Molly, how long have you been seeing Hudson?"

"Was the wedding planned or was it spontaneous?"

"Hudson, what does Dane think about all this?"

Damn.

They are relentless.

I've been with the team for years and have never seen anything like this. Sure, there was that blip with Aiden, but even that was controlled. Nothing like this. That was one lone reporter out to get him. This is something else entirely.

I keep my head down, my sunglasses hiding my eyes as I cling to Hudson's arm. His presence is solid and steady, and he doesn't say a word as we push through the crowd.

Got to hand it to him. He has a way of comforting me like no one else can. Walking through these animals, I actually feel safe with him. *Does that mean something?* Yeah, I think it does. What? I'm not sure, and I'm not ready to broach that topic, but I know it does.

"Hudson, over here!" one of them shouts, shoving a microphone toward his face.

He turns, his expression cool and unreadable. "No comment."

"But—"

"No comment," he repeats, his hand dropping to wrap tightly around my waist.

The reporters continue their shouting.

With each step we take, they become more persistent, but Hudson doesn't stop.

Instead, with his head held high and his arm wrapped around me, he leads me to his car.

When we get to it, he opens the passenger door for me like a gentleman.

I've never wanted to admit it, but he's not a bad guy.

He's actually a pretty fabulous guy.

"Hex, get in." His voice sounds tight. My guess is he's super pissed and trying to not give the press a show.

I do as he says, and he closes the door behind me before rounding the car and sliding into the driver's seat.

As we pull away from the chaos, I finally let out the breath I've been holding.

beautiful collide

He glances over at me. Our eyes lock. "You okay?"

I nod even though I'm not.

My heart pounds in my chest. "Thanks."

"For what?" he asks.

"Helping me."

He didn't have to, and I appreciate him.

He shrugs before turning to face the road. "It's my job."

"No, it's not. I don't deserve it, but thank you."

The car goes quiet. It's almost like my words shut him up.

I pivot in my seat and watch him.

He's looking forward, hands on the steering wheel.

His jaw is set, and it's almost like he didn't hear me, but then I see a slight twitch.

He did, and my words affected him.

The silence stretches between us, heavy and loaded. Finally, I can't take it anymore, needing to say so much and not willing to wait.

I bury my head in my hands. "Now what?"

He sighs. "Honestly, no clue."

I shake my head. "This is a disaster."

"Maybe, but it doesn't have to be."

"You really think we'll be okay?" I ask, my voice small.

The car rolls to a stop at the light, and he looks at me. "I know we will."

And for a moment, I almost believe him.

chapter sixty-seven

Dane: Are you serious, Molly?

Molly: I know. I KNOW. Please don't yell at me.

Dane: Yell at you?? Do you even still consider me your brother, or did you trade me in for Hudson??

Molly: Oh my God. You're being dramatic.

Dane: DRAMATIC? I found out my sister MARRIED my teammate FROM THE PRESS.

Molly: I'm sorry. It wasn't supposed to happen like this.

Dane: What, you accidentally said "I do"?

Molly: Okay, fair point. But it's a long story, and I didn't know how to tell you.

Dane: You just tell me, Molly. That's how.

Dane: Remember me? Your brother? The one who raised you?

Molly: You're right. I should've told you. I'm sorry.

Dane: . . .

Molly: You're mad.

Dane: I was mad. Now I'm just worried about you. Are you okay? For real.

Molly: Yeah, I'm okay. Promise.

Dane: If you need anything, you tell me. No exceptions. You hear me?

Molly: I hear you.

Dane: Good. I've already got the team's PR on this. We'll spin it. Damage control is what they're good at.

Molly: Thank you. I didn't mean for any of this to happen.

Dane: I know. I'll deal with Hudson later.

Molly: Please don't kill him.

Dane: No promises.

Molly: Dane.

Dane: Fine. He lives. For now.

Molly: Thank you.

Dane: Just don't make me an uncle anytime soon.

Molly: BLOCKED.

Dane: 😂 Love you, kid.

Molly: Love you, too, big brother.

chapter sixty-eight

Hudson

*N*OW, WHAT DO WE DO?
I wish I had answers to how this happened, but I don't. This leads me to pacing the room and staring at Molly.

She sits on my couch with her legs crossed and her arms folded.

Neither of us has spoken since we arrived, and I'm starting to worry we won't.

Which doesn't bode well for solving this.

Narrowing my eyes, I take her in. Her jaw is set, and her brows furrowed.

This I can work with.

She's pissed, but this is different. *This is stubborn determination.*

A look I have come to know all so well.

Yep, I can decipher the many looks of Molly Sinclair.

I've been watching her long enough, after all.

Stalker much.

I'm used to this version of Molly. She's planning, and when she's like this, she's unstoppable.

beautiful collide

My lips part into a grin.

She's really something else.

Can't wait to see what she comes up with when she establishes a plan she thinks I should follow.

I watch her for a beat. She's in the zone.

I can practically see the wheels in her head turning as she tries to devise a plan.

"If you keep thinking that hard, you might hurt yourself."

She rolls her eyes. "Well, one of us has to."

I laugh. "Not nice, Hex."

But she's right. We do need to think of something.

"It's not," she admits, her gaze drifting to the family photos on the wall. "What are they going to say about this?"

"Maybe they won't find out." Yeah, okay. And maybe I'll retire from hockey and join the cast of *Stars On Ice*.

I stride across the room and toward the couch. Once there, I plop down on it.

"Seriously, Hudson," she deadpans.

"No." I stretch out, making myself comfortable. We have a lot to discuss, and who knows how long it will take.

"Shit." She sighs before going quiet. I want to agree with her, but I need to stay strong and pretend this will all work out.

It doesn't help anyone for us both to be confused.

"All right, Hex." I break the silence. "Let's talk about this mess."

She stiffens, her arms tightening around herself. "Where do we even start?"

"Well . . ." I lean forward, resting my elbows on my knees. How do I say this? If I blurt it out, she might get upset. Oh, who am I kidding? She will get upset no matter how I say this. There is no world where she doesn't. "First off, you should know something."

She looks at me, her eyes wary, like she's bracing for bad news.

"We can't get an annulment."

"What?" She sits up so fast from where she was reclined, I'm afraid she might have pulled a muscle.

"This whole marriage thing?" I say, keeping my voice steady. "It's good for me."

Her brow furrows, and I can see the confusion and disbelief in her expression. "What?"

"Image-wise," I clarify. "It's good for my reputation. You know what people think of me. The playboy, the party guy, the guy who can't keep his name out of the tabloids. But now? Now I'm a family man. Married to a teammate's sister. It's like the ultimate PR makeover."

Her mouth falls open slightly, and I can tell she's trying to figure out if I'm serious.

"Are you saying we should stay married for your reputation?" she asks, her voice sharp.

"Not exactly," I say, holding up my hands. "I'm saying it's worth considering not doing it right away. I just got my first endorsement offer that wasn't from a condom company. Seven figures, Molly. That's not nothing. And it's not just about the money—it's about showing people I'm not who they think I am."

"Let me get this straight." Her jaw tightens, and she shakes her head. "You want me to be your PR stunt?"

"That's not what I mean." Shit, that did come out wrong. "Look, this could work for both of us. It will be temporary, but we can figure it out. You're already stuck with me, so—"

"Seriously, Hudson," she snaps. "You get an endorsement deal, and what about me? What do I get out of this deal?"

I sound like a real asshole when she puts it that way.

My mind short-circuits.

Think.

Think of something to say that won't make her storm out the door.

I open my mouth and then shut it.

Nope.

Nothing.

There's no fixing this.

beautiful collide

I really put my foot in my mouth this time.

I'm about to say anything—hell, I'll beg for her forgiveness—when her phone buzzes on the coffee table.

She picks it up, glances at the screen, and freezes. "It's your mom."

"What?" I sit straight up. "Why is she calling you?"

"I don't know," she says, staring at the phone like it's a ticking time bomb. Finally, she presses the speaker button.

"Molly, sweetheart." My mom's voice fills the room, bright and cheerful. Her normal, happy self. I don't even have to hear what she says to know this won't go well. "Oh, I'm so glad you picked up."

"Hi, Mrs. Wilde." Molly glances at me like she's hoping I'll save her.

"Call me Mary." My mom laughs. "We're family now, after all."

Shit.

She knows, and by the look on Molly's face, she's come to the same realization as I have.

I groan, dragging a hand down my face. Of course, she knows. *It's all over the news.*

Plus, if that isn't bad enough, Anna practically stalks me. She even has a damn Google alert that tells her whenever someone posts about me.

"Anna saw something online," my mom continues, oblivious to my growing mortification. "When she told me, I thought she was joking, but then I was like . . . well, that makes sense. I'm not blind."

"What do you mean?" Molly croaks.

"I could see the way Hudson looked at you that night at dinner. It was obvious something was going on. It makes sense. You're perfect for him, after all."

I look over at Molly, who is currently mouthing the word, "Perfect." Her eyes are wide, and she looks very confused, but she shakes her head after a second.

Molly bites back a laugh. "Thank you."

"Oh, honey, I'm so happy for you both." Jeez, my mom is

gushing. I need to put an end to this, or she's liable to say something really embarrassing.

"Hi, Mom," I cut in, making my presence known and hoping that's enough to stop her.

"Hudson, what am I going to do with you?"

"You're going to have to be more specific, Mom."

"You keeping this a secret. Why didn't you tell me?"

"Uh . . . surprise?" I scratch the back of my neck. God, I sound awkward. Not what I want Molly to see, but whenever my mom is around, I revert to a momma's boy.

She laughs. "Well, you'll have to come visit soon. I want to hear all about the wedding. And, Molly, I need to know everything—how did he propose? Was it romantic? Did he cry?"

Molly laughs nervously, and I groan again. "Mom, please."

This woman is going to be the death of me.

"Oh, hush, now," she says. "Molly, dear. Welcome to the family. We're so lucky to have you."

Lucky to have her.

My throat tightens, and I glance at Molly, who's staring down at her lap, her expression unreadable.

"Thank you," she whispers, and I wonder if my mom even heard her.

"Well, I'll let you two go. I'm sure you're both very busy." My mom giggles.

Great, my mom has her head in the gutter.

Knowing her, she will probably start wondering when we will give her grandbabies. "But don't be strangers. And, Hudson, don't mess this up. Molly's a keeper."

The call ends, and the silence in the room feels heavier than before.

Molly sets the phone down slowly, her hands trembling slightly. "I can't do it," she says suddenly, her voice shaking.

"Can't do what?" I ask, frowning.

"I can't divorce you," she says, meeting my eyes. "Not after that. Not after hearing how happy your mom is. At least not yet. I don't want her to know the truth. We can just keep this up a little longer, and then we can—"

"Molly..."

"Hudson. You don't understand. She welcomed me into her family like I've always been part of it." Her voice breaks. "She's so excited, Hudson. I can't take that away from her. It won't be forever, but long enough for you to get your deal and for your mom not to hate me."

My chest tightens, and I stare at her, unable to speak.

She doesn't have to do this.

She doesn't owe me—or my mom—anything. But the fact that she cares enough to stay, even if it's only for a short time, hits me harder than I expected.

"You don't have to do this for her," I say quietly.

"I know." Her voice is steadier now. "But I want to. Your family . . . they're incredible. They care about you so much. And if I can help make this whole thing easier, I will."

I swallow hard, my throat burning. "Why are you like this?" My voice sounds rough, and I wonder if she can hear how moved I am by her words.

"Like what?" She frowns.

"Caring," I say. "About my family. About me."

She laughs softly, shaking her head. "Because someone has to."

The words hit me like a punch to the gut, and all I can do is stare at her.

"Molly," I say, leaning closer. "You know this changes everything, right?"

She nods, her eyes meeting mine. "Yeah. I know."

Fuck. I'm in way over my head. Because when the time comes, I'm not sure I'll be able to let her go.

chapter sixty-nine

Molly

Cassidy: MOLLY SINCLAIR, EXPLAIN YOURSELF.

Josie: I wake up, check my phone, and BAM. "Hudson Wilde marries teammate's sister in Vegas." What is happening???

Cassidy: You MARRIED him??? Like . . . legally??

Molly: Can everyone calm down? It's not a big deal.

Cassidy: Not a big deal??? GIRL, it's literally a headline. I had to re-read it three times to make sure I wasn't hallucinating.

Josie: Do we call you Mrs. Wilde now? Or do you prefer Hex Wilde?

Molly: I knew I shouldn't have told you two about Hex.

Josie: To be fair, we loaded you with booze first.

Cassidy: Hex Wilde sounds like a supervillain. Fitting, honestly.

Molly: Stop. Both of you.

Josie: Oh, we're just getting started.

Cassidy: Wait, wait. Tell me there was Elvis. There had to be Elvis.

Molly: I'm not answering that.

Josie: 😂 THAT'S A YES.

Cassidy: I am crying. Vegas weddings and Elvis?? This is iconic.

Molly: I hate you both.

Josie: No, you don't. You're just mad we found out through TMZ instead of you.

Cassidy: So mad. You couldn't even send a "Hey, I married Hudson Wilde" text?

Molly: You're acting like this was planned! It wasn't. It just . . . happened.

Cassidy: "It just happened." That's your explanation? You tripped and fell into holy matrimony??

Josie: Did Hudson dare you? Tell me he dared you.

Molly: No, there was no dare!

Cassidy: So you chose this. Voluntarily.

Josie: Questionable decisions were made.

Cassidy: Extremely questionable.

Molly: Are you two done?

Josie: I'm never done. But seriously, Molls . . . are you okay? Like, for real?

Cassidy: Yeah. The media is going nuts. We're joking, but you know we're here if you need anything, right?

Molly: I'm fine. I promise. It's just . . . a lot.

Josie: I bet. Having your entire life plastered across the internet sucks.

Cassidy: And having Hudson as a husband can't help.

Molly: You have no idea.

Molly: Actually, Hudson is great.

Josie: I will say, you two are kind of . . . weirdly cute together? Like enemies-to-lovers, Vegas edition. You could write a book.

Molly: Don't. Start.

Cassidy: 😊 She's flustered. Did we hit a nerve, Mrs. Wilde?

Molly: Stop calling me that.

Josie: No chance.

Cassidy: Never happening.

Molly: You two are the worst.

Josie: But we love you. And if you need to hide, cry, scream, or plot Hudson's murder, just say the word.

Cassidy: We'll bring snacks and bail money.

Molly: I appreciate you idiots.

Cassidy: Anytime.

Cassidy: Now, seriously, does Hudson know how to say "I do," or did he just nod like an overconfident frat boy?

Molly: I'm leaving this chat.

Josie: 😊 That's not a denial.

Cassidy: We'll take that as confirmation.

Molly: I'm blocking you both.

Josie: Love you too, Mrs. Wilde.

Cassidy: Forever and always.

chapter seventy

Hudson

T HE GRAVEL OF THE DRIVEWAY CRUNCHES UNDER THE TIRES OF my Mustang. We probably should have driven Molly's car, but since we hauled ass out of Redville right after I rescued her, there was no time to go back to her place.

Driving up this path in my car always makes me cringe.

A paved road would be so much better for my car. Not that I can change it.

They can't afford it, and although I have offered, they will never take my money.

It's annoying as all hell.

I work hard, and I just want to help them.

But as we pull up to my parents' farmhouse, the sight of it never fails to hit me in the chest, even after all these years.

It's the same house I grew up in, but now it's weathered by years of neglect. I wish my father and mother weren't so prideful.

The small and quaint house has faded white paint and a wrap-around porch that faces the soybean fields.

"This is where you grew up?" Molly's been quiet since we left the main road, her eyes fixed on the scenery.

"It is."

"It's beautiful."

I narrow my eyes and shake my head as I roll to a stop. Is she seeing what I'm seeing?

The peeling siding.

The roof begging to be replaced.

Now, as I turn off the engine, she leans forward in her seat, her gaze sweeping over the house, the barn, and the fields in the distance.

"Crop farming?"

"Yeah, soybeans."

"I didn't even know that was something people grow out here."

I turn to face her. "It's actually one of the most prominent crops grown in Illinois."

Her lips curve into a smile. "The more you know," she jokes. "Well, it's beautiful. When I was a girl, and I used to have panic attacks, I would imagine myself no longer in the—" She stops herself, and I wonder what she was going to say. Her jaw looks tighter, but then she exhales and looks back out toward the property. "I used to imagine myself going to a farm like this. In the dream, I'd sit under a large tree, sun in my face, wind blowing my hair, and I'd be drinking a big glass of lemonade."

"That's pretty specific."

"It was a good dream." She looks wistful, and I want to give her that dream.

I want to make her happy.

The realization hits me in the gut. My head starts to spin with what that means for the future and how I can give her everything she wants.

An idea comes to me, a crazy one.

Maybe this is where I can help her.

Maybe this is the place to make Molly's dreams come true.

"Come on." I open the door, then walk around until I'm by her side, opening hers wider for her before reaching my arm out and grabbing her hand until she's standing outside the car.

"Hudson, I'm capable of getting out of a car."

"Yeah, I know. But you're my wife."

"Is it because your mom is peeking out the window and watching us?" Molly groans, and I laugh.

"Of course it is."

Stepping around to the back of the car, I pop the trunk and grab our bags. "Let's get inside before Mom bans us from eating dessert since we are late."

"Would she do that?"

"Hell yeah, she would. She wields the control over who gets her famous cookie bar like a power-hungry demon."

Molly laughs. "That's mean."

I shrug. "It's the truth. Wait. You'll see. Dad is always in the doghouse; he never gets seconds."

Molly laughs nervously, and I can't help smiling. She's out of her element, but she's here. With me.

We aren't even up the path to the main house when the screen door swings open. My mom steps out, her hands on her hips and a grin on her face.

She's wearing her usual faded jeans and a T-shirt, this one with a giant soybean on her chest. Her hair is pulled back into a messy bun like she doesn't have a care in the world.

I love that about my mom. She's not one to change who she is for anyone else.

The king of England could be coming to our house for dinner, and she would still look and act the same.

"Hudson. Molly, you're here. Finally." *Way to play it cool, Mom.*

With Molly in tow, I climb the stairs and pull my mom into a hug. "Hey, Mom. You remember Molly?"

My mother swats me on the arm. "Of course, I remember my daughter-in-law." I look back at Molly and see that she looks a little tense, but it's short-lived because soon Molly is being pulled toward my mom, who's hugging her like her life depends on it. "You know this is the most proud you ever made me, Hudson."

"You weren't this proud when I got called up to the pros?"

She doesn't answer.

Molly shifts in her arms.

"Mom. Let her go. I don't think she can breathe."

"I'm fine, Hudson," Molly says, meeting my stare and practically begging me to shut the hell up. "Hi, Mrs. Wilde."

"I already told you. It's Mary." She lets Molly go finally. "I have so many stories to tell you. And pictures to show you. I've been waiting for this day for a long time." My mom turns to me, narrowing her eyes. "I thought you'd be bringing a girlfriend home, not a wife. But this will do."

"Gee, thanks, Mom. Happy to have your approval."

"Shh, Hudson. Or there will be no death by chocolate for you tonight," my mom fires back, making Molly laugh.

"What? No. That's unfair."

She places her hands on her hips and challenges me to continue.

Molly watches us like a person watching a tennis match, her gaze bouncing back and forth. "Stories, huh?"

Damn. She caught that.

"Only the good ones, okay, Mom?"

"No promises," she says before giving Molly a once-over. "You're even prettier than I remember."

Molly blushes, stammering out a thank-you, and I feel a weird sense of pride swell in my chest.

"You guys go get settled in Hudson's old room—"

"Mom, it might be better if Molly sleeps in the guest room since I only have a twin bed," I say. While I'd love to sleep in a bed with Molly, I want her to be comfortable and sharing a twin isn't ideal.

"Oh, about that. . .Don't you remember. I turned the guest room into a craft room."

I narrow my eyes but don't say anything.

beautiful collide

Since when?

Something tells me this is a new renovation...

One that happened just for us.

As the night winds down and the sun dips lower in the sky, I can't help but stare at Molly.

She seems so much more relaxed than she did back in Redville.

It's almost like the whole reporter debacle from earlier today never happened.

She's laughing at one of my dad's corny dad jokes, many about the farm, which I bet she doesn't even understand, but she's a good spirit about it all.

My mom busies herself clearing the table, swatting away any attempts to help.

"Hudson, grab the death by chocolate pie from the counter." My mom motions to the kitchen.

"Yes, Mom." I push back from the table and catch Molly's eye. She's already helping stack plates despite my mom's protests.

She fits in perfectly.

It's like she's known them all for years.

I grab the pie, then set it down in front of her.

Mom starts serving everyone a slice.

Molly takes a seat at the table. "That's . . . um. Too much." Molly's eyes are wide.

The piece takes up half the plate. Mom does love to cut the slices very generously.

"Trust me when I say it's not enough. It's the best dessert you'll ever have," I promise as Molly takes a small bite.

Her eyes widen. "This is incredible."

"See, Hudson? At least your wife appreciates my baking." My mom beams.

"I just called it the best pie she'd ever eat, Mom. Jeez." I raise my hands in surrender. "Get off my case."

We all eat in silence, other than the groan of appreciation that slips out of my dad's mouth.

He's really annoying when he eats Mom's pies, but I don't call him out since Molly is here.

After dessert, Molly stands to help clear the plates again.

"Stop helping," Mom says. "Hudson, take Molly outside."

I glance at Molly. "I'd like that." She smiles.

"Come on." I grab her hand and lead her toward the back door. "We'll start with the short tour of the property."

The gravel crunches under our feet as we cross the driveway.

Molly looks around, her gaze lingering on the horizon, where the sky glows in shades of orange and pink.

"It's beautiful," she murmurs.

"This is the best time of day," I admit. "It's peaceful."

"It is."

We walk toward the fields, the sky darkening as the stars begin to peek out. Molly stops every so often to take in the scenery.

She looks deep in thought, and I wish I could hear her thoughts and know what she's thinking. Instead, I give her space.

After a few more minutes of walking in silence, I take her right hand in mine and lead her to the large oak tree at the edge of the property.

"This is it," I say, stopping beneath the tree. "The place from your dream."

As the words leave my mouth, I thank fuck that none of the boys from the team are here to hear me. I'm laying it on thick with cringe, but the thing is . . . Molly deserves it.

She looks up, her eyes softening as she takes in the wide trunk and the large branches that act as a canopy. "It's perfect."

"It's almost perfect."

Molly raises an eyebrow, clearly not understanding, but then I reach into my pocket and pull out a small thermos I snagged before we left the house.

Her eyes widen as realization must hit her. "Not quite

lemonade, but close enough." I pour her a cup of iced tea and hand it to her.

She laughs, shaking her head. "You thought of everything."

"Not everything. But it's a start."

She sits beneath the tree, her back against the trunk, and I join her.

We sit in silence, the only noise coming from the sounds of the farm as day turns into night.

"This is nice," she says, her voice barely above a whisper.

"Yeah," I agree, looking at her instead of the horizon. "It is."

chapter seventy-one

Hudson

AN HOUR LATER, WE'RE BACK IN THE HOUSE. WE STILL HAVE to unpack before bed, but since I'm not ready to call it a night, I decide to show Molly around a bit.

The impromptu tour isn't just for her. It's for me too.

I want to see her eyes when I tell her the stories of this place. When I share my memories with her, will she get it? Will she understand how much this house means to me?

How much I want her to feel like she belongs here?

I hope so.

I lead her into the living room first. Unable to resist a little drama, I give the summary with all the flair of a teen at drama camp. "The living room," I announce, sweeping my arm like I'm unveiling something grand. "Where many a family movie night went down and where my dad once fell asleep during *Home Alone* and woke up convinced burglars were breaking into the house."

She laughs, the sound warm and effortless, and I can't help but grin. "Sounds like fun," she says.

"The stories I can tell." I point to a dent in the wood floor. "That's from when Anna tried to skate . . . with skates on."

Her mouth drops open. "In the house?"

"Yep. Let's just say Mom was pissed."

"I bet." Molly laughs so hard, I can't help but laugh too.

It's not just a house to her anymore, and that matters to me more than I expected it to.

Next, we head to the kitchen.

"I know this isn't a new room, but a tour isn't a tour unless I tell you a story in each room."

"Is that so?" she teases.

"It is." I point my hand to the oven. "For example, that's where I accidentally set a fire and almost burned down the house."

Molly gasps.

"Don't worry. We put it out."

"You think?" She rolls her eyes.

I run a hand along the counter as I talk. "This is where Mom makes the magic happen. Her cinnamon rolls are legendary. One time, Mason tried to bribe her into making them for the whole team. Maybe you'll get lucky, and she'll make some while you're here." I throw in a wink.

"Did it work?" she asks.

"Of course it did," I reply with a laugh. "Mom can't resist feeding people. But Mason had to help clean the barn in exchange. He lasted ten minutes before he bailed. Pun intended."

Her laughter fills the kitchen, and I feel a swell of pride. I don't know what it is about making her laugh, but it feels like winning a game in overtime. Like I'd do anything just to hear it again.

After a quick stop in the dining room, where I point out the chair I broke when I was ten trying to pull off an "epic dive," we head upstairs. The air feels quieter up here, more personal. She's walking through memories I haven't shared with anyone in a long time.

We stop in the hallway, and I gesture to my door. "Obviously, you know that's my room."

"Hard to miss the hockey shrine when I first walked in there," she says dryly, her eyes sparkling as she gestures to the posters and trophies lining the walls.

"Hey, those were my glory days," I say, feigning offense.

She rolls her eyes but smiles anyway, and I feel like I'm fourteen again, trying to impress someone I like. God, I'm pathetic. But also? I kind of don't care.

"And this," I say, stopping in front of the door across the hall, "is Anna's room."

I push the door open, and she peeks inside. The bright and cheerful room is full of books, art supplies, and Anna's signature chaos. Photos and postcards cover the corkboard on the wall, a patchwork of her life.

"She's the artistic one in the family." That is obvious from the state of her room. But I still point out a sketch pad on her desk. "Always painting or drawing something."

"That's amazing," Molly says, turning to look at me.

"She's amazing," I say simply because it's true. "Sometimes she's a pain in the ass, of course, but I love her."

We head back into the hallway. "Now, where is this *craft* room?"

I'm sure it's obvious to Molly that there is no craft room, or at least there never was. Neither one of us is in any denial that something was up with my mother.

I'm curious to see what her play is. I'm pretty sure I know, but seeing and thinking are too different things.

I point at the door across from mine. "So, this is it, the *famous* craft room," I say, pushing open the door to what used to be the guest room.

Molly steps in behind me, her arms crossed. I pivot to look at her and bite back a laugh.

I can practically hear her thoughts as she surveys the mess inside. The twin bed is shoved haphazardly against one wall.

Yeah, no one is buying this, Mom.

If the bed's location isn't bad enough, the mattress is leaning slightly off the frame.

She didn't even bother to make this look believable.

The "sewing machine"—that's the main reason she needed this room for her crafts after all—sits on a tiny folding table dead center in the middle of the room, like anyone will believe it belongs there.

This is ridiculous.

I love my mom, but she's gone too far this time.

A pile of fabric in colors ranging from baby pink to blinding neon green is thrown on the floor in a pile.

That must have taken her one minute to set up. And for the final selling point, someone crammed an old rocking chair into the corner of the room right next to a stack of yarn that looks like it might collapse at any moment.

I turn to face Molly because I need to see her reaction to my mother's treachery.

Molly's mouth twitches, and I know she's trying not to laugh. "Wow. This is some craft room."

I run a hand through my hair, trying to hide my grin. "It's been like this for *years*."

"Years?" Molly echoes, clearly amused. "My best guess is it looks like she converted this room this morning."

"You don't say." There is no hiding the sarcasm in my voice. Not that I'm trying.

Molly picks up a piece of fabric before setting it back down. "Right. A total coincidence that the room is packed with so much stuff there's barely enough space to breathe, let alone sleep."

Mom is a diabolical genius. That's for sure.

"Exactly." I lean against the doorframe. "Completely unrelated to the fact that she wants us to share a room."

Molly gives me a look. It's a cross between half amused and half exasperated. "Your mom is a mastermind, isn't she?"

"She's something all right."

"Two words come to mind." She laughs. "Lovely and funny."

"Yeah, let's go with that," I say with a chuckle. "She's definitely determined."

Molly shakes her head, glancing around the room one last time. "Well, I guess that settles it. The guest room's out of the question."

"Guess so." I push off the doorframe. "Come on. Let's get you settled in my room."

We step into my old bedroom, and I suddenly feel like I'm fifteen again, awkward and unsure of what to say.

Despite having an active social life in high school, I never brought a girl home. Which makes my mom's meddling even funnier.

I watch Molly surveying the room for the second time as though she thought the hour outside would change the fact that there still is only one tiny twin bed for us to share.

At least the bed still sits in the corner. That way, we have a wall to lean on so no one falls off the bed when we sleep.

It still looks the same as when I lived here.

Nothing has changed.

Not the navy blue comforter.

Or the hockey posters lining the walls.

This is so embarrassing.

There is literally a signed poster of a player I idolized as a kid.

Can this get any worse?

Why yes, it can.

Trophies and medals still line the shelves.

It's a shrine to my childhood.

I watch Molly as she takes it all in. She stops at the desk, where a photo of Anna and me sits. We're both grinning like idiots, holding up a snowman we built in the backyard one winter.

"This is so . . . you." Molly smirks.

"What's that supposed to mean?"

She glances at me, a faint smile tugging at her lips. "I don't know. It's just . . . it feels like stepping into your head. It's kind of nice."

"Nice?" I repeat, raising an eyebrow. "I was going for impressive."

She rolls her eyes. "Sorry, there is nothing impressive about that." She points her finger toward the bed, making me laugh.

"Touché."

Molly walks over to the bed and sits. "This is going to be . . . interesting."

"Interesting is one word for it." I cross my arms at my chest.

She sighs, brushing a stray strand of hair out of her face. "Okay, ground rules. No snoring, no hogging the blankets, and absolutely no crossing the invisible line down the middle of the bed."

I smirk, tilting my head. "Invisible line, huh? Sounds complicated."

"It's not," she says firmly. "You stay on your side; I stay on mine. Simple. No sex in your parents' house."

"You're no fun." The thought of being this close to her all night without crossing that line sounds like its own brand of torture.

"Do we have a deal?" She holds out her hand.

"Another deal." I wink.

"Oh, shut it." She shakes her head. "Yes or no?"

I hesitate for a second, then step forward and shake her hand. Her skin is warm against mine, and I forget how to let go.

"Deal," I say finally, my voice quieter than I intended.

She pulls her hand back quickly, clearing her throat as she stands. "Good. Now, let's figure out where to put my stuff."

After unpacking her bag and finding room for her things in my closet (barely), we settle into an awkward rhythm.

I sit on the edge of the bed, watching as she arranges her toiletries on the small desk by the window.

"This feels like something you would see in a movie about summer camp," she mutters, lining up her travel-size bottles of shampoo and lotion. "I never went, so I wouldn't know, but I imagine it like this."

"Except at camp, you don't usually have to share a bed with your bunkmate," I point out.

She glares at me over her shoulder. "Oh, yeah, well, don't remind me."

I laugh, leaning back on my hands. "Relax, Hex. It's just a bed."

"A bed we'll be sharing for lord knows how long while we hide away from the press," she says, turning to face me. "This is your fault, you know."

"My fault?" I say, feigning offense.

"Yes," she says, crossing her arms. "If you hadn't dragged me into this whole farm hideout plan, I'd be at home in my perfectly comfortable apartment, in my perfectly comfortable bed."

"Where the paparazzi would still be camped outside your door," I point out.

She sighs, her shoulders sagging. "Okay, fine. You're right. But that doesn't mean I have to like it."

"Fair enough," I say, standing and walking over to her. "But hey, look on the bright side."

"What bright side?" She narrows her eyes.

"At least my mom likes you." I grin. "That's more than I can say for most people I've dated."

Her cheeks flush, and she looks away, pretending to straighten a bottle of lotion. "One, it sounds like you've never brought a woman home before . . . and two, that's because your mom doesn't know the full story."

"Maybe." I lean against my desk. "Or maybe she just has good taste."

She glances at me, and something unspoken passes between us.

"Well," she says, breaking the silence. "We should probably get ready for bed."

"Yeah. Good idea."

"Are you sure this will work?" she asks.

beautiful collide

"Nope," I say, grinning.

She groans, climbing onto the bed and lying down on one side. "If you kick me in your sleep, I'm moving to the couch downstairs."

"Noted," I say, lying down beside her.

The bed creaks under our weight, and neither of us speaks. The room is quiet except for our breathing. "Thanks for coming here." I turn my head to look at her.

"Thanks for bringing me." She smiles at me, and my heart thumps in my chest. "Good night, Hudson."

"Good night, Hex."

chapter seventy-two

Molly

H E'S TOO CLOSE. EVERY MOVE HE MAKES, I FEEL. THE STEADY inhale of his breath, the way his chest rises and falls, the warmth radiating off his body.

I'm supposed to be sleeping, but I can't. *Not like this.*

This is torture.

His mom is a diabolical genius because, in this tiny bed, all I can think about is how much I want him.

The soft fragrance of his cologne filters through my nose like an aphrodisiac. It beckons me to cross the tiny space that separates us and do what I want.

And all I want to do is kiss him.

"I can hear you thinking over there," he murmurs, his voice low and teasing.

"No, you can't," I shoot back, even though my pulse betrays me. It's hammering in my ears so loud he might actually be able to hear it.

"Sure, I can. It's so loud, I wondered if I had a superpower and can read your mind."

"You're not funny."

"Yet you said, 'I do.'"

"Har, har. Go to sleep."

"Whatever you want, Hex."

I feel him shift, and before I can react, his arm wraps around me, pulling me closer.

Now, my head rests on his chest, and I can hear the steady rhythm of his heartbeat, slow and even.

This man does crazy things to me.

Be strong.

There is no having sex in his childhood bed with his parents down the hall.

Just as I'm about to turn over and try to scoot as far away as possible, he presses a soft kiss to the top of my head, lingering just a second too long, and my breath catches.

Calm down, girl.

Just because he kissed your head doesn't mean he wants to—okay, maybe he does.

Because, at this exact second, I can feel his hand begin to trace a slow, deliberate path down my back, his fingers barely grazing my skin through the thin fabric of my shirt.

Okay, that means he does, right?

If I'm reading this right, he wants me. Now the question is, am I willing to risk his parents hearing just to feel him inside me right now?

"Hudson," I whisper, but I don't pull away.

His hand pauses for the briefest moment before continuing its gentle exploration, the warmth of his palm leaving trails of fire on my skin.

"What?" he murmurs, his voice rough with something I don't dare name.

"This isn't . . ." My voice falters as his finger dips lower, brushing against the curve of my hip.

"Isn't what?" He's teasing now, and I'm ready to snap.

I lift my head to meet his gaze, and the intensity in his eyes steals whatever words I thought I had.

He shifts again, his free hand coming up to cup my cheek, his thumb brushing across my skin with a tenderness that makes my chest ache.

"Say the word, Hex," he whispers, his voice barely audible. "And I'll stop."

I don't say anything. Instead, I lean in, closing the gap between us, and press my lips to his.

The kiss starts soft and tentative but doesn't stay that way.

Soon, his fingers are entangled in my hair as we devour each other's mouths.

Maybe if he weren't such a good kisser—oh, who am I kidding? I still wouldn't be able to stop.

I want Hudson Wilde.

I want him with every fiber of my bones.

Right here. Right now.

He pulls back just enough to rest his forehead against mine, his breathing uneven.

"You're impossible, you know that?"

"You're the one who started this," I counter, my voice trembling but steady enough to challenge him.

He laughs softly, the sound vibrating through my body where it's pressed against his. "And I'm the one who's going to finish it."

I'm about to say is that so, when he silences me again. His mouth seals onto mine.

He pulls me on top of him, and the moment he does, I know I'm lost to this man.

I need him, and I need him now.

Without another thought, I push my body up, giving myself the room to place my hand between us.

beautiful collide

With each swipe of my tongue, I almost forget what I'm doing, but I'm a determined woman, slowly working my way to pulling his extremely hard cock out from his briefs. Once in my hand, I begin to stroke him from root to tip, getting him ready for me.

"What are you doing, Hex?" he asks.

"Taking what I want," I respond, matter-of-fact.

"Is that so?"

"Yes, now be quiet so no one hears."

He must agree with my crazy plan because the next thing I know, I feel his hands on my hips as he pulls my sleep shirt up and pushes my panties down.

Once I'm bare to him, I don't waste any time. I'm so hot and bothered, it won't take me long.

I lift my hips and align his cock with my entrance, then I sink down until his hard length is buried inside me.

"You feel so good," he groans on a whisper.

The feeling of us joining is sublime, but I need to move and chase the high that only Hudson can give me.

I rock back, and his cock almost slips out, then he thrusts back in. His hands grip my ass, helping me rise and fall on his dick.

Over and over again, I rock, grinding down, rubbing my clit each time on his pelvic bone.

It's too much. My body feels like it's floating away. My inner walls start to quiver and quake, gripping him harder and tighter as I fall over the edge. I fall forward, and he takes over, thrusting upward until his cock jerks in me, filling me with everything he has.

"Fuck. That was good," he whispers before the room falls silent except for our breathing, tangled and uneven. Exhausted, I close my eyes, vowing to get up in a moment, but for now, I let out a small sigh as we lie together, the outside world forgotten.

chapter seventy-three

Molly

THE FOLLOWING MORNING COMES FASTER THAN I EXPECT, AND surprisingly, I feel great.

As shocking as it seems, I slept. And honestly, it was probably the best sleep of my life.

I'm going to try not to read into why. *Hudson.* It's all him.

Even now, just thinking of waking up in his arms, has a smile spreading across my face.

Damn, I got it bad. So bad, that I really want to tell him that we should forgo going outside and go for round two instead.

The screen door slams shut behind me as Hudson steps out onto the porch, his boots thudding heavily against the wooden planks.

He turns to face me, that easy grin plastered on his face, and gestures toward the property stretching out before us.

"Well, Hex." Hudson shoves his hands into his pockets. "Ready for the next part of your grand tour of the Wilde farm?"

beautiful collide

I glance at him, squinting against the late-morning sun. In the fresh light of the day, the farm looks so peaceful.

It's obvious why Hudson loves to come here.

Hell, I haven't been here that long and I already love it too.

The grass is sprawling. I've never seen anything like it. It's almost as though it stretches out all the way toward the horizon.

None of this feels real.

A picture-perfect red barn sits off in the distance, and I can just make out a weathered fence that wraps around the whole property.

It's unreal, straight out of my dreams.

"Do I have a choice?" I joke, raising a playful eyebrow.

"Not really," he says, his grin widening. "Come on. This is the fun part."

"The fun part?" Together, we walk farther onto the property.

"Welcome to the farm." He spreads his arms wide as he leads us toward our first stop.

Up close, the barn is exactly how I imagined it.

It's straight out of a movie, with red paint, a slightly crooked roof, and the faint smell of hay.

Perfection.

"You're going to love this." Hudson pushes open the doors.

The first thing I see is the stalls for the horses. "You have horses?" I say, shock evident in my voice.

"We do."

"Wow. You really are a man with secrets." I laugh before walking farther into the barn to see what else Hudson's been hiding from me all these years.

Obviously, it wasn't intentional since I never allowed myself to get to know him. But now that I am, I really like this side of him.

"This," Hudson says, pointing at a dusty corner near the back, "is where I learned how to skate."

I blink, confused. "In the barn?"

"Yep," he says, grinning. "My dad made me an indoor rink. I'd spend hours in here practicing."

"That's . . . surprisingly resourceful," I say, impressed.

He shrugs. "When you're a farm kid, you make do with what you've got. I didn't step foot on a real rink until I was eight."

"Eight?" I echo, surprised. "But you're so good. How did you catch up so fast?"

He smirks. "Talent, Hex. Pure, natural talent."

I roll my eyes because he's ridiculous.

Next, we visit the chicken coop, where a flock of hens cluck and peck at the ground.

"Meet the ladies." Hudson gestures grandly.

A laugh bubbles up. They have chickens. Of course, they do.

How did I peg him so wrong?

Everything I thought I knew about Hudson is the opposite of the truth.

I always assumed he was raised in an affluent family from a city. Which couldn't be further from the reality.

Wow. I was off.

Another giggle breaks loose when I see a feisty-looking hen flap her wings and glare at me. "They seem . . . territorial."

"They're harmless." He reaches down to pick one up. "Mostly."

I take a cautious step back as he cradles the hen in his arms like it's the most natural thing in the world.

"Wanna hold her?" He holds the hen out to me.

"Absolutely not." I cross my arms.

He laughs, setting the hen back down. "City girl," he teases.

"And damn proud of it," I shoot back.

The last stop on the tour is the pasture, where a couple of horses graze lazily.

"Do you ride?" Hudson asks as we approach the fence.

"No."

"Never?"

"Once when I was a kid," I admit. "But that was at a party, and it wasn't even riding. It was more like being led around in a circle."

"Well"—he leans on the fence—"maybe we'll change that while you're here."

I glance at him, half expecting him to be joking, but his expression is sincere.

"I don't know," I say, hesitant.

"You'll love it," he says, his voice soft. "It's one of the best feelings in the world. Don't worry, it won't be for a few days. Relax."

I stare at the horses, their movements calm and unhurried, and for a moment, I let myself imagine it—riding through the fields, the wind in my hair, the world quiet and peaceful.

"Maybe," I say finally.

Hudson grins, and I feel something in my chest loosen.

By the time we head back to the house, the sun is high in the sky.

I'm tired, my legs ache from walking, and I have dirt smudged on my jeans, but I feel . . . lighter.

"This place," I say as we climb the porch steps. "It's special."

"Yeah." Hudson holds the door open for me. "It is."

And as I step inside, I realize something I hadn't before.

For the first time in years, I feel like I belong.

chapter seventy-four

Hudson

Dane: So let me get this straight . . . you took your new wife, MY SISTER, to a farm for the honeymoon? A literal farm.

Mason: 🐄 Moo, bitches.

Aiden: I don't even know what to say.

Hudson: It's not our honeymoon.

Mason: Sure it's not. Just you, Molly, and a bunch of cows starting your married life in style.

Aiden: Nothing says "I love you" like milking goats.

Hudson: We don't even have goats.

Dane: You're not helping your case, dude.

Hudson: My mom invited us. She wanted to spend time with her new daughter-in-law.

Mason: Your mom invited you? On your honeymoon? Hudson, blink twice if you're being held hostage by your family.

Hudson: Find another joke Mason.

Mason: That's not a no.

beautiful collide

Aiden: Did she put you to work too? I bet Hudson's out there chopping wood and tilling fields while Molly's sipping lemonade, laughing at his misery.

Hudson: I'm not chopping wood.

Mason: Sure you're not. I can already picture you. Shirtless, flexing for Molly like some Hallmark movie farmer.

Aiden: "She fell in love with the farm boy. His abs were the real honeymoon."

Hudson: You guys are idiots.

Dane: At least tell me you took her somewhere nice before forcing her to do manual labor.

Hudson: I didn't force her to do anything.

Mason: So what you're saying is Molly is out there bonding with your mom while you're baling hay. That's the story?

Hudson: There's no hay. You're all unhinged.

Aiden: It's a farm. There's definitely hay.

Hudson: Can you all focus on something else?

Mason: Nope. You're the entertainment today, Wilde.

Hudson: You're all dead to me.

Mason: Is that you in the barn? Is that where you're texting us from right now?

Aiden: He's probably hiding from his mom.

Dane: Or hiding from Molly after she realized this is her "honeymoon."

Hudson: IT'S NOT A HONEYMOON.

Mason: Sure, Farmer Hudson. Now go tend to your chickens or whatever.

Hudson: I hate all of you.

Mason: Love you too, big guy. 🐄

Aiden: 🐔

Dane: 🧺

Hudson: What's with the basket?

Dane: It's for the eggs Molly's probably gathering.

Hudson: I'm blocking this chat.

Mason: No, you're not. You'd miss us too much.

Hudson: I'll send you all hay bales for Christmas.

Aiden: He admits it! There's hay!

Mason: HA.

Hudson has left the chat.

Mason: He'll be back.

Aiden: He always comes back.

Dane: Text me when he starts ranting about this in person.

Mason: Deal.

chapter seventy-five

Molly

THE CHILL OF THE RINK HITS ME THE MOMENT WE STEP INSIDE. It's freezing in here. Or maybe it's the contrast from the warm air outside, but damn I'm cold.

The crisp air tickles my cheeks as we make our way to the ice.

"This was the first rink I ever skated on," Hudson tells me as we stand beside the entrance.

His grin is wide enough to make my heart stutter.

He looks alive here, like the ice is where he belongs, where he's completely himself.

"All right, Hex." He nods toward the benches. "Let's do this."

"Do what?" I glance at him and then at the ice.

"Lace up, duh." He motions to the skates he's carrying.

"Wait, are we really doing this?" Can I sound any dumber? Of course we're skating. He's borrowed Anna's skates; what did I think he was going to do with them?

"Yes."

I let out a long-drawn-out sigh. "I haven't done this in years. Like since I was a kid. And even then, I was terrible at it."

"Which I find funny knowing who your brother is."

"Why? Not all siblings are the same. Look at you and Anna."

"You make a valid point."

"I always do." I smile. "Okay, so I'm warning you. I suck at this. No laughing."

"Would I laugh? Fine. I would. But I promise I won't. Plus, I'm here to help," he says, dropping onto the bench and motioning for me to sit beside him. "I'll make sure you don't break anything."

"Reassuring," I mutter, but I sit down anyway.

Hudson grabs a pair of skates from the bag he brought and slides them across the floor toward me. "These should fit."

I sigh, kicking off my sneakers and slipping my feet into the skates. They feel stiff and awkward.

"Have I mentioned I don't skate?" I deadpan, staring at my feet like I want to rip the skates off.

"Here." Hudson crouches in front of me. "I can't believe I'm saying this to you, of all people, but you're doing it all wrong. I'm literally mortified for you and your brother; you have no business working for an NHL player."

His words hit close to my own fears. I really don't have any business working for him.

My mood turns dark as intrusive thoughts try to push their way in, but I don't let them.

I will not ruin the moment.

Instead, I raise an eyebrow as he takes over. "Oh, so now you're an expert on tying skates?"

"Pretty much," he says, glancing up at me with a smirk. "You're in good hands."

I roll my eyes, but there's no denying the way my pulse quickens when he looks at me like that.

Once my skates are on, Hudson leads me to the edge of the

rink, his hand steady on my arm. The ice stretches out in front of us, smooth and slippery from what I can remember.

I see the irony, of course.

Dane loves being on the ice, and like most things I can't control, I hate it.

The idea of falling on my face isn't that enticing.

Yet here I am, stepping onto the ice, and the moment my skate touches it, I wobble.

This is pathetic.

I take another step out, and my legs spread so wide I look like a baby deer learning to walk.

Bambi's got nothing on me.

"How are you so bad at this? Your brother is legit the best enforcer in the league."

This is going to be annoying to explain. "I never got lessons. No one taught me."

Hudson halts his movements. "I'm confused. But then, how did Dane learn?"

I take a deep breath. "My dad taught him."

"And he didn't teach you?"

Of course, Hudson wouldn't understand this. His family practically belongs on the Hallmark channel. Wholesome, caring, and a far cry from how my formerly drunk father was.

"Why would he? Only Dane could go to the NHL." I don't finish the thought, but we both know it. That he didn't teach Dane out of love. He taught him out of greed. Only Dane needed to be the cash cow.

"No fear, Hex. If you suck at skating, that's cool. Luckily for you, I'll teach you."

"Gee, thanks."

"And the best part . . . you don't even have to worry about how you're going to pay me. I'm rich, and I accept other forms of payment." He waggles his brows at me.

I can't help but laugh.

If Hudson is good at one thing, he can always lighten the mood. It's his superpower.

"Ready?" he asks, and I shake my head.

"No." At least I'm honest.

"Come on, Hex. Don't be like that. It's easy. First rule is don't fall."

"Wow. That's some great advice you got there, Wilde," I say dryly.

He laughs, stepping onto the ice effortlessly beside me. "Have no fear, I'll help you." He reaches his hand out to me. I take a deep breath and grasp it.

"Now all you have to do is relax," Hudson says, his grip firm but gentle. "I've got you."

"Easy for you to say," I mutter, my eyes glued to my skates. "You aren't the one who most likely will fall on their face and break their nose."

"First off, do you think I'd let you break that cute button nose you have?"

"You're annoying."

"And you married me."

"Don't remind me," I deadpan.

He chuckles, guiding me slowly onto the rink. "You're overthinking it. Just let go and trust me."

Let go. Trust him. *Sure.*

The words hit harder than they should, stirring something deep in my chest.

Trust isn't something I give easily.

Especially not after everything I've been through. But there's something about him, something I can't put my finger on, that makes me want to try.

We start slow.

He pulls me toward him, wrapping his arms around me, and skates for us both.

I'm stiff at first, and every muscle in my body is tense.

Please don't let me fall.

He won't.

When has he ever?

Despite everything in our past and the little lie the first time we met, he never let me down.

I keep that thought in my head as I give my trust to him and kick off from one foot to the next, gliding across the ice.

"See . . ." He places a kiss on my hair. "Not so bad, right? Now let's try this." He lets go of me and starts to skate until he's facing me, but he's skating backward this time, taking my hands in his.

Yeah, I think I liked it better when his arms were wrapped around me.

"Nope." I glare at him. "I'm not ready for this. I'm totally going to fall."

He grins, his hands tightening slightly on mine. "I wouldn't let that happen." Something about the way he says it, so matter-of-fact, makes me believe him.

It takes a while, but after a few laps around the rink, I find a rhythm, and I'm no longer as wobbly.

Hudson lets go of one of my hands and pivots his body, so he is now skating beside me.

"All right." He slows to a stop. "Time to change it up."

That doesn't sound promising.

I stop awkwardly, nearly losing my balance. *Real smooth, Molly. Real smooth.* "Um, what?"

His lips part, and now I know I should be worried because the grin he gives me is mischievous as all hell. "I want you to close your eyes."

"Nope. That would be negatory." I immediately shake my head. "That is never going to happen."

"Molly." His voice is softer now. "Would I steer you wrong?"

"Yes." My answer comes out so fast that Hudson's lip twitches.

He inclines his chin down, looking me straight in the eye. "Molly . . ."

"Don't Molly me."

"Please trust me." Something about the way he says that makes my pulse race a little faster. Can I really deny him this?

I stare at him, my heart pounding. "Hudson, I can barely stay upright as it is."

"You're better than you think." He steps closer. "And I'm right here. I won't let anything happen to you."

The words sink in, heavy and reassuring.

I want to believe him. I want to trust him.

But the idea of giving up control, even for a moment, makes my chest tighten with anxiety.

He must see the hesitation in my eyes because he steps even closer, his hands resting lightly on my shoulders.

"It's just you and me." He squeezes lightly. "No one else. No cameras, no reporters, no pressure. Just us."

I take a shaky breath, his words melting the edges of my fear. Slowly, I nod. "Okay."

"Okay," he says, his smile widening. "Close your eyes."

I do, squeezing them shut as I feel his hands slide down to my waist.

"Good," he says. "Now let me guide you."

With my eyes closed, my other senses kick up a notch. I'm hyperaware of his presence as he steadies me and skates us around the rink. It feels as if the world centers around us, and we are the only people.

It's him.

His laughter.

His voice.

His strength.

He's shifted something in me.

The ice feels smooth and steady as Hudson guides me around, and for the first time in what feels like forever, I let go.

"You're doing great," Hudson says, his voice filled with pride.

I smile, the edges of my fear melting away.

"I have one more thing I want to try?" he asks, his tone teasing.

I open my eyes, narrowing them at him. "Evasive much? What does that even mean?"

Before I can get an answer, he bends slightly, his hands sliding down to my legs as he lifts me effortlessly into the air.

"What the hell?" My hands fly to his shoulders.

"Relax." He spins us in a slow circle. For a second, I feel dizzy, maybe from the movement or maybe from nerves, but the more we move, the more my mind lets go. "I've got you."

I feel high off life.

The world blurs around me, the motion making me feel weightless. As my inhibitions fade away, something shifts inside me.

Peace. *I feel at peace.*

For the first time in years, I feel free. Free from the fear, the anxiety, from everything I have held in my chest for so long.

A few minutes later, Hudson sets me down gently, his hands lingering on my waist as I find my balance again.

My heart races, but not from fear. From hope. Maybe he's right. *I can do this.*

"See?" he says, his voice soft. "Told you that you could do it."

I look up at him.

My breath catches at the way he's looking at me—*like I'm the only thing in the world that matters.*

And that's when it hits me.

I'm falling for him.

Hard and fast and against every ounce of logic I have left.

But standing here, on this ice, in his arms, I can't bring myself to care.

chapter seventy-six

Molly

Cassidy: Okay, spill. Is the rumor true? Are you at a farm?

Josie: Like . . . an actual farm? With cows and chickens? And dirt? Send a mushroom emoji if you're in trouble and need rescuing.

Molly: Yes, there are cows, and chickens, and dirt. And no, I don't need rescuing. Yet.

Cassidy: Yet?!!!! What are you even doing out there?

Molly: Mostly trying not to get eaten alive by mosquitoes.

Josie: OMG. How did this happen? Were you kidnapped?

Cassidy: Hudson. It's Hudson, isn't it? You're being held hostage by that man.

Molly: I am not being held hostage. I'm fine.

Cassidy: So you're willingly on a farm? Molly, I've known you long enough to know that willingly and farm do not belong in the same sentence for you.

Molly: I am here of my own free will. Mostly.

Josie: What does that even mean?!

beautiful collide

Molly: Look, it's not that bad. Hudson's parents are really nice.

Cassidy: This is worse than I thought. You're being charmed by the Wilde family. That's how they get you! First, they're nice. Then they're feeding you pie. And before you know it, you're churning butter.

Josie: 😄 I'm picturing Molly in a bonnet.

Molly: There are NO bonnets.

Cassidy: Yet.

Josie: So what do you even do on this farm all day?

Molly: Today, I helped gather chicken eggs with his mom.

Cassidy: You?? Chickens??? The same Molly Sinclair who once screamed because a pigeon flew too close to her face?

Molly: It startled me, okay?! And these chickens were fine. Mostly.

Josie: There's that "mostly" again . . .

Cassidy: Be honest, do you have to fight for your life out there?

Molly: No, but tomorrow might be worse. Hudson's taking me horseback riding.

Josie: Wait, you're getting on a horse?

Cassidy: Like willingly?

Molly: He talked me into it.

Josie: Do you even know how to ride a horse?

Molly: No. Absolutely not.

Cassidy: Molly.

Molly: I know! It's a terrible idea.

Josie: Girl, horses are huge. Do you even have the right clothes for this?

Molly: Hudson said he'd "take care of it," whatever that means.

Cassidy: Oh no. That man is going to put you in cowboy boots and a hat, isn't he?

Molly: If he tries, I'm walking back to Redville.

Josie: Please send pictures. I'm begging.

Cassidy: Seconded. I need to see this. For science.

Molly: You two are the worst.

Cassidy: Correction: We're supportive friends. Now, tell us—how scared are you?

Molly: Terrified. I don't even know how to sit on a horse. What if I fall? Or the horse doesn't like me? Or it runs off into the woods and I'm stuck foraging for food forever?

Josie: The horse isn't going to run off into the woods.

Cassidy: You're overthinking it. Hudson won't let you die. He'd probably throw himself off the horse first to protect you.

Molly: That's not helpful, Cass.

Josie: Seriously, though, you've got this. Just hang on, let Hudson teach you, and try not to die.

Molly: JOSIE.

Cassidy: And trust the horse. Horses know things.

Molly: What does THAT even mean?!

Cassidy: I don't know. It sounded wise.

Josie: If Hudson annoys you tomorrow, just "accidentally" steer your horse into his.

Cassidy: I second this plan.

Molly: I'm deleting this chat in case it gets SUBPOENAED.

Cassidy: So you're contemplating it . . .

Molly: Shut up.

Josie: You'll be fine. And if not, at least we'll get hilarious pictures from it.

Molly: 😑 You guys are the worst.

Cassidy: Love you! Don't die tomorrow.

Josie: Hudson better not let you fall. Tell him we'll come for him if he does.

Molly: Noted.

Cassidy: PS Don't forget to send the pics.

chapter seventy-seven

Hudson

As cliché as it sounds, there really is no fucking place like home.

I love being here.

Whenever I'm in Redville, I get lost in the frenzy of my life, and it's easy to forget this place.

This feeling.

My life is always so crazy that I can barely remember my own name, let alone anything else.

But the moment I walk back onto this property, the feeling of comfort that only this place can bring comes rushing back.

That's one of the reasons I want to help my parents so badly.

Sure, it's because I know that they need help, but a part of me, a bigger part than I want to admit, wants to help for selfish reasons.

Knowing that no matter how crazy my life gets, I'll always have the farm, has me desperate to help.

This place is such a huge part of my life. I don't want them to lose it. Why do they have to be so stubborn?

I'm practically begging them to take my money, but . . . *no*. They won't have it.

It's frustrating as all fuck.

I close my eyes and inhale deeply.

The smell of the barn hits my nostrils. To be specific, it's the fragrance of hay. This place always grounds me and reminds me how simple life can be.

Sure, I love being on the ice, and the rush of skating, but the farm brings a level of calm I can't get anywhere else.

But today isn't about me—it's about Molly.

And trying to help her see there is more to life than being afraid.

Behind me, I hear her boots crunching against the dirt.

She's almost to where I'm standing beside Gracie, our gentlest horse. Which makes her perfect for the task at hand.

She's steady and calm and exactly what Molly needs right now.

Shit, I just hope this goes well.

It should, though.

After the way she opened on the ice, I have a feeling like this will be the same.

There is also an ulterior motive for wanting her to do this.

I want her to love the farm.

I want her to see that she belongs here, even if she doesn't realize it yet.

"This is Gracie." I run my hand over the horse's smooth coat.

Gracie leans into my touch. "She's the best. And even better, she's perfect for you."

Molly stops a few feet away, her arms crossing tightly over her chest. Her fingers grip her jacket.

She's hesitant.

She's nervous.

Of course, she is.

Don't push her, Hudson.

She's not sold.

That's fine. She will be soon.

Gracie is a large horse, so I can understand being unsure, but she's by far the gentlest horse I've ever known.

"I don't know about this," she admits.

I move closer to her. "You don't have to ride her." I keep my tone easy. "We can just hang out here. We can just feed her carrots."

Telling her this is a calculated move. I know she will ride her, but I also know she needs to know she has a way out. *Just in case.*

This will give her the control she craves.

Molly shifts her weight, glancing back at Gracie.

I think she's going to say forget it. *Which is fine.*

But then she squares her shoulders and straightens her spine, and I know she's ready. *Good girl. Be as strong as I know you can be.*

I keep my exterior expressionless. I don't want to piss her off. That won't bode well for my plan. Molly is liable to say "fuck it" and leave if I do that.

"Fine, I'll at least feed her." Her voice is still quiet, but her determination is peeking out.

I can't help but smile.

There it is.

That spark.

She's amazing, and the crazy part is she doesn't see it.

She will.

I'll make her.

"All right," I say, keeping my tone warm. "Let's take it slow."

I grab a carrot from the nearby bucket and hold it out to her. "Hold it flat in your palm like this," I say, demonstrating.

Her fingers brush mine as she takes the carrot, and for a second, that tiny touch sends a flicker of warmth through me.

Focus, man. This is about her, not you.

When she mimics my gesture, I guide her hand toward Gracie's mouth.

Gracie takes the carrot gently from Molly's palm. Thank fuck too. One never knows how Gracie will react if she's hungry. While she would never hurt anyone, she gets pretty excited to eat. She's liable to snatch the carrot the way a hungry child might grab a candy bar at a chocolate shop.

"See? She likes you," I tell her.

"Well, I don't know if I like her yet," Molly mutters. "Not enough to ride her."

I narrow my eyes and tilt my head down. "Hex..."

"Saying my nickname won't get me on the horse any faster." She presses her lips into a thin line. She's not pissed, though, just pretending to be.

That's the Hex I know.

"Gracie," I correct.

"What?"

"The horse has a name. It's Gracie."

Molly rolls her eyes. "Have I ever mentioned you're insufferable?"

"Only every day since we've met."

"Well, you are."

"Enough stalling."

She crosses her arms at her chest. Defiant as always. "I'm not stalling."

"Sure you are."

"You ever think maybe I have no interest in riding a horse?"

"No."

"Wow."

"I think you're scared. And that's okay, but I'm here to tell you—you have no reason to be scared. Fear is just a lie we tell ourselves until we find the courage to rewrite the story.

"Now that we have that settled, let's start with getting you on her back, and we'll go from there," I say, grabbing the mounting block and setting it beside Gracie. I turn to her, extending my hand. "Come here."

She hesitates, staring at my hand and then at Gracie.

Molly trembles slightly, but she still places her hand in mine. She trusts me.

Don't screw this up.

I'm not sure why she's the way she is or what causes her panic, but I can tell that this moment is important.

For her.

For me.

"All right," I say, positioning myself beside her. My hands move to her waist, steady and deliberate. "I'll lift you. Just hold on to the saddle."

Before she can second-guess herself, I lift her, settling her onto Gracie's back.

She grabs the saddle horn tightly; her knuckles are so white I'm almost afraid she'll break something.

"Relax." I keep one hand on her leg. "I've got you."

She takes a shaky breath, and I see her grip loosen just a little.

"Perfect. You're doing amazing. Much better than I did my first time."

She looks at me over her shoulder, her brows furrowed. She clearly doesn't believe me. I'm not lying. It's true. "Please. You expect me to believe that?"

"Yep." I grin. "Believe it or not, the first time I got on a horse, I fell off . . . twice."

That earns me a reluctant smile, and something in my chest eases.

There it is.

A real smile.

"Okay," she says, her voice quieter now but steadier. "What's next?"

I grin. I love seeing her like this. "Next, we take a little walk. You ready?"

She nods, her hands tightening again.

As I lead Gracie out, I hold Molly tight. "Now close your eyes."

"What?" Her voice is full of shock.

I move my head so my lips are at her ear.

"Trust me, Molly. Believe I'll never let anything hurt you."

As her muscles loosen, I can feel that she is giving me her trust.

The feeling is unlike anything I have ever felt before.

chapter seventy-eight

Hudson

IT DOESN'T TAKE A ROCKET SCIENTIST TO KNOW SOMETHING IS wrong the moment I spot Anna when I enter the barn.

I came out here to grab the jacket I had left, but now it seems my trip will be for a different purpose.

To talk to my baby sister.

We aren't that close, but I'd still do anything for her.

I step closer to where she is, and she must hear me because she looks up from where she's sitting on an overturned bucket. Her arms hug her knees.

Her long hair spills down one shoulder, hiding part of her face, but I don't need to see it to know she's upset.

Anna's never been good at hiding how she feels. *Especially not from me.*

"Surprised to see you here."

"Why?" Her nose crinkles.

"You hate the smell of hay."

"Maybe I'm getting used to it."

"Doubtful." I step closer inside. "People don't just start to like the smell."

A beat passes, and Anna doesn't argue.

Yep.

She's not okay.

I drop down onto the ground right in front of her. "What's going on, Annie?"

She shrugs. "Nothing. Just . . . thinking."

"Well, that's not good. We try never to do that. It's against the family motto, after all."

Her lips twitch. Almost a smile. I'll take it. "Hudson, I'm fine."

"I'm calling bullshit. You're sitting alone in a barn. Which is legit the last place you would ever voluntarily be. So, yeah, I'm not buying it."

She doesn't answer. Instead, silence stretches between us.

"Please, Anna, talk to me." I drop my voice, hoping she hears my sincerity.

She lets out a sigh before finally lifting her head so that our gazes lock. Now, this close, I can see that her eyes are red-rimmed. She's been crying. Shit.

"I just . . . I don't know what to do," she finally says.

I incline my head down. "About what?"

"Everything." She swallows hard. "I graduated. My friends are all working or going off to college, and I'm just stuck. I don't know what I want to do with my life."

"You're not stuck," I say immediately. "You've got options. College, a job, whatever you want."

"But what if I want to leave here? What if I don't want to stay?"

"Then you leave."

"But how?" She bites her lip, her voice trembling. "How can I abandon Mom and Dad? They need me. Doesn't that make me selfish?"

I sit up straighter, my brows pulling together. "What are you talking about?"

Her hands grip her knees tighter. "You know Mom and Dad won't take your help. But the thing is, they work so hard, and I see it every day. If I go to school or move somewhere else, who will help them?" She shakes her head. "How can I be okay with that? How can I leave them here alone?"

The guilt in her voice guts me.

Anna's a good kid, but this isn't her responsibility. She needs to put her life first.

I push my hand through my hair, exhaling roughly. "Anna, you can't put that on yourself."

"Then who will? They're struggling, Hudson. You know it as much as I do. And you're not here all the time. You're off playing hockey. It's not fair to leave them with no one."

I grit my teeth.

She's not wrong.

I've offered to help.

I've begged them.

They wouldn't let me do anything. Not pay the mortgage or fix up the farm.

And for what?

They are barely making ends meet and now Anna is crying because she's afraid to leave them.

"I'll take care of it," I say firmly.

Anna laughs bitterly. "Hudson, you've tried. They won't take your money."

I lean forward, resting my elbows on my knees as I meet her gaze. "I'll find a way, okay? It's not on you to hold this place together. You don't have to give up your future just because Mom and Dad are stubborn."

"It's not fair to put this on you either. You have enough going on."

beautiful collide

"Just trust me," I say softly, because what else can I say? "I'll take care of it. You don't have to worry."

I want to tell her more, but now is not the time.

There's so much she doesn't know. For years, ever since I went pro, I've been putting money aside for her. To help her.

She doesn't know that Mom and Dad will only take help from me if it's for her.

Her shoulders slump, and for a second, she looks so young. "Hudson . . ."

"No objections. I'll handle it. That's what big brothers are for."

She snorts, making a face. "Cringe."

I stand, then hold out my hand to her. "Come on. Get off that bucket. Mom's cooking chili."

She takes my hand, letting me pull her up. "Fine, but only because chili is my favorite."

"Obviously." I playfully roll my eyes.

Together, we walk back toward the house.

The whole time, I'm thinking about how I'll broach this with Mom and Dad again. Our parents might be stubborn as hell, but not more than I am. I'll make them take my money.

Somehow.

"Hudson?" Her voice cuts through my thoughts.

"Yeah?"

Anna looks over at me, her lips twitching into a grin. "You need to get me ice cream after dinner."

I laugh, shaking my head. "Oh, is that so?"

"Yep." Anna laughs.

"No."

"Fine. I'll steal your car and buy it myself."

"With what money?"

"The money you give Mom and Dad for me." She smirks, clearly enjoying teasing me. "I'm not stupid. I know you've been being sneaky and giving them money for me."

I run a hand over my face. "You could've said something."
"Why? It was more fun letting you think I didn't know."
"Unbelievable."
But as she skips ahead, laughing, I can't help but smile.
Maybe everything will be okay after all.

chapter seventy-nine

Molly

SUNLIGHT FILLS THE BARN WITH A SOFT GLOW AS HUDSON leads me to my *surprise*. When he finally stops, my eyes go wide.

No way am I going up there.

I wipe my sweaty palms on my jeans and glance at the ladder Hudson wants me to climb.

"Nope."

"I'll be right behind you. Trust me."

My heart is racing, though I'm not entirely sure why. Maybe it's the climb. Or perhaps it's Hudson asking me to trust him again.

This man seems to think pushing my limits is his job.

"You don't have to if you don't want to." His calm voice wants to reassure me. It's sweet, and I might complain, but he does have a point. Each day that he has pushed my limits, I have felt amazing after, so maybe he's on to something. "But I know you can do it," he says, sealing the deal.

I put my hand on the ladder but pause, my grip tightening.

Backing down isn't an option.

Not again.

Not this time.

I need to challenge myself.

Trust that I will be okay and not just because Hudson is behind me, but because I know in my heart, I'll be safe.

"Fine. I'll do it." The words come out quickly, despite my uncertainty.

I don't want to change my mind.

I need to do this. So I do. I take a step up, then another, and another until I'm at the top.

Once on solid ground, I stop short, surprised by what I find.

The space is unexpectedly charming, with sunlight pouring in through a large arched window.

It feels like we are in another country. It's magical.

He really pulled out all the stops.

In the center, Hudson has set up a blanket, and on top of it sits two Mason jars filled with pale yellow lemonade. There is also some wrapped bundle that I have to assume is food.

He steps up behind me, his larger-than-life presence filling the small space.

"Fancy," I say, turning over my shoulder to look at him.

Hudson shrugs, grinning like this is no big deal. "Hey, I have standards." He leads me to the blanket, then drops down and pats the spot beside him for me to sit.

For a second, I hesitate. But finally, I lower myself beside him, legs folded awkwardly beneath me.

After a second, he unwraps the bundle, revealing slices of red apple and a handful of sugar cubes nestled in a cloth.

"Snacks for the horses?" I shoot him a sideways glance.

"And us." He pops a sugar cube into his mouth like it's a piece of candy.

"You can't be serious. You want me to eat raw sugar?"

beautiful collide

"Yeah, what of it?" he says, holding a sugar cube out to me. "You know you want to."

I hesitate, narrowing my eyes at him.

He's a pain. He's fully aware I won't back down when he words it like that. I pluck it from his hand, the tips of my fingers brushing his.

It's a small thing, that touch, but it lingers more than it should.

I place the cube on my tongue, my brows furrowing as it dissolves. It's sweet.

Very sweet, but it makes me feel giddy. *Must be having a sugar high.*

"See?" Hudson says, his grin widening. "Not so bad."

"Not bad," I admit.

We fall into a comfortable silence, sharing the slices of apple.

I glance at Hudson out of the corner of my eye. The sunlight catches on his face. He's beautiful.

Something about him makes me ache in a way I don't want to name.

How does he do it?

How does he do this to me?

For a second, my heart races, but then I take a breath.

It's funny. I would never expect Hudson to be so comfortable here. I wonder if he misses Redville. Or is this enough?

"You ever get tired of this?" I ask suddenly, the words spilling out before I can stop them.

Hudson blinks, turning to look at me. "Of what?"

"This." I gesture broadly at the barn. "The quiet, the farm . . . everything."

"Never," he says without a second's hesitation, leaning back on his hands. "It's home."

The word hits me hard, and it's difficult to keep steady. *Home.* The word feels foreign. I drop my gaze to my hands, the weight of the word pressing into me.

I've never had that—not really. Home isn't a place for me. It's just . . . somewhere I end up. That's not true. I have Dane.

Had.

He now has Josie.

Must be nice.

Where does that leave me?

But for a second, I allow myself to believe—just a little—that maybe I could have this.

Hours later, Mason jars still in hand, Hudson shows me the rest of the property. Eventually, we stop to sit down and drink our lemonade.

"Pretty great, right?" he says, tilting his chin toward the horizon. The sun is currently a beautiful shade of pink as it dips low into the sky.

I smile faintly and let my eyes follow his. The fields stretch endlessly. It's green as far as the eye can see.

"It's beautiful." I sigh.

It really is beautiful. Too beautiful, maybe.

Like something out of a dream I would never let myself have.

We fall into silence—not awkward, not tense, just quiet.

Everything about this moment is perfect.

The way the air smells of wildflowers to the soft breeze in the air that tugs at the loose strands of my hair.

Hudson's hand reaches out and tucks the piece behind my ear, and when he does, I let him.

I love being here with him.

It feels right.

"Do you miss this?" I gesture around us, making it clear I'm talking about the farm.

Hudson takes a deep breath before looking out over the fields.

"Every day," he admits on a sigh. "But what other choice do I have? Hockey's the dream, you know? Always has been." He pauses. "But this . . . this is home."

There's that word again.

Home.

And it lands as heavy right now as it did before.

I tighten my grip on the jar. My throat feels tight, and I'm not sure why.

"What's that like?" I ask, my voice barely more than a whisper.

Hudson turns toward me, his brows pulling together in a gentle crease. "What do you mean?"

"Having a place that feels like home," I say, keeping my eyes fixed on the horizon. My voice is steady, but it feels like I might break. "I don't think I've ever had that."

There it is.

I did it.

I said the one thing I never thought I'd say out loud.

Why did I say it now? Why does he make me feel like it's safe to admit it?

The easy humor in Hudson's expression fades.

He sets his jar down on the ground beside him, turning fully to face me. His eyes search mine, and I resist the urge to look away.

"You know"—his voice is quieter now—"home doesn't always have to be a place." He leans in slightly, just enough that I can feel the shift in his presence. "Sometimes it's just . . . people. The ones who make you feel safe."

My chest tightens, the weight of his words pressing against something fragile inside me.

A lump rises in my throat.

I try to swallow but can't.

I break his gaze, not wanting him to see the tears filling my eyes. *I won't let them fall.*

"I'm not sure I've had that either."

Hudson doesn't rush to fill the silence. He doesn't look away, doesn't fidget. He just stays there, solid and present, until finally, he speaks.

"You do now," he says, his voice calm but so certain it feels like a promise.

My breath catches, the air hitching painfully in my chest.

I tighten my grip on the Mason jar, holding it like it's the only thing keeping me steady. Slowly, I turn back to him, my eyes locking on his.

The weight in my chest that I've carried for so long—the feeling of not belonging . . . it feels like it might crack open.

That I might crack open.

chapter eighty

Molly

TONIGHT IS THE PERFECT NIGHT TO SIT OUTSIDE.

It's breezy out, but the stars are in full effect.

I sit on the blanket in the middle of the field with Hudson, my knees tucked into my chest.

It's peaceful. So peaceful that I can't believe a place like this exists in this world.

This must be what heaven is like.

Then why does my mind refuse to settle?

Maybe it's the company? And what being with him means.

Hudson is beside me, leaning back on his elbows, his face tilted up to the night sky.

Normally, being near him calms me.

But not tonight.

Tonight is different.

It's time.

I feel his attention even when he's not looking at me, and the weight of what I need to say presses harder with each passing second.

"Hey," he says softly, breaking the silence. "You okay? What's going on?"

I stare out at the horizon, tightening my grip on the edge of the blanket. "I've been thinking." My voice is barely above a whisper. "About . . . everything."

He turns his head, and even though I can't see him, I feel his eyes on me. "That sounds heavy."

"It is." I force a small, weak smile. "But it's not bad heavy. It's just . . . time."

Hudson shifts to sit upright, his arms resting on his knees, his focus fully on me now. "Time for what?"

"To tell you." The words catch in my throat, and I take a moment to steady myself. "About my childhood. About why I . . . struggle with certain things."

He nods. "You don't have to, Hex."

"I know." I tilt my head up to the sky and inhale deeply. "But I want to." Hudson stays quiet, so I continue. "When I was thirteen, my parents died in a car accident. I was in the car—me, my mom, my dad. My dad was driving to pick up Dane . . . and he was drunk."

His jaw tightens, but he doesn't interrupt. He just listens.

"I survived with just a few scrapes and bruises," I continue, my voice cracking slightly, "but they didn't make it. The worst part is that I remember it. The screaming, the sound of the car crashing . . . everything."

Hudson's hand finds mine, his warmth grounding me. He doesn't say anything, doesn't push—just holds on.

I swallow hard, blinking back the tears threatening to spill. "After the accident, my uncle became my legal guardian. He moved into our house with Dane and me, but . . . Dane didn't stay long. Dane and him—" I pause, the words lodging in my throat. "They didn't get along. Dane was eighteen but still in high school. He was

beautiful collide

barely old enough to take care of himself, let alone me. But when my uncle kicked him out . . ."

"Wait." Hudson cuts in gently, his brow furrowing. "Kicked him out? What the hell? I never knew you lived with anyone but Dane."

I nod, pressing my lips into a thin line. "Yeah. He didn't like Dane challenging him or telling him how to take care of me. So he kicked him out, and I was left alone with him."

Hudson's hand tightens around mine, and I feel the anger radiating from him beneath his calm exterior.

"Dane fought for custody," I say quickly, rushing to the next part before I lose my nerve. I can't tell him all Dane had to do to get me, but I tell him what I can. "He worked multiple jobs, hired a lawyer—he did everything he could. But for months, while he was fighting, I had to stay with my uncle. And he . . . he didn't want to take care of me."

Hudson exhales sharply, his jaw clenching. "What did he do?"

I close my eyes briefly, forcing myself to say it. "To keep me out of his way, he used to lock me in the closet. Sometimes for hours. I don't know if it was because he didn't want to deal with me or if it was just easier for him. All I know is that I was alone. In the dark. And I couldn't do anything about it."

"Did he ever . . . um, hurt you?"

"He did. But mainly, he would just leave me in the closet."

Hudson straightens, his eyes blazing with fury. "Molly . . . Jesus Christ."

"It's why I freak out in tight spaces," I say quickly, needing to explain before his anger consumes the moment. "Why closets, small rooms . . . why it's hard for me. Why I need to have control. But this week . . ." My voice softens as I look at him. "This week has been different."

"What do you mean?"

"You've helped me more than you know," I say, my words trembling but honest.

"How?"

"You didn't push me," I say. "You didn't force me to confront it. You just . . . made me feel safe. Sitting in the barn, riding Gracie. Skating . . . I didn't feel trapped. I felt like I could breathe."

Hudson's eyes soften, his hand still firmly holding mine. "Molly, I didn't do anything special. You did that yourself."

I shake my head, tears brimming in my eyes. "No. I didn't. I couldn't have. Not without you."

He stays silent for a moment. Finally, he sighs, his voice low and raw. "I hate that you went through that," he says quietly. "I hate that someone could do that to you. Whatever happened to your uncle?"

"He's gone . . . Out of our lives. Most likely drunk somewhere." Hudson narrows his eyes at my words. "Let's just say he won't be bothering me anymore."

It's not my story to tell. It's Dane's, and I need to respect that.

"I'm glad you told me."

I wipe my eyes with the back of my hand, forcing a shaky laugh. "You're not going to use this as leverage to win a game of charades, are you?"

He laughs softly, the sound easing the tension. "Oh, absolutely. Next time you hesitate, I'm pulling the 'you trusted me with your trauma' card."

I roll my eyes, laughing despite myself. "You're ridiculous."

"Yet you're still sitting here with me," he teases.

I glance at him, my heart pounding. "Yeah," I say softly. "I am."

He shifts closer, his hand never leaving mine. "You're stronger than you think, you know that?"

"I don't feel strong," I admit.

"Maybe not yet," he says. "But I see it. You're not just surviving anymore, Molly. You're living."

My throat tightens, and I can't bring myself to speak. Instead, I lean into him, letting my head rest against his shoulder. Hudson's arm slips around me, holding me close as the stars shimmer above us.

beautiful collide

For the first time in years, I feel safe.

Hudson turns to face me instead of the sky.

"You're staring," I murmur, breaking the quiet, though I can't bring myself to look away.

"Yeah," he says shamelessly. "I am."

I turn my head to face him, and the edges of my lips tug up despite myself. "The stars are up there, you know."

"So?" he says, his voice lower now, soft and teasing. "I'm looking at something better."

I laugh, rolling my eyes. "That's so cheesy."

"True, though," he says, leaning a little closer.

The space between us shifts, the air thickening. His hand moves, brushing against mine, where it rests on the blanket. It's the lightest touch, but it sends a ripple through me, my breath catching before I can stop it.

"You okay?" he asks, his voice barely a whisper.

I nod, even though my heart is racing. "Yeah. Just . . . you make me nervous sometimes."

His brow furrows slightly, though his eyes stay soft. "Why?"

"Because you make me feel things I'm not used to feeling," I admit, my voice trembling slightly, the vulnerability of the words hitting me as I say them.

His lips curve into a small, reassuring smile, and his fingers lace with mine. His hand is warm, grounding, steadying me in a way I didn't realize I needed. "You don't need to feel that way with me, Hex."

The silence returns, but it's not empty.

It feels full.

Things are changing.

I can feel it in the air, and by the way he reaches his free hand and brushes it against my cheek, I think he feels it too.

"You're . . . special." His blue eyes lock on mine.

"Special?" What does that mean? "How so?"

Hudson laughs. "Are you fishing for compliments?"

"No. Just curious."

"Beautiful. Caring. Amazing. Is that enough for you? Or would you like me to keep going?" he jokes.

I laugh softly, shaking my head. "I'm going to need you to create a PowerPoint presentation."

"I'll get right on it. But in all seriousness, you're all those things and more."

"You're just saying that because you're biased."

"No," he says, his voice steady and very serious. "I'm saying it because it's true."

His thumb traces along my jawline.

The feeling is sublime.

My pulse hammers in my ears, and my body buzzes with anticipation.

He leans in.

The world seems to still as I wait for his lips to brush against mine.

Then they do, and everything in my life feels complete.

The kiss is soft at first, tentative, like he's giving me the chance to pull away.

But I don't.

Instead, I press closer, my hands sliding up to his shoulders, clutching the fabric of his shirt.

This is everything. Everything I never knew I wanted, yet it feels so right.

He deepens the kiss until it becomes more urgent, more consuming.

His hands move to my waist, pulling me closer, and the warmth of his touch seeps through every layer of my being.

"I want you." His forehead rests against mine.

"I want you, too."

He pulls his mouth away from mine before he trails his lips down my neck, lingering at my collarbone.

It's all too much.

The way he kisses me. The way he trails his fingers down my skin.

It feels like I'm hovering over my body, and he's the only thing that tethers me to reality.

"Hudson." My fingers tangling in his hair.

Hudson's hands slide under my shirt, caressing my skin. Shivers run across my skin.

I lift my arms, allowing him to gently remove my top. Now, the cool night air allows the goose bumps to rise on my skin.

"You're so beautiful." His hands move to my back, unclasping my bra with surprising deftness. As it falls away, he gazes at me with awe.

"This is everything I ever wanted," Hudson tells me, and I shake my head in confusion. "Us being together on the farm." The words are supposed to make me understand, but instead, they confuse me more. How long has he dreamed of us together?

Has it been as long as I've dreamed of him? *Since the very beginning, even when I wouldn't allow myself to.*

I gasp as his mouth finds my breast, arching into his touch. "Hudson," I moan softly.

He lavishes attention on me, alternating between gentle kisses and playful nips that leave me breathless.

When he's at my belly, he pauses. Looking up at me, he stops. Then he dazzles me with his heart-stopping smile as he hooks his fingers into the waistband of my shorts.

I lift my hips, allowing him to slide them off along with my underwear.

Hudson kisses the inside of my thigh. "You're perfect," he murmurs against my skin.

Despite knowing what he's about to do, I'm not at all prepared for the feeling when he latches his mouth around my clit.

For some reason, it feels different tonight under the stars.

I've laid myself bare tonight. That's why. He sees the real me.

He licks and sucks me into his mouth.

Drawing gasps and moans from my mouth.

He never breaks his stare.

He watches me through every quiver, every moan. He watches me as I fall apart and then puts me back together.

Afterward, he gathers me in his arms, holding me close as I catch my breath. I've never felt so cherished, so completely and utterly loved.

"You okay?" Hudson brushes my hair back from my face.

I smile up at him. "Never better."

In one fluid motion, I flip us over to straddle him. His eyes widen in surprise as I pin his hands beside his head.

"Molly, you don't have to—" he protests, but I silence him with a kiss.

"I want to," I whisper against his lips. "Let me make you feel good too."

I trail kisses down his neck as I unbutton his shirt, savoring the warmth of his skin. Hudson shivers beneath me, his breath catching as I explore his body.

I take my time. When I reach for his belt, Hudson gently grasps my wrist. "Are you sure you want to do this out here?" he asks softly.

I nod, smiling. "Yes, Hudson. I know what I want, and what I want is you."

He lifts his hips, allowing me to slide off his jeans and boxers. I take him in my hand, stroking from root to tip. Hudson groans, his head falling back.

Slowly, I move to hover above him, and once I align myself with his dick, I lower myself onto him.

Hudson's hands grip my hips, steadying me as I adjust to the sensation.

When I start to move, the world falls away until there's nothing but us and how this feels.

I throw my head back as pleasure builds within me.

Hudson moves with me, our bodies finding a perfect rhythm.

"God, Molly," Hudson groans. "You feel incredible."

Suddenly, Hudson surges up, wrapping his arms around me as he flips us over. He intertwines our fingers, pressing my hands into the blanket beside my head as he enters me again.

We move together. Every thrust sends waves of pleasure through me, building and building until I'm crying out his name.

Hudson follows soon after, burying his face in my neck as he finds his release.

When it's over, I'm lying against his chest, his steady breathing grounding me. His fingers trace lazy patterns along my back, and I tilt my head up to see him.

"You're quiet," he murmurs, his voice low, his lips brushing against my hair.

I smile against him, my heart full in a way I've never known. "I don't have words."

"Good ones or bad ones?" he teases, his tone light but full of affection.

"Good ones," I say softly, tilting my head to meet his gaze. "Really, really good ones."

He grins, leaning down to press a kiss to my forehead. "Good."

I shift slightly, resting my chin on his chest as I search his face. "You make me feel safe, Hudson. And that's not something I've ever had before."

His expression softens, his eyes glinting with an emotion I can't name.

chapter eighty-one

Hudson

THIS SHOULD BE FUN.

Molly is on the couch, sandwiched between Anna and a leaning tower of board games, begging to fall.

She looks relaxed, or she's trying to, but I can see the slight tension in her shoulders, the way she's scanning the room like she's still figuring out the rules.

Something tells me she's never had a game night, and my heart breaks for her.

I look around the room, and a smile lines my face.

Dad is by the fireplace, poking at the logs.

I'm not sure why he's making a fire in the middle of the summer, but I guess once you hit a certain age—apparently my parents' age—you're always cold.

Mom, on the other hand, is making a ruckus in the kitchen, and I wonder what kind of trouble she's concocting right now.

A second later, I get my answer as she comes bustling in with a tray of mismatched mugs and cookies.

beautiful collide

I'm about to ask Mom if she needs help when Anna slaps the Monopoly board onto the coffee table. "Monopoly first," she declares. "Winner gets bragging rights; loser does dishes for a week."

I smirk, all thoughts of helping Mom long gone. "Convenient that you're terrible at dishes." I lean against the back of the couch.

Anna glares. Grabbing the nearest pillow, she hurls it at me.

I dodge easily.

She's terrible at throwing.

Molly takes a mug from Mom before turning her attention back to the conversation. "What's the catch?"

"The catch"—I plop down next to her, making the cushions dip—"is that Anna cheats."

"I do not cheat," Anna fires back, looking genuinely offended, which is weird because it's the truth. Anna has never, in her eighteen years of life, not cheated when playing a board game.

"She literally hid the free parking cash under the board last time," I say, turning to Molly.

Molly laughs, and when she does, it feels like everything is right in the world.

"Noted." Her gaze flicks toward Anna.

"All right." I crack my knuckles as Anna starts handing out money. "Let's get this over with."

"You sound so confident," Molly teases, neatly stacking her colorful bills into precise piles.

"He's always confident before I crush him." Anna's voice is sugary sweet, but I know better. She doesn't have a sweet bone in her body when she's playing.

She continues to pass out game pieces as I lean toward Molly, dropping my voice so only she can hear. "Just a heads-up, Anna's strategy is to distract you with her 'charm' so you don't notice her skimming from the bank."

"I do not skim," Anna yells, throwing her hands in the air. *So much for being quiet.* "It's called playing smart."

I grin back. "Let's see if you're still this cocky when I own every property on the board."

An hour later, I do not own every property on the board.

Far from it.

Molly's completely bankrupt, Anna's sitting on an empire of hotels, and I'm one bad roll away from total disaster.

"Pay up," Anna says, holding out her hand like a queen collecting taxes as I land on her hotel-stacked Boardwalk.

"You're the worst," I groan, slamming my last pathetic stack of cash onto the table.

Molly can barely breathe, laughing so hard she's clutching her stomach.

I turn to her, feigning outrage. "You were supposed to be on my side."

"You're on your own," she says through fits of laughter, tears threatening to spill from her eyes.

"You're ruthless," I mutter, but I can't stop the grin tugging at my lips.

Anna stretches dramatically, standing up and tossing her hair over her shoulder like the reigning champion. "Monopoly is too easy. Let's play charades."

"You mean cheat at charades," I call after her, dodging yet another pillow.

It doesn't take long for charades to turn into absolute chaos.

Anna's "dancing giraffe" has everyone crying with laughter, and Mom's over-the-top impression of a bodybuilder has Dad practically falling out of his chair.

But the real show is Molly trying to waddle across the room, arms pinned to her sides, attempting to be a penguin.

"Penguin," I whisper, leaning in just enough to make her jump.

"Stop sabotaging me!" she hisses, swatting at me, but she's laughing too hard for me to take her seriously.

"Not my fault you're a terrible penguin." I grin when she glares at me.

"You're going to regret this." She narrows her eyes at me.

"Oh, I'm terrified," I deadpan.

By the time Anna declares herself the victor again, the room is filled with groans.

Of course she won. She cheated.

Molly is now curled up in the corner of the couch.

Anna stretches with a yawn. "I'm done. You guys suck."

"Thanks for cheating . . . again."

Anna makes sure to flip me off before she heads up the stairs.

As Mom and Dad follow, the room feels quieter, softer.

The only sound is the occasional pop of the fire. I glance at Molly, who's staring into her mug like it might tell her the mystery of life.

"You held your own tonight," I say, breaking the silence.

She shrugs, her eyes still on the mug. "It was fun. Your family's great."

"You say that like it surprises you."

She hesitates, her fingers tightening around the mug. "It does a little," she admits softly.

"What do you mean?" I ask, leaning closer.

She's quiet for a second, and then she sighs. "Not everyone grows up with this," she says, her voice softer than I've heard all night. "My uncle wasn't exactly the game night type."

Her smile is forced, and it twists something in my chest. I reach over and take the mug from her hands, setting it on the table. "Molly," I say gently.

She looks at me, her eyes shadowed with something I don't fully understand but want to.

"It's just . . . different here," she says finally. "I didn't realize how much I missed out on until tonight."

"You deserved this kind of family," I say, my voice firmer than I intended. "You still do."

She glances away, her fingers twisting in her lap. "I'm just glad

I get to borrow yours for a while," she says, trying to sound light, but the crack in her voice gives her away.

"It's not borrowing," I say, reaching out to brush my hand against hers. "You're part of this now. Whether you realize it or not."

Her breath catches. Slowly, she looks back at me, her eyes wide and unsure.

"Hudson—" she starts, but I cut her off, curling my fingers around hers.

"You don't have to say anything," I tell her quietly. "Just know that you're not alone anymore."

Her eyes glisten with tears she quickly blinks away, but when she squeezes my hand, I know she believes me.

chapter eighty-two

Molly

H UDSON LEANS AGAINST THE COUNTER AS HE WATCHES ME work.

Despite the season being over, I still have plenty of things to do for Dane. Something that Hudson doesn't understand.

"I don't get it, Molly," he says, breaking the silence. His voice is low and measured, but I can hear the edge beneath it. "Why are you still doing this to yourself?"

"Doing what?" I ask as I stand from the table and head over to the sink.

"This." He gestures to my computer. "Living your entire life for Dane. Putting his career before your own life."

My chest tightens, and I force myself to focus on rinsing my coffee mug. "You don't understand," I say quietly.

"Then help me understand," he says, stepping closer.

I sigh. "What do you want me to say, Hudson? That I owe him everything? That he fought for me when no one else did? That I wouldn't even be standing here if it weren't for him?"

"That's not what I'm saying," he counters, his voice steady but firm. "I know what Dane's done for you. I know he's your brother, and you love him. But you don't have to spend your whole life repaying him like it's some kind of debt."

"It's not a debt." My voice rises more than I want. "It's loyalty. Something you wouldn't understand."

As soon as I say the words, I regret them.

His eyes flash. He wants to snap, but he doesn't. Somehow, he refrains. "This isn't about loyalty, Molly. It's about you. Your life. Your dreams. Do you even have those?"

I open my mouth to argue, but the words catch in my throat. I can't speak. His words hit too close to home. To the fears I have.

"That's what I thought."

I shake my head. "I didn't let you in so you can then throw it back in my face," I say, my voice trembling.

"I'm not throwing anything at you," he says quickly. "But you're letting it control you. You've been through hell, Molly, and you came out stronger. But now you're letting that same pain keep you stuck. You're living in Dane's shadow because it feels safe, but you deserve more than that."

"Don't," I say sharply. "Don't tell me what I deserve. You don't know what it's like to be me. You don't know what it's like to feel like everything you have could disappear in an instant."

"You're right." His voice softens. "I don't know what it's like to be you. But I know what it's like to watch you. To see you playing small when you're capable of so much more. And it kills me, Molly. It kills me to see you hiding in Dane's shadow when we both know he'd be the first one to tell you to step out of it."

My chest aches at his words because it's true.

How many times has Dane tried to fire me?

How many times have I refused?

"You don't get to judge me, Hudson. You don't get to decide what's best for me."

"I'm not trying to judge you," he says. "I just want you to see yourself the way I see you."

"Stop." My voice trembles. "Just stop."

He takes a step back. We stare at each other, the weight of everything we're not saying hanging heavy in the air.

Finally, I turn and walk out of the kitchen, my footsteps echoing down the hall.

An hour later, I have no idea where he is.

Most likely with his family, but I don't feel comfortable looking for him.

So, instead, I lie awake in bed *alone*.

I hate how I let him get under my skin. It's not like he said something I haven't thought about myself for years.

It's just I'm not ready to acknowledge those thoughts out loud yet.

The door creaks open, and I freeze, my heart pounding as Hudson steps into the room. He's quiet, his movements careful as he crosses to the bed and slides in beside me.

I stiffen, but he doesn't say anything at first. He lies there, the warmth of his presence both comforting and infuriating.

"I'm sorry," he says finally, his voice low and rough.

I don't respond right away, the anger still simmering beneath the surface.

"I shouldn't have pushed you like that," he continues. "I just . . . I hate that you put everyone else first."

I roll over to face him.

"I don't know how to be any other way," I whisper. "It's all I know. Dane is everything to me. I owe him my life."

Hudson shifts closer, his hand resting lightly on my arm. "You don't owe him your entire life, Molly. He doesn't want that. I mean, he tries to fire you once a week, right? Maybe it's his way of telling you he wants more for you."

"You think so?"

You think so too.

"I know so," he says. "Dane loves you. He wants you to be happy."

"But—"

"No. Buts," he says, his voice barely above a whisper. "You're smart, strong, stubborn as hell . . . and you deserve the whole world."

Tears sting my eyes, and I look away.

"Molly." His hand brushes against mine. "I'm sorry I hurt you. I just care about you."

I let out a shaky breath, my anger melting away in the face of his sincerity.

"I think I'm scared," I admit, my voice barely audible. "If I'm not Dane's assistant, then who am I?"

"You're Hex, you're Molly Sinclair. You're the best person I know." He closes his hand over mine. "But you don't have to be scared. Because you don't have to do this alone. You have Dane. You have me. Hell, you have the whole team. Mason and all."

"Mason, that's not a good endorsement." I laugh.

"No, it's not," he chuckles, pressing a kiss to the top of my head, his arms tightening around me. "You're going to be okay, Hex," he says softly.

"We're going to be okay."

"Yeah, we are."

chapter eighty-three

Hudson

The sun's almost down by the time I finish up the last of the chores for the day.

My dad always says farming is honest work—it humbles you, grounds you, and doesn't give a damn how tired you are.

Today, I believe it.

My muscles ache in a way that even training camp can't replicate, and all I want is a long shower and maybe a beer if I can wrestle one out of Dad's fridge.

But before I head inside, I catch a faint sound drifting from the barn—soft laughter, followed by the familiar voice of my mom.

Curiosity gets the better of me.

Mom's laughter is different than usual, and I swear I hear another voice.

Molly.

I head toward where they are, my boots crunching against the gravel path.

The door is cracked open. I move quietly, not because I'm

trying to sneak up on them, exactly, but because I'm . . . curious. *Yeah. Just curious.*

I'm spying.

As I peek inside, I spot them near the back corner of the barn.

My mom's carrying a basket of eggs while Molly crouches down beside one of the hens, murmuring something.

"You're good at this," Mom says with a smile. "Most people are too jumpy to collect eggs."

Molly looks up and grins. Fuck, she's gorgeous.

"Guess I'm good under pressure. And I had a good teacher." Molly lays it on thick, and my mom loves it.

"Sweet talk will get you everywhere, dear," Mom jokes. "It will also get you seconds of dessert." She winks.

I lean against the doorway, folding my arms as I watch them.

Molly looks so at ease here.

She looks like she's done this a thousand times.

Her pants are streaked with dirt, and one of my mom's old flannel shirts hangs loosely around her shoulders.

She's got hay in her hair, too, but it doesn't seem to bother her.

She's . . . beautiful.

It's stupid to think that, standing here watching her with chickens and eggs, but there it is.

She's fucking gorgeous.

The most beautiful woman I have ever seen.

I'm about to step in when Molly's voice stops me.

"Growing up, I used to dream of doing stuff like this." Her voice is practically a whisper, and I have to strain to hear it. "Not a farm, necessarily, but . . . stability."

Mom doesn't respond right away.

I want to jump in and rescue my girl from the pain that's in her voice.

But I don't. I let her continue with this moment with my mom.

"You didn't have that growing up?" Mom finally asks.

Molly shakes her head. "Not really. After my parents died, it was . . ." She trails off. "It was rough. I worried about everything. Money, mostly. I didn't care about being rich—I just wanted us to be okay, you know? I wanted to know that Dane would have food on the table and a roof over his head."

Her words shock me. I never knew this about her. My chest tightens at her words.

Mom sets down her basket, turning to give Molly her full attention. "That must've been hard for a little girl to carry all that."

"It was," Molly admits. "But Dane did his best. He worked so hard to take care of me. And when he went pro, everything changed. For the first time, I wasn't worried anymore. I wasn't anxious about where the next meal would come from or whether the person I loved most in the world was okay." She pauses. "That's all I ever wanted. To know that the people I care about are safe and stable."

I swallow hard.

God, my throat feels dry.

Molly isn't just telling her story—*she's telling their story*.

My parents' story.

The one they never say out loud, but regardless, I know it.

And now here's Molly, sitting in our barn, subtly trying to convince my mom that sometimes it's okay to let someone help.

To let me help.

My chest feels tight. Maybe my mom will finally understand.

"That's a beautiful way to look at it, Molly. But . . ." She hesitates, choosing her words carefully. "Sometimes pride gets in the way."

"It doesn't have to."

"That feels like admitting defeat." My mom sighs.

Molly looks up at her. "It's not defeat, though. It's love."

My mom stays quiet, listening. I want to walk in there and ask her what she's thinking. Tell her I love her, and like Dane and Molly, I just want to help them, but I don't.

"It was hard to let Dane help me," Molly continues. "But I did because it meant something to him, too. It made him happy to take care of me. To give me the stability I didn't have before."

Mom nods slowly as if considering her words. "I suppose I never thought of it that way."

Molly smiles again—small, hopeful. "You gave Hudson everything. A home, love and stability, and a family. You worked so hard to make sure he didn't have to carry those same worries." She pauses, her tone careful, like she's testing the waters. "And now he has a chance to give that back. Not because he has to, but because he loves you. Because it means something to him."

My breath catches.

Holy crap, Molly.

It's like she knows exactly how to get through to my mom without pushing too hard or making her feel uncomfortable. She's walking the fine line between honesty and persuasion, and I've never seen anything like it.

She's remarkable.

Mom doesn't respond right away.

Instead, she picks up the basket of eggs, her hands moving slowly, thoughtfully. "You're wise for someone so young, Molly," she says finally.

Molly shrugs, her smile turning wry. "I had to grow up fast. You learn a lot when you don't have a safety net."

Mom nods, and there's a long moment of quiet between them.

I take that as my cue to step in before I start feeling like even more of an intruder. I push the barn door open a little wider, letting it creak loudly against the metal tracks. Both of them look up, startled.

"Well, isn't this cozy." I try to keep my voice light as I stroll in.

Molly rolls her eyes immediately, her guard snapping back into place. "Were you eavesdropping?"

"Me?" I feign innocence, grabbing a stray piece of hay and twirling it between my fingers. "Nah. I was just looking for you two. Thought you might've run off with the chickens."

Mom gives me one of her disapproving looks. "Hudson, don't tease."

"I'm not teasing," I protest, flashing a grin. "I'm just saying, I didn't expect to find you in here getting life lessons with the hens."

Molly shoots me a look, her lips twitching like she's fighting back a smile. "I'm sure you were just worried I'd make a better farmer than you."

"Highly unlikely," I retort. "But you keep telling yourself that, Hex."

Mom gives us both a look that screams behave, but there's a softness in her expression.

"I'll take this inside," Mom says, holding up the basket. "Dinner is in an hour, so don't stay out here too long."

"Got it, Mom."

As soon as she leaves, the barn feels quieter, the air humming with something unspoken. Molly stands and dusts off her pants, avoiding my gaze.

"You didn't have to do that," I say finally, my voice low.

She glances up at me, her expression unreadable. "Do what?"

I step closer, watching her carefully. "Whatever that was. With my mom. You didn't have to say all that."

Molly shrugs. "I wasn't saying it for you."

"Maybe not," I admit, tilting my head. "But you meant it, didn't you?"

She doesn't answer, but she doesn't have to.

Because I realize that Molly Sinclair—my little Hex, the woman who has spent years driving me insane—might just be the best damn thing to ever happen to me.

chapter eighty-four

Hudson

THE SUN ISN'T EVEN UP YET, BUT THE FARM IS ALIVE.

I head toward the barn, the cool morning air biting at my skin.

Dad's already there, of course, waiting like he's been up for hours.

Most likely, he has.

He always beats me to it, no matter how early I get out of bed.

The man is a legend.

Too bad the farm hasn't been profitable enough for him to retire yet or that he won't let me help, because when I see him here, at this insanely early hour, I want to beg him to take my money.

His hands are currently wrapped around a chipped coffee mug, steam curling into the crisp air.

"Look who finally decided to join the party," he says, his voice carrying that familiar mix of humor and pride.

"First off. It's too early to make jokes." I smirk, rubbing the sleep from my eyes. "Also, you could've—you know . . . waited for me."

"Not my style," he says, taking a sip of his coffee. "Ready to get to it?"

"As I'll ever be." I roll up my sleeves.

Today is going to suck.

But I wouldn't miss this.

It's worth it to spend time with Dad.

Working with Dad was my dream a long time ago. If it weren't for hockey, I'd probably be doing it.

I'd be happy doing it too.

Because out there, it's just Dad and me.

Dad climbs into the cab of the combine.

Once he's seated, he settles into the driver's seat.

I take my place beside the auger cart, ready to guide the process.

"Remember the first time I let you help with the harvest?" Dad asks over the noise.

I shake my head in jest. *Of course, I do.* "Yeah, and you yelled at me for almost running over your boots."

"You were so scrawny back then," he says with a chuckle. "Could barely lift a bag of beans without tipping over."

"Hey, I've bulked up since then." I flex.

He laughs, the sound warm and familiar.

It reminds me of why I love this place.

Even if it interferes with the beginning of the hockey season.

The morning flies by as we work.

Sweat drips down my back, and my hands ache.

I don't mind, though.

"All right, switch."

I shake my head, wiping the sweat from my forehead. "I've got it. Take a break."

"Hudson," he says, giving me a look. "I can handle it."

"And I can handle it better," I shoot back. "Go sit down. Drink some water. I'll finish this pass."

He hesitates, but eventually, he nods. "Fine."

"Thanks, old man." I climb into the cab.

"Who are you calling old man?"

I smile while pointing at him before setting back to work.

Everything is running smoothly until it isn't.

The machine jerks suddenly.

A loud, sickening screech fills the air.

I slam the brakes.

"What the fuck?" I climb down to see what the hell is going on.

The auger is jammed.

I crouch down, trying to get a better look.

"Hudson." Dad jogs over. "What's going on?"

"Auger's jammed." I point at the mess. "I'll clear it out."

"Wait." He frowns. "We should call someone. That's not safe."

"I'm not calling anyone," I say firmly. "It'll take too long. I've got it."

"Hudson." His voice is low and serious. "You're not supposed to be doing this kind of work. Your contract—"

"I know what my contract says," I snap. "But we have no choice."

His jaw tightens, but he doesn't argue.

"Just keep an eye on the controls," I say.

The space inside is tight and hard to maneuver.

Sweat drips into my eyes.

I'm almost done when it happens. The machine jolts.

Pain explodes through my wrist.

My vision blurs for a moment.

Fuck.

The pain is unbearable.

"Hudson!" Dad's voice is panicked, but I can barely hear him over the pounding in my ears.

I pull back, cradling my wrist as I stumble out of the auger.

Blood drips onto the dirt, the bright red stark against the pale dust.

"Shit," I mutter, my knees buckling.

Dad's there in an instant, his hands on my shoulders as he helps me sit down. "Let me see."

I hold out my arm, and his face pales when he sees my wrist.

There's blood everywhere.

Shit.

This is bad.

"Dammit, Hudson," he says, his voice shaking. "What the hell were you thinking?"

"I was thinking I didn't want you doing it," I say through gritted teeth.

He grabs his phone. "We need to get you to the house."

The walk back to the house is a blur. By the time we reach the porch, I'm sure I'll pass out.

"Mary!" Dad calls, his voice urgent.

The living room is quiet.

This is hell.

The tension is thick enough to cut with a knife.

I sit on the couch holding a towel to my arm.

This is bad.

The blood is soaking through.

This is really bad.

I try to keep my face neutral, but it's damn near impossible.

"Why didn't you call me sooner?" Mom's voice rises as she paces the room, her hands fluttering uselessly.

"Mom, I'm fine." My tight voice betrays me. I'm not fine. I'm in a fuck load of pain.

"Fine?" She spins toward me. "You're bleeding all over my floor, Hudson."

"What happened?" Molly asks. Shit, when did she come into the room?

She's the last person I want to see me like this.

All eyes snap to her. No one speaks.

"He-he got hurt. The auger jammed, and he—" Dad finally says.

"I tried to fix it." Not that I think anyone will care right now. But for some reason, I feel defensive.

"You what?" Her eyes narrow as she stares me down.

"It isn't a big deal." I try to shrug but end up wincing. *Real smooth, Wilde.*

Goddamn, that hurts.

"It wasn't a big deal," she repeats, her voice rising, "yet you're sitting here bleeding like you're the star of *The Texas Chain Saw Massacre*?"

"Hex, please," I say softly, trying to calm her down. "I'm fine."

"You are not fine." Her green eyes blaze. "You need a doctor."

"I can't," I say firmly, meeting her gaze.

"What do you mean, you can't?"

I glance at Dad, then back at her. "It's against my contract," I admit, my voice low. "If the team finds out I was doing farm work, I could lose my job."

Her eyes widen, and she blinks at me, trying to process what I've just said. "Your contract forbids you from . . . what? Doing anything useful?"

"Anything dangerous," I correct, glaring at her like it's a perfectly reasonable clause.

"And this qualifies," Dad mutters.

Molly lets out a frustrated breath. She's quiet for a moment before running her hands through her hair. "Okay, so what's the plan, then? Because you can't just sit here bleeding out."

"We'll clean it up and wrap it properly," Mom says. "Then we'll figure out the rest."

I clench my jaw, looking away. She doesn't need to know how bad it is.

"It's deep," Mom admits quietly. "He needs stitches."

"And we're just . . . not going to do that?" Molly sounds pissed.

"We can't." My tone leaves no room for argument. "If I go to a hospital, they'll ask questions."

"Hudson, this isn't just about you. If this gets infected—"

"It won't," I say, cutting her off. "We'll take care of it."

She glares at me. "This is ridiculous."

"And risk my contract?" I say through gritted teeth as my mom cleans the wound with antiseptic. "No way."

"You're risking your life instead," she snaps. "Great. Just great."

"I'm not risking anything," I grit out through the pain. "I need this job, Molly."

The words hang heavy in the air.

"This is not okay," Molly says.

"No, it's not," I admit, my voice softening.

She doesn't say anything to that; she just focuses on holding my arm steady while Mom works.

Once the wound is cleaned and wrapped, I lean back in the chair.

I feel like shit. Everything hurts.

"All right," I say, sounding more confident than I feel. "What's next?"

"Next?" Molly repeats, crossing her arms. "Next is figuring out how you're going to hide this from the team."

"I have two weeks before practice starts," I say. "I'll keep it covered, take it easy, and hope for the best."

"Hope for the best?" she practically growls. "That's your plan?"

"It's worked so far," I say with a faint smirk.

She glares at me, her frustration bubbling over. "Hudson, this isn't a game. If the team finds out—"

"They won't." My voice is firm. "I'll make sure of it."

She looks like she wants to argue, but she doesn't.

I wish she understood.

This isn't just about pride. It's about survival—for me and for my family.

"Fine," she says finally, her voice tight. "But if anything gets worse, you're going to a doctor. Contract or no contract."

"Deal," I say, though we both know I don't mean it.

For now, that's enough.

After a minute, she breaks the silence. "Why did you do it?"

I open my eyes, meeting her glare. "Would you rather I let my dad do it?"

Her expression softens. "You're impossible," she mutters, sitting down beside me.

"As you've told me many times." I grin despite the pain.

She rolls her eyes. "Don't scare me like that again."

"I'll try not to." I rest my head against the back of the couch.

As the exhaustion pulls me under, I feel her hand brush lightly against mine, and for a moment, the pain doesn't seem so bad.

chapter eighty-five

Hudson

BAD IDEA.
Fuck, that was a bad idea.

All I did was tug at the straps of my gear... No big deal, right?

Except it is a big deal because now, my wrist I've been trying to rest screams in protest.

It's been a week, but I guess I'm still not healed.

If that weren't bad enough, the cold air in this damn rink is brutal. It feels like I'm being stabbed.

"You okay?" Molly asks.

"Fine," I lie.

While I know I should tell her the truth—that my wrist feels like someone poured acid on it—I don't. I pretend I'm okay. *Healing beautifully.*

I'm full of shit.

Molly sits on the bench a few feet away, bundled in one of my hoodies.

She looks adorable as always, drinking a steaming hot cup of coffee.

As cute as she is, she's a drill sergeant. She's watching me like a hawk, her brows furrowed. She's trying to pretend she's not worried.

She's a bad liar. I'm not.

"You sure about this?" she asks, her voice soft but edged with concern.

"Yeah," I lie, pulling on my gloves. The motion sends a fresh wave of pain up my arm, but I grit my teeth and keep going. "Just need to see where I'm at."

Molly doesn't look convinced. "Hudson—"

"I'm fine. I need to do this."

Her lips press into a thin line, but she doesn't argue.

She knows better than to try.

The moment I step onto the ice, I feel better.

This is my sanctuary.

When I'm here, everything fades away.

But today, even the ice can't quiet my brain.

I grip my stick and push off.

The first few strides feel good. But when I try to stickhandle, my left arm refuses to cooperate.

The puck slips away, skittering toward the boards, and I curse under my breath.

"Fuck."

"Take it easy," Molly calls from the bench.

I ignore her, skating after the puck and gripping my stick tighter.

The motion sends a searing pain through my arm.

Shit. Shit. Shit.

My grip falters, the stick slipping in my hands.

This isn't just bad. This is fucked.

I keep going, though.

I refuse to admit defeat.

So instead, like the genius I am, I push through the pain.

Passes, shots, drills—I can't do shit.

Everything hurts.

Everything sucks.

I can't play.

My body is betraying me.

By the time I've circled the rink for the third time, my arm is throbbing, and sweat is dripping down my face despite the cold.

I glance toward where Molly stands now, her arms crossed tightly over her chest. Her eyes meet mine. Wow! Even at our worst, she's never looked at me like this.

I'm screwed.

Molly is about to rip me a new one for pushing my body too hard.

I skate toward her slowly.

Each move feels harder than the last.

My breath comes out in short, painful gasps.

When I reach the bench, I lean on my stick, trying to mask how my legs shake.

"Hudson," she says softly, stepping closer. "You're done."

"I'm fine," I say automatically, even though we both know it's a lie.

She shakes her head, her expression fierce. "No, you're not. You're hurt, and you're pushing yourself too hard. Get off the ice."

I want to argue and tell her I'm fine and need more time, but the words die on my tongue. She's right. I know she's right.

With a heavy sigh, I skate to the bench and sit down, pulling off my gloves and cradling my injured wrist.

Molly sits beside me, her eyes scanning my face like she's trying to read my thoughts.

"You can't keep doing this," she says quietly. "You're only going to make it worse."

"I don't have a choice," I mutter, my voice bitter. "Practice starts in a week. If I can't perform, I'm done."

"Why are you pushing so hard? What's going on? This is more than just about the team."

My head dips down.

"Talk to me, Hudson."

I let out a sigh. "It's the farm."

"I don't understand."

"I'm afraid they're going to lose it. I need the money to help them."

Her hand brushes against mine, tentative but steady. "We'll figure it out," she says. "Together."

I glance at her, the sincerity in her eyes cutting through the fog of my frustration. I let myself believe her.

The next couple of days are hell.

Molly doesn't let me push myself the way I want to, forcing me to slow down and focus on healing.

She sets up a makeshift rehab schedule, using every resource she can find online to help me work through the pain.

Molly is incredible. I don't deserve her.

"You need to let the muscle rest," she says, her tone firm as she wraps my arm in an ice pack for the third time today.

"I don't have time to rest," I snap, the frustration bubbling over.

She doesn't flinch, her hands steady as she secures the ice pack in place. "You don't have time not to. If you go back too soon and make it worse, you'll be out for the whole season. Is that what you want?"

I grit my teeth, hating that she's right. "No."

"Then trust me," she says, her voice softening. "We'll get through this. You just have to let me help you."

I don't say anything, but I nod, the weight of her words settling over me.

Mornings start early with gentle stretches and mobility exercises that make me feel like an old man. Molly stays by my side through all of it, her patience endless even when I snap at her out of frustration.

"You're doing great," she says one morning, her voice calm as I struggle to lift a light dumbbell with my injured arm.

"Yeah, right," I mutter, the pain sharp and unrelenting.

She kneels beside me, her hand resting lightly on my shoulder. "You're stronger than you think, Hudson. You just have to give yourself time."

I glance at her, the softness in her eyes making my chest ache. She believes in me, even when I don't.

By the third day, there's a small glimmer of hope. My grip is steadier, the pain more manageable, and I can handle basic movements without feeling like my arm is being stabbed with a knife dipped in acid.

"You're getting there," Molly says as I practice stickhandling with a ball in the living room.

"Barely," I mutter, but the words feel less bitter now.

She smiles, leaning against the wall. "You're stubborn, but it's working in your favor for once."

I chuckle, shaking my head. "Don't get used to it."

Her laugh is soft, and for a moment, the tension between us fades.

That night, as we sit outside watching the stars, I find myself thinking about how much she's done for me.

She didn't have to stay or put up with my temper or my endless frustration.

But she's here, fighting for me when I can't fight for myself.

"I don't deserve you," I say quietly, the words slipping out before I can stop them.

She glances at me, her brow furrowing. "What are you talking about?"

"All of this," I say, gesturing vaguely. "I'm a mess, Molly. And you're still here."

She sighs, her gaze softening. "You're not a mess, Hudson. You're human. And I'm here because I want to be."

Her words hit me harder than I expected, and I can't speak.

"Thank you," I finally say, my voice sounding rougher than normal.

She smiles, her hand brushing against mine. "We're a team, remember?"

I nod, my chest tightening with a feeling I've never felt before, something I'm not ready to name.

chapter eighty-six

Molly

D**AMN, IT SMELLS GOOD IN THIS KITCHEN.**
  I stride inside and find Hudson's mom standing in the kitchen cooking up a storm.

Onions sizzle in a pan, the bread is in the oven, and the unmistakable scent of homemade tomato sauce bubbles on the stove.

"Can I help?" It's the same question I've asked every day since we've been here, and just like every other time, Mary doesn't turn around, too busy sautéing. Instead, she points at whatever she wants me to do.

A cutting board with carrots already on it. Great, I can do that. With a smile on my face, I make my way over and start chopping.

I love this.

I feel so at home here.

Which is kind of nuts.

But it's the truth, nonetheless.

Hudson's family farm has brought me comfort.

The pace here is slower, the expectations lighter, and for once, I feel like I can breathe.

It's a bit brisk today, and I'm happy I packed my old letterman jacket to keep me warm. I haven't worn it in years, but I'm thankful I did, 'cause I'm cold.

"Where'd you get that old thing?" Mary's voice cuts through my inner rambling. I turn toward her to see her glancing over her shoulder from where she's stirring the sauce with a peculiar look on her face.

I pause mid-slice, looking down at the jacket. "Oh, um, I've had it for a while," I say casually, though my heart does a little flip.

Mary wipes her hands on a dish towel and then squints at me. "You found Hudson's jacket?"

I blink. What is she talking about? "What do you mean, Hudson's jacket?"

She gestures toward the sleeve. "That's his high school hockey jacket. He loved that thing. Wore it everywhere."

My heart starts pounding. "This . . . this was Hudson's?"

Mary picks up the edge of the sleeve and inspects it. "Yep. See this little stitch here?" She points at it. "I sewed that up for him when it tore one day after a game."

The room tilts slightly, my mind racing. "What happened to it?"

Mary scrunches her nose, like she's trying to remember. "If I remember correctly, he came home one day and said he lost it."

My legs feel unsteady, my chest tightening. "How long ago was that?"

"Oh, must've been years now." Mary turns back to the stove. "Before he graduated from high school, I think. Why?"

High school.

Holy shit.

Could it really be . . . *his*?

My mind flashes to that day. I can still feel the heavy weight of the jacket being draped over my shoulders.

The warmth and comfort I needed.

It was Hudson.

All these years, the stranger who saved me, who gave me something to hold when I was falling apart . . .

It was him.

"Molly?"

I swallow hard, my pulse racing. "I-I need a minute," I stammer, backing toward the door.

Mary nods. Her brow furrows, but she doesn't press. "All right, but come back soon. Dinner will be ready in thirty minutes."

I barely register her words as I push open the door and step outside.

The next thing I know, I'm striding toward the barn.

My heart pounds so hard it feels like it might burst, but I don't stop. I can't stop.

I need to see him. *Now.*

When I reach the barn, I push open the door.

"Hudson." My voice is shaking.

He turns around to face me. "Hey, Hex. What's—"

I close the distance between us, and before he can utter another word, I grab his face and kiss him.

He freezes for half a second, then kisses me back.

"Not that I'm complaining." His voice is low and husky. *Freshly kissed.* "But what was that for?"

Tears prick at my eyes, and I take a shaky breath. "It was you," I whisper.

His brow furrows. He has no idea what I'm talking about. It's clear as day that he thinks I've lost it. "What was me?"

"The jacket," I say, stepping back slightly and gesturing to it. "You gave this to me."

His eyes widen, then his mouth drops open. "That was you?"

I nod, tears filling my eyes. "I was about to have a panic attack. I had just seen my uncle. I was sitting there, trying to hold it together, and then you—" My voice catches, and I press a hand to my mouth, trying to steady myself.

Hudson takes a step closer, his hands reaching out to rest on my arms. "I didn't even see your face," he says, his voice thick with emotion. "I just . . . I saw someone who looked like they needed it more than I did."

My chest tightens. My heart is ready to explode. "Do you realize what you did for me that day? This jacket. I held on to it every time things got bad back then. And now . . ." I shake my head, tears streaming down my face. "Now I know it was you." He pulls me into his arms, holding me tightly as I bury my face in his chest. "Fate," I whisper against him.

"What?" he murmurs, his voice low and soothing.

"Fate." I pull back to look at him. "Fate brought you to me that day. And it brought us back together all these years later. Don't you see? Every time I've needed someone, every time I've been on the edge, you've been there . . . Even when we didn't know it."

He cups my face, his thumbs brushing away my tears. "You're right. It's fate. It's always been fate."

"This is just . . ." I can't think of the word I want to say. This moment feels too much for simple words.

"Proof."

"Proof of what?" I raise a brow.

"That you're stuck with me. I'm not going anywhere, Hex. Not now, not ever."

A laugh bubbles up, and I rest my forehead on his chest. "You're such a pain in the ass."

"And you're my favorite bad luck charm."

I laugh again, the sound light and free, and for the first time in years, I feel like I'm exactly where I'm supposed to be. With him. *Always with him.*

chapter eighty-seven

Hudson

Mason: Yo, TMZ says you're back in Redville, Hudson. That can't be true because I'm your best friend, and you would've told me. Right?

Aiden: TMZ, huh? Always a credible source.

Hudson: . . .

Dane: 😂 Busted.

Mason: UNREAL. You're really back? And you didn't say anything? Traitor.

Hudson: Relax. It's not that deep.

Mason: Not that deep?! I thought we had something special.

Dane: Mason's probably crying into his protein shake right now.

Aiden: Someone cue the sad violin music.

Mason: Screw all of you. I'd NEVER keep secrets like this. Right, Hudson?

Hudson: 🙃

Dane: Deflecting? Interesting.

Mason: Don't change the subject. Hudson, hop on Xbox. I'm feeling generous enough to let you win once tonight.

Hudson: Can't. Busy.

Mason: What kind of lame excuse is that?

Hudson: Molly wants to hang out.

Aiden: 😂 Oh my God, he really said that.

Mason: Dude. DUDE. You're officially one of those guys.

Dane: He's domesticated. Newlywed syndrome in full swing.

Mason: Next thing we know, he'll be baking sourdough bread and watching HGTV.

Hudson: You fuckers are ridiculous.

Aiden: Admit it, Hudson. You've been tamed. Molly's got you doing dishes and lighting scented candles.

Mason: He's probably calling her babe every five minutes, too.

Dane: I swear if you're wearing matching pajamas . . .

Hudson: 🖕

Mason: Nah, for real. Hudson can't hang anymore. He's gone soft.

Hudson: Oh, I'll show you soft the next time I bodycheck your ass into the boards.

Mason: Big words for a guy who's too "busy" to play Xbox. Go cuddle your wife.

Aiden: He's probably got a face mask on while watching rom-coms right now.

Dane: Don't judge.

Aiden: Dane?

Dane: Um, nothing.

Hudson: You're all jealous. It's fine.

Dane: Jealous? Nah. I'm just waiting for you to start a "Hudson & Molly" couple account with vlogs of your farm trips.

beautiful collide

Mason: 😂 "Day in the life of Hudson Wilde, Former Hockey Bad Boy Turned Trad Husband."

Hudson: I hate you all.

Mason: Love you too, buddy. Let us know when Molly gives you permission to play with the boys again.

Aiden: Or when you're done picking out throw pillows.

Hudson: 🖕🖕

Mason: PS If you do start baking sourdough, send me a loaf.

chapter eighty-eight

Molly

I SIT IN MY CAR OUTSIDE DANE'S HOUSE.

My car is still running.

I should go. I shouldn't be here. I shouldn't be doing this.

My hands grip the steering wheel. I know what I'm doing is wrong. Hudson will be pissed if he knows I interfered, but what other choice do I have?

I can't sit back and watch Hudson hurt himself, and that's what he will do if I don't speak to my brother.

I can help him.

Like he's helped me.

Taking a deep breath, I cut the engine and step out of the car.

There's no backing out now.

Well, technically, I can still turn around, but I won't be doing that. Hudson has done so much for me. It's my turn to do something for him.

I march up to the front door, and when I'm there, I knock before I lose my nerve.

In the past, I would have used my keys, but with Josie living here now, that's not going to happen.

My foot taps on the pavement as I wait.

Luckily, it only takes a moment for Dane to answer, his broad frame filling the doorway.

His brow furrows when he sees me. "Molly? What are you doing here? You okay?" Always the protector.

"I need to talk to you." He narrows his eyes at my words. "It's important."

He steps aside, motioning for me to come in.

"What's going on?" he asks, closing the door behind me.

I turn to face him, my hands clasped tightly in front of me. "It's about Hudson."

His jaw tightens, and I can see the wheels turning in his head. He's ready to kill him. Down, boy. "What about him?" he grits out. "What did that asshole do to you?"

"He didn't do anything to me. He's hurt." I bite my lip. "He got injured on the farm a week ago. His wrist—"

"Wait, what?" Dane cuts me off, his voice sharp. "How bad is it?"

"Bad," I admit, my stomach twisting. "He won't go to a doctor because he's afraid Coach will be pissed. He's been hiding it, but with practice starting soon . . . I don't know how he's going to pull it off."

"That idiot," he mutters under his breath. "Why didn't he tell anyone?"

"Because he's stubborn." I sigh. "And because he's an idiot who thinks he has to do everything on his own. But he can't. He needs help."

"And I'm supposed to help him." It's a statement, not a question, and a pissed statement at that.

I nod. "Obviously. For one, you're my brother, but also, and more importantly, it's literally your job to protect him. Which means you can make sure no one hurts him. You can buy him time to heal."

Dane crosses his arms. "And what if someone finds out? What if he hurts himself more?"

I swallow hard. It feels like there is a lump in my throat. "If that happens, then we figure it out. But right now, none of that matters. All that matters is he has someone who's got his back."

Dane lets out a heavy sigh. "All right. I'll do it."

My shoulders slump forward. "Thank you."

"But"—he holds up a finger—"there's one condition."

I knew it was too good to be true. "What condition?" I ask.

"You have to agree to let me fire you." If my brother feels bad about his demands, he doesn't let on. Instead, his expression is blank, and for a second, I think he's joking. But when he doesn't laugh, my stomach drops.

"What?"

"You heard me." His tone is firm. "You've been living your life for my career, and it's time to stop."

"This isn't about me," I say, my voice trembling. "It's about Hudson. He needs you."

"And I'll be there for him," Dane says, stepping closer. "But only if you promise to let me do this. To let me fire you. For real this time."

I shake my head. He can't do this, can he? *Yes, he can.* "Seriously?"

"Yes, seriously. I've never been more serious," he says, and panic rises in my chest. "Molly, I love you. But you deserve more than this. You deserve your own life."

I look away, my hands clenching at my sides. "Dane, please." *Don't cry.*

"Promise me." He won't change his mind on this. This is the deal. The price to pay.

"Fine," I whisper, the word barely audible. "If that's what it takes to keep Hudson safe, I'll agree."

Dane nods. "Thank you, Molly. You're doing the right thing," he says quietly.

"Am I?" I ask, my voice cracking.

He nods, his eyes steady. "Hudson will be okay. And so will you. Trust me."

I force a smile, though it feels hollow. I'm not sure he's right. Only time will tell.

chapter eighty-nine

Hudson

I'VE BEEN DREADING TODAY.

Sure, I'm excited to be back on the ice, but I'm still not up to full speed.

My wrist still hurts, and if I take any hits, I'll be fucked.

Hopefully, since it's only a practice, I'll be okay.

The whistle blows, sharp and demanding. I adjust my helmet, flexing my injured wrist as subtly as I can.

I hope nobody notices, especially Coach.

It's still stiff, but it's manageable. Hopefully, with the adrenaline coursing through me, the pain will be dulled. I'm a glass-half-full kind of guy.

Fifteen minutes later, practice is in full swing, and for the first time since my injury, I'm on the ice with the team.

I've been careful to hide the extent of my injury, but now if anything happens, I won't be able to hide it. Which puts me on edge.

I already feel that my shot's a little weaker and my stickhandling slower, but I've worked hard to make it look like nothing's wrong.

At least, I think I have.

Here's to hoping.

"Wilde, move your ass!" Coach shouts from the bench.

Maybe I spoke too soon.

I bite back a curse and push harder, forcing myself to close the gap as Aiden sends the puck flying toward me. I catch it on my blade and send it back, ignoring the twinge in my wrist as the vibrations from the pass ripple through my hand.

"Nice, Hudson!" Aiden calls, skating past me.

I nod, gritting my teeth as I adjust my grip on the stick. Every movement feels worse than the next, and if I don't catch a break soon, Coach will for sure find out.

It's not even a minute later that the puck is flying my way again, but this time, Dane is there, real close, blocking Wolfe, who's coming after the puck and, in turn, me.

Dane's been . . . different today.

Not off in the sense that he's not doing his job—if anything, he's playing harder than usual. But there's something about the way he's moving, the way he's interacting with the team.

He's everywhere.

Every time someone gets near me, Dane is there, his stick tapping the ice or his body shifting into their path. It's subtle enough that no one else seems to notice, but I do.

He's practically playing shadow, blocking anyone who even thinks about breathing in my direction.

At one point, Wolfe goes for a check, and Dane cuts in, bumping him just hard enough to redirect him.

"Chill, man," Wolfe says with a laugh. "What's up your ass?"

Dane shrugs. Not even bothering to answer him before skating away without a word.

I have to agree with Wolfe. Something is up with Dane, but since I'm benefiting from it, who am I to ask questions?

Every time he blocks someone from hitting me is another minute I have to heal.

Practice ends, thank fuck. I hit the locker room with the rest of the guys. However, my movements are much slower than theirs.

My wrist... and now my whole arm fucking kills.

When I was on the ice, it hurt, but not this bad.

I blame it on the adrenaline.

"Nice job." Aiden nods at me. He's not a man of many words.

"It's good to be back. I missed you, man. How's married life?" Mason grins as he heads toward the showers.

"It's good."

I need to get out of here, but before I head out, I catch Dane's eyes.

He's all the way across the room, but even from this distance, I can tell something is wrong with him. Or still wrong with him, maybe.

I nod, but he just turns away, heading out without another word.

By the time I get home, the house smells like chicken soup and fresh bread. My mom's recipe. Molly is in the kitchen stirring something on the stove, her hair pulled back in a messy bun.

She's been here every day since the injury, taking care of me like it's her full-time job. I didn't ask her to.

Hell, I tried to tell her she didn't need to. But Molly, being Molly, ignored me and moved herself in anyway, which is fine by me. If it were up to me, she'd never leave.

"Hey," she says without turning around. "How was practice?"

"Decent." That's the best I can do. Anything else would be a lie.

Molly turns to face me. "What happened?"

She scrunches her nose as she stares at me.

"Well, it was kind of weird, though. Dane was acting like my personal bodyguard."

Her hand stops moving, and the spoon clinks against the pot.

"What do you mean?"

"I mean, he didn't let anyone near me." I lean against the counter. "It's like—"

"Like what?"

"Like he was blocking only me."

She shrugs. "Maybe he's just being protective. You know how he is."

"Yeah," I say slowly, watching her carefully. "It's just . . . different. Even for him."

Molly finally looks at me, her face neutral. "Maybe subconsciously he could tell you weren't at your best."

It feels like she's leaving something out.

What?

I have no clue, but it feels that way.

About twenty minutes later, we finally sit down for dinner. While we eat, neither of us speaks. It's quiet, the only sound is that of the spoons clinking the bowls.

Something is definitely off with Molly, though.

She's been quieter than usual, her focus entirely on her food.

"You're not eating much." I glance at her half-empty bowl.

"Neither are you," she shoots back, raising an eyebrow.

I chuckle, leaning back in my chair. "Touché."

She gives me a small smile, but it doesn't quite reach her eyes.

Interesting.

Later, as I sit on the couch icing my arm, Molly brings me a cup of water and sits beside me. She doesn't say anything; she just tucks her legs under her and stares at the TV.

"What's going on with you?" I ask.

"Just tired," she responds.

"You sure?"

She nods, but I don't believe her.

"Maybe it's me." I nudge her. "Maybe I'm too high maintenance. You don't have to take care of me, you know."

She turns to me, her brow furrowed. "I want to."

I don't know what to say. "Thank you," finally slips out, but my voice is quieter than I intended.

She smiles, and this time, it feels real. "You'd do the same for me."

"Yeah," I say, leaning back against the couch. "I would."

The silence settles around us.

Comfortable.

Peaceful.

Everything I've ever wanted.

I don't know what I did to deserve her, but I'm not about to question it.

chapter ninety

Molly

THE EARLY MORNING SUNLIGHT STREAMS IN THROUGH THE curtains. My eyes blink, confused about what day it is and why my alarm hasn't gone off.

But then it all comes flooding back. Today is the first time in years that I don't have an alarm clock set or a list of things I need to do.

No. Today is my first day of being unemployed.

There's no checklist.

No emails to answer.

No schedule to organize.

There's nothing.

It feels odd.

I'm actually at a loss for how I feel.

On the one hand, it's nice to be able to catch a few extra hours of z's, but on the other, now what do I do with my life?

Who am I, if not Dane's assistant?

Flipping over in the bed, I look at Hudson's spot—it's empty.

I'm all alone.

Hudson probably left a few hours ago for practice.

Grabbing my robe, I throw it on, head downstairs, and grab a cup of coffee before taking a seat. The house is quiet except for the soft hum of the fridge in the kitchen. I sit at the table drinking.

I should feel relieved.

Then why don't I?

This is a blessing.

Then why doesn't it feel that way?

For years, I've worked tirelessly for Dane, putting his needs above my own.

Now, I finally have a chance to focus on myself. To figure out what I want.

But the truth is, I have no idea where to start.

The first day is the hardest. After I get dressed, I leave the house with no destination in mind, just walking aimlessly down the quiet streets of Hudson's neighborhood.

The air is cool, and the early fall leaves crunch beneath my boots as I walk.

I used to dream about what it would be like not to work for Dane.

Now I'm scared to find out.

Sure, I haven't worked for him for a few days here and there, but never more than two months.

What do I do now?

Where do I work?

I stop at a small park and sit on a bench.

A group of kids play, their laughter so loud I can't help but smile.

When was the last time I felt that carefree?

I can't remember.

No. That's not true.

At the farm.

At the rink.

With Hudson.

beautiful collide

All the days blur since Dane fired me.

Sometimes I end up at the same park. Other times, I find myself wandering through shops. I walk a lot. Never a destination in sight. Hudson doesn't ask what I do all day, and I don't offer. He has his own shit to worry about. Like his wrist.

But every evening, when he comes home, he looks at me like he's trying to figure out what's going on in my head.

"You doing okay?" His arm rests in a sling while we half-watch a TV show.

"Yeah," I say automatically, even though it's not entirely true.

His eyes linger on me for a moment before he nods. "If you need anything..."

"Thanks."

He doesn't push, and I'm grateful.

One afternoon, I find myself at a small bookstore. That's where I find a book that piques my interest.

Finding Purpose After the Unexpected.

I pick it up, turning it over in my hands. The irony isn't lost on me, but something about the title tugs at my chest.

Back at the house, I sit at the kitchen table and start to read. I don't know what I'm expecting.

Maybe the secret to life.

A magical solution.

Heck, maybe even a roadmap, but the pages are filled with actual stories of people who almost lost hope but found their way.

One passage stands out: "Sometimes, starting over doesn't mean finding something new. It means rediscovering what you've always loved."

I stare at the words for a long time. What have I always loved?

The truth is, I don't know.

chapter ninety-one

Molly

Tonight, I cook dinner again.

It's a simple pasta dish, nothing fancy, but whenever I cook now, I think of Mary.

One of my favorite things about going to the farm was spending time with his mother in the kitchen.

I always imagined that's what my life would be like if my mom hadn't died.

It was special to have those moments with Hudson's mom.

A part of me wonders what the future will bring. Will there be more family games and walks around the farm . . .

"What's got you so deep in thought?" Hudson asks as he walks into the kitchen.

"Nothing." I look over my shoulder and smile at him.

All of this feels so domestic.

And I love it.

It feels like we have a future together. It's felt like this ever since the day I unburdened myself to him. Now, how do I broach the topic? How do I know if he feels the same way?

I know we are currently staying married until the ink is dry on his endorsement deal, but this feels like it can be more, like it can be forever.

"So what is all this?" He grins, walks over, and presses a kiss to the top of my head.

"Dinner." I laugh.

"Looks amazing." He makes his way to the already set kitchen table and drops into the chair.

For the next few days, I try to keep busy.

I do chores around the house.

Little things to give me a sense of control.

I organize Hudson's kitchen, rearranging the spices and utensils in a way that makes sense to me.

I clean out his fridge, throwing away expired condiments and wiping down the shelves.

While cleaning, I open a drawer to grab a blank notebook. While removing it, I notice the business card he tried to give me once.

Why does he still have it?

I'm not sure how I feel about it. My eyes narrow as I stare at it like it's a bomb ready to explode.

I close the drawer.

Pretending I never saw it.

But in the back of my mind, I know it's there, and for some reason, it doesn't feel as frightening as it did before.

Maybe one day, I'll fish it out and call the number on the card.

Maybe . . .

But not now.

With the notebook in hand, I take a seat at the island in the kitchen and start to make a list. It's not much—just a few ideas of things I might want to try.

Writing, volunteering, maybe even taking a class. The list feels small and insignificant, but it's a start.

As I look at it, a strange sense of hope stirs in my chest.

I feel like I'm moving forward, even if it's just an inch at a time.

The sound of footsteps startles me.

Hudson walks over, placing a kiss on my forehead like he's done every night since I've taken up residence at his place.

Of course, I still have my apartment, but I stay here for appearance, or at least that's what I tell him and myself.

"What's this?" he asks, picking up the notebook.

I shrug, suddenly self-conscious. "Just some ideas."

He reads it silently, his eyes scanning the page. When he looks up, there's a small smile on his lips.

"This is good," he says, his voice warm. "Really good."

I nod, and my cheeks feel warm. "Yeah. I think it's time."

"For what?"

"To figure out who I am," I whisper.

His smile widens, and he sets the list I made back down. "You got this."

And for the first time, I believe him.

chapter ninety-two

Hudson

WHAT THE HELL IS GOING ON?
 Why is there barking coming from my house?

The TV.

Obviously, Hex is watching something, or at least that's what I tell myself as I walk inside.

I'm not dumb. I know it's not that at all, because I can totally also hear Molly cooing at the same time.

Jeez, what has she got herself into this time?

Not working is one thing.

Creating lists is another.

Now this . . .

The farther I make it into the house, the more I'm one hundred percent sure it's a dog.

The barking is way too high-pitched and chaotic to be anything else.

I'm about to step into something I'm not prepared for.

Great.

When I turn the corner, I realize how screwed I am. There, in the living room, is Josie. She's crouched down, playing with a floppy-eared puppy.

"Look." Josie waves at me like she hasn't seen me in years. "Isn't he cute?"

I blink, taking in the scene.

She points at the dog, and I shake my head, but then I hear the distinct sound of a second dog and I pivot to find the source. That's when I see a smaller dog sitting on the couch, and lo and behold, Molly sits next to it. Her hand rests gently on its head like the puppy is already hers.

"Nope." I run a hand through my hair. This is bad.

Molly looks up, and I can tell she's trying not to laugh. "Hi, Hudson."

Damn her and her innocent smile.

"Hi, Hudson?" I move closer to her. "No, absolutely not."

"What?" She acts like she has no clue what I'm saying no to.

"You don't get to act casual about this. There are dogs in my house. Plural. Explain."

Josie jumps up, scoops up her squirming puppy, and holds it against her chest. "We adopted them. Aren't they adorable?"

I blink at her, then look back at Molly, who suddenly finds the dog sitting with her very interesting.

"You what?" This is not happening.

"We adopted them." Molly finally meets my gaze. "You remember the adoption event? Well, they were still looking for homes, so . . ."

"You went behind my back and brought a dog into the house?"

"It's not behind your back." Molly raises an eyebrow. "You're standing right here."

Josie bursts out laughing, and I shoot her a glare. "You're not helping."

"Don't be mad," Josie says, and I return my attention to her.

She's currently flashing me her most innocent smile. *Don't fall for it.* "Look at this face." She tilts her puppy toward me.

Molly stands with her puppy in hand and walks up to me. She places a kiss on my lips, which is followed by the white fluff ball in her hands licking me too.

"Dammit." I wipe my face. "That's cheating."

"Well, that's my cue to leave. Have fun with your new pup," Josie says as she moves to leave the room.

Molly waves as Josie heads out the door. Once we're alone, I look over at Molly. Both she and the dog are giving me puppy eyes.

This is cruel torture.

How can I say no to this?

I cross my arms. "All right, Hex. Spill."

Molly sighs, patting the dog's head as she looks up at me. "It's not a big deal, Hudson. I've wanted a dog for a while, and this one needed a home. That's all."

"That's all?" I narrow my eyes. "Molly, you don't just adopt a dog. So what's going on?"

She hesitates, her fingers stilling against the dog's fur.

"Molly," I say, my voice softer now. "Talk to me."

She lets out a slow breath, her shoulders sagging slightly. "I told Dane about your injury."

The words hit me like a slap, and for a moment, I just stare at her, trying to process what she said. "You what?"

"I told him," she says again, her voice firmer now. "He's the enforcer. Your defender. He can protect you on the ice. You needed someone to have your back, and now you do."

"Why didn't you tell me?"

Because you would have objected.

"I knew you'd be mad," she admits.

Welp, she's right about that.

It's true. I would have been.

I rake a hand through my hair, pacing the length of the room. "Jesus, Molly. You went behind my back—"

"I did it for you!" she shouts, cutting me off.

I almost stumble. In all the years I've known Molly, and despite everything we have been through, she's never yelled. Sure, she's snapped. But yell, no.

Something else is happening here. "And you're welcome, by the way, because Dane's been keeping everyone off your ass during practice, hasn't he?"

Why is she acting like this? I start to walk. Why would she be so defensive about this? It's almost as if . . . then it hits me square in the chest.

I stop pacing, turning to face her. "So, that's why you let him fire you?"

Her mouth opens, then closes, and the guilt in her eyes tells me everything I need to know.

"You traded your job for me," I say quietly, the weight of it settling in my chest.

"It wasn't like that," she says, but her voice is weak. *She did.*

"Don't lie to me, Molly. Please, be honest," I say, stepping closer. "You've spent years fighting to stay in that job, and now, suddenly, you're okay with him firing you? It's because of me."

She looks away. "It's done, Hudson. Can we not make a big deal out of it?"

"A big deal?" I repeat. "You gave up everything for me, and you don't want to make a big deal out of it?"

"It's not everything," she says, but her voice trembles, giving her away. It is. "It's just a job. I'll figure something else out."

I shake my head, closing the distance between us. "Molly, you didn't have to do that. I didn't want you to do that."

"I know." Her eyes glisten with unshed tears. "But I did it anyway. Because I care about you. And because someone had to."

Her words hit me like a punch to the gut, and for a moment, I can't speak.

"You're unbelievable," I say finally, my voice thick.

She frowns, confused. "What?"

beautiful collide

"You're unbelievable," I repeat, stepping even closer. "You drive me crazy, Molly. You're stubborn and frustrating, and you make me want to pull my hair out half the time. But you're also the most selfless, infuriatingly wonderful person I've ever met."

She blinks, her mouth opening slightly.

"And I love you for it," I say, the words spilling out before I can stop them. "You beautiful, chaotic storm. You collided into me, flipped my world upside down, and made it feel like home. I love you, Molly. Every maddening, incredible part of you."

Her eyes widen, and she stares at me like she can't believe what I just said.

"You . . . you love me?" she whispers.

I nod, my chest tightening. "Yeah. I do. And if you think for a second that I'm going to let you keep sacrificing yourself for me, I won't."

Her expression becomes more serious. "I love you too."

"Yeah, obviously."

Her lips twitch, and she lets out a laugh. "You're such a pain in the ass."

"Takes one to know one." I grin.

She laughs again, and it's the most beautiful sound I've ever heard.

"So," I say, glancing down. "What's the deal with this little guy?"

"It's a *she*. And she doesn't have a name yet." Molly scratches behind the dog's ears.

"No name?" I say, mock scandalized. "Well, we've got to fix that."

She raises an eyebrow. "What do you suggest?"

"Hmm." I rub my chin, pretending to think. All the funny names Anna has come up with over the years as she begged for a dog come to mind. "How about . . . Fluffypants?"

Molly snorts. "Absolutely not."

"Fine," I say, smirking. "What about Bark Twain?" Anna came up with that one when she was eight. It was one of my favorites.

She groans, shaking her head. "You're the worst."

I grin, looking down at the dog. "All right, Twinkie, it is."

Molly pauses, her hand stilling on the dog's head. "Twinkie?"

"Yeah," I say, my smile softening. "You know, like the ones we ate during the tornado. The ones that kept us alive."

She stares at me for a moment, then bursts out laughing. "Okay, Twinkie it is."

The dog wags her tail, clearly approving of the name.

And as Molly leans into my side, her head resting against my shoulder, I realize that this—her, me, Twinkie . . .

It feels like home.

chapter ninety-three

Hudson

When I get home today from practice, I find Molly sitting cross-legged on the couch.

I expect to find Twinkie on her lap. Instead, she has her laptop balanced there.

Twinkie is on the cushion next to her, fast asleep, despite the sound of her fingers typing furiously.

She's been like this every day for the past three days.

Every day since I told her the full extent of what's going on at the farm.

Now, she searches for a solution to a problem that isn't even hers to solve.

She hasn't stopped trying to figure out a way to fix it—for me.

"Hudson," she says, breaking the silence, and I expect her to tell me another idea.

"Yeah?"

She closes the laptop and sets it aside, her eyes locking on to mine. "I think you need to tell Coach."

Um, where the hell did that come from?

I was sure I was safe from hockey talk because she's been avoiding it, but fuck.

I shake my head. "Tell Coach? Yeah, that's going to be a no."

She sits up straighter. "Hudson, you can't keep doing this. Hiding your injury, playing while hurt."

I shake my head, standing and pacing the room. "You don't understand, Molly. If Coach finds out I was working on the farm, I could lose everything. My spot on the team, my reputation—"

"Your health." She cuts in. "You could lose your career permanently if you keep hiding this. Is that what you want?"

I stop pacing, my chest tightening. "Of course not."

"Then you need to tell him." She exhales. "Please, Hudson. Ask him for help. Tell him. I know you don't know Robert like I do, but he's a good man. A really good man."

That's easy for her to say. She's known Coach Robert since she was a teen. The man is practically a father figure to her. To me . . . well, I'm the reckless player he wishes he could throw off the team.

I run a hand through my hair.

I can't do it.

I can't come clean.

But maybe she's right. Perhaps I need to.

"You really think I should?" I ask.

"I do." She stands up and crosses the room to stand in front of me. "Because I know you, Hudson. And I know that you're tired of hiding. Tell him. I promise it will be okay."

"Fine, I'll do it."

The following morning, I'm standing outside Coach's office.

My heart pounds in my chest.

Maybe I'm having a heart attack.

Now I'm being ridiculous.

Stop dicking around and go in there.

It's time.

And if I get let go, at least Molly will be there for me.

I take a deep breath.

Knock on the damn door.

"Come in."

With slow moves, I push the door open. It feels heavy today, but I know it's just nerves.

Once it's open, I step inside and make my way to his desk. He's already sitting there with a stack of papers in front of him. He looks up, and when he does, I swear I start to sweat.

Fuck. *Man the fuck up, Hudson.*

He raises an eyebrow. "Wilde." He leans back in his chair. "What brings you here?"

Even though he hasn't told me to sit, I do. "Coach, I need to talk to you about something."

His brow furrows. "This sounds serious."

I let out a breath. "It is." *Shit, how do I say this?* "I'm hurt," I admit and then I tell him everything.

About the farm.

About the money.

About the accident.

When I get to that part, Coach's jaw tightens.

"And you've been practicing with this injury?" he asks, his voice low. Fuck. He's pissed.

This is it. Time to kiss my career on the Saints goodbye. It's been a good run.

I nod. "Yeah."

He rubs a hand over his face. "Hudson, this is reckless, even for you. You could have made it worse."

"I know." I nod. "I screwed up. But I didn't know what to do. The farm's barely holding on. I needed to help them, and the only way I can is with hockey."

Coach is silent for a moment, his gaze heavy. Finally, he lets out a long sigh. "All right, I have an idea."

I sit up straighter, my heart pounding. He hasn't kicked me off the team yet. That's got to be a good sign.

"You're sitting out the first three games," he says firmly. "Without pay. You're going to focus on getting that wrist healed."

Holy fuck.

This is the best outcome I could have prayed for.

"Thank you, Coach."

"I'm not done." His eyes narrow. Fuck, I celebrated too soon. "You're also going to let me make a few calls. I have connections. I think I can help you find more endorsement deals. Maybe one that can help the farm."

My eyes widen, and for a moment, I can't speak. "You'd do that?"

"You're one of my best players, Wilde," he says. "But more importantly, you're a good kid. You made a mistake. Everyone makes mistakes."

"Thank you."

"Don't thank me yet." A small smile tugs at his lips.

When I walk out of Coach's office, I'm already feeling better.

I find Molly where I left her, waiting by the car.

"And?" She taps her foot on the pavement impatiently.

God, I love this woman.

I smile, the first one in days. "Good. He's making me sit out the first three games, but he's also helping me find another endorsement deal. One that could also help the farm."

"Oh my God." She gasps. "This is amazing. I'm so happy for you."

"Yeah, it is. And it's all thanks to you."

She shakes her head, stepping closer and wrapping her arms around my neck. "You did this, Hudson. You should be proud of yourself. God, I love you so much."

I kiss her head. "Molly Sinclair-Wilde. Hex. You're my favorite bad luck charm." I wink.

She laughs softly, her arms wrapping around me. "Always."

chapter ninety-four

Hudson

Mason: Morning, Princess Hudson. How's the royal wrist today?

Aiden: Should we get you a throne? Or maybe one of those bubble wrap suits?

Hudson: ☹ You're all hilarious.

Dane: Don't forget fragile. He's fragile AF.

Mason: He's like a glass ornament. One wrong move and CRACK.

Aiden: A glass ornament. With sparkles.

Hudson: I hate all of you.

Mason: Nah, you love us.

Dane: Not as much as we love seeing you get wrapped in the bubble wrap of shame by Coach.

Aiden: Bet you're sidelined for two weeks just because someone looked at you wrong.

Hudson: I'M FINE.

Mason: "I'm fine" is what people say when they're absolutely not fine.

Dane: You're not fine, Hudson. And don't give me that BS. You should've told us.

Hudson: Told you what?

Dane: About the injury. About the farm. About whatever stupid thing you were doing that landed you in this mess.

Aiden: You think we wouldn't have your back? You think we wouldn't help?

Mason: We're teammates, dude. That makes us family.

Dane: And family doesn't let you pull dumb stunts alone.

Hudson: . . .

Mason: What? Nothing to say now?

Hudson: I didn't want anyone to worry about me.

Dane: That's the dumbest thing you've ever said.

Aiden: Yeah, we're going to worry regardless. It's our default setting, considering your string of life choices.

Mason: You're not invincible, Wilde. None of us are.

Hudson: I know. I just didn't want to let anyone down.

Dane: You let us down by not telling us. We're a team. You should've trusted us.

Hudson: You're right. I screwed up. I'm sorry.

Mason: You're sorry? You're also a massive idiot.

Aiden: Huge. Like Olympic-level idiot.

Hudson: Jesus Christ, do you guys ever stop?

Dane: Nope.

Mason: Never. We're relentless. Like your bad decisions.

Hudson: I take back my apology. You're all assholes.

Aiden: Assholes who care about you.

Hudson: Thanks. For real.

Mason: Anytime, Princess.

Hudson: I'm muting this chat.

Dane: Go ahead. You'll still be hearing us chirp you at practice.

Aiden: Oh, 100%. We're just getting started.

Hudson: Great. Looking forward to it.

Mason: Love you, glass princess. Stay unbroken.

Hudson Wilde has left the chat.

Dane: He'll be back. He always comes back.

SEASON FIVE

epilogue

Hudson

THE CROWD IS BUZZING.

Excitement courses through the air.

Today is my first game back since my injury.

It's also the first time I've felt like myself since I got hurt.

Being on the ice is like being home.

As I step out onto the ice, it feels right.

I love everything about this. The way the ice glistens under the bright spotlights. The anticipation building as fans wave their signs and scream for their favorite players.

It's all part of why I keep playing.

Normally, that's enough for me to want to play hard, but tonight, it's something else.

Tonight, hockey isn't the only thing on my mind.

Tonight isn't just about the game.

Tonight is about her.

Molly.

She's somewhere in the family box. In the past, she never

wanted to sit there, but now, since my family is there, she wants to be with them, and knowing her, she's probably having the best time with my sister.

Things have been great with my family. I have no complaints, and lately, I can't stop smiling. It helps that my parents are now swimming in dough. Ever since Molly spoke to my mom about me helping them, they became more open to it.

Thankfully, Coach came through, getting me an endorsement deal with a large organic grocery store. The connection has brought the farm a ton of new business, which has been great. They used the money to hire help, and now they have time to travel, see the world, and rack up a retirement fund. All thanks to Hex's help.

The way she loves my family is how I know that I've made the right decision.

My heart pounds as I glance up at the booth, searching for her. And then I see her leaning over the railing, her hands clasped together as she talks to Josie and Anna.

She's beautiful in a way that still knocks the wind out of me.

She's effortless.

Radiant.

Mine.

A whistle from Mason snaps me out of my thoughts. "You ready for this?"

I turn to see him grinning like an idiot, his stick resting on his shoulder. Aiden and Dane are behind him, smirking, clearly in on the plan.

"Yeah," I say. I keep my voice steady despite the fact that I feel anything but. "Let's do it."

The first period flies by in a blur.

We're up by two.

The crowd is going nuts.

I love it.

Love being back on the ice.

As the second period winds down, my focus shifts.

beautiful collide

During the intermission, I make my way to the locker room with the team, the adrenaline coursing through me like a live wire. Dane slaps me on the back as we pass through the tunnel.

"You nervous?" he mutters so no one hears.

"A little," I admit. "But it's a good kind of nervous."

He smirks, shaking his head. "Good luck, man."

As the third period begins, my nerves pick up. Not because of the game, though.

Nope, my nerves are because of the clock. I'm watching it, counting down the seconds.

It's almost time to put my plan into action.

When we finally win—which obviously is a bonus since my plan would have happened regardless, but this is better—the crowd cheers.

But I have something bigger to celebrate.

The announcer's voice booms over the speakers as the team lines up at center ice for the traditional post-game thank-you to the fans.

My heart pounds as I grab the microphone. It's a well-thought-out plan, and luckily for me, Coach Robert was happy to speak to the GM and let me do this. The suits were excited too. The marketing team even more so.

None of that matters to me. I'm not doing it for views or likes. I'm doing it because I need to.

"Hey, everyone." My voice echoes through the arena. "Can I have a moment of your time?" The crowd quiets at my words, all curious about what I'm about to say. "Before we wrap up tonight, there's something I need to say. Something I've been waiting a long time to do."

I glance up at the family box, locking eyes with Molly. Her brow furrows, her lips parting in confusion, and I know she's trying to figure out what's happening.

"Molly," I say, my voice steady despite the way my chest is pounding. "Can you come down here?"

Again, this is not normal or protocol, but since we've won two Cups, and the crowd is sure to go nuts, I have a lot of leeway in what I'm allowed to do.

The crowd cheers, their excitement rippling through the arena as the spotlight shifts to her.

Josie nudges her, grinning, and Molly looks mortified.

"Come on. Don't make me come up there."

She groans, but she finally starts moving, making her way down the stairs.

Security leads her to the ice.

When she reaches me, I can't help but smile at the way she crosses her arms. She looks confused and maybe a little pissed.

Fuck, I love this girl.

"What are you doing, Hudson?" she whispers under her breath.

"You'll see." I take her hand.

The crowd falls silent, the weight of the moment hanging heavy in the air.

I take a deep breath, turning to face her, my other hand resting on her shoulder. "Molly, when I met you, I thought you were my hex." This is the first time I've publicly called her this, but it feels fitting and right. "You kind of lived up to the name at first."

The crowd laughs, and Molly glares at me.

But despite that, I can see a flicker of amusement in her eyes.

"But then, something changed." My voice softens. "You didn't hex me. You saved me. You've been there for me in ways I didn't even know I needed. You saw me at my worst and refused to let me give up. You've been my constant, my support. And as it turns out, you're my good luck charm."

Her eyes widen.

I drop to one knee, pulling a small box from my pocket.

The crowd gasps.

"I know we've technically done this before. But this time, I want to do it right. Molly, will you stay married to me? Not because of

beautiful collide

circumstance, but because I'm crazy about you? Because there's no one else in this world I'd rather call my wife."

The arena is dead silent for a beat, and then someone from the crowd yells, "Wait, aren't they already married?"

Laughter ripples through the stands, but my eyes stay locked on Molly.

She's quiet. Way too quiet. But then, finally, she lowers her hand. "Yes. Yes, I'll stay married to you."

The crowd erupts into cheers as I slip the ring onto her finger and then pick her up and fling her over my shoulder.

"I can't believe you just did that," she laughs.

"Believe it. You're stuck with me, Hex."

"Good. Because I wouldn't want it any other way."

Molly

Six months ago, I was lost.

My identity was so tightly wound around other people's lives that I couldn't see my own.

I thought being fired by Dane was the end of me.

Now, I know that none of my fears were real.

That I was scared, holding on to trauma, and not willing to let go.

Turns out, I did use that card that Hudson gave me.

It took a long time to muster up the strength, but then I did.

When Hudson found the strength to tell Coach about his injury, I found the strength to take the steps to heal myself.

It's been a long road, but every day, I get closer to finding the closure I need and live in the moment, not the past.

Today, I sit in a hotel room in New York, laptop balanced on my knees. I should be working, but Hudson's laughter drifting from the adjoining room has me smiling instead.

The guys are all playing cards.

The sound makes me feel alive.

Who knew this was where I'd find my extended family.

Because that's what they have all become . . . *my family*.

This is my life now.

I close my laptop, leaning back in my chair and letting out a satisfied sigh. My latest project for the Saints social media team is done—photos, interviews, and short videos ready to upload.

Somehow, this job fell into my lap just when I needed it most.

I get to travel with the team, highlight their personalities, and showcase the work they do off the ice.

It's more than a job. It's a purpose.

And it fits.

Plus, I get to work with Josie, who has quickly become one of my best friends. Cassidy being the other, but she's often busy with school.

"Molly." Hudson's voice booms as he leans into the room, his grin wide enough to light up the entire city. "Get your ass out here. We're starting a new round, and Mason is already crying about losing to me."

"I'm not crying," Mason yells from the other room. "You're a cheater."

I laugh, setting my laptop aside. "Oh my God, fine. I'm coming."

Hudson's gaze softens as he meets my stare. "You good?"

"I'm great," I say, standing and stretching.

He watches me closely, studying. He's silently asking me about my panic attacks.

With the therapist's help, the panic attacks that used to grip me have become rare. And when they do come, I know I'm not alone.

I cross the room and walk right into Hudson's open arms, resting my forehead against his chest. "I love you."

He kisses my hair. "I love you too, Hex."

Together, we make our way to our friends. The card game is already chaos, and round two hasn't even begun.

Josie is perched on the arm of Dane's chair, whispering into his ear. Cassidy is laughing so hard she's nearly crying.

"Just admit you all cheated," Mason grumbles.

Aiden raises an eyebrow. "How can we all cheat? Maybe you just suck, Mason. That sounds more plausible."

Mason throws his cards down dramatically. "You know nothing."

Hudson leads me to the couch, and we sit down.

He throws an arm around my shoulders, pulling me close. "This is what I love," he murmurs.

"What? Watching Mason and Aiden bicker like an old married couple?"

"That, and this." He gestures to the group. "All of us together. It feels right."

I glance around the room, my chest tightening.

He's right. *This is right.*

And as we sit here, surrounded by the laughter of our *family*, I know one thing for certain.

I'm not that scared, broken girl in the closet anymore.

I'm Molly Wilde—free, loved, and exactly where I'm meant to be.

The End

He just wanted a decent book to read ...

Not too much to ask, is it? It was in 1935 when Allen Lane, Managing Director of Bodley Head Publishers, stood on a platform at Exeter railway station looking for something good to read on his journey back to London. His choice was limited to popular magazines and poor-quality paperbacks – the same choice faced every day by the vast majority of readers, few of whom could afford hardbacks. Lane's disappointment and subsequent anger at the range of books generally available led him to found a company – and change the world.

'We believed in the existence in this country of a vast reading public for intelligent books at a low price, and staked everything on it'
Sir Allen Lane, 1902–1970, founder of Penguin Books

The quality paperback had arrived – and not just in bookshops. Lane was adamant that his Penguins should appear in chain stores and tobacconists, and should cost no more than a packet of cigarettes.

Reading habits (and cigarette prices) have changed since 1935, but Penguin still believes in publishing the best books for everybody to enjoy. We still believe that good design costs no more than bad design, and we still believe that quality books published passionately and responsibly make the world a better place.

So wherever you see the little bird – whether it's on a piece of prize-winning literary fiction or a celebrity autobiography, political tour de force or historical masterpiece, a serial-killer thriller, reference book, world classic or a piece of pure escapism – you can bet that it represents the very best that the genre has to offer.

Whatever you like to read – trust Penguin.

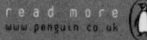